P9-CBC-021

THE
DIVIDE

**Center Point
Large Print**

**This Large Print Book carries the
Seal of Approval of N.A.V.H.**

THE DIVIDE

NICHOLAS EVANS

CENTER POINT PUBLISHING
THORNDIKE, MAINE

This Center Point Large Print edition
is published in the year 2005 by arrangement with
G. P. Putnam's Sons, a division of Penguin Group (USA) Inc.

The text of this Large Print edition is unabridged.
In other aspects, this book may vary from the original edition.
Printed in the United States of America.
Set in 16-point Times New Roman type.

ISBN 1-58547-687-0

Library of Congress Cataloging-in-Publication Data

Evans, Nicholas, 1950-
　　The divide / Nicholas Evans.--Center Point large print ed.
　　　p. cm.
　　ISBN 1-58547-687-0 (lib. bdg. : alk. paper)
　　　1. Large type books.　I. Title.

PS3555.V253D57 2005b
813'.54--dc22

2005017273

While the author has made every effort to provide accurate telephone numbers and Internet addresses at the time of publication, neither the publisher nor the author assumes any responsibility for errors, or for changes that occur after publication. Further, the publisher does not have any control over and does not assume any responsibility for author or third-party websites or their content.

ACKNOWLEDGMENTS

I am greatly indebted to the following for their kindness, patience, and help with my research: Charles Fisher, Glenys Carl, Blaine Young, Bruce Geiss, Alexandra Eldridge, Buck & Mary Brannaman, Daisy Montfort, Andrew Martyn-Smith, Jill Morrison, Dennis Wilson, Sarah Pohl, Barbara Theroux, Doug Hawes-Davis, Dan Pletscher, Tom Roy, Elizabeth Powers, Sara Walsh, Jake Kreilick, Jeff Zealley, Gary Dale, Roger Seewald, Rick Branzell, Sandi Mendelson, Deborah Jensen, Sonia Rapaport, Richard Baron, Pat Tucker & Bruce Weide, Fred & Mary Davis, and George Anderson.

Many thanks also, for support of several crucial kinds, to Ronni Berger, Aimee Taub, Ivan Held, Rachael Harvey, Elizabeth Davies, Gordon Stevens, Larry Finlay, Caradoc King, Sally Gaminara, Carole Baron, and Charlotte Evans.

For Charlotte

And after he had made all the other creatures of the earth, only then did the Creator make man and woman. And he fashioned their bodies that they should know each other's flesh but their souls that they should forever be strangers. For only thus divided might they find their true path.

—CALVIN SASHONE, *Creative Mythology*

ONE

ONE

T hey rose before dawn and stepped out beneath a moonless sky aswarm with stars. Their breath made clouds of the chill air and their boots crunched on the congealed gravel of the motel parking lot. The old station wagon was the only car there, its roof and hood veneered with a dim refracting frost. The boy fixed their skis to the roof while his father stowed their packs then walked around to remove the newspaper pinned by the wipers to the windshield. It was stiff with ice and crackled in his hands as he balled it. Before they climbed into the car they lingered a moment, just stood there listening to the silence and gazing west at the mountains silhouetted by stars.

The little town had yet to wake and they drove quietly north along Main Street, past the courthouse and the gas station and the old movie theater, through pale pools of light cast by the street lamps, the car's reflection gilding the darkened windows of the stores. And the sole witness to their leaving was a grizzled dog who stood watch at the edge of town, its head lowered, its eyes ghost-green in the headlights.

It was the last day of March and a vestige of plowed

snow lay gray along the highway's edge. Heading west across the plains the previous afternoon, there had been a first whisper of green among the bleached grass. Before sunset they had strolled out from the motel along a dirt road and heard a meadowlark whistling as if winter had gone for good. But beyond the rolling ranch land, the Rocky Mountain Front, a wall of ancient limestone a hundred miles long, was still encrusted with white and the boy's father said they would surely still find good spring snow.

A mile north of town they branched left from the highway on a road that ran twenty more with barely a bend toward the Front. They saw mule deer and coyote and just as the road turned to gravel a great pale-winged owl swerved from the cottonwoods and glided low ahead of them as if piloting the beam of their lights. And all the while the mountain wall loomed larger, a shadowed, prescient blue, until it seemed to open itself and they found themselves traveling a twisting corridor where a creek of snowmelt tumbled through stands of bare aspen and willow with cliffs of pine and rock the color of bone rearing a thousand feet on either side.

The road was steeper now and when it became treacherous with hard-packed snow the boy's father stopped so they could fit the chains. The air when they got out of the car was icy and windless and loud with the rush of the creek. They spread the chains on the snow in front of the rear wheels and his father climbed back into the driver's seat and inched the car forward until the boy called for him to stop. While his father knelt to fasten the chains, the boy stamped his feet and blew on his hands to warm them.

"Look," he said.

His father stood and did so, brushing the snow from his hands. Framed in the V of the valley walls, though far beyond, the peak of a vast snow-covered mountain had just been set ablaze by the first reach of the sun. Even as they watched, the shadow of night began to drain from its slopes below a deepening band of pink and gold and white.

They parked the car at the trailhead and they could see from the untracked snow that no one else had been there. They sat together beneath the tailgate and put on their boots. The owner of the motel had made sandwiches for them and they ate one apiece and drank steaming sweet coffee and watched the shadows around them slowly fill with light. The first few miles would be steep so they fitted skins to their skis to give them grip. The boy's father checked the bindings and that their avalanche transceivers were working and when he was satisfied that all was in order they shouldered their packs and stepped into their skis.

"You lead," his father said.

The journey they had planned for that day was a loop of some fifteen miles. They had made the same trip two years before and found some of the best skiing either had ever known. The first three hours were the hardest, a long climb through the forest then a perilous zigzag up the northeast side of a ridge. But it was worth it. The ridge's south face was a perfect, treeless shoulder that dropped in three consecutive slopes into the next drainage. If all went well, by the time they reached the top, the sun would just have angled onto it, softening the top half-inch of snow while the base remained frozen and firm.

These backcountry ski trips had become their yearly ritual and the boy now looked forward to them as much as he knew his father did. His snowboarding friends back home in Great Falls thought he was crazy. If you wanted to ski, they said, why not go someplace where there's a ski lift? And in truth, on their first trip four years ago in the Tetons, he feared they were right. To a twelve-year-old it had seemed like a lot of effort for precious little fun; too much up and not enough down. At times he had come close to tears. But he kept a brave face and the following year went again.

His father was away from home on business much of the time and there weren't many things they ever got to do together, just the two of them. Sometimes the boy felt they barely knew each other. Neither of them was much of a talker. But there was something about traveling together through these wild and remote places that seemed to bind them closer than words ever could. And little by little he had come to understand why his father enjoyed the uphill as much as the down. It was a curious formula of physical and mental energy, as if the burning of one fueled the other. The endless rhythmic repetition, sliding one ski past the other, could send you into a kind of trance. And the thrill and sense of achievement when you reached that faraway summit and saw a slope of virgin spring snow reveal itself below could be close to overwhelming.

Perhaps he came to feel this way simply because each year he had grown stronger. He was taller than his father now and certainly fitter. And though not yet as wise in his mountaincraft, he had probably become the better skier. Perhaps that was why today, for the first time, his father was letting him lead.

For the first hour the trail was darkly walled with lodgepole pine and Douglas fir as it rose ever higher along the southern side of the winding canyon. Even though they were still in shadow, the climb soon had them sweating and when they paused to gather breath or to drink or to shed another layer of clothing, they could hear the muted roar of the creek far below. Once they heard the crashing of some large creature somewhere in the timber above them.

"What do you think that was?" the boy said.

"Deer. Moose, maybe."

"Would the bears be waking up yet?"

His father took a drink from his canteen then wiped his mouth with the back of his glove. This was prime grizzly country and they both knew it.

"Guess so. Days have been warm enough this past week."

An hour later they had stepped out of the trees and into the sunlight and were picking their way across a gully filled with the crazed debris of an avalanche, jagged lumps of frozen snow and rock skewered with trees sundered from their roots.

They reached the ridge a little before ten and stood side by side surveying in silence all that unfolded below and around them, mountain and forest quilted with snow and the flaxen plains beyond. The boy felt that if he squinted hard enough he might even defy science and all the world's horizons and see the backs of their own two selves, tiny figures on some distant snowy peak.

The shoulder below them looked as good as they had hoped. The sun was just upon it and it glistened like white velvet strewn with sequins. They took off their skis and unhitched the skins from which they carefully brushed the snow before stowing them in their packs. There was a cold breeze up here and they put on their jackets then sat on a bench of rock and drank coffee and ate the last of the sandwiches while a pair of ravens swirled and called above them against the lazuline sky.

"So what do you think?" his father asked.

"Looks pretty good."

"I'd say this is about as close to heaven as a man can get."

As he spoke one of the ravens banked before them, its shadow passing across his face. It landed a few yards from them along the ridge and the boy tossed a crust of bread toward it which made the bird flutter and lift again, but only for a moment. It resettled and with a cocked head inspected the crust then the boy then the crust again. It seemed almost to have summoned the courage to take it when its mate swooped in and snatched it instead. The first bird gave a raucous call and lifted off in pursuit and the boy and his father laughed and watched them tumble and swerve and squawk their way down into the valley.

As with the climb, the boy led the descent. The snow felt as good beneath his skis as it had looked. The sun had melted the surface just enough to give purchase and he quickly found his rhythm. He spread his arms and opened his chest to the slope below as if he would embrace it, savoring the blissful swish of each turn. His father was right. It was as near to heaven as you could get.

At the foot of the first of the three slopes, where the gradient leveled a little, the boy stopped and looked back to admire his tracks. His father was already skiing down beside them, carefully duplicating each curve, keeping close and precisely parallel, until he arrived alongside and the two of them whooped and slapped each other's upheld palms.

"Good tracks!"

"Yours are coming along too."

His father laughed and said he would ski the next slope first and that when he got to the next level he would take some photographs of the boy's descent. So the boy watched him ski down and waited for the call and when it came he launched himself into the sunlit air, giving all he had for the camera.

From where they stood next, at the foot of the second slope, they could see all the way down into the drainage, where the sun had yet to seep. They knew from the last time they had skied here that the creek that ran along the bottom was a series of pools and steep waterfalls. It had been warmer then and there had been a lot less snow and, except for some crusted ice at the pool edges, the running water had been exposed. Now, however, it lay buried beneath all the heaped snow that had funneled into the creek and all they could see were contours and ominous striations.

His father looked at his watch then shielded his eyes to peer at the sun. The boy knew what he was thinking. Half the slope below them was still in shadow. The air down there would be colder and the snow not yet transformed. Maybe they should wait awhile.

"Looks a little icy," his father said.

"It'll be okay. But if you're feeling chicken let's wait."

His father looked at him over his sunglasses and smiled.

"Okay, hotshot. Better show me the way then."

He handed the boy the camera.

"Make sure you get some good ones."

"They'll only be as good as your skiing. Wait till I holler."

He put the camera in his jacket pocket and grinned at his father as he moved off. The snow for the first few hundred feet was still good. But as he came closer to the rim of the sunlight, he felt the surface harden. When he turned there was almost no grip and no swishing sound, only the rasp of ice against the steel edges of his skis. He stopped where the sun met the shadow and looked up the slope where his father stood against the sky.

"How is it?" his father called.

"Kind of skiddy. It's okay."

"Wait there. I'm coming."

The boy took off his gloves and pulled the camera from his pocket. He managed to get a couple of shots with the zoom as his father skied down toward him. The third picture he took would later show the exact moment that things began to go wrong.

His father was starting a right turn and as he transferred his weight the edge of his left ski failed to bite and slipped sharply downhill. He tried to correct himself but in the process stepped too hard on his uphill ski and it skidded from under him. His body lurched, his arms and ski poles scything the air as he tried to recapture his balance. He was sliding now and had twisted around so that he was facing up the slope. For a moment he looked almost comical, as if he were pretending to ski uphill. Then he jerked and flipped backward and fell with a thump onto his back and at once began to gather speed.

It briefly occurred to the boy that he might try to block his father's slide, or at least check or slow it, by skiing into his path, but even as he thought it, he realized that the impact would surely knock him over and that he too would be carried down the slope. In any case, it was already too late. His father was accelerating so fast there would be no time to reach him. One ski had already come off and was torpedoing away down the mountain and now the other one came off and the boy moved quickly and reached out with a pole, almost losing his balance. He managed to touch the ski but it was traveling too fast and rocketed past him.

"Stand up!" he yelled. "Try and stand up!"

It was what his father had once called to him when he was falling. He hadn't managed to stand and neither could his father now. As he careered past, facedown now and spread-eagled on the ice, his sunglasses scuttling alongside like an inquisitive crab, he shouted something but the boy couldn't make it out. The father's ski poles, one of them badly bent, were still looped to his wrists and trailed above him, flailing and bouncing on the ice. And still he was gaining speed.

The boy began to ski down after him. And though he was shaky with shock and could feel his heart thumping as if it would break loose from its roots, he knew how vital it was not to fall too. He kept telling himself to stay calm and tried to summon all the technique he had ever learned. Trust the downhill ski, even though it slips. Angulate. Chest away from the mountain, not into it. Finish each turn. Angulate, angulate! Look ahead, you idiot, not down at the ice, not down at your skis.

There was no grip at all now, but after a few first tentative turns he found he could control the slide of his skis and his confidence began to return. Mesmerized, he watched the dark and diminishing figure sliding away and down into the shadow of the valley. Just before he disappeared from view, his father cried out one last time. And the sound was high-pitched and chilling, like an animal frightened for its life.

The boy slithered to a halt. He was breathing hard and

his legs were shaking. He knew it was important to remember the exact point at which his father had vanished, though why he had vanished, he couldn't yet figure out. Maybe there was some sudden drop you couldn't see from above. He tried to picture the last time they had skied the slope but couldn't recall whether the lower part of the drainage grew steeper or leveled out. And he couldn't help thinking about what might happen when his father hit the bottom. Would the snow heaped in the creek bed cushion his fall or would it be frozen like rock and break every bone in his body? In all his fretting, the boy had already lost the mental note he had made of precisely where his father had disappeared. In the shadow below everything looked the same. Maybe there were some marks on the ice that might lead him to the place. He took a deep breath and eased himself forward.

On the very first turn his downhill ski skidded badly and he almost fell. His knees were like jelly and the rest of him was locked with tension and it took him some time to trust himself to move again. Then, a few yards down the slope ahead of him, he saw a dark streak maybe six inches long on the ice. In a barely controlled side-slip he made his way toward it.

It was blood. And farther down the slope there was more. There were scuff marks in the ice too, probably where his father had tried to kick a grip with the toes of his boots.

Had the boy been able to ski this same slope in good snow, it would have taken him no more than four or five minutes. But on sheet ice with legs atremble, all he could manage was a side-slip so tense and fearful that it took the best part of half an hour. So slow was his descent that the sun overtook him and he watched the band of shadow retreat below him and the trail of blood turn vivid on the pristine snow.

Now, in the glare, he could see that the trail disappeared over a sudden rim and that there was something lying there. And drawing closer, he saw his father's sunglasses, perched on the edge of a last steep section of mountain, as if they had stopped to watch the climax of the show. The boy stopped and picked them up. One of the lenses was cracked and an arm was missing. He put them in his pocket.

The slope below him fell sharply some two hundred feet into the valley bottom which even as he watched was filling with sunlight. He peered down, expecting to see the crumpled form of his father. But there was no sign of him nor sound. Just a dazzling white silence.

Even the trail of blood and scuffing had vanished. There was a sudden rushing of air and the pair of ravens swooped low over his head and down toward the creek, squawking as if they would show him the way. And as the boy watched their shadows cross the creek he saw one of his father's skis and a dark hole in the rumpled blanket of snow.

Five minutes later he was down there. There was a crater, some ten or twelve feet across, its edges jagged where the frozen snow had cracked and given way. He wasn't yet close enough to see into it.

"Dad?"

There was no answer. All he could hear was a faint trickle of water somewhere below him. Cautiously, he maneuvered his skis sideways, testing the snow with each small step, expecting that at any moment it might collapse and swallow him. It seemed firm. Then he remembered his avalanche transceiver. This was exactly what it was for, to help you locate someone buried in the snow. He took off his gloves and unzipped his jacket and pulled the transceiver out and started fiddling with the knobs. But his hand was shaking and his head so blurred with panic that he couldn't remember how the damn thing worked.

"Shit! Shit! Shit!"

"Here! I'm here!"

The boy's heart lurched.

"Dad? Are you okay?"

"Yeah. Be careful."

"I saw blood."

"I cut my face. I'm okay. Don't come too near the edge."

But it was too late. There was a deep cracking sound and the boy felt the snow tilt beneath his skis and in the next instant he was falling. He caught a brief glimpse of his father's bloodied face staring up at him as the lip of the crater crumbled and then he saw nothing but the white of the snow cascading with him.

The next thing he knew, his father was hauling him out of the wreckage, asking him if he was hurt. At first the boy didn't know the answer but he said he didn't think so. His father grinned.

"Good job, son. You just made us a way out."

He nodded and the boy turned and saw what he meant. The collapse had created a kind of ramp for them to climb. They sat staring at each other, his father still grinning and dabbing his cheek with a bloody handkerchief. There was a long gash but it didn't look deep and the bleeding had almost stopped. The boy shook his head.

"Didn't think I'd find you alive."

"Hope you got that picture."

"Wow, Dad. That was some fall."

The walls of the hole in which they sat were layered with shelves of bluish-white ice, which their two falls had shattered. It was like being in the cross section of some giant frosted wasp nest. The floor felt firm and when the boy brushed away the snow he saw they were on solid ice. His skis had come off when he fell and lay partly buried in the snow. He stood and gathered them up. His father slowly stood too, wincing a little as he did so. The sun was just creeping in on them.

"I guess we ought to have a look for my skis," he said.

His pack was lying on the ice just next to where the boy had brushed away the snow. A shaft of sun was angling onto it. The boy stooped to pick up the pack and as he did so, something caught his eye, a pale shape in the translucent blue of the ice. His father saw him hesitate.

"What is it?"

"Look. Down here."

They both kneeled and peered into the ice.

"Jesus," his father said quietly.

It was a human hand. The fingers were splayed, the palm upturned. The boy's father paused a moment then brushed away a little more snow until they saw the underside of an arm. They looked at each other. Then, without a word, they got to work, brushing and scraping and pushing away the snow, creating a window of ice through which, with every stroke of their gloves, they could see more of what lay encased.

Tucked beneath the upper arm, half-concealed by a naked shoulder and peering shyly up at them with one blank eye, they now could see a face. From the swirl of hair, captured as if in a photograph, it looked like a young woman. She lay at an angle, her legs askew and slanting away into the darker ice below. She was wearing some kind of crimson top or jacket that was rucked and twisted and seemed to have torn away from her arm and shoulder. The fabric trailed from her as if she had been frozen in the act of shedding it. Her flesh was the color of parchment.

TWO

Sheriff Charlie Riggs looked at his watch. He figured he had about fifteen minutes to get through the stack of paperwork that lay menacing him from the only clearing in the jungle of his desk. If he didn't get away by two, he wouldn't be able to drive into Great Falls and be back in time for his daughter's tenth birthday party. He had to go to Great Falls to pick up her present, which he should have done yesterday, but as usual a dozen damn fool things had popped out of nowhere and he hadn't been able to. The present was a custom-made, hand-tooled saddle that he'd ordered in a fit of extravagance a couple of months back. How he had ever believed he could afford it, he had no idea. The thought of how much it was going to cost made him wince.

He heeled his chair closer into the desk, shoved aside a couple of stale coffee cups and picked up the first file. It was a draft of yet another report on the use of methamphetamine in Montana. The door to his cramped little office was open and out in the dispatch room all the phones seemed to be ringing. Nobody was answering them because it was Liza's day off and the new girl, Mary-Lou (who hadn't really gotten the hang of things yet), was at the counter talking with old Mrs. Lawson, whose dog had again disappeared. The old biddy seemed to have left her hearing aid at home because Mary-Lou was having to shout and say everything twice. Through the window he caught sight of Tim Heidecker, one of his not-so-sharp deputies, parking his truck. It was odds on that as soon as the boy stepped inside he'd come barging in with a whole bunch of dumb questions. Charlie slipped from behind his desk and quietly closed his door. It was ten to two already.

It wasn't so much his daughter's disappointment that he worried about. He and Lucy got along just great and

26

he knew she'd understand. What bugged him was that he would be handing yet another weapon on a plate to her mother. He and Sheryl had been divorced nearly five years now and she had remarried, happily, by all accounts, though how anyone could be happy with the slack-jawed jerk she'd shacked up with was a mystery. What continued to amaze Charlie was how, even after all this time—and even though it was she not he who had walked out—Sheryl could never resist the slightest opportunity to take a jab at him. And she seized on anything that involved Lucy with thinly disguised glee. It wasn't enough that Charlie should have been a lousy husband, he had to be a useless father too.

The use of methamphetamine is on the increase, he read. Well, well. Who would ever have guessed? He often wondered how much the people who wrote these darned reports got paid for restating the blindingly obvious. Hell, you could spend five minutes on the Web or go down to the bookstore and find out how to make the stuff in your own kitchen. Maybe he was just getting too old and cynical.

"I'm sure he'll show up, Mrs. Lawson," Mary-Lou was saying out at the counter.

"What was that?"

"I said, 'I'm sure he'll show up.'"

He heard Tim Heidecker answering one of the phones. The chances of his being able to handle whatever it was on his own were about a million to one against. Sure enough, within a minute there was a knock on the door and, before Charlie could hide, it opened to reveal the boy's irritating face.

"Hey, Chief—"

"Tim, I'm real busy right now. And please don't call me Chief."

"Just got a call from the Drummond place, you know, up there on the Front—"

"I know where the Drummond place is, Tim. Can you tell me later, please?"

"Sure thing. Just thought you ought to know."

Charlie sighed and let the report flop on his desk.

"Tell me."

"Couple of skiers just showed up out there, say they found a body up Goat Creek. Young woman, frozen in the ice."

Ned and Val Drummond's ranch was a small spread that lay close by the north fork of the creek. Beyond them, apart from one or two cabins that only got used in summer, there was only wilderness. It took the best part of an hour for Charlie and Tim Heidecker to drive out there and the best part of another to interview the two skiers. They seemed good people and were well aware how lucky they'd been. If they hadn't managed to find that other ski, the father would have had a hard time getting out. His son would have had to come down alone to raise help. But they were smart and well prepared, which was more than could be said for a lot of the idiots who got into trouble up there and had to be rescued.

The father was able to pinpoint on the map where

they'd found the body. Charlie had brought out a couple of snowmobiles on the trailer and for a while he toyed with the idea of going up at once to take a look. But the sun was already getting ready to disappear behind the mountains and when it did, the light would go fast and the temperature would plummet. If it was frozen into the ice like they said it was, the body wasn't going anyplace. Better leave it till morning, he figured, work out a plan and go up with all the right gear. In any case, he wanted the father to come along too and though Val Drummond had done what she could to patch it up, that cut on his face needed stitches.

They all sat drinking mocha coffee in the Drummond's dark, log-walled kitchen. Charlie had known Val since they were kids and had always had a soft spot for her. In fact they'd once had a little romantic moment after a high-school dance. Even now he could picture it clearly. In her early forties, she was still a fine-looking woman, tall and athletic in that kind of horsey way. Ned was shorter and ten years older and talked too much, like people with a lot of time on their hands tended to, but he was okay. Val had volunteered to drive the boy's father to the medical center to get some stitches and had said he and his son were more than welcome to stay the night. Both offers had been gratefully accepted. Everyone agreed to meet at eight the next morning when they would go up and check out the body.

Just as they were saying their good-byes, with a sinking feeling in his gut, Charlie remembered Lucy's party. There was no signal on his cell phone up here so he asked Val quietly if he could use the landline. She showed him into the living room and left him there. Charlie figured the party would still be going on but there was no way he was going to get there before it finished. He dialed Sheryl's number and steeled himself.

"Hello?"

She always sounded quite pleasant until she knew who was calling.

"Hey, Sheryl. Listen, I'm really sorry. I—"

"Nice of you to call, at least."

"Something cropped up and I couldn't—"

"Something more important than your daughter's tenth birthday party? I see. Well, there you go."

"Can I speak to Lucy?"

"They're all busy right now. I'll tell her you called."

"Can't you just—"

"Are you bringing the saddle over?"

"I . . . I didn't have time to—"

"Okay. Fine. I'll tell her that too."

"Sheryl, please—"

"Nothing changes, does it, Charlie? I've gotta go. Bye now."

They heard the snowmobiles long before they saw them. At last the headlights eased into view, strobing through the trees far below them then climbing the steep slope out of the forest and bouncing up alongside the creek toward them, the yellow beams shafting the dying blue light of the valley.

The closest they had been able to park the search-and-rescue vehicle was at a trailhead nearly three miles down the valley. It was a converted school bus decked out with a lot of fancy equipment. Ordinary radios weren't reliable in these steep canyons so the bus had one with a 110-watt booster, powerful enough to relay messages between those in the mountains and the sheriff's office thirty miles away. Everything they needed had to be ferried up from the trailhead by snow-mobile. The two that were heading up toward them now were bringing chainsaws, blowtorches, and some pow-erful lamps so Charlie and his men could go on working into the night.

He had a team of ten, three of them his deputies and the rest search-and-rescue volunteers, apart from the Forest Service law-enforcement guy who meant well but was young and new to his job and mostly got in the way. Protocol, however, dictated he be there because the girl's body had been found on Forest Service land. They had worked in shifts, going down to the bus every few hours for rest and food and drink—all except Charlie, who stayed with the body the whole time. They brought him food and hot drinks every now and then, but he was tired and cold and by now more than a little grouchy at having to wait almost an hour for the equip-ment.

They had been at it all day. First, they had cordoned off the whole area, then systematically searched it, pho-tographing and videotaping the scene from all angles. They hadn't found a single clue as to how the body might have come to be there. With all that snow and ice

Charlie hardly dared hope for one. Maybe when the thaw came they would find something. Clothes or a shoe or a backpack, maybe. Even footprints in an underlayer of snow or mud, if they got really lucky.

The two skiers had brought them here at dawn and showed them where the body was. Floating down there in the ice, she was as ghostly a sight as Charlie had ever witnessed and as the county coroner as well as sheriff he'd seen his fair share of bodies over the years. The skiers hadn't hung around longer than they had to. The father had fifteen stitches in his cheek which had bruised up like a beetroot. He was keen to get home. The boy had looked pale and still a little in shock. He'd be going home more of a man than he left.

It wasn't until the early afternoon that they were ready to start trying to cut the girl out. It turned out a whole lot trickier than Charlie had figured. The body would have to be driven over the mountains to the state crime lab in Missoula, a journey that would take a good three hours. With warmer weather forecasted, they all agreed that the best way to preserve it was to keep it encased in ice. Until now they had been working with spud bars, carefully chipping the ice away fragment by fragment so as not to miss any item of evidence that might be frozen there. But it was like mowing a hay-field with a pair of scissors and Charlie decided that unless they changed their method, they would be here for weeks.

The snowmobiles were coming up the last hundred yards beside the creek now, both of them towing sleds stacked with the equipment. Charlie and those who had been waiting with him walked over to meet them. The headlights flashed on the yellow-green fluorescent vests that they were all wearing over their black parkas. As night was falling, so was the temperature. Even in his insulated boots his feet felt numb. What he'd give to be at home in front of the fire with the new book he'd just started. As he trudged through the snow, he took off his gloves and tried to blow some warmth back into his fingers. His mood wasn't much improved by seeing Tim Heidecker climbing off the first snow-mobile.

"What took you so long?"

"Sorry, Chief. Snowmobile got stuck down the creek."

"Why didn't you radio?"

"We tried. Couldn't get anyone to hear."

"Well, let's get moving."

They had brought him some hot soup and some candy bars which made him feel a little more benign. He stood sipping the soup and issuing orders every now and then while they rigged up the lights to the little generator and positioned them. Above him the mountains dimmed to looming shapes against a sky that slowly filled with stars.

Soon the crater into which the skiers had fallen was a cocoon of light in the enfolding night air. Its floor had been brushed of all snow and through the burnished black ice the young woman, with her swirled hair and her arm stretched out and her torn red jacket trailing behind her, looked like a leaping dancer captured in obsidian.

It took another six hours to cut her out. One of the chainsaws jammed and twice they had to radio down for more blades. And because the ice crazed and went opaque when they cut into it, they kept having to stop and to use the oxyacetylene torches to melt it so that they could see what they were cutting into. They sliced a wide trench parallel to where the young woman lay and placed a sled there and began to lever her onto it with wooden poles. But her sarcophagus of ice was too heavy and there was a terrible creaking and cracking and one end of the sled broke through and tilted into the running water of the creek below. For a few long and perilous minutes, it seemed as if she was going to slide off and disappear through the hole but the men managed to slip ropes around her and hold her safe until they got the poles beneath the sled and propped it up and righted it.

They trimmed more ice from around her to lighten the load but the block was still too big for a body bag so they radioed down for tarpaulins and wrapped it up like a parcel and fastened it with duct tape and ropes. And just before midnight three snowmobiles and half a dozen men, all straining at the ropes, succeeded at last in hauling the sled and its black-shrouded cargo from the hole.

Getting her down to the bus took another hour and it was nearly three by the time they had her loaded into the back of Charlie's truck, insulated with blankets and sheets of cardboard. A couple of his deputies volunteered to accompany him over to Missoula but Charlie declined. They'd been working their butts off for almost twenty-four hours, and he thanked them all and ordered them off to their beds. He felt himself in that strangely energized state that lay beyond tiredness and, for some reason he didn't fully understand, he wanted to be alone.

He drove down through Augusta and turned right onto Route 200 at a lonely crossroads where only a month earlier he had helped lift two dead teenagers from a wrecked car. Two straight roads met in the middle of nowhere and there were even traffic lights but it remained a place where people regularly managed to die. The memory unsettled him and got him musing about the dead girl who lay behind him, still frozen in her ballerina leap. The image had imprinted itself in his mind and he tried to clear it but couldn't.

He kept wondering who she was and how she came to be there. He remembered a suicide up there once, not far from Goat Creek, a boy of seventeen who had taken off all his clothes and neatly folded them and placed them in his pack along with a rambling poem he'd written that tried to explain why he had to kill himself. He'd thrown himself off a cliff and his remains were found a month later by some bow hunters. Maybe this young woman was another such case. Or maybe she had fallen by accident. No hikers or skiers had been reported missing but that didn't necessarily make it suspicious. Most likely she'd been on her own and was from somewhere far away and hadn't thought to tell anyone where she was going. These things happened. Hopefully the body was in good enough condition to get an ID.

Charlie wondered about her parents or some other loved one and what they must be going through, the daily agony of not knowing where she was. He couldn't help imagining the same thing happening to Lucy. His only child just vanishing like that and he and her mother not knowing if she were alive or lying murdered at the bottom of a ditch. How would he handle it? Hell, it would drive any parent insane.

He crossed the Continental Divide at Rogers Pass and started the winding descent toward Lincoln. But so lost was he in the dark meanderings of his head that he took a bend too fast and almost ran into a pair of white-tailed deer. He stamped on the brake and the truck slithered and snaked across the road. He heard the body sliding forward behind him and as he skidded to a sideways stop across the verge, it slammed into the back of his seat with such force that his neck whiplashed and he saw stars.

Charlie sat for a few moments, collecting himself and waiting for his heart to settle down. If the road hadn't been gritted, he'd have been flying off it into the tree-tops. He drove the rest of the way at forty miles an hour with an oldies radio station on full blast to keep bad thoughts at bay, his neck throbbing to the beat.

The state crime lab was a smart brick building just off Broadway on the way to the airport. He'd had his office phone ahead to make sure there would be someone there to admit the body and to warn them it was a heavy one. They had obviously gotten the message because the two guys who came out to meet him looked like Olympic weight lifters.

"So this is our Jane Doe," one of them said as the three of them struggled to load her onto the gurney. "Man, talk about on the rocks. You got more ice than body here."

"Freshness is our byword," Charlie said.

They wheeled her straight into the cold room and Charlie signed a form and wished them goodnight.

The eastern sky was paling to shades of pink and dove gray as he drove back into town. There were one or two cars and trucks about now. He briefly considered driving home but concluded it wasn't wise. Now the job was done, tiredness was falling heavily upon him and his neck hurt like hell. He found a motel near the interstate and took a room barely bigger than a pool table. But it had a bed and that was all he cared about. He shut the beige plastic blind, shed his jacket and boots, and crawled under the covers. Then he remembered he hadn't turned off his cell phone and wearily went to get it from his jacket. The screen showed that he had voicemail. He got back into bed, lowering his neck carefully onto the pillow. He switched off the bedside lamp and accessed the message.

It was Lucy. She said she hoped he was okay and that she was sorry he hadn't been able to get to her party. She told him she missed him and loved him very much.

It was dumb, Charlie knew, and not at all like him, and it was only because he was so ragged with tiredness. But, alone in the darkness, if he'd allowed himself, he could easily have wept.

THREE

She had been waiting nearly a quarter of an hour and was starting to feel foolish. Across the sunlit white stone floor of the small piazza, a group of schoolgirls, some of them licking ice creams and all impossibly pretty, kept staring at her and although Sarah barely understood a word of Italian, she was sure they were talking about her. The girls were supposed to be listening to their teacher, a nervous-looking woman with tightly pinned hair who was reciting from a book. She was no doubt briefing them about the gallery that they—and Sarah, if her date showed up—were about to visit.

She took her cigarettes out of her purse and lit one. She would give him twenty minutes. That was what Benjamin used to say. If someone kept you waiting, allow twenty minutes, then go. It was polite yet assertive, he said. Any longer and people would believe you had no self-respect. It irritated her that she should still think to behave according to his rules after four and a half years of living without him. But it was too ingrained.

In so many different situations, whether buying clothes or choosing from a menu or expressing a view on almost any subject, she would catch herself wondering what Benjamin would say. Then, to punish herself, she would deliberately go the other way, opt for a color or entrée she knew he would hate, or voice an opinion that would have him howling in protest. The trouble was, after so many years together, their views almost always coincided. The cost of her rebellion could be counted in the number of ghastly new outfits that hung unworn in her closet.

It was her last day in Venice and she didn't want to waste it waiting for a virtual stranger, a man at least twenty years her junior who, in any case, had probably forgotten all about her. She had planned to spend the day browsing the shops, buying gifts for a few people back home. And to get this done in time to meet the young man, she had risen, breakfasted, and left the hotel before eight.

They had met the previous morning on the ferry to Torcello. Her tour group had split up for the day and only a handful had wanted to make the hour-long trip across the lagoon. They were mostly retired couples or pairs of friends, either from New York City or New Jersey. All were a good ten years older than Sarah and she had little in common with any of them. There was too much moaning about the hotel food and how expensive everything was. All week she had kept her distance, politely declining offers to include her. Her best friend Iris, with whom she had booked the trip, had cancelled at the last moment because her mother had a stroke. Sarah probably should have cancelled too. But she'd never been to Venice and was reluctant to miss the chance.

On the ferry she chatted for a while with the merry widows—two women from Newark who never stopped laughing—and then escaped aft to find a seat where she could quietly read her book and gaze out across the green water at the vaporettos chugging by.

The young man had come on board when the ferry stopped at the Lido. He took a seat across the aisle from her, facing the same way. He was probably in his mid- to late twenties, conservatively dressed in a white shirt and pressed charcoal pants. He caught her looking at him and gave her a beautiful smile. She smiled back politely and quickly looked down at her book, hoping the glow she could feel in her cheeks didn't show. Out of the side of her eye she saw him pull a sketchbook from his black leather bag. He flipped through it until he found the page he was looking for and then took out a pen and set to work.

Sarah could see it was a precise drawing in black ink of an old palazzo. There were patches of crumbled stucco and ornate scrollings at the windows. He was filling in the detail, perhaps from memory or perhaps simply from his own imagination. Whichever it was, the work was impressive. Again he caught her looking and graciously showed her what he was doing. They began talking. In robust, if flawed, English, he told her he was from Rome and that he came to Venice every spring to visit an aged aunt. The picture was of her house.

"She must be very grand," Sarah said.

"I make it look much grander than it is. She like that."

"You draw very well."

"Thank you, but I know I am too technical. I am a student of . . . *architettura*."

"Architecture. My husband was an architect."

"Oh. He is no longer?"

"No, I mean, he *is* an architect. He's just no longer my husband."

When they reached Torcello, they found themselves walking together along the path that wound from the dock to the ancient church of Santa Fosca. The early spring sun was hot and reflected brightly on the white cement. Sarah took off her sweater and tied it around her hips like a teenager. She was wearing a sleeveless pink T-shirt and a white linen skirt.

The young man said he had come that day to draw Torcello's famous bell tower. He seemed to know a lot about the history of the island. It was settled, he said, in the fifth century, much earlier than Venice itself. It had once been a thriving place, with a population of twenty thousand. But malaria had driven people away and most of the buildings had fallen into ruin and disappeared. These days only a few dozen people lived there.

Outside the church, he showed her the crudely carved stone throne that was supposed to have belonged to Attila the Hun.

"Do you think he really sat on this?" she said.

"Not for very long. It looks not very comfortable."

"Maybe that's what made him so mean."

They went inside the church. It was cool and dark and filled with a reverential hush. They stood in awe for a long time before a golden mosaic of the Madonna and Child. He whispered to her that in his opinion it was the most beautiful thing to be seen in all of Venice, except perhaps for the Scuola Grande di San Rocco. He asked her if she had been there yet and, when she said no, offered to show it to her the following day. Flattered and amused by the attention of this handsome, diffident man who, with his perfect skin and perfect teeth and clear brown eyes, was young enough to be her son, she agreed. They arranged to meet. She left him settling down to draw the bell tower and only when they shook hands to say good-bye did they tell each other their names. His, appropriately, was Angelo.

And now here she was, waiting as agreed, like a fool, outside the Scuola Grande or whatever the damn place was called, being giggled at by a bunch of schoolgirls who probably, given that she was smoking and trying too hard to look chic in her shades and her little navy Armani dress, had her down as some sort of superannuated hooker. She checked her watch again. He'd had twenty-two minutes (those two extra minutes a pathetic defiance of her ex-husband) and that was enough. She squashed her cigarette under her shoe, stuck out her tongue at the most insolent of the schoolgirls, and strode off.

Three minutes later she heard her name being called and looked back to see Angelo running over the bridge she had just crossed. She waited for him to reach her and gave him her coolest smile. Through his panting he managed to explain that his aunt had been taken ill that morning. Bless him, Sarah thought, surely he could do better than that. But he seemed so genuinely contrite and distressed for having kept her waiting that she couldn't help but forgive him. Okay, she was a pushover, but what the hell? He was a lot better company than the merry widows, who had probably written her off anyway as too damn snooty.

The Scuola Grande was filled with Tintorettos. The upper hall was vast and dark and sumptuously furnished in red velvet and polished walnut that gleamed in the pooled light of the wall lamps. There were perhaps fifty or sixty people there and all, even the schoolgirls who were now there too, stood peering in silent wonder at the paintings that adorned the walls and ceiling. The pictures themselves were dimly lit and Sarah had to put on her glasses to make out the religious themes they depicted.

Angelo was as diligent and informed a guide as he had been the previous day on the island. He whispered to her that the place was built in the early fifteen hundreds and dedicated to San Rocco, the patron saint of contagious diseases, in the vain hope that he might save the city from the plague. Tintoretto, Angelo said, had spent almost a quarter of a century decorating it. It was the kind of information that could easily have been plundered from any guidebook and the cruel thought occurred to her that perhaps he made a habit of picking up female tourists of a certain age.

The most renowned of Tintoretto's paintings, *The Crucifixion*, was in a small adjoining room and they stood there for a long time staring at it. Sarah had never known quite what to make of religion. Her mother was a lapsed Catholic and her father a lapsed atheist, now teetering in his seventies over the edge of agnosticism into an as yet amorphous realm of belief. Benjamin had always denounced any form of religious belief as a convenient excuse for not thinking. And though Sarah was less zealous in her skepticism, her attitude on this—and so many other issues—had been infected by his.

So perhaps it was, again, some futile, half-conscious attempt to excise his influence, to mark herself out as an independent mind, that she allowed herself to be so moved by the painting. It was a tumult of suffering and beauty, each cluster of characters busy in its own drama. And the nailed Christ, winged and crowned with light against the stony sky and gazing down from his cross at his executioners, radiated such serenity that Sarah found herself filled with a confused and nameless longing.

Behind her glasses her eyes began to brim but she managed to keep the tears from spilling. She was sure, however, that the young man at her side noticed. He had been saying something about Tintoretto's habit of putting a self-portrait into his pictures but he broke off and walked away a few paces to study another painting. Sarah was grateful. If he'd tried to touch or comfort her she would certainly have lost control and started to sob. And she had done enough crying these past few years.

It mystified, even slightly angered, her that a mere picture could bring her so close to the brink and she used the anger to chastise and compose herself.

Stepping again into the sunlight was a relief. They wound their way to the Grand Canal just in time to catch a vaporetto to the Rialto Bridge where Angelo said he knew a good little restaurant. Venetians ate there, he said, not tourists. It turned out to be a modest place, halfway along a narrow alley. White-coated waiters, all of whom seemed to Sarah curiously small, scurried between the tables with trays stacked with fresh seafood and steaming pasta. The one who took their order did so with a curt politeness.

She told Angelo to choose for her, that she liked almost everything. He ordered a salad of sweet tomatoes, basil, and buffala mozarella and then some grilled whitefish whose name meant nothing to her but which, when it arrived, looked and tasted a little like striped bass. They drank a whole bottle of white wine which he said was made from grapes that grew along the eastern shore of Lake Garda. It was cool and creamy and Sarah drank too much of it and began to feel a little lightheaded.

She had never felt comfortable talking about herself. It was a subject about which she felt there was nothing to say that could possibly be of interest to anyone. Of course, after Benjamin left, she had gotten a lot better at it. Iris and the handful of close friends who rallied around her hadn't given her much option, urging her to explore with them the failure of her marriage, examining every wretched corner and wrinkle of it until there seemed to be nothing left to say and they all grew sick of it.

And yet long before that, almost as long as Sarah could remember, when she and Benjamin had been—at least, as far as she was concerned—happily married, she had developed a simple technique to avoid revealing too much about herself. She would ask questions instead and soon discovered that the more direct and startlingly personal the question, the more likely it was that the person asked (especially if it happened to be both a stranger and a man) would start talking about himself and forget to ask her anything. And this was what she was now doing with Angelo.

She asked him about Rome, about his studies, about what kind of architecture interested him; about his aunt (whose sickness, surprisingly, seemed to be authentic); and finally even got him talking about a German girlfriend called Claudia to whom some day he hoped to be married. At which point, the disparity between his confessions and her almost total reticence became so great that he placed his palms upon the white crumb-strewn tablecloth and demanded a few answers from her.

He asked if she worked and she told him about selling the bookstore and what a relief it was after all these years to be free of it.

"You didn't like it?"

"I loved it. Books are my great passion. But small independent stores like we were have a hard time competing nowadays. So now I don't sell them, I just read them."

"What are your other great passions?"

"Mmm. Let me see. My garden. Knowing about plants."

"And now you have sold the bookstore, you can enjoy all these things. You are . . . How do they say? A lady of pleasure."

"I think what you mean is a lady of leisure."

Sarah smiled and looked at him over the rim of her glass while she took another slow sip of wine, realizing as she did so that she was flirting. It was about a hundred years since she had felt like flirting with anyone. She thought she'd forgotten how to. But she was enjoying it and, in that moment, had he asked her if he might come back with her to her hotel room for a shared siesta, she might even have found herself saying yes.

"So you were married," he said.

"Correct."

"But no longer."

"Correct."

"For how long were you married."

"A lifetime. Twenty-three years."

"And you live in New York."

"On Long Island."

"And you have children?"

She nodded slowly. Here it was. The most compelling reason to avoid questions. She felt pleasure draining from her through the hole he had just unplugged. She cleared her throat and replied quietly in as level a tone as she could.

"One of each. A boy and a girl. Twenty-one and twenty-three."

"And what do they do? They are students, yes?"

"Uh-huh."

"At college?"

"Yes. Kind of. Can we get the check?"

She needed to leave, to be outside again. And alone. And she saw that, of course, he was puzzled by this abrupt change in her. How could the mere mention of children so snap a woman's mood? It was the subject above all others to which they normally warmed. The poor boy would misinterpret it, naturally. He would probably assume she was embarrassed to admit that she had children not much younger than himself. Or conclude that she wasn't really divorced at all, just out for a good time and that the mention of children had struck some chord of guilt. She felt sorry for him and sorry too for fracturing what had been so easy and pleasant between them. But she couldn't help it. She stood up and took a credit card from her purse and placed it on the table in front of him, ignoring his protest. Then she excused herself and walked off to find the restroom.

Outside, bewildered, he asked her if she would like to visit another gallery and she said no and apologized, pretending that the wine had made her feel unwell, that she wasn't used to it. She thanked him for being so sweet and such a fine guide and for all the wonderful things he had shown her. He volunteered to accompany

48

her to the hotel but she said that, if he didn't mind, she would rather go alone. She said good-bye and offered him her hand and he looked so forlorn that instead she put both hands on his shoulders and kissed him on the cheek, which only seemed to confuse him more. When she walked off he looked quite bereft.

Back at the hotel, the lobby was quiet. A young British couple was checking in. They had the shy felicity of honeymooners. Sarah collected her key and walked toward the elevator, her heels clacking sharply on the white marble floor.

"Mrs. Cooper?"

She turned and the concierge handed her an envelope. She pressed the elevator button and while the cables clanked and whirred behind the glass door, she opened the envelope. It was a message from Benjamin in Santa Fe where he now lived with that woman. He had phoned at eight that morning and again at ten. He wanted her to call him back. It was urgent, he said.

FOUR

Ben and Eve had been in bed watching an old Cary Grant movie on the TV when Agent Kendrick called. It was a little after nine. Eve had lit candles and the flames were catching a draft from somewhere, sending shadows tilting and wobbling on the rough whitewashed walls and across the paintings and swaths of cloth that hung there. Pablo was asleep in his bedroom next door. Ben had only a short while ago looked in on him and stumbled through toys to tuck another blanket around his skinny shoulders. The boy shifted and murmured from some unknown corner of a dream, then settled again, his long dark curls spread like an aura on the pillow.

It was Saturday and they'd had the kind of perfect spring day that seasoned residents of Santa Fe took for granted but Ben continued to find miraculous. The dry desert air laced with the scent of lilac and cherry, the sky a clear deep blue and the light—that vivid, washed, almost shocking New Mexican light with its shadows sharp across adobe walls, the kind of light that could make even a color-blind philistine want to pick up a paintbrush—still, after four years of living here, could induce in him something close to euphoria.

The three of them had driven out in the Jeep for a late breakfast at the Tesuque Village Market then browsed the stalls of the flea market, Pablo running ahead of them like a scout, finding things and calling them to come and look. Eve bought an antique dress in purple and brown and orange swirls, cut on the bias. There was a hole under one arm and she haggled the woman down to thirty dollars and whispered as they walked away that it would be easy to fix and was worth at least a hundred.

In the mellowing sun that afternoon in the little backyard, the cherry tree groaning with an absurd overload of pink blossoms, they barbecued tuna steaks and sweet red peppers and zucchini while Pablo played chasing games with the little Swedish girl from next door. Eve's house was one of an enclave of six that stood on the south-facing side of a valley of sage and pinyon that funneled down into the town's west side. It was on one floor and made of cracked adobe, its angles rounded and its doors of ancient, grizzled pine. Both house and yard could have fit three times over into the house on Long Island where Ben had lived all those years with Sarah and where she now lived alone, but he already preferred it. He liked its spare, worn functionality, the way it belonged to the land that surrounded it. He liked it too because it was Eve's and even more because it wasn't his. It made him feel—as Pablo also made him feel—unencumbered, that his association was entirely of his own choosing. And this, of course, made him feel younger and more footloose than a man of almost fifty-two years deserved.

Just when the food was ready to be served the children came running up the path, all excited, saying the hummingbirds were back. They had seen one down by Eve's studio where the yard became more jungle than garden. Eve asked them what kind they thought it was. It was too early for the rufous, she said, and from what they were able to tell her they concluded that it must have been a black-chinned. After supper, with Pablo bathed and in his pajamas, they rummaged for the feeder jars in the closet and filled them with sugar water then hung them from a low branch of the cherry tree.

Pablo wanted to wait up to see if the birds would come and while Eve took a bath Ben sat with his arm around him on the couch, reading *Treasure Island* and breathing the warm, sweet smell of him, another man's child he had come to love as his own. The boy was nearly eight but small and skinny and looked younger. The hummingbirds never came and when it was dark Ben carried him slack and sleeping to his bed.

It was Eve who answered when Kendrick called. And Ben knew from her face and from her voice what kind of call it was. She handed him the phone and muted the TV. She sat up and swung her legs out of the bed and Ben reached out to try to make her stay. She always moved away and found something to do when his other life called. When he had once mentioned this she said it was only to give him space, but he suspected it was also to protect herself. She whispered now that she would make them some tea and be right back.

Special Agent Dean Kendrick worked out of Denver and had become Ben's main contact with the FBI. There had been others with whom he had talked during the past three and a half years that Abbie had been on the run and many more, he was sure, who had watched him and followed him and bugged his phones and e-mails and monitored his bank accounts, faceless men and women who probably knew more about his habits than he did himself.

The ones whose names he knew and whom he had called for news every few weeks were civil enough though rarely friendly. But Kendrick was different. He seemed genuinely sympathetic and had almost become a friend, though Ben had only ever met him once. They even called each other by their first names now. Maybe he was just better at his job than the others. He certainly made Ben feel more at ease and, of course, if he felt that way, he might more likely let something slip, some secret snippet of information that might help them catch and convict his daughter. Ben only wished he had such a secret.

"Ben, how're you doing?"

"I'm fine. How are you doing?"

"I'm okay. Do you have someone with you?"

It seemed an odd question, given that he'd just spoken with Eve.

"Yeah. We're just watching a movie. Why?"

"I've got some news. About Abbie. They were going to get one of our guys in Albuquerque to drive up and tell you in person but I thought you'd rather hear it from me."

He paused. Ben was way ahead of him.

"I'm afraid it's not good news."

But still his heart chimed. What was good news or bad news when it came to Abbie? And good or bad for whom? She hadn't called any of them—not him, nor Sarah, nor even her brother Josh—in almost three years now. If the FBI had caught her that would surely qualify as good news, wouldn't it? He swallowed.

"Uh-huh?"

"They found her body up on the Front Range in Montana, west of Great Falls. She'd been there awhile. Ben, I'm really sorry."

Cary Grant was about to get beaten up by two heavies. He was trying to charm his way out but it wasn't working. Ben's brain felt closed. His daughter dead? He could see it almost dispassionately as a concept but it wasn't something he was going to let into his head. It wasn't possible. Eve appeared in the doorway with two mugs of green tea. She stopped there and stood very still, her loosened hair raven against the pale of her shoulders, steam curling from the mugs, the candlelight dancing in the creases of her peach satin robe. Watching with those still brown eyes, knowing.

"What kind of condition . . ."

Ben couldn't allow himself to finish the thought. His little girl decaying, a carcass picked at by savage animals. No.

"I mean, are you sure it's her?"

"A hundred percent. Fingerprints and DNA. Ben, I'm so sorry."

There was a long silence. Ben felt as if he were watching his world unhinge and twirl slowly away from him. Eve put down the tea and came to sit beside him on the bed. She laid a cool arm around his shoulders. Kendrick waited and when Ben was ready they talked some more. About practical things, from which Ben began to fashion a fragile shield from the shock. Kendrick delicately asked if he should let Sarah know, but Ben said he would do it himself and that, in any case, she was in Italy. From his weekly phone call to Josh two days ago, he knew she wasn't due home until Monday.

Kendrick said once more how sorry he was and that he would call again in the morning. They could decide then what to do about funeral arrangements and what to tell the media. There would, of course, have to be some sort of statement.

"Yes," Ben said. "Of course."

Ben thanked him and hung up and sat there staring at the TV. The credits were rolling. He found the remote and killed the picture. And only then did he start to weep.

An hour later, lying with his head still cradled on Eve's breast, her nightgown patched with his tears, they began to discuss what was to be done. Ben wondered if it might be best not to tell Sarah until she got back. Spare her all those long hours on the plane with no one to comfort her, cloistered alone with her grief. Maybe he should fly to New York and meet her off the plane and tell her then. But Eve, clearer-headed than he and, as a mother, wiser in such matters, said he couldn't leave it that long. Sarah had a right to be told straight away and would hold against him any failure to do so.

In Venice, they calculated, it was now six o'clock in the morning. Too early to call. Let her sleep, Ben thought. Give her two more hours without the pain. Without this new pain. He would phone at midnight. They could then decide between the two of them how to break the news to Josh and the grandparents and whoever else needed to know.

While they waited, he told her what Kendrick had said about releasing the news to the media. A couple of years ago, Abbie Cooper, little rich girl turned ecoterrorist, wanted all across America for murder, had been big news. There had been whole TV shows devoted to her, with dramatized reconstructions of what she was alleged to have done. For months Ben had to field half a dozen calls a week from reporters, mostly trying to follow up on some new angle. But as time went by and there was still no arrest, they seemed to lose interest and the circus had moved on. Maybe they wouldn't make too much of a meal out of her being found dead. Or maybe they would.

At midnight, when he called Venice, he was told that Signora Cooper had already left the hotel. And when he called again two hours later she still hadn't returned. They waited, fading in and out of sleep, holding each other while the candles burned low and guttered and one by one died. Once, while Eve slept on beside him, facing away from him, a curve of hip warm against his belly, he woke and wept again while a slice of moon traversed the window.

He was jolted from his sleep just before seven. Eve was standing beside the bed, handing him his ringing cell phone.

"It's Sarah," she said.

He saw the name on the little screen and so disoriented was he by sleep that for a moment he wondered why she might be calling. Then the leaden reality reassembled. Their daughter was dead.

Eve was already dressed. Sunlight flecked with dust was slanting in through the window behind her. He sat up and took the phone and she kissed his forehead and walked out. She had left a mug of coffee on the bedside table. He could hear Pablo calling from the kitchen. He pressed the green button on the phone and said hello.

"Benjamin?"

Her voice sounded tight and throaty, barely recognizable. She was the only one in the world who ever called him Benjamin.

"Sweetheart—"

She had reprimanded him more than once for calling her that—*Whatever I am to you now, Benjamin, I'm certainly not your sweetheart*—but it was hard to break a habit of so many years. This time she cut in on him before the word was fully uttered.

"What is it?" she said. "Is it Abbie? Have they found her?"

It startled him that she should know. But it was only to discuss their children that they ever talked nowadays. Then Ben realized that by *found,* she meant alive. He swallowed, still struggling to clear his head.

"Sarah—"

"For heaven's sake, Benjamin! Tell me!"

"She's dead."

"What?"

It was more an intake of breath than a word. How could he blurt it out like that? Kendrick had broken the news to him with so much more finesse. He stumbled on.

"They found her body. In Montana. Somewhere in the mountains."

"No. Abbie. Oh, no. No . . ."

She began a low, moaning wail and then tried to say

something but couldn't. And because the sound was so harrowing he began to talk, just to keep it from his ears. He talked and went on talking, trying to seem calm and clear, telling her what he knew, about the DNA and the fingerprints and where the body was being kept and about the decisions that they were going to have to make, until she screamed at him and told him to stop. At that his voice cracked and he lost control, as if all his words had emptied and weakened him.

And, separated by so many thousand miles and by distance of another kind far greater, they sobbed as one but each alone for the young life they had together spawned and loved and separately lost.

The funeral home, so Ben had been told, was only a short drive from Missoula Airport and he had already resolved that he would go there as soon as his flight got in. He hadn't told Sarah he was going to do this and he knew he should probably wait until she arrived from New York so they could go there together. But when he landed and switched on his cell phone there was a message from her saying she was having to take a later flight. She wouldn't be getting into Missoula until the evening, by which time the funeral home would be shut. That meant going there with her tomorrow. He couldn't wait that long.

Despite Kendrick's assurance that the identification was one hundred percent certain, there lingered in Ben's mind just a sliver of doubt that they might have made a mistake. He'd once read about a case where this had happened. Someone had mixed up two sets of samples and put the wrong names on them. He had to see her, see with his own eyes that it was Abbie.

He had brought only hand baggage and was one of the first off the flight. The chirpy young woman at the Hertz desk welcomed him like an old friend but that was probably just how they were trained.

"On vacation?" she asked.

"No, I'm here . . . to see my daughter."

"That's nice. She's at UM, right?"

"She was, yes."

It took her only a few minutes to process the paperwork. She told him the bay number of the car and handed him the documents and keys.

"So, you're all set. You have a great time."

Ben thanked her and went out through the double glass doors. The sky was vaulted in slate-colored cloud and the air felt warm and restless as if at any moment it might rain. Abbie used to say the weather in Montana was like Forrest Gump's box of chocolates: You never knew what you were gonna get. He remembered that first visit to Missoula, more than five years ago, when he and Sarah had flown here with her to check out the university. It was late October and when they arrived it was eighty degrees. They woke the next day to a foot of snow and had to go out and buy warmer clothes. At a store on North Higgins they had bought Abbie a cerise Patagonia ski jacket that cost more than two hundred bucks. God, she'd looked so beautiful that day. So confident, so full of joy.

Ben stopped himself. He mustn't think about her that way. There was too much to be sorted out, important decisions to be made, people to talk to, the sheriff, the local FBI people, find out what they thought had happened. If he let himself remember her like that, all aglow and happy, then he would be sure to lose it and be unable to think straight. Above all, Sarah would need him to be strong. He didn't want to let her down, give her yet another reason to hate him.

The car was a little silver Japanese thing. He had to shift the seat all the way back to get his legs under the steering wheel. Sarah would probably think he was being cheap and should have rented something bigger. They hadn't seen each other in more than a year and he already felt dread welling in his stomach. He started the car up, reversed from the parking bay and slowly headed out toward the highway.

The second time they had spoken on the phone, before Sarah flew home from Italy, she had fully regained composure. She was cool, almost businesslike. Not a tear was shed by either of them. Ben had been expecting a discussion but it was more like listening to a series of announcements. The body would be shipped back to New York, she said, and that was where the funeral would be, where all Abbie's loved ones lived. The *all* excluded Ben, of course, but he let it pass. And it would be a burial, which was how Sarah's family had always done these things. Ben had been planning to suggest a cremation, with the ashes scattered here in Montana, the place Abbie had so often said she loved best in all the world. But he wasn't going to get into a fight about it.

There was more to come. Sarah had already phoned Josh in New York. He was, she informed Ben, "devastated but okay." How to break the news to their son was another thing Ben had been expecting to discuss. He was furious. He had been all set to fly to New York to do it in person and now wished he hadn't waited. Moreover, Sarah had also organized for the boy to go stay in Bedford with her parents. Indeed, they had already driven to the city to collect him. Sarah would see him, albeit briefly, when she got back, then fly on to Missoula. Josh, she said, would not be coming with her.

Ben had thus been thoroughly preempted and excised. And, as usual, he swallowed his anger and said nothing. It was a technique Sarah had used over and over again since he left her and she now had it honed to perfection, excluding him from important decisions about their children with such a casual—sometimes even friendly—aplomb, that to complain seemed churlish. The underlying message was always the same: By leaving, he had revealed his total lack of love for them and had thereby forfeited all rights of consultation.

Sometimes she did it so brilliantly, he couldn't help but be impressed. And though it surprised him that she should choose to do it now, in their shared desolation, he realized later that she had in fact surpassed herself. For now he would have to call Josh in the enemy camp of his former in-laws. George and Ella Davenport had always considered him unworthy of their golden daughter and his desertion had vindicated their contempt. Ben was now properly consigned to some lower stratum of cheats, liars, and ne'er-do-wells.

Immediately after he had finished listening to Sarah's list of decisions, he called Josh's cell phone.

"Hey, Joshie."

"Hi."

"I was going to fly over and tell you about Abbie, but Mom says she already told you."

"Yeah."

"How are you doing?"

"Okay, I guess."

There was a long pause. Ben thought he could hear whispers in the background.

"Are you with your grandma and grandpa?"

"Yeah. We're in the car."

"Oh. Right. Well, say hi to them for me."

"Okay."

"Mom says you're not coming out to Missoula."

"What's the point?"

His voice was so flat and colorless that Ben wondered if the boy had taken too many of those antidepressant pills he'd been on for the last few months. Or perhaps he was just dazed by the news or embarrassed to talk in front of Ella and George. Ben cursed himself for not going to New York. It was he who should be with his son at this time, not those two.

"Well, I guess you're right. Listen, will you call me when you've got a moment to yourself?"

"Okay."

"Bye, then. I love you, son."

"Yeah. Bye."

The Valley View Funeral Home and Crematory—
"Serving Missoula's Bereaved Since 1964"—
stood between a used-car lot and a sinister-looking bar
called Mountain Jack's. It was skirted by a thin strip of
lawn doing its best to appear elysian. Ben parked in the
otherwise empty lot and, thrusting his hands into his
jacket pockets, walked toward reception. The building
was all Palladian pillars and swirled cream stucco, a
curious hybrid of temple and hacienda that at any other
time would have made the architect in him smile.
Beyond it, away to the west, lightning flickered against
the gunmetal shroud that had lowered itself over the
mountains. The air smelled of wet dust and just as he
reached the cover of the portico a first few plump rain-
drops began to smack and speckle the asphalt.

The reception area was a hushed expanse of mush-
room-pink carpet and magnolia walls, decorated with
elaborate arrangements of fake flowers and framed
prints. Away in the far corner, a muted TV was entertaining a coffee table and a pair of empty couches in
blue velour. Ben pressed the soundless button at the
reception desk and while he waited wandered with
soundless footsteps, inspecting the pictures. All were
landscapes and all featured water of some kind—a
river, lake, or ocean. There was a unifying, bland tran-
quility to them, nothing too poignant or risky, no sun-

sets or stormy skies, not a hint of hell or eternal judgment. He wondered if they ever censored the pictures to suit the special sensibilities of their clients. Maybe they had already done it for him because there sure wasn't a single snowy mountain on the walls.

"May I help you?"

A young man with a friendly round face and a body that seemed too long for his legs was heading across the mushroom pink toward him. Ben introduced himself and saw a fractional retuning in the man's smile. He wasn't overdoing it, just finding the right calibration of professional sympathy. This was the Jim Pickering both Ben and Sarah had spoken with on the phone.

"Your wife called to say you weren't going to make it today."

"She had to get a later flight. I flew up this morning from Albuquerque. We're not married anymore."

He didn't know why he had volunteered that, but the man nodded, readjusting the smile again, just a touch more concern.

"Is it inconvenient for me to see . . . ?" Ben couldn't finish the sentence. Should he say Abbie? My daughter? The body?

"Not at all. We're all ready for you."

"I just wanted to, you know, make sure—"

"I absolutely understand."

He asked Ben if he would mind waiting a moment and hurried off the way he came. He disappeared down a corridor and the silence reasserted itself. The place had the best soundproofing Ben had come across in a long time. He caught himself wondering what materials they had used. What was the matter with him? Waiting to see his daughter's body and thinking about goddamn acoustics?

Jim Pickering came back and asked Ben to follow him. As they walked a sequence of corridors, he explained that they had embalmed the body, as Mrs. Cooper had requested, and that the search-and-rescue people over the mountains had made the process a lot easier by keeping so much ice around her during recovery and transportation. The results, he said, were consequently a lot better than in the circumstances one might have expected. Whether the man was making a modest professional boast or simply trying to allay anxiety, Ben couldn't decide.

"We didn't have any clothes, so she is in what we call a hospital gown. And, of course, we didn't have any reference for hair and makeup, so you'll see we've gone for quite a natural look. There is scope for some minor adjustment, should you wish. And the casket is only temporary. Mrs. Cooper didn't say whether you would be interested in purchasing one from us or from the funeral home back east. We do have quite an extensive range."

"I'm sure."

"Well, here we are. This is our viewing room."

He stopped in front of some white double doors, his hands poised to open them. He was looking at Ben for the signal to proceed.

"Are we ready?"

Ben nodded.

The room was about fourteen feet by ten, and lit with a roseate glow by four tall uplighters, their tops flared like lilies. The plain, pale wood casket stood open on a waist-high table. From the doorway, all Ben could see of its interior was a band of pink satin lining.

"I'll leave you," Jim Pickering said. "I'll be just along the corridor. Take as long as you need."

"Thank you."

The doors closed quietly behind him. Ben stood there a moment, trying to conjure a trace of his earlier, absurd hope that the body would be someone else's. But he knew it was Abbie. He could feel his blood pulsing fast and insistent in his ears and an icy weight turned in the pit of his stomach. He swallowed and stepped forward.

It was almost three years since he had seen her. Her hair then had been dyed black and cut short and spiky, as if to advertise her anger. But now it was back to its natural reddish blond and longer and neatly combed so that it framed her slender neck and softened her. The face, with its pert nose and prettily arched eyebrows, was light-years from the hostile, screaming contortion that had haunted his head since that terrible night. Death, perversely, had warmed her. The funeral makeup had given her skin a clever, healthy luster. There was even, in the tilt of her chin and in the dimpling at the corners of her mouth, a curious imminence. As if something in a dream had amused her and at any moment she might smile or wake and tell him what it was. And open those eyes. Gray-green and flecked with hazel. He wished he could see them just one more time.

The only other body Ben had ever seen was his father's, almost twenty years before. And the undertakers then had gotten it all wrong—his hair, his expression, the way he knotted his necktie, everything. They had plastered on so much rouge and mascara and lipstick that he looked like some frightful, unwigged drag queen.

But in her white gown, like the bride she would never be, his daughter looked only serene and innocent and utterly beautiful.

"Oh, sweetheart," he whispered. "My little sweetheart."

He gripped the rim of the casket and bowed his head and closed his eyes. And the sobs came quaking through him and he didn't try to fight them. Alone now, he would allow himself this, and later be the stronger for Sarah.

How long he stood there, he couldn't tell. When he could cry no more, he straightened himself and walked across to a little table where a box of tissues had been placed. And when he had dried his face and composed himself, he walked once more to the casket and leaned in and kissed his daughter's cheek. She smelled of nothing and her flesh against his lips was as cold as stone.

FIVE

Sarah let the waitress fill her cup with coffee for the third time, and tried not to watch the two men across the table finishing their breakfasts. The sight and smell of all that egg and bacon and fried potato was making her feel queasy.

Jet-lagged, she had taken a sleeping pill sometime after midnight and all it did was plunge her into a shallow semi-coma fraught with anxious dreams. She woke twisted in her sheets like a mummy and with a blurred and aching head that two heavy-duty painkillers had failed to clear. Outside it was still raining. It hadn't stopped since she arrived.

Benjamin had met her off the plane and driven her to the hotel in the ridiculous little car he'd rented. Why he had to be so cheap, she had no idea. But she hadn't mentioned it. On the flight she had given herself strict instructions to be civil. But, God, it was hard. Even the sight of him now, eating his breakfast and talking trivia with this sheriff character, made her feel angry. He had grown his hair longer and bought himself some trendy little wire-rimmed glasses. All very Santa Fe.

Benjamin had booked them adjoining rooms at the Holiday Inn Parkside and after checking in last evening they had borrowed an umbrella and walked over to a Japanese restaurant on North Higgins. The food was fine but the conversation hideously stilted, perhaps because they were both trying so hard to avoid talking

68

about Abbie. Benjamin had seemed barely able to look her in the eye and kept asking all sorts of eager questions about Venice. She wanted to scream at him to shut up. Who on earth *was* he? This polite stranger who had shared her life for all those years and was now treating her like a guest with whom he'd gotten trapped at a cocktail party.

She knew she was being unfair and that it was probably her fault that he behaved that way. Some curious defense mechanism seemed to have clicked on inside her brain. Being cold and brittle and angry with him was the only way she could cope. Allow herself to be any warmer or more receptive to comfort and she would lose her foothold and fall off the edge, spiral into the black whirlpool she knew was waiting for her below. Her little girl dead, lying cold in a box . . . No, she wasn't going to let her head go there. But when he put his arm around her on their way back to the hotel she almost had. And again when he kissed her goodnight in the dingy corridor outside her room and they went off to their lonely, separate king-size beds, so thinly partitioned they could hear each other's every shuffle and cough and flush of the john.

Sheriff Charlie Riggs didn't have an office in Missoula, which was why he had suggested they meet for breakfast here at The Shack. It was a place Abbie had once taken them to, tucked away on West Main and just another short, wet walk from the hotel.

The sheriff had been there waiting for them, his rain-soaked Stetson and a white plastic bag beside him on the bench of the little wooden booth. He stood to greet them, a tall man, even taller than Benjamin, but bulkier, with a bushy mustache that was going to gray. His eyes were gentle and had in them a sadness that Sarah suspected was permanent, not merely contrived for their benefit. He had those old-fashioned Western manners that she had always been a sucker for, politely nodding when he shook her hand and calling her ma'am.

He declared at once how sorry he was about Abbie.

"I have a daughter myself," he said. "Can't even bear to think of such a thing happening."

"Not wanted for murder just yet, I hope," Sarah said with a withering brightness before she could stop herself. The poor man winced and Benjamin looked away.

"No, ma'am," the sheriff said quietly.

They sat down and the two men chatted about the weather and nothing much else until the waitress came and took their orders. Then, leaning forward and talking in a low voice so as not to be overheard, Sheriff Riggs had taken them through what had happened. He told them about the skiers finding Abbie in the ice and how the autopsy at the crime lab hadn't been able to establish either how she came to be there or how exactly she had died. He asked if they had any ideas about why she might have been in that part of the world and Benjamin said they hadn't. Abbie had suffered head injuries, the sheriff went on, as well as a broken leg and a dislocated shoulder. And there was water in her lungs, which suggested she might have drowned. The best guess at the moment was that the injuries had been sustained in a

70

serious fall, the cause of which remained unknown.

"You mean, someone could have pushed her?" Benjamin said.

"That has to be one possibility, yes sir." He glanced at Sarah, no doubt gauging her sensitivity to such talk. She felt vaguely affronted.

"What about suicide?" she said.

Benjamin looked at her in surprise.

"Abbie would never do that," he said.

"How would you know?" she snapped.

They both stared at her. The spite just seemed to come spouting out of her of its own accord. She hurried on, trying to soften it.

"I mean, how can any of us know? She's been missing so long, we don't know what might have been going on."

"You're right, Mrs. Cooper," Charlie Riggs said gently. "It has to be another possibility we can't yet rule out." She could tell he was getting the measure of how things stood between her and Benjamin. He probably already had her down as a prize bitch. She would have to get a grip and curb her tongue.

"Anyhow," the sheriff went on. "I want you to know that this is a top priority. We're going to keep going up there while the snow starts to melt. Hopefully we'll find something that'll help build us a picture of what happened."

If either of them wanted to go see where Abbie was found, he said a little awkwardly, he would be happy to show them. Benjamin thanked him and said he might well come back in a week or two to do that. How absurd and pointless, Sarah thought but managed to stop herself from saying. She couldn't think of anything worse—except seeing the body itself, which they were planning to do later, though she wasn't at all sure she could handle it.

The sheriff seemed about to say something else when the waitress arrived with the food. If so, he thought better of it and not a lot more was said while he and Benjamin ate. Sarah had ordered some wheat toast but didn't even touch it. What she really craved was a cigarette but she wasn't about to dent her dignity further by stepping out into the rain to have one.

When they had finished, Charlie Riggs said that if they didn't mind, he would take them along to the Federal Building on Pattee Street to meet the local FBI agent who had a few routine questions to ask them which might help them all find out what happened to Abbie. Sarah said that would be fine. Then, looking a little uncomfortable, he reached for the plastic bag beside him.

"These are the clothes your daughter was wearing when we found her," he said. "I didn't know if you'd want them, but one of the girls in the office washed and ironed them. The jacket's torn pretty bad. In the fall, I guess. Anyhow."

He handed the bag to Benjamin, who instead of just thanking him and putting it to one side, pulled out the red ski jacket and opened it up. Sarah could see his eyes filling as he looked at it. For heaven's sake, she thought.

Not here, not now. If he lost control, she would surely follow. She silently reached across and took the jacket from him and stuffed it back into the bag.

Charlie Riggs cleared his throat.

"There's one other important thing I haven't yet told you," he said. His voice was grave and he paused as if searching for the right words.

"Something they discovered in the autopsy that you probably didn't know. At the time of her death, Abbie was two months pregnant."

O ver the years, Charlie had met more than a few FBI agents and had gotten along fine with nearly all of them. There had been one or two who came on too strong or a little patronizing but the rest had always been courteous and decent and good at their jobs. Jack Andrews, the last one he'd had dealings with in the Missoula office and whom the Coopers had met when their daughter first disappeared, Charlie had liked a lot. But his successor, this young upstart Wayne Hammler, was something else.

They had been sitting in his stuffy little office for most of an hour and during that time he had barely let anyone else get a word in edgewise. Even with his GI's haircut and snappy blue blazer, he looked about fifteen years old. Maybe that was why he felt he had to pontificate to them like a pompous polecat. Right now he was giving the Coopers a speech about *interagency synergy* and *forensic information analysis systems,* whatever the hell they were. All he'd really done so far was go through again what Charlie had already told them. Mr. Cooper still seemed to be listening politely, but for the last ten minutes his ex-wife had been staring out of the window.

Charlie had been staring at her. It was kind of hard not to. He wondered how old she might be. These East Coast city women took care of themselves. Mid-forties, maybe. She was tall and elegant and had clearly once been a great-looking woman. In happier circumstances, if she put on a few pounds and let that cropped blond hair grow a little, she still could be. The dark blue dress suited her and Charlie would have put money on those little diamond studs in her ears being the real thing. All in all, Sarah Cooper was what his daddy used to call "a class act." Mind, that sharp tongue of hers sure seemed to have her ex-husband on eggshells. Charlie knew from his own dealings with Sheryl how the poor guy must feel. But he'd seen bereaved mothers behave like this before. Anger was probably just her way of hanging by her fingernails to sanity.

But now and then, behind that cool façade, he'd gotten a glimpse of how fragile and wounded she was. And it moved him to see a creature so graceful in so much pain. The look in her eyes when she learned about her daughter being pregnant was close to heartbreaking and it was still there now as she gazed out at the rain. Since Charlie broke the news, she'd barely spoken a word.

Ben Cooper bore his grief more visibly. He seemed like a decent enough guy. They must have once made a

fine couple, the kind you saw in those society magazines, sitting on a yacht or by a swimming pool, happy
and perfect and probably on the brink of divorce.
Charlie wondered what had gone wrong between the
two of them, whether it was all about their daughter or
whether they had traveled some other special route to
sadness of their own devising. There was a story there,
he had no doubt, along with the same old story shared
by himself and countless others, of guilt and grudge and
shattered hope.

He followed the woman's gaze. The rain had gotten
heavier and there was a wind now too. The trees outside
were starting to come into leaf and through the frantic
branches he could see squalls thrashing the roofs of
three U.S. Mail vans parked below in the street. A
young woman in a clear plastic poncho was pushing a
boy in a wheelchair along the sidewalk, trying to keep
him dry with a red umbrella. Charlie looked again at
Mrs. Cooper and found she was looking at him. He
smiled and with his eyes tried to apologize for
Hammler who was still droning on behind his immacu-
lately organized desk. There was a little chrome pot of
perfectly sharpened pencils and a matching tray for his
staples and paper clips. The little creep even had a
coaster for his coffee cup. Charlie remembered
someone once saying that you should never trust a man
with a tidy desk. Hammler's was borderline obsessive.

Mrs. Cooper didn't smile back. Instead she turned
and glared at her ex-husband. Whether it was because
of the polite attention the poor guy was giving

Hammler or for some other transgression, Charlie couldn't tell.

"So, that's where things stand as far as the investigation goes," the agent was saying. "Now, if you don't mind, I need to ask you both some questions."

"Okay," Mr. Cooper said. "If it'll help. Go ahead."

Hammler had his questions all neatly listed on a legal pad, squarely placed with a new pencil in front of him. The first was about when the Coopers had last seen or heard from their daughter. Charlie had already asked and he pointed this out to Hammler but to no avail. Mr. Cooper answered patiently, if a little wearily, but Charlie could see his ex-wife starting to seethe. Finally, when the agent began asking about Abbie's character and personality and whether they would describe her as being *prone to bouts of depression,* she exploded.

"Listen. You people have asked us all of this God knows how many times. We came to hear what you had to tell us, not to go over all this old stuff again. If you want to know these things, look at the files. It's all there. Everything Abbie ever did or said or had for breakfast is there. Just look it up."

Hammler blushed. Charlie nearly cheered.

"Mrs. Cooper, I'm well aware how difficult a time this is—"

"Difficult? Difficult! You haven't the slightest idea."

"Mrs. Cooper—"

"Who the hell do you think you are!"

She was on her feet now and heading for the door.

"I'm not listening to any more of this bullshit."

All the men had stood up too. Hammler looked like a kid who'd just been mugged for his candy. He started to say something but Mrs. Cooper, swinging the door open, turned to face them and cut him off.

"When you've got something new to tell us, I'm sure we'd be only too delighted to hear from you. But this morning, Wayne, we're a little pressed for time. We have to go pick up our dead daughter and ship her home for the funeral. So if you'll excuse us, we'll go now. Come on, Benjamin."

And she was gone. Her footsteps echoing angrily down the corridor. Hammler's jaw was jutting and he seemed about to head off in pursuit. Charlie stepped forward and gently restrained him.

"Let her go," he said quietly.

"But there's a lot to—"

"Later. It's not the right time."

Ben Cooper was just standing there with his head bowed, looking forlorn and embarrassed. Charlie picked up the poor guy's coat and laid a hand on his shoulder.

"Come on," he said. "You'll need a lift."

The sheriff parked outside the hotel and they sat in his truck for a few minutes with the rain drumming on the roof. He reassured them again that he would do everything in his power to find out how Abbie died. Ben was in the front and kept glancing over his shoulder at Sarah who hadn't said a word and didn't even seem to be listening. She sat hunched by the back window, silhouetted by the silver rivering of water on the glass. Her hair was wet and straggled and the collar of her white raincoat turned so high it looked as if she might at any moment vanish.

The sheriff apologized again for the FBI man and promised to call as soon as he had any news. They thanked him and went inside to check out and collect their bags. While Ben paid the bill, Sarah stood alone under the portico and when he had finished and came out to join her, she didn't wait for him to come along-side but turned and walked ahead of him out to the car, heedless of the rain, her arms folded tight to her chest. Ben noticed the backs of her calves were spattered with mud and the sight touched him and made him want to say something comforting, even if it was only to declare his admiration for the way she had stood up to that little FBI creep. But he was too wary of her now and didn't trust himself to find the right words or tone.

As they drove slowly out along Broadway to the funeral home, the repeating thud and swish of the wipers made the silence between them so loud that Ben could bear it no longer.

"How the hell could she be pregnant?" he blurted.

With a week's notice, he couldn't have come up with anything more crass. Sarah turned and looked at him and he swallowed and stared ahead and braced himself for the blistering put-down. But she said nothing.

Jim Pickering was waiting in the reception area to welcome them. He was wearing a smart suit in a mid-dling shade of blue, dark enough to be formal but not somber. From one glance at Sarah he seemed to sense that it was best to keep words to a minimum and soon he was leading the way once more to the viewing room.

Ben asked if she wanted him to go in with her and was neither surprised nor offended, only relieved, when she said she would rather see Abbie alone. The image of the girl in her white gown was etched in his head and he doubted he could bear the etching of another, of mother and daughter together. Instead, he went with Jim Pickering into the office along the corridor to do the paperwork.

There were documents to sign and details to be given for the death certificate and forms to complete for the shipping of the body to New York. The only airline able to ship bodies out of Missoula was Northwest, which meant connecting through Minneapolis. Jim Pickering had made the necessary arrangements. Abbie's casket, he explained, would be placed in something called an "air tray," a box with a plywood bottom and a cardboard top.

At dinner last night, Sarah had casually announced that her father would be meeting them at La Guardia and that it might be better if Ben flew back to New Mexico from Minneapolis.

"I was thinking I'd stay over in New York until the funeral," he said. "You know, help arrange things, spend some time with Joshie."

"We can handle it."

"I know you can. I'd just like to be involved."

"Please don't make an issue of this."

"I'm not, I—"

"There's nothing that can't be sorted out by phone. Come if you want, I just can't face a scene between you and Daddy at the airport."

"I suppose it's okay if I come to the funeral?"

"Why do you have to be so hostile?"

Ben narrowly avoided saying something he would regret. But he was getting tired of being bullied and excluded and on this issue he wasn't going to give in. There was a job to be done. And he wanted to see Josh; he had to see him. Any father would feel the same.

"Listen," he said as steadily as he could. "She's my daughter too. And there won't be a *scene*. I can handle your parents. I've done it for years. I want to come with you. Please."

She sighed and raised her eyebrows but that was the end of it.

The paperwork was done now, but Sarah still hadn't emerged from the viewing room, so Ben walked along to the room where a selection of urns and caskets stood on display. As he wandered around inspecting them, it occurred to him that perhaps he should have opted for something more lavish than the plain wood casket. Even now, Sarah was probably thinking, yet again, that he had been cheap. The more splendid ones cost around four thousand dollars. But they looked so pretentious and too grown-up. No doubt somewhere, he mused darkly, they had a special range for the younger deceased. The only thing he liked was an ornate bronze urn sculpted like a mountain, with pine trees and three deer—an antlered male, a female, and a cute little fawn. It was kind of Disney, but much more like Abbie. But, of course, they weren't cremating her.

"Shall we go?"

Sarah stood framed in the doorway, Jim Pickering hovering discreetly behind her. She was wearing sunglasses, her face as pale as her raincoat. Ben stepped toward her. He wanted to put his arms around her. It seemed the most natural thing in the world. But she read his intention and with the smallest gesture of her hand signaled that he shouldn't.

"Are you okay?" he asked stupidly.

"Fine."

"I was just having a look here and wondering if we should get a better casket," he blundered on. "I mean, I like the plain one, but . . ."

From behind her shades, she gave the room a quick, derisive scan.

"There's nothing here. I'll get one at home."

The plane took off on schedule into a clear blue sky. The rain had stopped just as they arrived at the airport as though it had been laid on only for their visit. From the windows of the departure lounge they had seen the wagon trundle Abbie out across the damp asphalt to the plane where four young men, chatting all the while, lifted and stowed it.

Now, as the plane banked and headed east, the forest skidding in vivid shades of sunlit green across the portholes, Sarah thought of the body tilting coldly in its narrow case below her in the dark of the hold. The fact of her daughter's death remained too vast to grasp and perhaps that was why her mind kept flitting strangely to these lesser facts, the circumstantial detail of the girl's unliving presence.

Standing alone by the open casket at the funeral home, she had been shocked, not at the sight of the body, so prettily, so ridiculously prepared, but at her own sense of detachment. She had been expecting it to be the moment when the bolted floodgates of her grief would at last open. But it had been like watching herself in a movie or through thick plate glass, through which no emotion seemed able to pass. She had put on the sunglasses, which still she hadn't removed, not because her eyes were ravaged by tears but because they weren't. She felt like an impostor. And that was probably why she had so cruelly shunned Benjamin's embrace afterward. She saw—and not without pity—how much it hurt him.

Poor, wretched Benjamin. She took a sideways look at him now, sitting across the aisle. The flight was less than half-full and the seats had arms that could be hoisted out of the way. At Sarah's suggestion, to give themselves more space, they had each occupied an empty row. He was staring out at the mountains, lost in thought. In his mournful way, he was still a handsome man, though the longer hair made him seem to be trying too hard to look young. He wasn't as gaunt as the last time she had seen him and the extra weight suited him. She was glad she could assess him like this now, almost objectively, without yearning for him to come back. She didn't really even hate him anymore.

He must have felt her gaze, for he turned to look at her, cautiously. To mask her thoughts, Sarah smiled and, like a whipped dog sensing forgiveness, he smiled back. He got up from his seat and crossed the aisle to sit next to her. Sarah moved her purse to make space.

"We just flew over the Divide," he said. There was more than one meaning to what he had said and he quickly tried to clarify. "I mean, the Continental Divide."

Sarah glanced briefly out of her window.

"Well," she said. "The other Divide must be somewhere pretty close then."

"No. It's some way south and west of here."

"Oh."

It was the place where it all began. Or began to end. The Divide guest ranch where they had come summer after summer and had the best vacations of their lives. The place where Abbie had fallen in love with Montana and become so determined to go to college there. And where, six years but what now seemed like a lifetime ago, Benjamin had fallen in love (or whatever it was) with Eve Kinsella and set about the destruction of their marriage.

For a while neither of them spoke. The flight attendant was wheeling a wagon of drinks and snacks toward them along the aisle. They both asked for water. The piped air of the cabin was cold and smelled fake and antiseptic.

"Talk to me," he said quietly.

"What?"

"Please, Sarah. Can't we just talk a little? About Abbie?"

She shrugged.

"If you like. What is there to say?"

"I don't know. I just think that if we talked about it, we might be able to . . . give each other a little comfort, I suppose."

"Oh."

"Sarah, you know, we mustn't blame ourselves—"

"Blame ourselves?"

"No, I don't mean—"

"Benjamin, I don't blame myself at all. Not at all."

"I know, I just—"

"I blame you. You and you alone . . ." She broke off and smiled. There was that woman too, of course. She could see in his eyes that he read the thought. "Well, maybe not quite alone."

"Sarah, how can you say that?"

"Because it's true. Abbie didn't die because she fell or jumped or got pushed off a cliff or whatever it was. She died, Benjamin, because of what you did to us all."

TWO

Six

The Divide was a place that seemed to want to keep itself secret. It perched concealed at the head of a split and tortuous valley that descended to another far grander where a highway followed the curves of the Yellowstone River. Beside this highway, for those who could spot and decipher it, there was a sign of sorts. But the gnarled cottonwood to which it had long ago been nailed had all but consumed it and the words now looked like a parasitic scarring of the bark. Some thirty yards on, a road of pale gravel branched away beside a creek and the only clue that it led anywhere was a battered tin mailbox.

Lost Creek, whose course the gravel road followed, was well named. In summer it ran dry or at best was barely a trickle and its banks were rife with chokecherry and willow scrub, their leaves layered with a white dust churned from the road. The water was plundered for the hay meadows that stretched away on either side and for cattle ponds farther upstream where the land began to rise and the grassland filled with sage.

Even with the snowmelt of spring, even in its highest reaches, Lost Creek never truly found itself. But its sibling, across the dividing spine of pine-clad rock that gave the ranch its name, was thirstier and flashier by far. Named for some long-forgotten but doubtless ebullient pioneer, Miller's Creek brimmed and tumbled for five dramatic miles of bouldered curves and waterfalls and swirling, trouty pools.

It took fifteen minutes to drive up from the highway and only in the last half-mile did the ranch reveal itself. Just as the gradient seemed to be growing too steep and the forest too darkly encroaching, the road broke abruptly from the trees into a bowl of lush pasture where glossy quarter horses ambled and grazed and swished their languid tails at flies. Beyond them, on higher ground and dustier, stood a cluster of whitewashed clapboard stables and a red sand arena and corrals with bleached wood fences. And above all this, encircled by flower beds and lawns, the mountains rearing grandly behind it, was the ranch house itself.

The building was long and low and made of logs and fronted for its entire length by a deck some ten feet wide with tables and chairs where in the evening guests liked to gaze out over the treetops and watch the mountains on the east side of the valley catch the last ochre glow of the lowering sun. The creeks divided behind the house and moated it on either side where both were simply bridged to oval meadows stolen from the forest. Along their perimeters, discreetly placed among the ponderosa pines were two tennis courts and a swimming pool and twenty log cabins, each with its own porch.

Montana had ritzier ranches, with finer cuisine and glitzier guests. But there were few, if any, so beautiful. The Divide didn't advertise or tout for business for it had no need. Its guests came by word of mouth and returned again and again. And thus it was with the Cooper family. For the last two weeks in June, they always took cabins six and eight. This was their fourth visit and it would be their last, the vacation that would change their lives forever.

Today was Ben's forty-sixth birthday and he was dragged from his dreams into it by the most wretched rendition of *Happy Birthday* he had ever heard. His head was clouded from too many beers and too little sleep and the out-of-tune singing entered it like a rusty corkscrew. He opened an eye to see Sarah smiling from the pillow beside him. She leaned over and kissed him on the cheek.

"Morning, birthday boy," she said.

"So that's what they're singing."

The sun coming through the red-and-white curtains cast a glaring checkerboard pattern on the bare wooden floor and across Ben's bare feet as he shuffled to the door, pulling on his bathrobe as he went. Abbie and Josh and a ragged choir of conscripts were gathered in the meadow just below the cabin porch, and they cheered as he emerged, shielding his eyes against the sun.

"Oh, it's you guys," he said. "I thought there was a pack of sick coyotes out here."

"Happy birthday, Daddy," Abbie called.

87

She had mustered her friends and a couple of their favorite ranch hands. There were eight or nine of them, all grinning and wishing him a happy birthday and making smart remarks about his age. Abbie came up the steps with Josh and they kissed him and handed him a big box wrapped in paper decorated with little cattle brands. Sarah was out on the porch too now, wrapped in her matching white bathrobe. She came to stand between her two children and draped her arms around their shoulders. They were all tanned and their hair tinted even blonder by the sun. Ben had never seen them so radiant, so golden.

"It's kind of from all of us," Abbie said.

"Well, thank you. Do I get to open it now?"

"Of course."

There was an envelope on top and he opened that first. It was one of those cards parents had to pretend to find funnier than they truly did. It had a picture of a dinosaur skeleton on the front and inside said *Happy Birthday, You Old Fossil.* Ben nodded and smiled.

"Thanks," he said. "I love you too."

Inside the box was a fine Stetson made of beige felt.

"Wow, that's what I'd call a hat."

He put it on. They cheered and whistled. It was a perfect fit.

"Goes great with the bathrobe," Abbie said.

"How did you know my size?"

"We just went for the biggest," Josh said.

Everyone laughed and Ben made as if to grab him but the boy dodged easily out of reach.

"Mr. Cooper?"

Ty Hawkins, one of the ranch hands, stepped forward, holding out a little package. Abbie's two best friends, Katie and Lane, were giggling behind him and had clearly put him up to it. He was a mild-mannered young man with a shock of blond hair and the kind of rugged yet innocent good looks that had weakened the knees of just about every female on the ranch. Especially Abbie. She had made sure she was in his riding group every day since the vacation began.

"The girls reckoned you'd probably need this to go with it."

Ben opened the package and pulled out a patterned leather cord, braided with horsehair. He knew what it was, but didn't want to spoil the joke.

"What's this for?"

Ty smiled. "I think it's supposed to hold your hat on."

"They're called sissy straps," Katie trilled.

Ben Cooper's birthday had become a ritual of these ranch vacations and while he considered himself a good sport and enjoyed the attention, he sometimes felt it unfair that his notching of years should be so routinely public. Last year they had given him a red toy Porsche in a box emblazoned with the words *Ben's Meno-porsche*. Though he wasn't as neurotic about aging as some men he knew, he couldn't say it was a process he relished; the way your bones creaked when you got out of bed and how your hair seemed to get bored of growing on your head and sprouted in your ears and nose instead. Yesterday in the shower he had discovered his first gray pubic hair and he was trying not to see it as symbolic.

"We better be getting back to work," Ty said. "Are you riding this morning, Mr. Cooper?"

"If you've got a horse man enough for this hat."

"We've got a stallion needs breaking, if that's okay?"

"No problem. Saddle him up."

Ben's riding was another family joke. He brought to it, as he did to most sports, more enthusiasm than skill. Abbie, who had ridden since she was six and had inherited her mother's effortless elegance, said that on a stationary horse he looked like Clint Eastwood, but morphed, as soon as it moved, into Kermit the Frog.

Ty and the other wrangler said they had better go start saddling the horses for the ride and everyone else agreed to meet at the ranch house in twenty minutes for breakfast. Ben and Sarah lingered on the sunlit porch to watch the little crowd drift and disperse across the meadow.

Lane and Katie were ragging Josh about something and he was pretending to be mad but clearly lapping up the attention. It was good to see. In the past year the boy's hormones had gone into overdrive. He had started to shave and was growing so fast he could hardly keep up with himself. Fortunately the clothes he liked to wear were mostly big enough for two of him.

Josh had always been the one Ben and Sarah worried about. Perhaps it was simply the contrast with his sister, who had every gift one could wish upon a child. Whereas Abbie had so far breezed through life, her brother seemed to snag himself at every turn of the trail. The very slouch of his shoulders suggested how heavily the world weighed upon him.

He was a gentle soul and sweet-natured and had many other fine qualities, but he lacked his sister's natural grace and good looks. And though Ben would never have admitted it to anyone, for he knew the emotion to be inappropriate, the love he felt for the boy had always been tinged with something akin to pity. He had witnessed too many disappointments, seen him reflect his own failure on the success of others, watched him watching from the sidelines while peers, brighter or sportier, better-looking or simply more extroverted, gathered the garlands. Ben suspected that Sarah felt the same, but they had never been able to discuss it without it escalating into a row. She was fiercely defensive and took as a personal slight any implication that her son might be less than perfect.

Last summer Josh had been almost chronically shy with Katie and Lane. But judging by the way he was romping off across the meadow with them now, that seemed to have changed. And watching them, Ben dared to hope that things might at last be falling into place for the boy. Children all seemed to have a particular age when they found their stride. Maybe, at last, this was Josh's. Katie gave him a shove now and ran ahead with Lane, the two of them laughing and taunting him and, like an overgrown Labrador puppy, Josh rollicked off in pursuit.

This left Abbie and Ty walking on their own.

Unaware that they were being watched, they moved closer together. Now she leaned closer still to whisper something and he laughed and she tucked her thumb into the back pocket of his Wranglers. Ben and Sarah looked at each other.

"Looks like our girl won the contest," he said.

"Ever known her lose?"

"He seems like a nice enough guy."

They stood watching, neither of them saying anything more, until all that remained in the meadow was a fan of footprints in the dew, the chime of the girls' voices fading on the windless air of the morning.

In the cabin's cramped, log-walled bathroom, while Sarah showered, Ben stood and shaved before the basin mirror wearing nothing but his new hat and a resolve that today things were going to be different between them. Be nice to her, he told himself. Stop being such a grouch and giving her—and yourself—such a hard time. Forget how it's been for the past week and start over.

"I can't get over Joshie," Sarah said from behind the glass.

"What do you mean?"

"The way he is this year. How he's blossomed."

"Yep. Amazing what getting laid can do for a fellow."

"You don't mean it?"

He didn't. He was just being mischievous.

"Why not?"

"Benjamin, the boy's only fifteen years old, for heaven's sake."

"I know, some guys have all the luck."

He said it without thinking, without any conscious attempt to needle her. But judging by her silence, that was precisely how she had taken it. He tried to change the subject and didn't quite succeed.

"How serious is Abbie about this young cowboy?"

"I don't know, but she'd better be careful she doesn't get him fired. They're pretty strict about that kind of thing here by all accounts."

"What kind of thing?"

"You know, consorting with the guests."

"Consorting?"

"You know what I mean."

She normally laughed when he teased her about her euphemisms, but not today. The rush of water stopped and the shower door opened. He watched her in the mirror step out and reach for a towel, studiously avoiding any eye contact.

At forty-two, she was still slim and firm-breasted and even after twenty years of marriage the sight of her naked body rarely failed to stir him. Perhaps this was because his access to it had always been so much less than his desire. Things had long been thus between them and her evasions of his lust had grown deft and mechanical. As now, when he turned and stepped toward her and she briskly wrapped the towel around her so that by the time he reached her she was covered. He held her by the shoulders and she smiled defusingly and pecked him chastely on the lips.

"That's a really great hat."

"Thank you, ma'am."

"Do you honestly think Josh and Katie are . . ."

"Consorting? Of course."

"Shouldn't we talk with him about it?"

"Sure, if we really want to embarrass him."

He was still holding her and tried to stem her defensive talk with a kiss.

"Benjamin, I'm serious."

"Can we talk about this later? There's another male member of the Cooper family that needs a little attention."

He was aroused now and pressing himself against her. She glanced down and arched an eyebrow.

"Precisely which member are we talking about here?"

"Him. Forget about me. This is entirely altruistic."

"Later. I want to give you your present."

"You're the only present I want."

He held her closer and kissed her neck and she let him but stopped his hand when he tried to unhitch her towel.

"Later."

He kissed her mouth. But she wasn't going to relent. She put her hands on his chest and gently fended him off.

"Benjamin, we'll be late for breakfast."

He let go of her and turned away and saw himself in the mirror, sullen and tumescent and suddenly fatuous in the hat. He took it off and spun it onto a chair.

It was the same old thing. The same predictable cycle of slight and sulk, of sexual rejection and injured pride that had dogged their marriage for almost as long as he could remember. Despite knowing how things stood, he still concocted these foolish, romantic notions about how it might be different once they were on vacation together. It was as if he actually wanted to be disappointed.

Sarah had disappeared into the bedroom and a few moments later, protectively robed, her hair wrapped in a towel, she came back with the gift, prettily wrapped and tied with a red ribbon. He was drying his face and pretended not to see her. She had probably bought him a shirt and would probably apologize for it and predict that he wouldn't like it. He probably wouldn't but would pretend, unconvincingly, that he did.

"If you don't like it, they're happy to change it."

"Oh, thank you."

He took it from her and put it down on the chair.

"I'll open it later. We'll be late for breakfast."

And with a sideways glance to gauge the impact of his spite, he stepped into the shower and shut the door behind him.

They rode that morning to The Outlook. It was one of their favorite places, a high buttress of red rock that reared above the forest like the brow of some vast and noble warrior surveying his domain. It was a long ride and steep in its first twisting miles up through the canyon. But after an hour the land leveled into high pasture and that was where they were now, crossing a wide and shallow valley where the horses liked to run before they stopped to rest and take water.

The grass this year had grown long and lush with copious spring rain and the horses had to hoist their heads as they loped through it, parting it with their chests like warm-blooded boats through an ocean of green. Including Sarah, there were nine riders and, as usual, she was last in line. Apart from Jesse, the ranch hand who was guiding them up front, she was by far the best rider, but she liked to go last so that she could stop whenever she liked without bothering anyone. And that was what she was about to do now. Spangled in the grass she had noticed some white and yellow flowers that she didn't recognize. She wanted to pick a couple so that she could take them back to the ranch and check them in her new edition of *Plants of the Rocky Mountains.*

She mentally stored the names of plants—both their common and Latin names—in much the same way that she stored the names of books and writers. But this summer at The Divide, there was such hectic abundance, she couldn't locate them all. Riding up through the canyon, she had identified arrow-leaved balsamroot, paintbrush, and shootingstar. But these she had just spotted were new to her. She let the others lope ahead, slowed to a walk, and circled back.

She and Benjamin were riding with the Delstock parents and two women from Santa Fe who had arrived the previous evening. Abbie and Josh and all the kids were riding with Ty, making their way to The Outlook by a different route. The Delstocks was Abbie's collective name for the Bradstocks and the Delroys, the two families they had met here three years ago on what was for all of them a first visit. Their children—in every case, a boy and a girl of roughly matching ages—had formed an immediate bond and so had the parents. They had reconvened every year since. The fact that for the other fifty weeks of the year, except for the occasional phone call at Christmas or Thanksgiving, they might as well have lived on different planets only seemed to intensify the friendship.

Tom and Karen Bradstock were from Chicago and were both lawyers in private practice, though of very different kinds. Karen represented the poor and oppressed, Tom their rich oppressors or, as Karen put it, "assorted corporate gangsters." He had the salary and she the social conscience and this was the subject of a perpetual war between them, waged in public with wit and mock outrage and the support of anyone either could enlist. In almost every other way, in as much as one could ever judge these things, they seemed well matched. Both were big and loud and zestful, with a kind of mutual, almost brazen sensuality that Sarah sometimes found embarrassing.

The Delroys, from Florida, were hipper, skinnier, and altogether more mysterious. Phil (whom everyone, even his wife, called Delroy) ran his own software company whose precise purpose nobody seemed able to establish, except that it was "entertainment-oriented." Tom Brad-stock often taunted him by saying this was a euphemism for porn, but Delroy would just give one of his inscrutable, black-eyed smiles and let the mystery hang. He was tanned like a beach bum and tied his graying black hair in a ponytail. On his right shoulder he had a tattoo of a Chinese symbol whose meaning, again, he would never disclose. He had that laconic, laid-back sense of humor that some women seemed to find attractive, though not Sarah, who found it all a little too contrived.

Maya Delroy was an alternative healer. It had something to do with "kinetic focus" but when she tried to explain what that meant, Sarah's attention always seemed to wander, which probably indicated that she was in need of a session herself. Maya was airy and lithe and wore a lot of red and amber and yellow and early every morning laid a little rush mat on the grass outside her cabin and did yoga. Most of this qualified her to be the kind of woman that Sarah would normally pay good money to avoid. But there was an undermining edge to Maya's alternativeness, a sort of scurrilous, self-mocking wit that redeemed her, almost as though the whole spiritual image was one big put-on.

Benjamin's theory was that the Bradstocks and the Delroys were so unalike that they probably wouldn't have bothered to get to know each other if it hadn't been for him and Sarah bridging the divide between them. The fact was that none of the three couples had more than a few trifling things in common and it was probably this very disparity, along with their children's complementary ages, that made their annual two-week friendship work.

They had all ridden far ahead now and out of sight.

The sun was high and hot and there was barely a breeze to ruffle the grass or shift the few floating cotton clouds from the mountains. In search of perfect specimens, Sarah had dismounted. She took off her straw hat and tilted her face at the sun and, shutting her eyes, tried to let the peace of the place seep into her. All she could hear was the hum of insects and the swish of the horse's tail and the chomp of his teeth on the sweet-stemmed fescue. Like all the others, he was a quarter horse, a sturdy fourteen-year-old bay, named Rusty for his color. He wasn't the best ride on the ranch and because the head wrangler knew how well she rode, each year she was offered better. But the horse was brave and big-hearted and she would have no other.

She opened her eyes and rubbed the sweat from his neck. It was time to move on. She picked her flowers, one yellow, one white, and stowed them safely in the little tin she kept for this purpose in the breast pocket of her white cotton shirt. She knew the place where the others would be resting the horses before they started the last leg of their ascent to The Outlook so she didn't need to hurry. She swung herself into the saddle and nudged Rusty into a gentle walk, filling her lungs with the hot green scent of the grass and thinking, as she had been all morning, about Benjamin.

The power of human habit never failed to astonish her. How was it that two intelligent, decent people who basically loved each other could get so locked into a pattern of behavior that neither of them—or so she presumed—enjoyed? It was as if each knew the role he or she was expected to take and had no choice but to play it. Sarah had often wondered if Benjamin felt as miserably miscast in their drama as she did. She ever the frigid bitch and he the libidinous brute. As the years had gone by, like actors in some tired TV soap, they had become caricatures, marooned in their own sad clichés, unable to contemplate any other way of being with each other. God, how tired of it she was.

For more than a week he had virtually ignored her. Simply because on their first night here, after all the hours of traveling and then staying up too late partying with the Delstocks, she had felt too tired to make love. Could he not have waited until morning? Could he not have just given her a cuddle? If he had, without forcing the issue, she might, despite her tiredness, have been coaxed into what he wanted. But with Benjamin, nowadays, there was no such thing as just a cuddle. It always had to lead to sex. And women didn't work that way. At least, she didn't.

He hadn't always been like this, though the change had been too gradual to pinpoint. For sure, he had always wanted more sex than she felt able to give him. But wasn't that the way things were with most couples? Sarah had never been the kind of woman (though she'd often wished she were) who talked candidly about these things to friends, but she had the impression that most women felt the same—at least, after those first heady eighteen months or so when you couldn't get enough of each other. Once passion had given way to familiarity and then kids and the plain old routine of living, things changed. Sex became more of a comfort.

That didn't mean she found it boring or that she couldn't be stirred. There had been times, particularly in the old days if they were away on their own somewhere, when their lovemaking had been thrilling. But back then, when the kids were much younger, he had been more patient, gentler, more understanding. Now, if she didn't switch on immediately, she was made to feel cruel and cold and sexless.

Perhaps this impatience was something that afflicted all men when they reached middle age and saw their youth ebbing away. Perhaps this first glimpse of their own mortality made them more demanding and desperate to prove themselves, made them interpret even the gentlest deflection of desire as a dagger thrust at the heart of their manhood.

Whatever it was, Sarah resented it more and more. It was so unjust. So disrespectful. And the routine that went with it was almost unbearable. The sulking. The dark, brooding silences. Were these supposed to make her feel more inclined to make love with him? And the hypocrisy of it all. For in public—in front of the children and the Delstocks, in particular—he was all sweetness and light. Only the other night Abbie had been rhapsodizing about how lucky they were to be such a happy family. The happiest family she knew, she had boasted. Neither she nor anyone else had apparently noticed that her father had barely spoken a direct word to Sarah in more than a week.

And nobody, of course, saw how it was when they were alone, how he only ever broke the silence if he was lucky enough to have spotted something to criticize. Otherwise he shuttered himself off behind his newspaper or his *Architectural Digest*—or that wretched biography of Le Corbusier that he'd been trying to read for the last six months—and behaved as if she existed only in the coldest, most remote margins of his consciousness.

Of course, Sarah knew she was actually at its very center. And she also knew that it made him seethe if she inhabited her exile blithely, as if she had no inkling of his rage and resentment or simply didn't care. Perhaps, again, this was how it was with all marriages. Each partner found an appropriate weapon and learned how best to use it. His was icy silence. Hers—and she knew it was the more potent—was pretending not to notice.

Anyway, this time Sarah had been determined to hold out for as long as she could. She felt guilty about what had happened that morning. It was, after all, the poor man's birthday and though he hadn't apologized (for he never did), it must have been hard for him to suspend his sulk like that and come on to her when she stepped out of the shower. But the stubborn streak in her, that notorious Davenport obstinacy that had helped make her father's fortune, had clicked in and told her not to succumb. All he wanted, after all, was to fuck her and why the hell should she let him after all those days of being ignored?

It would resolve itself, no doubt, as it always did. Eventually, the tension would become so unbearable that she would crumble and cry and blame herself, telling him he ought to go out and find someone else, someone younger and sexier and more normal. And she would sob and so, probably, would he. And they would have sex. And it would be tragic and desperate and seismic.

She could see the others now, way ahead across the rippling grass. There was a stand of aspen where some were taking shade while the others watered the horses in a rocky pool of the stream below. The pale stems of the trees seemed almost aglow against the hazed blue of the distant mountains.

Tom Bradstock and Delroy were down with the horses talking with Jesse and the two women from Santa Fe. Benjamin, wearing his new hat, was sitting in the shade, talking with Maya and Karen. Jesse saw Sarah and called out and the others turned to look and everyone waved. Except Benjamin, who just sat there and stared, as if assessing her, for such a long time that even at a distance she felt disconcerted and self-conscious. She wondered what he thought of what he saw and whether he still loved her. For in spite of how he hurt her and punished her, she had no doubt about her feelings for him. She loved him and always would.

SEVEN

Ty and his band had been playing for almost an hour and Abbie still couldn't get over how awesome they were. The place was totally rocking. All the tables and chairs had been cleared in the big dining room, the band was at one end, the bar at the other, and everyone who could still stand was dancing—kids, parents, grandparents, not to mention the staff. Nobody was dancing with anybody in particular, just with whoever happened to be in front of them at the time. Even though all the doors and windows to the deck were wide open, the place felt like an oven and they were all drenched with sweat, but nobody seemed to care.

The band was called Hell to Breakfast, a name Abbie didn't quite get, but at least it was unusual. Their own stuff was amazing, though tonight they had been playing mostly goldies for the oldies, a lot of Rolling Stones and Beatles and Eagles numbers. At the moment they were into a great version of "Born in the USA." Abbie was dancing with Lane Delroy and her brother Ryan. He and Abbie had had a bit of a thing going last summer but thank heaven he was over it and cool about it and they were now just good friends again. Everyone was laughing at Ryan's dad, Delroy, who Abbie secretly found a little creepy. He was one of those guys who was always putting his arm around you, not quite feeling you up but almost. Right now he was trying to coach

Katie Bradstock and her mom to do some funny kind of African tribal dance.

Abbie's mom was dancing with Tom Bradstock, who had this hilarious Blues Brothers shuffle going, while her dad was into his Bruce Springsteen impression with Maya Delroy. A few years ago Abbie would have been mortified at the sight of her parents making such a spectacle of themselves, but now she was proud of them. It was good to see them so happy and having fun.

And all the time her eyes kept coming back to Ty. He was almost too good to be true. Not only was he sweet and sensitive and looked like Brad Pitt (well, okay, at a distance, a little), he also played the guitar and sang like some real live rock star you might see on MTV.

The other day when he had casually mentioned that he and some of his friends from college had a band and that, if she wanted, they could come and play at her dad's birthday party, Abbie hadn't expected anything remotely as good as this. He looked gorgeous in his blue jeans and his white pearl-buttoned shirt all patched with sweat. She was dancing for him and felt his eyes upon her wherever in the room she moved. Only five more days until it was time to go home. She was going to miss him badly. Especially after last night.

Every evening after the last ride, the horses were turned loose and a couple of the ranch hands would ride up behind them to see them safely to the pasture. Yesterday it had been Ty's turn and on the flimsy pretext that his buddy wasn't feeling too good, he'd asked Abbie to ride with him instead. It was the first season he had worked at The Divide and from the moment they laid eyes on each other, it had been obvious that there was a connection and that if they allowed it, something might happen between them.

For days Abbie had been going down to the stables to help him with the horses and after a lot of talk and touching each other as if by accident, two days ago, they had finally kissed. The problem was, there was scarcely a moment they could be alone together and for the sake of his job they had to be discreet. Lane and Katie knew but nobody else. And even though Abbie suspected they were a little jealous, they had covered for her yesterday evening.

The sight of the horses thundering up through the sagebrush, churning a cloud of red and sunlit dust behind them, was awesome. They needed no herding and Abbie and Ty just followed on. Once they were up in the pasture, they had ridden across to a low hill and lain together in the sweet-smelling grass below the trees and watched the horses graze their lengthening shadows. He was tender and more hesitant than she had expected, almost shy. And though she had only once made love before, with a boy from school at a party earlier that year, she guessed that for Ty it was the first time and surprised herself by taking the lead, helping him when he fumbled with the condom, telling him not to worry when he quickly came. It was a lot easier and better the second time.

In the twilight as they dressed, they heard voices and before they could pretend to be doing something more innocent, two figures appeared as if out of nowhere. It was the women from Santa Fe whose names, Abbie had later discovered, were Lori and Eve. It was their first evening, and they were hiking around, exploring. There was no doubt they had seen her and Ty clearly enough to recognize them and to figure out what they were up to, but they acted as if they hadn't and without a word veered off and headed down toward the ranch.

On the ride that morning, when they reached The Outlook, Abbie was appalled to see the two women were there waiting with her mom and dad and the Delstocks.

"I guess I'd better start looking for another job," Ty said quietly as they climbed down from their horses.

But if the women had spread the word, there was no indication. Of all the men, Katie's dad was the biggest tease and could always be counted on to blurt out anything embarrassing. And it was he who took it upon himself to introduce Eve and Lori to Ty and the kids, none of whom they had, supposedly, yet met.

"And this is the lovely Princess Abbie," Tom Bradstock said.

The women smiled and said a warm hello and Abbie, never normally shy, nervously said hello back with just enough eye contact to see that there was no hint of a knowing look.

"And this is Ty, Montana's best-looking cowboy heartthrob."

Ty shook their hands and only then, when there was still no betraying look or smart remark from Katie's dad, did Abbie relax a little and begin to think they might have gotten away with it.

Right now, watching him singing and playing his guitar, she wanted the whole world to know. Everyone was yelling the final chorus of "Born in the USA" and it felt as if the roof was about to lift. When the music stopped there was a great cheer and Ty waited at the microphone, grinning and glistening with sweat, until he could be heard.

"Thank you very much," he said. "We're going to take a break now. Some of you folks sure look as if you could handle one too. That was just the warm-up. We'll be back in a while and play some real rock and roll."

There was fruit punch at the bar but Abbie just wanted water. Somebody handed her a bottle and she walked out to the deck which had been prettily strung with tiny white lights. It was too crowded and noisy and she eased her way through to the wide wooden steps that led down to the lawn. The low-angled lamps in the flower beds cast swaths of light across the grass but Abbie chose to stand in the shadow between, enjoying the cool of the air on her flushed cheeks and of the grass on her bare feet. She tilted back her head and finished the water in one long draft, staring up at the stars. Even as she looked there was a falling star and an instant later another.

"I hope you made two wishes."

She had thought she was alone and the voice startled her. For a moment she couldn't figure out who it was and then she saw Eve, smiling from the shadows.

"Oh, hi. But if you saw them too, I think we should get one each."

"Okay, it's a deal."

Eve shut her eyes and presented her smiling face to the sky. Since last evening Abbie had been too embarrassed to take more than a furtive glance at the woman. She was probably in her mid- to late thirties, tall and long-necked, and tonight she had her long, dark, wavy hair all bundled up in a silk scarf, the same sage green as her dress. There was something unusual about her face, with its slightly overlong nose and wide mouth. If not exactly beautiful, she was certainly striking, especially now when she opened her eyes again. There was a stillness, a directness, about the way she looked at you that Abbie found a little unnerving.

"Did you make your wish?"

"Not yet. I've got so many I don't know which one to go for."

"How wonderful to be young. As you get older they sort of whittle down and you end up wishing for the same thing every time."

"You mean, all the others come true?"

"No. Some do. But I think you just focus on the one that matters."

"The one that can never come true."

Eve laughed. "Maybe that's it."

Neither of them spoke for a few moments, just stared at the sky, waiting for another star to fall. Tom Bradstock's laugh boomed out from the deck behind them.

"You're from New York, right?" Eve said.

"Yes. Long Island."

"Are you at college?"

"Next year."

"Do you know where yet?"

"My mom and dad are all set on Harvard."

"But you're not."

"No. I want to come to college out here."

"You mean here in Montana?"

"Maybe. Somewhere in the West anyhow. I so love it out here. Colorado, Oregon, maybe. I don't know. Thing is, I'm really interested in wildlife and the environment and that kind of stuff. And I want to be somewhere it hasn't all been destroyed. By the way, my mom and dad don't know about this yet, okay?"

"Don't worry."

"And they don't know about, well . . ."

"Abbie, I'm so sorry about what happened. We were just taking a look around. We had no idea—"

"It wasn't your fault. Only I'd be really grateful if you—"

"I promise, neither Lori nor I have breathed a word to anyone. It's none of our business. I'm just sorry we embarrassed you."

"No, I'm sorry."

"Well, why don't we both stop being sorry and forget it."

"Okay."

Because of what had happened, Abbie had been ready to dislike the woman and was surprised to find how nice she was. Ryan Delroy and Katie's brother Will had started a ridiculous rumor that she and her friend Lori must be lesbians—or, as Will would have it, with all his father's political correctness, "beaver bumpers"—simply because they were on vacation together.

"You're from Santa Fe, right?"

"That's right. At least, that's where I live now. I grew up in California."

"And you're the painter and Lori owns the gallery, right?"

"Right. Kind of handy, huh?"

"What sort of stuff do you paint?"

"Hmm. Well, it's mostly figurative but not what you'd call realistic. More psychological, exploratory. I guess you could say I paint what's going on in my life. It's like therapy, but cheaper. Lately I've done a lot of paintings that are about my son."

"You have a son?"

"Yes. He's called Pablo and he's nearly two and, of course, the most wonderful child that ever was born."

"So where is he now?"

"With his father. We don't live together."

"Oh. You must miss him—Pablo, I mean."

"I do. But it's only a week and they always have a lot of fun together. Look, another star! Did you see it?"

"Uh-huh."

"Well, it's yours. I'm already sorted."

"I bet I know what you wished."

"Oh, really? You're a mind reader too?"

"No. It's just that my dad says, when you've got kids, all you ever wish for is that they'll be healthy and happy. And now I know you've got a son. So, I bet that's what you wished."

"Healthy and happy sounds like two wishes."

"Okay, well, you'd better have this one too."

B en was leaning against the wooden rail of the deck where Tom Bradstock was entertaining a small crowd with one of his stories. Ben had gone to get some more drinks, so hadn't been there at the start, but it was about a rat that had taken up residence in a house Tom and Karen lived in when their kids were little. The exterminator had put poison down and a few days later, in the middle of the night, they heard strange splashing noises coming from the kids' bathroom.

"So I go in and look around and listen. Nothing. Then I lift up the lid of the john and there he is, looking up at me. The rat. And he's big, you know, the size of a small dog. I'm not kidding. Well, okay, a very small dog. Apparently the poison makes them thirsty and that's where he'd gone for a drink. Anyway, I shut the lid and try to flush him away, but when I open it again, there he is, still staring at me, all wet but clinging on for all he's got."

He twitched his nose in an impression of the rat and everyone laughed. Almost everyone. Ben was standing next to Karen and he heard her sigh and when he looked at her she gave him a wry smile and shook her head.

"God," she said quietly. "If I had ten dollars for every time I've had to listen to this story, I'd be a wealthy woman."

"By now Karen has come to see what's going on. So I tell her . . ."

Karen mouthed to Ben: "Karen, go get my toolbox."

". . . Karen, go get my toolbox."

Ben grinned. The story went on and, though a little long, it was good and Tom told it well. Just as he was trying to kill the rat with a claw hammer and it was squealing and squirming around, little Katie, four years old, came to the door all sleepy-eyed and said she wanted to go pee-pee. She asked what her daddy was doing and he said, as if it was the most natural thing in the world to be standing there stark naked with a bloody hammer in his hand at three o'clock in the morning, that the john was broken and he was just fixing it so she'd have to use Mommy and Daddy's bathroom instead.

"I mean, if the poor kid had found a rat down the toilet or seen it all bloody and writhing, she'd never have wanted to go again, would she? Anorexic for the rest of her life. So. Karen takes her to do pee-pee and puts her back to bed while I finish the job. Then I take the body downstairs and wrap it in newspaper and put it in the garbage, then wash all the blood off my hands and the hammer in the sink. Like a murderer, which, of course, is exactly what I now am. Then I go back upstairs and get into bed. And I'm lying there for the rest of the night, wide-eyed, staring at the ceiling . . ."

Karen turned to Ben again and wearily mouthed the punch line: "Feeling like Anthony Perkins in *Psycho*."

". . . like Anthony Perkins in *Psycho*."

The story went down well. Then Maya Delroy started telling one about a close encounter she had once had with a scorpion but she didn't have Tom's gift and Ben didn't bother to listen.

"Is it just men or do women tell the same stories over and over?" he asked Karen.

"You tell me."

"I don't think Sarah does it."

"I don't either."

"But I probably do. Every guy has his party-piece stories."

"Well, there you go."

"So why don't women?"

"They don't feel they have to impress everyone with how witty and clever they are."

"And men do?"

"Of course. All the time."

"So, there's Maya telling a story. Isn't she trying to impress?"

"No. She's just telling a story."

Ben shook his head and smiled and took a swig from his bottle of beer. He'd always liked Karen, her subversive humor, the way anything and anyone were apparently legitimate targets.

"How long have you two been married?" he asked.

"Two hundred years this fall."

"Go on. You guys seem great together."

"We are. Basically. But isn't marriage hell? I mean, who invented it? Two people having to put up with each other year in, year out, slowly boring each other to death. The snoring, the farting. I mean, really, we're supposed to be this highly evolved, super-smart species, and that's the best deal we can come up with?"

"I think it's supposed to free the mind for higher things."

"What, marriage?"

"Yeah. Otherwise, we'd spend all our creative energy chasing each other around."

"Sounds okay to me."

Ben laughed.

"No, but seriously," Karen went on. "What's the point of marriage nowadays? I mean, the original idea was that it kept men around longer. You know, to provide meat for their kids and chase off the saber-toothed tigers. But women can handle pretty much everything on their own now, even the tigers. Then there's sex, I guess. Which was why our parents' generation got married. But then the pill came along, so that's that reason gone."

"This sounds suspiciously more like an argument against men than marriage."

"Hell, no. Men are fine. Though now you come to mention it, maybe we don't need quite so many of you. You know, we could keep a few prime specimens in cages. To keep the species going and satisfy our carnal needs."

"Sounds great."

"You figure you'd qualify?"

"Shall I impress you with one of my stories?"

Karen touched his arm and laughed. Delroy was

coming up the steps from the lawn and joined the little crowd listening to his wife's scorpion story. He was all pink-eyed and smiley. One of the few things about which he made no secret was his fondness for grass. Most evenings, after supper, he would slip quietly away into the trees for a smoke. The standing joke was that he was bird-spotting. Ben, who hadn't smoked pot or even a cigarette since college, had lately felt an unaccountable urge to accompany him but had as yet been too shy to ask.

"Hey, Del," Tom Bradstock called quietly. "See any three-toed woodpeckers out there tonight?"

Delroy smiled. "A whole damn flock of them."

Maya was winding up her story. It didn't seem to have anything resembling a punch line but no doubt there was some deeper, more karmic message that Ben had missed. He hadn't really been listening. He had been thinking about what Karen had said and watching Sarah. She was farther along the deck, talking and laughing with Lane and Katie and a couple of the boys from the band. He had always admired, even faintly envied, the easy rapport she had with kids their age. Elegant as ever in her cream linen shift, her hair tucked neatly behind ears each studded with a single pearl, she looked like she'd stepped out of a Ralph Lauren ad. Amused yet slightly aloof. Perfectly unattainable. Watching her, he felt curiously detached, almost as if he was studying a stranger. He became aware that Karen was studying him.

"So, how are you?" she said.

"Me? Terrific. Why?"

"Because you're so obviously not terrific."

"How do you mean?"

"There's something different about you this year. You seem . . . I don't know. Preoccupied. A little sad, maybe."

Ben lifted his eyebrows and gave her a wary smile.

"I'm sorry," Karen said. "It's none of my business."

"No, it's okay. But really, I'm fine. I guess work hasn't been that great for a couple of months. And I seem to have forgotten how to sleep."

"What's that all about?"

"Nothing. Listen, honestly, I'm good. Hell, it's my birthday. I'm having a great time."

"Well, Ben, that's just . . . great."

She looked away and took a drink and Ben felt mean for being so tight and defensive. But what could he have said? That he sensed his world sliding slowly away from under him? That he felt isolated and hollow and bereft and didn't know why? There was no easy way to chat about these things. Not, anyway, with a woman who, despite the candor with which they all often talked during these two weeks each summer, was hardly a close friend. In fact, he couldn't imagine talking to anyone about it. And this was not because he had a fear of confiding but because he wouldn't know where to start.

Watching Abbie and Josh walk away across the meadow that morning, he had shared their palpable joy. But the image had lodged in his head all day and—in its contrast with what had followed—transmuted into something stark and symbolic. Two happy young adults, striding off on their own, strong and confident, while their parents retreated to a space that was increasingly cold and empty of all but echoes. Playing the picture over and over again, like the trailer for a movie he didn't want to see, he'd had a premonition of profound loss.

If he was honest with himself, it was all about Abbie. Although he would never have admitted it to anyone, she had always been his favorite, just as Josh was Sarah's. Perhaps that was how it always divided in foursome families—father teamed with daughter, mother with son. It had certainly been that way when he was growing up. And with damaging results, for his mother's blind adoration of him had made her husband jealous, blighting their marriage and erecting a wall between father and son that neither of them had ever been able to scale.

Ben had always been determined that the same shouldn't happen between him and Josh. And it hadn't. They got along fine. But though he loved the boy dearly, it was a love of a different order from the love he felt for Abbie. She was the light that had for so long sustained him. And now, as its beam swung outward and began to shine forth into the world, he sensed the shadow encroaching.

There was little logic to it, for he took genuine pride in his children's burgeoning independence. He remembered and sometimes liked to quote the words from

Kahlil Gibran's *The Prophet*, which Martin—his best friend and business partner and Abbie's godfather—had read at her christening, about how parents should never feel they owned their children. Rather, they should consider themselves the bows from which their sons and daughters were sent forth as living arrows. Ben believed this and believed, moreover, that it was right and should be so. But what no one ever told you was what happened to the bow once the arrows had gone. Was that it? Was that all? Did it then just get propped in a corner of the closet to gather dust?

The selfishness of the thought shocked him now and to extinguish it he gulped the rest of his beer and put the bottle down on a table. Karen had moved away and was talking with somebody else. As he walked through the crowd along the deck, faces turning and smiling at him and wishing him a happy birthday, he saw Abbie coming up the steps. She was wearing blue jeans with a little pale pink top that showed her hips and tummy. She looked sensational. She saw him and came to him and threw her arms around his neck and hugged him.

"What's that for?" Ben said.

"Nothing. You just looked like you needed it."

He held her away from him by her bare arms to inspect her. She seemed to glow.

"Are you having a good time?" he said.

"The best. Are you?"

"Of course."

"Why aren't you wearing your hat?"

"I didn't want to make the other guys jealous."

"Where's Mom?"

"Over there, flirting with the band."

"Aren't they amazing?"

"Not bad. Except that lead singer."

"I know. They've got to get rid of him."

She grinned and narrowed her eyes a little and he could tell she was trying to figure out how much he might know.

"Ty's asked me if I'd like to go visit his ranch on Thursday. Would that be okay?"

"He's got his own ranch? Well, that changes everything."

"It belongs to his parents. Thursday's his day off. It's in Wyoming, quite a long way, so we'd have to leave Wednesday evening. Would you mind?"

Ben shrugged. "I guess not. See what your mom says."

Abbie reached up and kissed him on the cheek.

"Thanks, Daddy."

She went off to find Sarah. Ben turned to watch her go.

"You must be very proud of her."

He turned back and saw Eve standing in front of him, smiling. She had probably been there all the time he was talking with Abbie.

"Isn't it funny how you can always tell when they want something? Yeah, well. As daughters go, I guess she's not too bad. You're Eve, right?"

"And you're Benjamin."

"You've obviously been talking with my wife. Everybody else calls me Ben."

"Ben."

He held out his hand and she shook it with a mock solemnity, perhaps because they had already been introduced on the ride that morning. Attractive women often made him act a little gauche. Her hand felt cool.

He had noticed her the moment she walked into the dining room the previous evening. And though they hadn't spoken on the ride, he had spent a lot of time slyly watching her. He had noted the slow, slightly sardonic smile, the low voice that wasn't quite a drawl, the unflinching way she fixed you with those dark eyes, as if she knew more about you than you might wish—which, given that she'd been talking with Sarah, couldn't be discounted.

"Abbie said you come here every summer."

"Yes. This is our fourth visit. Probably time we went someplace else."

"Why's that?"

"Oh, I don't know. I guess I just mean it's good to move on, do something different."

"The kids all seem to love it."

"Yeah. You wouldn't believe the hard time Abbie gave us the first year when we said we'd booked into a dude ranch. She's always been an outdoors kind of kid but she was going through that phase when all girls seem to want to do is hang out at the mall. All her friends were going on vacation to Europe or Hollywood or Miami and she was going to a *dude ranch?* I can remember her sulking in the backseat as we came up the drive, saying, *Wow, look, a cow. Wow, look, another cow.*"

Eve laughed. "She saw the light, obviously."

"It took about five minutes."

There was a short pause. They smiled at each other, and he realized he was staring too intently at her mouth.

"Can I get you a drink?" he said.

"No, I'm fine, thank you. But go ahead if you . . ."

"No. I'm fine too."

They stood there for a few moments while Ben scanned for something to say. Everyone except them seemed to be laughing and talking. Eve was looking around as if she wanted to escape, then looked back and caught him staring at her.

"Sarah told me you're an architect. Do you design houses or . . . ?"

"Sometimes. Not as often as I'd like. My partner gets to do most of the exciting stuff. I look after the boring business stuff, chase people who owe us money, that sort of thing. I do the occasional remodeling job to keep my hand in. And a new build every now and then. I've been working on one lately, as a matter of fact."

"What is it?"

"Oh, just a little housing development. Out in the Hamptons."

"I didn't think anyone did 'little' in the Hamptons."

"Well, strictly speaking it's not quite the Hamptons. And the problem is, it's not little enough. It's a small plot, really pretty. Lots of trees, perfect for a couple of medium-sized houses. But the developers now want to get rid of all the trees, double the number of houses, and make them twice as big. It'd be just another ridiculous bunch of McMansions."

"McMansions. I like that."

"You haven't heard that before? They're everywhere now. Actually, what these guys wanted was more Garage-Mahal."

She laughed.

"Anyhow, it probably isn't going to happen. At least, not with me. There was this colossal fight just before we came out here. I walked out of a meeting. You know, the prima-donna architect. Just got up and left. Never done it before in my life, but I'm definitely going to do it a lot more."

"It felt good?"

"It felt wonderful."

"Sarah told me you designed your own house."

"Uh-huh."

"Tell me about it."

Why she should be interested, he couldn't imagine. He wondered for a moment if he was being patronized.

"Well, you know that amazing Frank Gehry building in Bilbao?"

She nodded eagerly. "The Guggenheim Museum?"

"Well, it's absolutely nothing like that."

She laughed again and it seemed real. God, he felt witty.

"It's tiered and white and has a big lawn in front with a wonderful Korean dogwood and a looped brick driveway. It's got oak and limestone floors and a ridiculously over-the-top, kind of Audrey Hepburn sweep-down staircase, which was really just to impress my parents-in-law—"

"Did it?"

"Not at all. And a big studio for me out the back with slatted shutters I can close and fall asleep or watch TV without anyone catching me. And the garage is tucked away and covered with Virginia creeper so nobody can call it a Garage-Mahal."

"It sounds beautiful."

"Oh no. It's a Frank Lloyd Wright rip-off, built on the cheap in the wrong place and I'd love to tear it down and start again. But it's home and it kind of works."

There was a loud blast of feedback from the sound system inside and then Ty's mellow voice at the microphone, inviting everybody to roll up their sleeves and get back on the dance floor. Ben was about to ask Eve if she wanted to dance when someone grabbed him from behind by the elbows. He turned and saw that it was Sarah.

"Come on, birthday boy. You haven't danced with me all evening."

"I couldn't get past all those young cowboys."

"Well, buddy, now's your chance."

She rarely drank and never too much, but her cheeks were flushed and the exuberance seemed slightly strained. She turned to Eve and gave her a conspiratorial smile that Ben found puzzling.

"Will you excuse us?"

"Of course."

"I hear you play tennis. Shall we play tomorrow?"

"I'd love to."

"Good."

Sarah hauled him by the hand toward the doorway to the dining room and just as he was about to follow her in, he turned and saw Eve still watching them. She smiled and he smiled back. And in that fleeting connection something happened inside him. It was only much later that he would come to acknowledge it for what it was and even then he would hesitate to give it so facile or slippery or grand a title as falling in love. But he knew it was a change, like the unlocking of a door or a footfall in an empty house.

The band began to play a tune he didn't know. Sarah led him to the dance floor and said something to him that got drowned in the music. He put his head close to hers.

"What was that?"

"I said, she's lovely."

"Who?"

"Eve."

He'd known exactly who she meant. It was his first deception. He nodded and shrugged, as if he hadn't until now considered it.

"Yeah," he said. "She seems nice."

Later, in bed, the lights out and his back turned in defensive rejection, he felt Sarah's fingers brush the hairs at the base of his spine then stroke slowly upward to the nape of his neck. And he lay still and cold as marble and, even as his loins stirred, he cruelly considered ignoring her. Reject the rejector, show her how it felt. He had done it often before and even though he knew it punished him as much as her and would only prolong their mutual suffering, giving them another night, another day, another week of cold resentment, he nearly did it now again.

But he didn't. Instead he turned and reached for her and found her, naked and cool and tentative. He held her for a while, the way he always held her and she lifted her thigh, as she always did, and placed it across his. The ritual, the feel, the smell of her so utterly familiar, the slow quickening of her flesh that never failed to thrill him.

But then, as if with some new resolve, she hoisted herself upon him and lowered her head and kissed him deeply, shockingly, her hair curtaining their faces. He angled his hips and slid himself into her and she leaned back until it bent him and hurt him and he cried out and had to grasp her hips to stop her. There was an urgency in her that he had never before known and that, were it not for its melancholy undertow, he might have taken for plain desire.

In the darkness above him he could just discern her slender shape, her breasts a parchment gray, nippled in charcoal, her ribs beneath like rippled sand. Her face was in shadow but he saw the glint of her eyes and it startled him, for whenever they made love she kept them shut, as if unwilling to witness herself so wanton.

They came quickly and together and she called out in a voice so low and feral he didn't recognize it. Then she went very still. For a long time she didn't move, just sat like a sculpture upon him, while their breathing slowed and faded and the silence folded in around them. Her head was tilted back so he could no longer see her face, only the silhouette of her chin and the pale fall of her neck and shoulders. Then she quaked and it was so violent and abrupt that for a moment he mistook it for some final spasm of her coming. But she was weeping. He reached up and laid a hand on her shoulder.

"What is it?"

She shook her head and seemed unable to find her voice. He raised himself on his elbows and as he did so she swiveled her body away.

"Sweetheart? What is it?"

"Nothing," she whispered.

He gently rolled her onto her side and tried to cradle her. And she started to sob. She had her arms tightly crossed, hugging herself, as if to stifle whatever private agony it was that came welling from her, convulsing her entire body. Ben had never heard a sound so dreadful.

"Tell me," he said. "Please, tell me."

"It's nothing."

EIGHT

They loped the horses through the sage and up a low bluff gashed red along its side where the rock had crumbled with the wind and rain. From the brow Abbie could see the glint of the river through the cottonwoods that lined its banks and see their jetsam of fluff drifting slowly on the hot noon air. They stood the horses awhile, Ty on her right and his father on her left, and watched the shadows of the clouds pass like ships of doubt across the pasture below and the billowed landscape beyond. Ty's father pointed east to where the river disappeared behind a distant shoulder of rock and said that this was where their land ended and their neighbor's began.

"And what mountains are those?" Abbie asked.

"The Bighorn. And, farther north, the Rosebud."

"It's so beautiful."

"It is."

"How long have you lived here?"

"Three generations. Ty's will be the fourth."

He seemed about to say more but then to reconsider and instead just rubbed his chin and stared in silence out across the land. High beyond the sparkling breaks of the river a great bird was spiraling slowly upward in a thermal, calling as if in lament at some great loss. Abbie asked what it was and Ty said it was a golden eagle and that she was lucky, for they weren't often to be seen hereabout. She already felt lucky. Earlier, riding higher in the hills, up where the forest began, they had seen a moose and some bighorn sheep and a black bear hustling her cub into the trees.

"Let's go find those colts," Ty's father said.

He nudged his horse forward and Abbie followed the swish of the gray mare's tail down through the boulders and the sage with Ty behind her. They had saddled her a smart bay gelding, his flanks now slick with sweat. Ty was riding a young strawberry roan he had started himself. They rode, all three, not with bits but with hackamores, a way Abbie had never ridden before. Never had she found a horse so easy yet so alive and utterly in tune. They were in a different league from those at The Divide, but then breeding and raising such horses was how Ty's father made his living. A Ray Hawkins quarter horse, she later discovered, would always fetch a premium.

Ray was probably about the same age as her father, Abbie figured, though too much weather had leathered his skin and made him look older. His eyes were the same pale blue as Ty's and when he smiled they all but vanished in the furrows of his face. He had that same quiet serenity she sometimes saw in Ty when he was concentrating on his work. In fact, so did Ty's mother and the horses and dogs and just about every living creature on the ranch. It was just a little bit spooky, as if they were in on some special secret. Maybe it was simply from living in such a wondrous place.

It had been a long drive the previous evening from The Divide. In Ty's old pale-green pickup, with the lowering sun behind them turning the plains and mountain peaks to gold, they had trundled east for hours along the interstate, past Billings and Hardin and Little Bighorn, then south and over the state line into Wyoming and the Powder River Basin. They talked a lot but were comfortable enough with each other by now to be silent too. Ty played her some of his favorite music, obscure country bands that Abbie had never heard of. She curled up beside him and slept and when she woke they were in Sheridan, bumping across the railroad and past an old steam engine, proudly parked beside it.

The Hawkins ranch sat in a cleft of hills some five miles out of town and was reached by a tortuous network of gravel road. It was dark when they got there and so it wasn't until morning that Abbie got to see what a spectacular setting it was. Ty's parents had waited up to greet them and though Abbie would rather have gone straight to bed, they insisted on serving an epic supper of cold ham and turkey, coleslaw, and baked potatoes, followed by blueberry pie and ice cream, all of which Ty devoured as if he'd been starved for weeks. And all the while, Ray and Martha, who had eaten earlier, sat by and watched and smiled and sipped their mugs of hot milk, saying barely a word, just listening as their son recounted between mouthfuls what had been going on at The Divide.

He was their only child and the pride shone from them. His mother looked like one of those Scandinavian women Abbie recalled from photographs of the early pioneers, freckled and blonde and buttoned to the neck, women who could with equal resolve and dexterity embroider a sampler or shoot a coyote between the eyes at fifty yards.

The colts they were now going to see had been turned loose in the last of the linked meadows that fringed the river. There were a dozen of them, and they lifted their heads and pricked their ears and watched while the three riders came closer. When he was still a hundred yards away, Ray stopped and left his horse to graze and went on foot toward them. The colts lowered their heads and shambled to meet him like a gang of blissed-out teenagers.

Ray stopped and let them come and when they reached him they circled around and nuzzled him and he stroked their necks and muzzles and rubbed their backs and spoke to them. He called to Abbie to come and both she and Ty got off their horses and joined him. And though a little shier with her than with Ty and his father, they let her put her hands on them and blow into their noses and savor their warm, sweet breath.

Back at the house over lunch, another sumptuous spread of cold meats and salad and home-baked bread, Abbie declared that she had never seen such a heavenly place in all her life. Ty's father smiled and nodded but his wife, pouring Abbie some more water, sighed and shrugged.

"It is now," she said. "How long it'll stay that way is another matter."

"What do you mean?" Abbie said.

Martha looked at Ray, as if asking his permission to go on. He didn't seem too keen. Ty looked as puzzled as Abbie was.

"What is it?" he said.

"Your mom's just talking about the drilling, that's all."

"Why, what's happened?"

"It's nothing. It won't happen."

"For heaven's sake, Ray. Tell him about the letter."

"What letter?" Ty said.

Abbie felt that she was intruding on some private family matter and wondered if she ought to excuse herself and pretend she wanted to go to the bathroom. Ty's father sighed and when he spoke it was to Abbie.

"There's a lot of drilling going on around here."

"For oil?"

"Gas. Coalbed methane. The land around here is full of it, all across the Powder River Basin. The gas gets trapped in the coal seams. Nobody bothered too much with it until fairly recently. But now they've found this real cheap way of drilling for it."

"You're not going to drill for it here?" Abbie said.

Ray gave a rueful laugh.

"No, Abbie, we're not. And even if we wanted to, we couldn't. Like most ranchers around these parts, when my granddaddy bought this land, the government only sold him the surface rights. They kept the mineral rights themselves and lately they've been leasing them off. We just found out somebody leased our land."

"Show Ty the letter," Martha said.

"Not now."

"Ray, he's got a right to—"

"Mom, it's okay. I'll read it later. Who bought the lease?"

"Some little outfit in Denver."

"And what do they plan on doing?"

Ty's father shrugged. "I guess we'll find out next week. They're sending a team to check things out."

"Don't let them."

"That's what I've been telling him," Ty's mother said.

Ray smiled. "You can't stop them. The law's on their side. They can drive around, dig, drill, do whatever they like. They give you a so-called 'surface damage agreement,' which everybody around here knows isn't worth the paper it's written on. But if we don't sign it, they can just go ahead anyhow."

"That's terrible," Abbie said.

"It probably won't come to much. A lot of these folks just buy the lease then just sit on it and don't do a thing."

He didn't sound as if he'd even convinced himself of this but he changed the subject and asked Abbie what it was like living in New York. She said it was okay and that she used to like it more than she did now. The problem was, the more time she spent out West, where there was so much space, the harder it was to go home.

"Ty says you want to go to college out here," Martha said.

"Definitely."

"That's great. How do your mom and dad feel about that?"

"I haven't told them yet. I think my dad'll be okay with it."

"Well, I'll tell you something, young lady," Ray said. "The way you handle a horse, I'd say it's where you belong."

It was the middle of the afternoon when they set off back to The Divide. As they drove out of Sheridan, Ty said he wanted to show her something and turned off the highway onto a winding gravel road. Ahead of them a great cloud of red dust rose into the sky and as they came around a bend they saw two giant yellow excavators hacking a crater into the hillside.

"They're digging a pit for the water," Ty said. "When they drill into the coal seam, it releases this huge amount of water. Which you'd think, in a place as dry as this, would be a good thing. But it's salt water and where it floods onto the land nothing can grow. Kills everything. See down yonder?"

He pointed down into the valley.

"Those white patches there, down by the creek? That's salt. Those were prime hay meadows, about a hundred acres. Friend of my daddy owns them. Now they're good for nothing. Used to be good trout fishing there too, but now there's not a single fish. All died. The gas companies line these big holes with plastic, like they're doing here. But they leak and spill, and they don't fix them because, basically, they don't give a damn."

They drove on and every so often Ty would point things out to her—well-heads, compressor stations, power- and pipelines, dirt roads gashed across the virgin landscape. They crossed over and down into another valley and stopped by a low wooden bridge where the water of another creek bubbled with methane released by the drilling. Ty told her how a friend of his had put a match to it one day and set the whole creek ablaze.

In other places, like the deserted ranch house he showed her on the way back to the highway, artesian wells that had functioned happily for forty years had suddenly started to bubble gas or run dry because some idiot gas drillers had ruptured the aquifer five miles away.

"Can't anyone stop these people doing this?"

"No. There's a pretty good protest group, but the problem is a lot of people think the drilling benefits the town. Creates jobs, brings business to the stores, that kind of deal. And that's bullshit. Often as not the companies ship in their own cheap labor and all the town gets is a whole lot of problems."

"Is this going on in Montana too?"

"Not yet. But it won't be long."

They didn't talk much after that. They headed north and west along I-90, while Steve Earle sang sorrowful songs on the stereo and a pale sun slid down ahead of them into its own coalbed of cloud. Ty said the weather looked set to change. Abbie had never seen him so heavy and forlorn. He switched on the headlights and she reached out and stroked the back of his neck.

"Two more days," he said. "And then you'll be gone."

A first few drops of rain spattered the windshield.

"I'll be back," she said.

It rained all of Friday and most of Saturday, and only a stalwart, slickered few—Abbie inevitably among them—ventured out on the last rides. Of the guests who didn't, the hardiest still plodded in their Gore-Tex down to the creek to cast a fly or hiked up the sodden trails through the woods, but mostly people simply sat around and read or played long games of Monopoly and Scrabble in the ranch-house lounge.

While Abbie went riding or hung around the stables "helping" Ty, Josh hung with the Delstock kids. This mainly involved lolling in one of their cabins (usually Lane and Ryan Delroy's because their parents didn't get uptight about the mess), listening to music and having sprawling, sardonic discussions on topics that segued surreally from world peace to thrash metal to nose rings and nail polish. Specifically, Josh lolled as often and as close as he could to Katie Bradstock. Which was what he was doing right now.

Over the course of the past twelve days, he had stirred himself up into a fever of yearning. There wasn't a moment of the day when his head wasn't full of her. She hummed and jangled through every nerve and vein of his body. The sight, the smell, even the thought of her gave him a strange, hollowing ache. He was an open walking wound from head to toe. A walking wound with a constant hard-on. So constant he worried it might be doing him damage.

Part of the problem was that he'd been waiting too long for something like this to happen. At school it seemed like every other kid his age (and younger) was getting laid, except him. He knew he was nobody's idea of a pinup but since last fall when he'd gotten rid of his glasses and started wearing contacts and shed a few pounds and gotten a little cooler with his clothes, he didn't think he looked so nerdy. And, thank God, he didn't get too many zits—though, come to think of it, that didn't seem to stop guys like Kevin Simpson, a complete duh-brain in tenth grade, from getting laid.

Of course, Josh wasn't so dumb as to believe all the stories that jerks like Kevin put out. A lot of kids pretended they'd done it when they hadn't. Whatever. This thing with Katie was doing his head in. The vacation was about to end and they still hadn't even kissed. He was pretty sure she wanted things to happen as much as he did. And a couple of times it almost had. Like the other night at his dad's birthday party, when they were dancing together and Ty's band started playing a slow number and she locked her arms around the back of his neck and smiled at him in a way that made him go all fluttery inside. And then Lane and Abbie came butting in and ruined things by dancing with them.

That was the real problem. They were all such a gang and always did everything together. Which was really cool and a lot of fun. But the downside was that there was hardly ever a moment when it was just him and Katie, just the two of them alone, when they might get to switch from being just friends into something more exciting. They had laughed and teased and talked and chased each other around and even tickled each other. But that was where it had gotten stuck. Like a scratched record. And neither of them seemed to know which button to press to move it on.

It was Saturday afternoon and all six brothers and sisters—including Abbie, back from the stables with straw in her hair—were sprawled on the shunted-together beds of Lane and Ryan's cabin. They were listening to the new Radiohead album, which Ryan said was "ultimate." Josh secretly felt that if he heard it one more time he might have to go out and hang himself. The room smelled of stale socks and cigarette smoke which they did their best to eliminate by keeping the back windows open and periodic blasts of Lane's Calvin Klein body spray for which they had promised to reimburse her, though probably wouldn't. Will Bradstock said it made the place smell like a Turkish brothel and seemed disappointed when nobody bothered to ask how he might know. They were all either too bored or too wasted from the night before when they'd snuck up behind the pool changing rooms and smoked the weed Ryan had stolen from his father's stash.

All except Josh. He was neither bored nor wasted. He was too busy thinking about his right thigh which for the last ten blissful minutes had been pressed against Katie. She was lying curled on her side with her back to him, raised on one elbow, her gorgeous butt nestled into him and a bare shoulder leaning gently against his chest. She was reading an old copy of *People Magazine* that was propped against Ryan who had fallen asleep across Abbie. Or maybe she was just pretending to read it because she hadn't yet turned a page.

Katie was wearing that sexy little yellow crop top and a denim miniskirt cut low around her hips to reveal six inches of tanned flesh. Sometimes, when she wiggled, you could also see the top of her panties, which were pink and lacy. Josh was pretending to read the magazine over her shoulder while in fact peering furtively down his nose into the gaping neck of her top where he could see her right breast bulge a little as it got cupped by her bra (which was also pink but seemed to be made of satin rather than lace). Her nearness, the pressure of her butt against his thigh, the sweet, warm, animal smell of her had given him a mega-boner, which, with a discreetly placed right hand, he was managing to flatten to his stomach.

The place where his thigh touched her butt was getting hot. She could have moved away but she hadn't. There was no way she could be unaware of it. She was probably enjoying it as much as he was. Man, he thought. Maybe this was the moment. The moment to show her how he really felt.

His heart began to pound. He hoped to God she couldn't hear or feel it. Go on, he told himself. It's the guy who has to make the first move. She's probably been waiting for it, dying for you to let her know how much you want her. And there was an obvious and simple way that would leave her no room for doubt. He took a long, deep breath and slowly slid the restraining hand from his stomach so that his hard-on pronged against her.

Katie Bradstock jumped as if she'd been jabbed by a cattle prod. She lifted a clear six inches from the bed.

"Josh!" she yelped. "Jesus!"

Everybody was staring at him. He felt his face starting to burn.

"What?" he said, trying for a tone of innocent shock and failing.

"What's the matter?" Abbie said, for all of them.

Katie was scrambling away across the bed, on her hands and knees over the tangle of startled bodies.

"Nothing," she said. "I just gotta go somewhere."

She was off the bed now and hurrying to the door and a few seconds later she was gone. There followed a long and bemused silence. Everyone was awake and alert now and looking at each other for some clue as to what had happened. Josh tried to look mystified, while his brain scrolled furiously for some half-plausible excuse.

Bugs, he thought.

"Maybe she got bitten."

He got to his knees, stupidly forgetting about his erection which was wilting fast but still tenting his shorts. He instantly and no doubt comically adopted a weird hunched posture to hide it, while he pretended to hunt for bugs among the rumpled bedclothes. On the stereo

140

Radiohead were coming to a suicidal crescendo. Abbie and Lane were already on their way out of the door in pursuit of Katie. Will and Ryan just sat there staring at him.

"What was that about?" Will said.

"No idea. I think she got stung or something . . ."

Ryan's eyes flicked languidly to Josh's crotch then back to his eyes, a slow grin sliding in.

"Yeah, right," he said. "I wonder what by."

Ben swung the last of the bags into the back of the rented truck and shut the tailgate. They had an earlier flight to catch than all the others who were checking out that morning and everyone had trooped down across the lawn to the parking area behind the stables to see them off. The ritual fond farewells were in full swing. Abbie and Katie and Lane, all close to tears, were hugging and kissing and making one another promise to call and e-mail. Their brothers were doing the more reserved and awkward male version of the same thing, calling each other *bro* and *man* and *dude* and sharing elaborate handshakes and slaps on the back.

Their mothers meanwhile were again going through that other annual ritual of promising to visit with one another. Ben heard Sarah say that this year they would *definitely* be visiting the Delroys in Florida. Maybe they could all escape the grandparents and meet up for Thanksgiving? And go skiing somewhere in February? None of this, of course, would ever happen and they all

141

secretly knew it. The mutual pretense simply made everybody feel better about parting.

It was a ritual in which, for reasons Ben didn't fully understand, the men never seemed to take part. Perhaps they were just too cynical. Instead, he and Tom Bradstock and Delroy were standing by the truck, looking on indulgently and discussing more manly and important matters, like check-in security procedure and how many air miles they had each clocked up. Tom had now started telling them about a sniffer dog that had taken a shine to him at Chicago O'Hare and headed straight for him every time he stepped into the baggage hall.

"I try to explain to the handlers that we're just good friends, but they don't believe me and haul me off to the booth for another search."

Ben listened just enough to be able to laugh in the right places. He was watching Josh and again feeling sorry for him. The boy had missed dinner the previous evening, claiming he wasn't feeling well. He hadn't even shown up for the usual end-of-vacation party in the bar afterward. All his earlier joy seemed to have ebbed away. Sarah said something had obviously gone wrong between him and Katie. And looking at the two of them now, studiously avoiding each other, Ben figured she must be right. On top of that, Abbie had been in tears before breakfast, having just said good-bye to Ty. Men and women, Ben sighed to himself. Lord help us all.

Then he saw Eve. He had looked out for her at breakfast, but she hadn't shown up and he had resigned himself to leaving without saying good-bye. It was probably better that way. But here she was, beautiful as ever in her riding clothes, walking down across the lawn. The morning ride was about to leave, the horses all saddled up in line outside the stables, some of the guests already mounting up. And for a moment Ben thought that was where she must be going. But then she gave a little wave and headed down toward the parking area. She looked at him and they exchanged a smile but she went to join the women.

Tom Bradstock had finished his story and had gone across to talk with one of the riders. Delroy was staring at Eve.

"What I'd give to be Adam," he said quietly.

It took Ben a couple of beats to understand what he meant.

"Oh, right. Yeah. She's nice."

"*Nice?* Ben, you are so . . . measured. I can think of a dozen things I'd call her before *nice.*"

Two nights earlier, Ben had plucked up the courage to accompany Delroy on his nightly stroll into the woods. Whether pot was stronger nowadays or it had simply been too long since he last tried it, Ben didn't know, but after just a few puffs his head started telescoping into itself, and he staggered in a clammy nausea back to his cabin and lay on the bed for what seemed like hours, convinced he was going to die. The humiliation was galling enough, but worse still was Delroy's apparent assumption that they had graduated to more intimate terms. *Measured?* How the hell would he know? They didn't even know each other. Ben looked at his watch.

"Well," he said. "I think it's time we were going."

As he walked over toward the women he heard Sarah ask Eve if she ever came to New York.

"As a matter of fact, I'm coming in September, for a friend's exhibition."

"Hey, well, we should get together," Sarah said.

"I'd like that."

"Maybe we could go see a show. Do you like musicals?"

"Love them."

While they swapped numbers, Ben rounded up the kids and everyone said their final good-byes. When Eve touched her cool cheek against his, he felt a twist of melancholy in his chest. She said how much she had enjoyed meeting them all. Not him, he noted, *them all.* Lori was still in bed, she said, but had asked her to say good-bye. The Coopers climbed into the truck and Ben turned the key.

"You make sure to call us," Sarah said to Eve.

"I promise."

She never would, of course. As they pulled away down the drive, the kids calling and leaning out of their windows to wave, Ben lifted his eyes to the mirror and took what he was sure would be his last look at her.

NINE

I t was match point and, as usual, Sarah's father was going to win. Nobody would be surprised. Even the lizards sunbathing along the court's perimeter looked on with a kind of weary fatalism. However, that George Davenport could still, at the age of sixty-eight, annihilate his son-in-law in two straight sets clearly gave him more pleasure than he could disguise. In his trim white shorts and polo shirt, his silver hair sleek and only the faintest glisten of sweat on his tanned brow, he bounced the ball and prepared to serve. At the other end, in his sodden gray T-shirt and floral boardshorts that he wore in childish defiance of Westchester court etiquette, Benjamin stood braced like a prisoner before a firing squad.

It was the Sunday of Labor Day weekend and the Coopers had driven that morning in sunlit gloom from Syosset to Bedford for the ritual lunch with Sarah's parents. Quite how the custom had endured all these years, when everyone involved—with the possible exception of Sarah's mother—so dreaded it, was a mystery almost as profound as her father's insatiable joy at beating, for the umpteenth time, so lackluster an opponent. Perhaps simply to prolong Benjamin's misery, he now served his first double-fault of the match.

"Forty—fifteen!"

Lunch was waiting on the terrace that spread grandly from the south-facing side of the house and, sensing what passed for a climax to the match, Sarah, her mother, Abbie, and Josh had wandered down across the manicured grass, bearing lemonade and a dogged, if somewhat strained, cheeriness. The court, like all else material at the Davenport residence, was immaculate. Groomed twice weekly by one of several gardeners, its brick and gravel surround planted with rose and hibiscus and sculpted cushions of lavender, it was surfaced with the very latest sort of synthetic grass which played, according to Sarah's father, even better than the real thing. That a man whose gifts to a grateful nation included several arcane varieties of hedge fund could so improve upon God's work would have surprised no one, least of all Benjamin, who, flushed and grimly sweating, now prepared to face a second match point.

"Go, Dad!" Abbie called from the shade of the court-side arbor.

"Quiet, please," her grandfather said. He wasn't kidding.

He served and this time it was fast and low and in and Benjamin lunged fitfully to his right and just got the edge of his racket to it, but only to hoist the ball back over the net in a high and easy lob.

With enough time for a man's life to spool in slow motion before him, his father-in-law watched the ball descend, his racket uncoiling like a cobra for the strike, and with a perfectly timed and blistering slam, dispatched the ball in one epic bounce between Benjamin's feet, over the wire netting behind him and into

146

the roses. With various degrees of irony, the four spectators cheered and applauded.

"Thank you, Ben!"

"Thank *you,* George."

Sarah watched the two most important men in her life shake hands at the net then walk toward the gate, her father with a patronizing arm draped across his son-in-law's sweaty shoulders.

"Life in the old dog yet, eh?"

"I'd say more than enough, George."

"Poor Benjamin," her mother sighed.

"So, Dad, what was the score?" Josh called, as if they didn't all know.

"Listen, it's called manners. You don't beat the host, didn't anyone tell you?"

"So how come you always lose to Grandpa at home too?"

The men were off the court now and stood toweling themselves beside the slatted teak table in the arbor, while Sarah's mother poured lemonade and answered Josh's question.

"The reason, Josh, is that your father knows very well that there isn't a man on God's earth who likes to win more than your grandfather. It's the cursed gene of the Davenports. Let's hope you haven't inherited it."

"Don't worry, Grandma," Abbie said. "Dad's loser genes will more than compensate."

"Hey, please," Benjamin said. "Everybody, feel free. Let's just call it National Get Ben Day."

He finished his lemonade and jogged off up to the

house to shower and change. Sarah's father, probably to indicate that he didn't need to do either of those things, strolled with the rest of them back across the lawn, grilling Abbie about her newly announced intention of going to the University of Montana. Sarah was less supportive than Benjamin on the issue, but at this moment didn't want to let Abbie down by siding with her father, who was predictably skeptical. Abbie was arguing her case well and Sarah decided to keep out of it and wandered ahead on her own. Josh was bringing up the rear with his grandmother, keeping her up to speed on how the Chicago Cubs were doing. On Friday he had received a letter from Katie Bradstock and had been all but euphoric ever since. He wouldn't disclose what it said but whatever had gone wrong between them was now right.

It hadn't rained for weeks, but the grass, with its state-of-the-art sprinkling system, was a dazzling, ludicrous green. A breeze had gotten up and was rushing in the scorched leaves of the big, old oaks along the driveway. Sarah closed her eyes and breathed deeply and tried to enjoy the warmth of the sun and the feel of the grass beneath her bare feet. But the knot below her ribs wouldn't loosen.

The place always made her tense. With its faux-colonial façade and preposterous number of rooms, it had never seemed like home. They had moved here from a much smaller and cozier place across town when Sarah was fifteen and her father's business was bought for an obscene amount of money by a big Wall

Street bank. What earthly need they had for such a palace, other than sheer ostentation, she had never been able to fathom. Particularly when they so rarely entertained and had already dispatched both her and her brother Jonathan off to boarding school. At the time Sarah had blamed the move on her mother, who came from grander New England stock. But as she had gotten older she had come to think—though would never have admitted it in front of Benjamin—that the real snob was her father. He was simply better at disguising it.

They had reached the steps to the terrace now and Sarah could hear that Abbie was getting exasperated. Why on earth, her grandfather was saying, when she had the pick of so many better colleges closer to home, would someone as smart as Abbie, a straight-A student, best at everything, want to go *someplace out the back of beyond?*

Sarah turned on him.

"Dad, it's Montana, for heaven's sake, not Mongolia."

"We just did a deal with some folks in Mongolia. It's a pretty switched-on place, as a matter of fact."

"It wouldn't have anything to do with meeting a certain young cowboy by any chance, would it?" Sarah's mother asked.

Abbie groaned and turned to glare at her brother.

"Josh, you little rat, what have you been saying?"

He held up his hands, all innocent.

"I didn't say a word!"

"You're such a pathetic liar. Maybe you should tell

everyone why suddenly you're such a fan of the Chicago Cubs. It couldn't have anything to do with your crush on little Katie Bradstock."

"*Little?* Oh, and we're so big and grown-up now, are we?"

"Children, children," Sarah said.

By the time they reached the terrace, the bickering had calmed and Abbie was reluctantly coaxed into telling her grandparents a little about Ty. She deftly managed to steer the conversation on to her visit to his parents' ranch, from which she had returned almost ecstatic, saying it was the loveliest place she'd ever seen, even more beautiful than The Divide.

Lunch was cold Maine lobster, flown down by special order the previous afternoon. There were also oysters and shrimp and a bewildering array of salads prepared by Rosa, who had kept house for Sarah's parents for the last nine years without, as far as Sarah was aware, ever once smiling. Benjamin said she was probably still waiting for a reason. The oval table was covered with a heavy white linen cloth and shaded by two vast cream canvas umbrellas. There was room for at least a dozen people and instead of grouping at one end, the six of them sat several yards apart, so isolated in their own space that if anything needed passing, Rosa had to be summoned from sullen standby in the wings.

Normally, the gaps would have been filled by Sarah's brother and his family. Jonathan was five years her junior and they had never been close. Like his father, he was in finance of some impenetrable sort and had recently taken a job in Singapore, hauling Kelly, his Texan wife, and their two identically spoiled twin daughters with him. As everyone chewed on oversized lobster and the silence grew more stubborn, Sarah was almost beginning to miss them.

Why did she persist in inflicting this annual penance on Benjamin and the kids when she hated it almost as much as they did? The past week had been blighted by a protracted argument with Abbie and Josh, who had both, until this morning, been refusing to come. At breakfast Sarah had finally delivered a tirade on the importance of family, heaping into it every weaselly, guilt-inducing gambit she could think of. Such as how they were prepared to take all their grandparents generous birthday checks and Christmas presents and yet weren't willing in return to spare them a paltry few hours for lunch. And how Grandpa wasn't getting any younger and wouldn't be around much longer (though, in truth, he was in obscenely good health and would probably outlive them all). She had even stooped so low as to mention Misty, the pony her grandparents had given Abbie when she was ten years old. Benjamin had kept out of it. But even though he didn't say a word, she could tell from his smug expression how much he was enjoying the revolution. It made her want to throw something at him.

But now they were here, the guilt had rebounded and she felt sorry for them all. Even Benjamin. He hadn't been exactly friendly for many weeks, not since they got back from The Divide. He'd been distant and preoccupied. He was having a hard time at work and she decided to attribute it to that. Perhaps it was her fault as much as his, for things weren't going well with the bookstore either. In fact, it was having its worst year ever. One of the big chains had opened a new store just a couple of blocks away and Jeffrey, her adored and devoted manager, who nowadays pretty well ran things on his own, was again talking about quitting. But although Sarah liked to talk about her problems, Benjamin didn't seem to want to listen anymore or to discuss his own. Her father, with the nose of a bloodhound, was asking him about work now.

"How's that Hamptons project of yours going?"

"It's not looking too good, as a matter of fact, George."

"What's the guy's name, I forgot."

"The developer? Hank McElvoy."

"McElvoy, that's it. I was asking Bill Sterling about him the other day. He says the guy's in trouble and the banks are calling it all in. Is that the problem?"

"No, actually, it was what I think they call *creative differences.*"

"Dad's a hero," Abbie called from across the table. "They wanted to cut down all these beautiful trees and he wouldn't do it."

"Seems a pity to lose a job for a few trees."

"Grandpa!"

"Well, you're probably well out of it."

"Yes, I probably am."

Benjamin took a mouthful of lobster and glanced at

Sarah. She smiled to show solidarity, but he looked away.

"Ella was telling me your firm just won some fancy award," her father went on.

"That's right. For the mall we did up in Huntington."

"Was that your design or Martin's?"

"Well, we all worked on it. But I guess you could say it was basically Martin's concept."

"He's a bright guy."

"Yes, he is."

"Oh, well. Give him my congratulations."

"Thank you, George. I will."

There was a time when such a thinly disguised put-down would have sent Benjamin into a fury. In the early days of their marriage, he would take only a certain amount and then pick a fight on another issue which, inevitably, her father would win. For, whatever the subject and no matter who was right or wrong, his technique of smiling and staying calm would eventually drive Benjamin so mad he would start yelling. But looking at him now, sitting across the table from her, still sweating from his humiliation on court, Sarah saw no sign of hurt or anger, just a weary resignation. It upset her more than any shouting match ever had or could.

And later, as she drove them home, it was Abbie and Josh who exploded, not Benjamin. Nor did he even so much as smile or seem to take any pleasure as they vented their anger and forced Sarah to promise on God's honor that this was the last Labor Day lunch they would ever have to endure. Without demur, she apologized and this seemed to disarm them and a tired silence descended. Josh put on his headphones to listen to his Walkman, while Abbie curled up beside him and was soon asleep. Benjamin leaned back against the headrest and stared blankly out of the side window. He looked so forlorn that she reached out and laid her hand on his arm but he didn't respond in any way and after a few moments she removed it.

"I thought age was supposed to mellow you," she said. "He gets worse and worse."

"He's always been like that."

"Everything he says has some kind of barb to it."

"It always did."

He closed his eyes and Sarah took the hint and drove on in silence. In the mirror she could see that Josh had fallen asleep now too. The freeway was clogged with holiday traffic so she exited and took what they called the "snake route" but it was just as congested and they crawled through the suburban sprawl, bumper to bumper, mile after mile. She switched on the radio but couldn't find a station that didn't irritate her or make her feel more alienated. The people in the cars around them all seemed to be talking and having a good time.

It was the old Volvo station wagon that did it. It was in the next lane and kept drawing alongside. It was just like the one they had once owned, only blue instead of white. Its roof was stacked with bicycles and camping gear, just like theirs used to be. Inside were a couple and two young children, a boy and girl, both blond and impossibly cute. Everyone was laughing and jabbering. Sarah tried not to look. She clenched the muscles in her face to stem the tears that nowadays welled so readily. And she stared resolutely ahead, scolding herself for being so stupid and sentimental and telling herself not to go there. Not to let into her head this image of her own lost happiness.

TEN

They had met during Sarah's sophomore year at Wellesley. A girl in her Shakespearean tragedy class, someone she barely knew and didn't even much like, was asked by a boy at Harvard to bring a busload of "chicks" into Cambridge for a party. There weren't many at Wellesley who answered happily to such a name and Sarah should have seen it as a warning, but she had nothing better to do, so tagged along.

It turned out to be one of those hideous fraternity affairs, crammed with drunk and obnoxious jocks, shouting and showing off and throwing up in the flower beds. Benjamin, standing alone in a corner, with his long hair and leather jacket, looked arty and interesting and, at the very least, sober. He was clearly older than the others, more man than boy, and obviously as appalled and alienated as she was. The two of them homed in on each other and seemed to bond before they even spoke.

His connection with the party turned out to be as tenuous as hers. He said he was there as transport. He had a car and had been cajoled by some guys who had been invited to drive them all the way from Syracuse where he was studying architecture.

"They said I should see how the other half lived."

He took a sip of the so-called fruit punch and grimaced. It had been laced, so rumor had it, with raw alcohol plundered from the chemistry labs. Someone put another Wings album on.

"Well, now you know," Sarah said.

"Yeah. At least they paid for the gas. This music is killing me. Shall we go somewhere else?"

They headed into Boston in his old Ford Mustang. It had a broken muffler and made so much noise that everyone turned and stared. They found a little Italian restaurant she had once been to and had steaming bowls of spaghetti vongole and a bottle of cheap Chianti and sat talking until the place closed. Sarah said she remembered a bar nearby and they went looking for it and when they couldn't find it just kept on walking. It was a clear fall night and the air was chilly and she surprised herself by tucking her arm into his. They must have walked for miles and never stopped talking the entire time.

He told her he came from Abilene, Kansas, where his parents ran a hardware store. He said he was fonder of the place now that he didn't have to live there, but that when he was growing up he couldn't wait to escape. He had an older sister he hardly ever saw and he didn't get along with his dad who was still mad at him for not becoming a lawyer. Sarah asked him if he had always wanted to be an architect and he said no, absolutely not. What he'd really wanted to be was an actor.

"Well, not an actor exactly," he corrected himself. "A movie star. A big, famous movie star. Like Paul Newman or someone."

"So what happened?"

"I wasn't any good. At college all I really did was drama. I was in all the plays. Got some good parts. But, thank God, I had a moment of revelation."

"Tell me."

"Really? Okay. I was playing Angelo in *Measure for Measure*—do you know the play?"

She knew it inside out but simply nodded.

"Okay. Well, you know when Isabella won't sleep with him, Angelo orders them to cut off her brother Claudio's head and they don't, but pretend they have and give some other poor guy the chop instead?"

"Barnardine."

"I'll take your word for it. Hey, that's pretty impressive. Anyhow, the director had them bring me the head in a basket and, of course, I don't know it's not Claudio's and I have to lift this cloth and look at what I've done. And he said, 'Ben, I want nausea, real nausea. And the dawning of guilt.'"

"The dawning of guilt. Sounds like a book."

"Yeah, the story of my life. So. Every night I used to look into the basket, at this ridiculous rubber head, all covered with tomato ketchup, and I tried, God, I tried so hard, but all I wanted to do was laugh."

"And did you?"

"No. Except on the last night when someone put an inflatable frog in the basket instead. No, I just faked it. Nausea, guilt. And I was fine. Got some great reviews. But I knew that if I couldn't feel it, I mean, really feel it in my guts, then I wasn't cut out to be an actor."

"Do you believe all actors really feel it?"

"No, but I think the best ones do."

In turn she told him about her family and growing up in Bedford—at which name he pulled a sort of mock-impressed face, as if he knew now who he was dealing with and this made her immediately start downplaying anything that hinted at money or privilege or connections. As if being at Wellesley wasn't already enough for him to place her.

She had never met a guy who listened so well. When at last, and more by luck than navigation, they found their way to where he had parked his car, it had been towed. By the time they got it back, dawn was breaking and they were both feeling hungry again. They drove out to the Massachusetts Turnpike and found a truck stop and ordered great greasy plates of bacon and eggs and hash browns.

It had been one of the best nights of Sarah's life. And when he said good-bye, kissing her chastely on the cheek, and headed off to pick up his friends and drive back to Syracuse, she knew—well, no, she thought, she dared to hope—that this was the man she would marry and have children with.

It wasn't only corny, it was absurd. Everybody knew

the joke about parents sending their girls to Wellesley to get their Mrs. But the idea was that you were supposed to net yourself some rich Harvard highflyer, not a Kansas storekeeper's son from what her father would call the University of Nowhere. Furthermore, she had only just turned twenty and was still a virgin. The only one in the entire college, she sometimes thought. It was the mid-seventies, post-pill and pre-AIDS, and everyone was at it like rabbits, or so it seemed. Except for Sarah Davenport.

It wasn't for want of offers, or because she was a prude or scared or uninterested. She knew her reasoning was quaint and probably a little dumb. Iris, her roommate, certainly thought it was both of these things, as well as plain crazy. They had been born in the same week of September and Iris constantly reminded her that being by five whole days Sarah's senior, she was infinitely the wiser. She was certainly the only person with whom Sarah felt able to have such intimate discussions. Iris had grown up in Pittsburgh, where, she maintained, absolutely everybody got laid at sixteen.

"Just get it over with, girl," she said. "Then get picky."

But Sarah felt it mattered. That she should love the man with whom she first went all the way might be an old-fashioned notion but it also seemed right. But though she'd had boyfriends and done with them pretty much everything else—or what she understood, from her talks with Iris, that this entailed—she was starting to feel something of an oddity. And these things had a way of getting out. She knew for a fact that one little creep she'd dated for a while had gone around afterward calling her a cock-teaser. And even though, according to what Iris had heard, he didn't have one worth teasing, it bothered her.

Had Benjamin suggested they make love, even in the back of his Mustang that very night, she would happily have done so. As it turned out, they didn't get even close to it for another five months. They spoke at least once a week on the phone and met a few times in New York to see a movie or some new art exhibition, each time followed by dinner and another good-bye peck on the cheek. And just as Sarah was growing resigned to the idea that all he had in mind was being her new best friend and that he probably had a girlfriend in Syracuse or back home in Kansas, he arrived unannounced in Wellesley on St. Valentine's Day with a vast and vaguely carnivorous-looking bunch of blood-red amaryllis and declared that he loved her.

It was only later that she discovered it wasn't quite as high-risk a venture as it seemed and that he had taken the secret precaution of calling Iris to check out if Sarah had other plans and, if not, how welcome he might be.

That summer he found work at a busy, if uninspiring, firm of architects on the Upper East Side where all they let him do was answer the phones and fetch coffee. Through a business contact of her father's, Sarah did the same for a company that made TV commercials. Neither of them got paid and—thanks to Sarah's allowance—neither much cared. They were too busy discovering each other.

An old Syracuse friend of Benjamin's was spending three months in Florence and let them use his apartment, a two-room shoebox on 93rd and Amsterdam. It was one of the hottest summers on record and the place had no air-conditioning. The sidewalks shimmered and steamed and that was pretty much how it was inside too.

Sarah had assumed, not from anything he'd said but more from his cool and worldly manner, that Benjamin was experienced with women. But in their first couplings, he seemed almost as new to it as she was and it was some time before they lost their reticence with each other. And though she couldn't quite understand why sex was supposed to be such a big deal, and even back then, even on those feverish nights, with the windows wide and the clamor of the street and of their own heated blood, couldn't match Benjamin's relentless hunger for it, she nevertheless had an almost giddy sense of relief and liberation.

It was in early July that she took him for the first time up to Bedford for the weekend to meet her parents, who by now knew about him and were curious. They had no idea, of course, that when their daughter stayed overnight in the city, as she increasingly did, she wasn't, as she claimed, staying with a friend from Wellesley. She had already told Benjamin enough about them to make him a little apprehensive. He had his hair cut specially for the occasion—which Sarah took as an act of devotion—and even wore a sports coat (though not a necktie) for dinner, which didn't quite do the trick for her mother, who was later overheard describing him as "charming, if a little Bohemian."

Sarah's father tried to camouflage his disdain for any college that wasn't Ivy League behind an overly enthusiastic interest in the University of Kansas where Benjamin had graduated before going on to Syracuse. Dinner was like an interview for a job. Her father knew as much about architecture as Benjamin knew about corporate finance but had obviously done some sly homework. While Sarah and her mother ate in silence, he cross-examined the poor guy for a full twenty minutes about Werner Seligmann, a Harvard professor who had just moved to Syracuse and would, in the years that followed, transform the place. Fortunately, Benjamin was already a fan and passed the test with ease. And although he probably lost a few points later by bumping into her mother as he tiptoed half-naked from Sarah's room, he made up for it the next morning by being thrashed for the first time by his future father-in-law on the tennis court.

They were joined for Sunday lunch by two couples who lived nearby. Both had young children who took to Benjamin as if they had known him all their lives. He teased them gently and played the fool and soon had them in fits of giggles. They wouldn't leave him alone. Many men of his age could do this, Sarah knew, but what struck her was how he was also able to talk with them, even about serious things and entirely on their level, without any trace of condescension. Her mother caught her staring at him and Sarah could see from the knowing smile that her intentions had been read.

They were married, sumptuously, in Bedford in the summer of Sarah's graduation from Wellesley. And never once, during those heady preceding months nor for many years after, did she falter from that first impression she had formed of him the night they met. She loved almost everything about him. His gentleness, his wit, his generosity, the way he sought her opinions and cared about what she thought and said and did. The way he would sit her down with a cup of tea if she had a problem and let her tell him all about it, without trying to solve it for her. She loved his passion for his work and was convinced that if there were any justice in the world, one day he would achieve great things.

Their interests didn't exactly coincide but they each seemed equally open to the things the other cherished. He read mostly nonfiction but she soon had him reading novels—Jane Austen and Henry James, as well as Updike and Bellow and Roth—and gave him a crash course in classical music. For a while he became almost obsessed with Mozart opera. She would never forget the tears streaming down his cheeks at the Met as they listened to the famous serenade duet in *Cosi fan tutte*. In turn, he took her to see obscure European movies by directors she had barely heard of, like Herzog and Fassbinder. And he played her all his Miles Davis and Neil Young records and took her to dark downtown dives to hear obscure punk bands so uniformly dreadful she felt like weeping too.

They seemed so closely in tune, so much a part of each other, that sometimes Sarah found it hard to know exactly where she ended and he began. Occasionally she worried that she was too malleable, that without realizing it, she was being quietly dismantled and remodeled. When they went shopping for clothes or for food or furniture or when they were redecorating the apartment, it was Benjamin's taste that nearly always prevailed. Not, however, against her will. She was only too happy to go along with it because, generally, she didn't know what she wanted and he always did. Confronted with a dozen different shapes of wineglass or twenty shades of blue, she would feel bewildered or her eyes would glaze over. Perhaps it simply didn't matter enough to her. And anyhow, she would justify, knowing about these things, having views about texture and color and shape was Benjamin's job, was in his very nature.

She knew this wasn't how it was with most couples. A lot of men were only too relieved to cede such decisions to women. And there was no doubt, Benjamin did have a tendency to want to control things. She remembered reading about such people once, when she took a psychology class at Wellesley. Their wish to control things often stemmed from a deep-seated insecurity, a worry that if they didn't appear decisive and keep tabs on everything, then chaos would erupt and overwhelm them. Perhaps Benjamin had some mild version of this.

If so, Sarah was happy to live with it. It wasn't as if he was a bully. And, frankly, it was often a relief.

He could be moody too, and difficult, especially when things weren't going well with his work. And there was a restlessness about him that probably should have worried her more than it did. And if they argued (which wasn't often and thus all the more upsetting when they did), he could be cruel and seemed to find it hard to apologize or forgive. They were both quick and clever with words but his tongue was the sharper and even when it was his fault he had a way of twisting things around so that it was she who ended up saying sorry.

In those early years, their worst arguments were about her parents. Perhaps inevitably, Benjamin carried a chip about them and resented being dependent on her trust money while he finished up at Syracuse and struggled through three cruel and tedious years of internship finally to qualify as a registered, penniless architect. He started referring to the house in Bedford as "the Country Club" and, in company, would sometimes joke that the key to success for an architect was to marry money. But Sarah knew such comments were preemptive and aimed at himself, not her.

The truth was that she disliked their reliance on her parents' money almost as much as he did. It made her feel redundant, as if it didn't matter if she made a success of her life or a hopeless mess. After college she was offered a job with the same company for which she had fetched coffee but because the initial contact had been her father's, not hers, she turned it down. Instead, she applied for and surprised herself by landing a research job with a TV company that made arts documentaries.

Her first project was a series for PBS about great American writers. Unfortunately, to qualify, they all had to be dead. So instead of her current heroes, Roth and Bellow and Updike, it was the usual high-school lineup of Melville and Twain and Scott Fitzgerald. The producer, a patronizing Englishman who wore white buckskin shoes and a toupée, said the reasons for this had to do with "budget and copyright and so forth," in a tone that suggested Sarah shouldn't trouble her pretty head about it. The alternatives she suggested were all dismissed. Henry James was too effeminate, Poe and Bierce too crazy, Hemingway too macho. Her quip that Edith Wharton was presumably too female didn't do her career prospects any good at all.

The money was derisory but at least she was earning it herself. She had always been a fast learner and within a couple of years was working for twice the salary with a younger, much trendier company in SoHo, producing a series of her own, this time about writers who were still alive, though in one case the interview was so stilted and boring she suspected he might have just been very well embalmed.

The life she and Benjamin led in their tiny rented apartment on the edge of Greenwich Village was frugal but happy. By now he was working for Dawlish & Drewe, a stuffy but sizable firm that did mostly small-scale industrial and commercial projects. He earned only a little more than she did and the work was routine, but he was soon getting himself noticed. He was one of the best draftsmen and model-makers in the office and found himself much in demand for presentations.

What made it fun was working alongside a bright and talented young architect who had been hired straight out of Columbia the previous fall. Short, dark, and (except for his polished dome of a head) excessively hairy, with mischievous black eyes and a brain as sharp as his dress sense, Martin Ingram had the kind of creative flair and ambition that were wasted on the likes of Dawlish & Drewe. His sense of humor was even more wicked than Benjamin's and at their adjoining desks they did cruel impersonations of the fussy, bow-tied Adrian Dawlish and the other senior partners. They became close friends and were soon plotting their escape to set up a partnership of their own.

Martin had grown up in Nassau County, in the town of Syosset, a name that for Sarah had only negative connotations. She had been taken there once as a child to visit a place called the Lollipop Farm, where she had been bitten by a goat, eaten too many lollipops, and thrown up all over the backseat of her mother's new car. For Martin, however, Syosset was pure, golden, apple-pie America, the kind of place where people never locked their doors and always helped their neighbors. He couldn't wait to get back there. He and his considerably taller wife, Beth—a commercial real estate agent with a loud voice and frizzy red hair, a woman Sarah tried hard to like—had it all figured out. When, at a date apparently already diaried, they had children, they were going to decamp to Syosset.

On the evening that the master plan was revealed (at least, to Sarah), the four of them were eating take-out pizza at the round glass table in the Ingrams' apartment, which was in a classier neighborhood than theirs and a lot bigger, though, in Sarah's opinion, way over-designed. Martin and Beth suddenly started going on about Syosset, extolling its virtues to Sarah in a way that for a while had her puzzled.

Among countless other assets, the place apparently had good schools, cleaner air, less crime, a brand-new public library, and a great deli called Bahnhof's on Jackson Avenue. Furthermore, Martin assured her, there were no longer any biting goats. Lollipop Farm had closed down in 1967. More to the point, he said—and this was when Sarah began to see where this was all heading—there was a dearth of decent local architects, thus plenty of potential for the embryonic ICA— Ingram Cooper Associates. The names had to be that way around, Martin said, since there was already a CIA.

"So do we get to move out there too?" Sarah said brightly. She was only joking, but from the pause that followed and from the look on Benjamin's face she could see that was exactly what he had in mind.

"Well, it's something we should talk about," he said.

"Oh, right. And when shall we do that?"

They did little else for weeks. And it escalated into a

full-blown fight. It emerged that he had already done a tour of the place with Martin and that he liked what he saw. He could imagine them living there, he said. Sarah accused him of concealing all this from her and of being a chauvinist for assuming his career should come first and for thinking he could decide where they lived. She didn't want to live in the suburbs, she said. Maybe it was just the slightly scornful way she uttered the word, but he accused her, for the first time, of being a Westchester County snob and it so infuriated her that she didn't speak to him for three days. A frost settled that neither of them seemed willing or able to thaw. They didn't touch each other for more than a month.

On a sunny Saturday morning in early spring, sullenly shunting a cart along the aisles of an uptown nursery where they had come to buy plants for their two square yards of roof terrace, Benjamin suddenly stopped and picked up a clematis.

"This one's for you," he said. He was smiling oddly, but for a moment she thought he was being genuinely friendly, that perhaps it was a peace offering. Then she saw the label. The name of the variety was *Arctic Queen.*

They got over their disagreement about where they would live. But this incidental act of spite lingered in Sarah's heart. It was the first time he had accused her of being frigid and it shocked and hurt her.

Abbie was born eighteen months later. And two years after that, in the same month that Ingram Cooper Associates got its first proper commission, along came Josh.

For each birth, Sarah organized her work so that she could take a few months off. Her career, if not exactly booming, was progressing well enough. One documentary had led to another. A film she made about David Hockney's joined-up photographs was even nominated for an Emmy. They were now living on the Upper West Side, in another rented apartment, more comfortable and spacious than their old Amsterdam love nest. But with two small children and a full-time babysitter they could barely afford, it was still cramped and less than perfect. Every morning Benjamin climbed into their old Volvo station wagon and slogged out through the traffic to Syosset.

True to schedule, Martin and Beth and their two young sons, born just ten months apart, were already living there, with Ingram Cooper Associates and its growing team housed in a long, glass-roofed studio set among the maples in their spacious backyard. And by Abbie's fourth birthday the Coopers had decided to join them. With a loan secured (despite Benjamin's reluctance) by Sarah's trust fund, they bought a small white clapboard house not far from the Ingrams and a few months later put down a deposit on a gently sloping, wooded acre at the edge of town, upon which Benjamin would build them a fine house to his own design.

Sarah would later find it hard to pinpoint the moment she warmed to the idea of the move. It was more a process of attrition, a growing unease about bringing up her children in Manhattan. Unlike Abbie, Josh was not an easy child. He was a magnet for any passing virus.

After a terrifying weekend when he was unable to breathe and turned blue and they had to rush him to the hospital, he was diagnosed with asthma. He was a timid and clingy boy, unsuited to the rush and clamor of the city. He screamed for an hour every morning when she left for work. And after their babysitter found him too hard to handle and quit, Sarah started turning down work to spend more time at home.

On summer weekends at Martin and Beth's, barbecuing under the trees and meeting their neighbors and watching Abbie and Josh run free and safe and happy with the other kids, Sarah came to believe that if she was going to become more of a full-time mother, this might not be such a bad place to do it.

The issue that clinched it—and over which Benjamin and her father had their first serious falling out—was education. Although ICA was doing well, it wasn't yielding enough to pay the fees of fancy Manhattan private schools. Her parents had reacted with a sort of condescending incredulity when Sarah first told them of the plan to move. Long Island, as far as her father was concerned, might be a good enough place to park a yacht, but it certainly wasn't somewhere one should choose to *live*. He had never been to Syosset but didn't need to in order to know the *sort* of place it was. And the fact that his daughter and grandchildren were being forced to migrate there was the long-anticipated proof of Benjamin's inability to provide for them properly. If they wanted to move out of the city, why not come up to Bedford?

In what turned out to be a last-ditch attempt to pre-empt the move, he took them to lunch at his club, a fusty place in which women had only marginally higher status than an ill-trained gundog. Benjamin's ego was already bruised and bristling before they so much as sat down. It was ninety degrees outside and he had turned up in an open-neck shirt only to be forced at the door to borrow a necktie and a blazer that was several sizes too big and smelled of cigar smoke. With more enthusiasm than she yet truly felt, Sarah had been telling her father all about the house they would build. He heard her out in silence, chewing grimly on his lamb chops.

"And the schools out there are amazing," she concluded.

He peered at her over his half-moon horn-rims.

"You're going to put Abbie and Josh through the public school system?"

"Yes."

"I'm astounded."

"Well, George," Benjamin said genially. "It was good enough for me."

Her father turned slowly and looked at him.

"Was it?"

"I'm sorry?"

"Was it good enough for you? I'm simply asking. I mean, I'm not meaning to be disrespectful. I'm sure the education you received was as good as the town of . . . I'm sorry, I forget . . ."

"Abilene."

". . . could provide. But have you ever thought what

172

you might be doing today if your parents had been able to send you somewhere better?"

It was so stunningly rude, Benjamin looked at Sarah and grinned. Oblivious, her father went on.

"Let's give them the best possible start in life, shall we? I'll pay."

Benjamin stood up.

"Thank you, George, but you won't. They're my children—and Sarah's, of course—and we'll do with them what we think best. Now, I'm sorry, but I have to go earn some money."

It was a tense moment but Sarah would always admire him for the resolute but dignified restraint with which he handled it and many similar occasions to come.

Life in the suburbs turned out to be better than Sarah felt she had any right to expect. The house Benjamin eventually built for them, in three separate stages, was exquisite. And around it, letting the trees and rocks already there dictate its design, Sarah created the garden it deserved. The children thrived. Whether it was Saturday morning soccer or horseback riding, the school play or summer camp in the Adirondacks, Abbie was always the effortless star.

With Josh it took longer. When he was just three he lost the top part of his right index finger when Benjamin inadvertently slammed a car door on it. He had a series of operations to make it look neater and it never seemed to hinder him in his writing or drawing or anything else. But it made him even more self-conscious and shy. He found school hard and was slow to make friends and had Abbie not been at hand to protect him, he might well have fallen prey to bullies. But though constantly in his sister's shadow, gradually he grew stronger and more confident, his asthma attacks less severe. He was a sensitive and loving child but with a kind of dogged resilience, doubtless born of so much early suffering. Benjamin, of course, never forgave himself for the accident, even after Josh started joking about it, holding up two fingers and saying in a dopey hippie voice *Almost peace, man,* which became a sort of private family greeting and farewell.

The price for shepherding her son through his tribulations—though she refused to so construe it—was Sarah's career. She had let it dwindle and the phone had finally stopped ringing. And when he was at last happy and healthy and secure and she started making calls herself, she found the world had moved on. Television had become even more ruthlessly commercial and nobody seemed much interested in the kind of films she had made. Nor were they strictly even *films* anymore. A whole new technology had taken over. Everyone was shooting documentaries on lightweight video; cutting rooms had junked the old Steenbeck machines and gone electronic. It wouldn't have taken Sarah long to learn how to adapt. But something held her back, a feeling that her life had moved on and that perhaps she should try something new.

It was Benjamin who came up with it. Arriving home one evening, he mentioned casually that he had just seen a *For Sale* sign outside the local bookstore. It wasn't the most inspiring of places and though Sarah, along with many friends and neighbors, used it out of loyalty, everyone moaned about the woman who owned it, how unimaginative, inept, and sometimes downright rude she was. Running her own bookstore had always been one of Sarah's fantasies, but until Benjamin suggested they buy it, she had always thought of it in much the same way that he had once dreamed of being Paul Newman.

"We can't afford it," she said.

"We can."

"I wouldn't know how to do it."

"You know darned well you'd be brilliant at it."

And she was. Within three years she had turned Village Books around and started to make a modest profit. She had Benjamin design an extension at the back and, long before anybody else was doing it, made it look like a den with floor lamps and comfy leather sofas and a little bar where you could get coffee and soda and homemade cookies. She turned one corner into a children's area with toys and a low table where they could sit and read or doodle with crayons. She set up new and quicker ordering systems and shamelessly used her old contacts, flattering and begging any writer she could think of to come and talk and sell a few books.

Benjamin and Martin, meanwhile, went from strength to strength. In the derelict downtown bakery that they had converted into a state-of-the-art studio, they now employed more than fifty people. Gradually, almost imperceptibly, and without any formal decision ever being taken, Benjamin now ran the business while Martin was its driving creative force. And though Benjamin wasn't altogether happy about this division of their labors and felt his fingers itch at the sight of some new design taking shape on the drawing board, he acknowledged that things seemed to work best this way.

"He's the genius and I'm the fixer," he would say.

And though Sarah would always contradict this, not just because she sensed he wanted her to but because she had always hoped that one day he would be a great architect, she came to accept that he was right. He was more an editor than a creator. If you showed him something, be it the draft of a letter or a newspaper ad for the bookstore or the design for some sensational new building that Martin was working on, he could immediately spot the weak points and know how to improve them. It was a rare talent but one he didn't seem to value in himself. Now and again, just to keep his eye in, he would become more hands-on with a project or even design something himself. And when this happened, Sarah saw the change in him, in his spirits and his energy, how it seemed to galvanize and brighten him.

He was the finest father to Abbie and Josh that she could ever have wanted. Whether it was helping with math homework or shooting hoops in the yard, ferrying them around town to violin lessons or Little League or dressing up as Dracula to entertain twenty kids at Halloween, he was always there for them. Sometimes, particularly during those three years when she was working long hours trying to turn the bookstore around and hadn't yet hired Jeffrey to help, Benjamin probably saw more of them than she did. She even found herself getting a little jealous when they turned to him for help with something rather than to her.

Her friends were always saying how great he was, how much more he did than their husbands, how lucky Sarah was to have him. But the remark that would always stick in her mind came from Iris. She and her stockbroker husband, Leo—who, when he wasn't working, seemed to spend most of his time on the golf course—lived in Pittsburgh, though in a neighborhood much classier than the one where she grew up. Iris had gone into journalism and was now an assistant editor on the *Post-Gazette*. A couple of times a year, with their three rowdy children but no Leo, she would fly to New York for a long weekend with the Coopers.

During one such visit, on a sunny Saturday morning, the two women were sitting at the kitchen table, drinking coffee and catching up on news, while Benjamin, who had already cooked breakfast for everybody, stacked the dishwasher, sorted the laundry, compiled (without any reference to Sarah) a grocery list, then cheerily packed all five kids into the car and headed off to the mall.

"Isn't that a little spooky?" Iris said.

"What?"

"He does everything. He *knows* everything. Men aren't supposed to know how much butter there is in the fridge. I bet he even knows the kids' shoe sizes."

"He does."

"And their friends' phone numbers?"

"Uh-huh."

"Leo doesn't even know their names. Does Ben know your dress size?"

"Yes."

"Your bra size?"

"I hate shopping. He buys most of my clothes."

"Does he know when your period's due?"

"Iris—"

"Does he?"

"Yes."

"It's not natural."

"Iris, for heavensake, it's not the nineteen-fifties."

"Don't get me wrong. It's fantastic—well, some of it—but it's not natural."

Not quite in the next breath, but soon enough afterward for it to be apparent that there was a connecting thought, she went on to tell Sarah something she had heard from a friend of hers in Pittsburgh, a hotshot divorce lawyer.

The gist of it was that there were two types of men who absconded from their marriages: the naughty and the needy. The naughty absconder was a simple, dick-driven creature who just couldn't help himself. However much he might love his family, it always came second to his main object in life, namely, chasing women. The needy absconder was basically insecure and forever trying to prove to himself how much everybody loved him. His family was, in effect, one big love machine that needed his constant control and attention. When his kids grew older and got lives of their own and didn't need him so much, he suddenly got scared and felt old and useless. So he ran off to look for a new love machine someplace else.

Iris relayed all this more as a joke than as a serious piece of social observation. But for days afterward, Sarah found herself thinking about it. And the more she did, the angrier she became at the implication.

She and Benjamin were happier than almost any couple she knew. Okay, maybe he was a little too fastidious, ever the architect. Everything in life had to be in the right place, at the appropriate angle, all balanced and neat and no rough edges. And she had to admit, he was a little needy. He liked to be liked. But didn't most men?

The idea of his being the sort who suddenly upped and left, if this was indeed what Iris had been suggesting (though, even as the thought occurred, Sarah was aware she was probably being a little paranoid here), was preposterous. They loved and trusted each other. And even though their sex life wasn't as exciting as he wanted and had for a long time been a source of some tension between them, she had never, not once in all the years they had been married, suspected him of cheating on her. He just wasn't the type. Any more than she was.

And in just about every other department, they were great together. Weren't they? So many wives and mothers were always going on about how dreadful their husbands were, how selfish and boorish and uncommunicative they were. But Sarah had never felt that way. She and Benjamin had always talked. About the people they knew, about their work, about all kinds of things. Mostly, of course, about Abbie and Josh. About their progress and problems and hopes, their triumphs at school, their disappointments. Their children were, she was proud to say, the center of their universe. Thank God they were. Surely, bringing up kids and doing all you could to make them happy and secure and fit for life was what marriage was all about? Could anything be more important?

Only much later, when the children were well into their teens and Sarah was starting to look forward to all the things she and Benjamin would soon be able to do, the places they would travel to, just the two of them, did she notice the shadow that sometimes seemed to fall on him. She would catch him staring at her or into the distance with a look of such desolation that she would think something terrible had happened, that he was about to tell her he had cancer or somebody they loved had died. She would ask him if he was all right and he would click on a smile and say of course he was, why?

On their wedding day, her father's older sister had taken Sarah aside and, with a quiet intensity, vouchsafed some advice. Elizabeth had always been her favorite aunt and had once been a renowned society beauty. She had never had children and had enjoyed what the family referred to as a "colorful" life, which

Sarah later realized was code for sleeping around. At the time, Elizabeth was on her third marriage (and subsequently died just after her fourth), so Sarah thought it both mildly amusing and a bit rich that she should presume to proffer guidance.

"Look after each other," she confided.

It wasn't exactly earth-shattering, but Sarah smiled politely and said of course they would. Elizabeth shook her head impatiently.

"No, you don't understand. *Look after each other.* As a couple. When you have kids, you'll want to put them first. Don't. Marriage is like a plant. To keep it alive you've got to water it and feed it. If you don't, when the kids are gone, you'll look in the corner and it'll be dead."

ELEVEN

E ve had never consciously intended to keep her promise to call the Coopers. And even after she had done so, she was reluctant to analyze her motives. With all the hurt that was soon to be unleashed, she didn't like to think of herself as the initiator. She preferred instead to believe it was all a matter of destiny. If not then and by those means, fate would doubtless have found some other way to bring her and Ben Cooper together.

During that week at The Divide she and Lori had become everybody's new best friends and Eve had been touched by the warmth of their welcome. Sarah, in particular, had sought to involve them from the start. Eve liked her well enough, but no more so than any of the other women. She was interesting and witty and clearly very bright, but there was a slightly stiff quality, not grand or superior, just a little cool and inaccessible. She gave the impression that even if you were marooned for ten years with her on a desert island, you probably wouldn't get to discover who she really was. But there was something about her husband to which Eve had felt herself curiously attracted.

It wasn't by any means immediate. In fact, at first, among all those new faces at the ranch, she hadn't really paid him much attention. He was one of the more interesting and artistic men there, for sure. She liked his sardonic take on life and how he asked questions about Pablo and about her work and her life in Santa Fe. And he actually seemed interested in the answers. But as the week progressed, even though she probably talked seriously with him on only two or three occasions, she began to sense a curious rapport.

In a group, when that Bradstock man or someone else was holding forth, she and Ben would catch each other's eye, exchange a wry smile. They had talked a lot about painting and there was no doubt that she was flattered by his interest in her work. What had touched her however, she later realized, was his sadness.

But he was married. How happily, she couldn't say, but it made no difference. He was out of bounds. Eve had always been strict about avoiding romantic entanglements with married men. Not so much from any moral scruple but rather because she knew from the experiences of several friends that it almost always ended in tears.

On the wall above the phone in her Santa Fe kitchen was a cork pinboard, a cluttered collage of obsolete notes and grocery lists, photos and postcards, along with Pablo's latest (and, naturally, brilliant) finger paintings. Among this chaos, which Eve never quite got around to tidying, was the invitation to the opening of her friend William's exhibition. It was at an important SoHo gallery, his first big one-man show, and he was a jangle of nerves, calling Eve almost every day for moral support. Pinned next to the invitation was the scrap of paper on which Sarah had written the Coopers' phone number. And one morning, in mid-July, after William had called, Eve caught sight of it and stared at it for a moment, then picked up the phone and dialed it.

It was Sarah who answered. And she sounded genuinely pleased to hear from her. After further consultation, during which Eve for no good reason found herself again pretending that she liked musicals, four tickets were duly booked for *Kiss Me, Kate* (four, because William, who really did love musicals, insisted on being Eve's date). A table was reserved for afterward at a place on Madison called La Goulue, which Eve didn't know but Sarah said she would adore.

When Eve's cab pulled up in front of the theater and she saw Ben Cooper waiting outside, sheltering from the rain with many others under the glare of the lights, she assumed Sarah must already have gone inside or had yet to arrive. She suddenly felt shy and almost asked the driver to go on and circle the block but people were clamoring for the cab so she paid and got out. She had no umbrella and so hopped as fast as she could through the puddles but still got drenched.

He didn't see her until she was close beside him, and when he turned and saw her, his face broke from a harassed frown to a smile so warm and welcoming that something turned over inside her. They tried to kiss each other on the cheek but both went for the same side so that their faces collided and they almost kissed on the lips instead. They joked about the rain and the traffic and then she told him she was sorry, but William wasn't with her. A big German dealer had breezed into the gallery just before it closed and said he wanted to buy the whole show.

"I would have called but it was too late."

"We wanted to call you too but Sarah couldn't find your cell number."

"Is she inside or . . . ?"

"She couldn't make it either. Some pain-in-the-ass author who was supposed to be doing an event tomorrow night at the bookstore just pulled out. She's got a hundred people coming and nobody to talk to them. So now she's melting the phones trying to find somebody else. I can't tell you how mad she is. She was so looking forward to seeing you."

So it was to be just the two of them. And though they both went through the motions of asking each other if they should call the whole thing off and go their separate ways, it was clear neither of them wanted to. There were people waiting in line for returns and Ben handed the two spare tickets to a young couple and wouldn't allow them to pay him.

The show was wonderful. How could she have ever thought she didn't like musicals? They came out exhilarated, both saying they hadn't realized where all those famous songs came from. It was still raining but somehow they managed to find a cab. Again they acted out the routine of asking each other if they should call it a day and go home. But, of course, they didn't. Sitting next to him in the cramped backseat of the cab on their way uptown to the restaurant, laughing and talking about the show, their legs touching and neither of them making any effort to move, she thought how handsome he looked and how good he smelled and then sharply told herself off.

The restaurant was crowded and they sat crammed in a corner next to a young couple who, somewhat disconcertingly, couldn't keep their hands or lips off each other. More by accident than design, Eve was wearing the same green dress she had worn on the night of Benjamin's birthday party. She thought how smart and different he looked in his black polo shirt and flecked charcoal jacket.

"Why does everybody in New York wear black?" she said.

"Maybe we're all in mourning."

"For what."

"Our lost innocence."

They ordered steak and salad and a delicious bottle of Margaux. He asked her how Pablo was and she ended up telling him all about the boy's father, Raoul, and how they had never really been a conventional kind of couple, more just good friends who made the mistake of becoming lovers. Though, given that the result was Pablo, she said it was without a doubt the best mistake of her life.

Then it was his turn to answer questions. She asked him about Abbie and Josh and this led to a long discussion about parenting and their own parents. Eve told him hers were still more or less happily married and lived in San Diego, a place she didn't much care for. Ben talked about his father and how they had never managed to get along.

"He thought I was an arrogant sonofabitch and he was probably right. I was. It's nearly fifteen years since he died and I've only just made peace with him. It's funny how these things go through phases. At first I was angry with him. I used to go on about how he never loved me and always criticized me. I actually really hated him for a while. Then, somehow, that passed and I just felt sad. And kind of cheated, you know? That we were never able to find each other. And now, it's funny, but I can honestly say I love him. And I know, in his own way, he loved me too. He just belonged to a different generation. Men weren't supposed to show their feelings like we do today. And he was so great with Abbie when she was a baby. He absolutely adored her. Used to sit her on his knee and tell her stories. So sweet and tender. I'd never seen him like that. It was like he was trying to give her the love he hadn't been able to show me."

He smiled. "Mind you, if you see photographs of me as a little kid, you can understand why he might have found it hard."

"Ugly, right?"

"More like obnoxious."

"Mine are ugly and obnoxious. Kind of Missy Prissy meets Barney the Bullfrog."

"Somehow I find that hard to believe."

"You mean because now I'm so drop-dead gorgeous."

It was a dumb thing to say and it came out all wrong, as if she were putting him down for making a pass, which wasn't how she had taken it. He looked embarrassed and smiled and took a sip of wine. The couple at the next table were spoon-feeding each other chocolate mousse.

"You know something?" she said, trying to put things right again. "If he was alive today, you two would probably be friends."

"You're right. I think we would."

She asked about his mother and he told her how he'd always been her favorite, how in her eyes he could never do anything wrong, how he could probably tell her he was a serial killer and she would still find a way of rationalizing it and admiring him for it. Her adoration, he said, had become something of a family joke.

"Not so long ago she came to stay and we were driving into town. She was sitting up front and Abbie and Josh and Sarah were in the back. And when I managed to park in what I have to say wasn't too challenging a space, she said, *Ben, you are such a fantastic parker.* Really. And I could see Sarah and the kids in the mirror, just cracking up. They still say it every time I park the damn car."

Eve laughed and he shook his head and smiled and took another sip of wine.

"It's fine," she said. "She loves you, that's all. And they say a boy can never be loved too much by his mother. It's empowering."

"Well, they're wrong. I did therapy for a few months after my dad died. And the guy told me that if you feel you are being loved for something that you know to be unjustified or false, in other words, if you know you are actually not the superhero the other person thinks you are, then it doesn't count. That kind of love doesn't empower you, it just makes you feel like an impostor. So just you watch out with that son of yours."

"He parks his tricycle better than any kid I know."

"Well, there you go."

He had already refused to let her pay for the theater so she sneakily paid the check on her way back from the restroom. It annoyed him a little but not for long. Outside the rain had stopped. The streets and sidewalks glistened and the air was washed and cool and smelled for the first time of autumn. They walked a couple of blocks and then he suddenly realized how late it was and that he was in danger of missing the last train home. They waved down a cab and Ben asked the driver to hurry to Penn Station. When they got there he stuffed a twenty-dollar bill through the screen and made sure the driver knew where to take her.

"I've had such a great time," Eve said. "Thank you."

"Me too."

They kissed each other on the cheek and this time got it right.

"Listen, I've got to run," he said, climbing out. "I'll call you—I mean, *we'll* call you, okay?"

"Okay. Go see William's show if you have a chance."

"I'll try. Bye now."

"Bye. Say hi to Sarah and the kids!"

But he was shutting the door as she spoke and seemed not to hear. Eve watched him jogging off into the station as the cab pulled away and when he had disappeared she leaned her head back against the seat and stared at the stained lining of the roof. As Lori always said, it was one of life's bummers: how the only nice guys she ever got to meet these days were either married or gay.

Eve called the following morning and was both relieved and a little disappointed when it was Sarah who answered. They agreed how sorry they were not to have seen each other. Sarah had found a less-well-known stand-in for her pain-in-the-ass author but was still anxious about breaking the news to her customers when they arrived. Eve was flying back to New Mexico that afternoon but she said she came to New York two or three times a year and on her next visit they would definitely get together.

"Definitely," Sarah said.

"And you and Ben should come out to Santa Fe sometime. Bring the kids, too."

"You know, I'd *love* that. I've never been."

On the flight home and over the days that followed she occasionally found herself thinking about Ben and about how much she liked him. Yet it wasn't with anything remotely like yearning or regret. The notion of their shared destiny had yet to take shape. Over the years she had taught herself that to look with longing down roads that were blocked brought only pain. And she thus simply accepted that this was how things were and that they could not be otherwise.

Nor, even if Ben had been single, would her attitude necessarily have been different. There was an intensity about him that interested her but daunted her too. And she didn't feel the need for that in her life right now. She had always, even as a child, been self-sufficient. Her parents had been caring but slightly remote, nurturing in all three of their children an independence that only later did Eve appreciate as their greatest gift.

It was a quality that others, men especially, often misinterpreted as lack of commitment, assuming that a love without need was somehow deficient. The only one who had ever fully understood was Raoul, who had clearly been carved from the same grain. Even during the two years that they lived together, it had been as two separate souls, each alone and content to be so. Like travelers whose different journeys had coincided along a stretch of the same trail.

Before Raoul, for virtually all her adult life, she had lived alone. But although she had known several sorts of pain, she had never once known loneliness as more than an idea or as a condition that affected others. She had always had her work and her friends and, sometimes, when it seemed right and uncomplicated and there was mutual desire, but desire for nothing more, there had been lovers.

One night, some ten days after she came back from New York, when Ben Cooper had faded from her thoughts and she felt fully reconnected with her life in Santa Fe, she dreamed about him. She was in a theater, not as gilded or grand as the one they had been to and the production felt more junior-high than Broadway. And Eve wasn't in the audience, she was onstage. It was her turn to speak but she hadn't had time to learn her lines. Then she caught sight of Ben in the front row beside an old woman she didn't recognize. He was mouthing something, trying to tell Eve the line, but she couldn't make it out and was getting more and more anxious. Then she woke up.

That same morning, on her way home from dropping Pablo at the nursery, she stopped for a newspaper at the Downtown Subscription on Garcia Street and there bumped into Lori. Sipping green mint tea in the sunlit yard, she recounted the dream. During their week in Montana they had agreed that Ben Cooper was one of the more attractive men on the ranch and Lori, with faked envy, had already elicited a detailed account of their evening in New York. After twelve years of Jungian analysis, she considered herself something of an expert when it came to the deciphering of dreams. This one, she declared, was as clear as Evian.

"The old woman sitting next to him," she said. "What was her demeanor?"

"Her demeanor?"

"Her attitude. Was she smiling, frowning or what?"

"I don't know."

"Eve, it's important. That was his mother. You obviously want to know if she approves."

"I don't."

"You do. That's why she was there."

"I didn't bring her. He did."

"You're not taking this seriously."

"I know. Anyway, approve of what?"

"You. You and Ben."

"Lori, give me a break. There is no me and Ben."

But even as she said it, a voice within her said there would be.

He checked in at the hotel just off the Plaza, a dark, folksy place that looked as if it had known better times. He had picked it without further research from a travel guide that claimed both JFK and Errol Flynn had once stayed there. As he dumped his bag in the cramped and overheated room, it occurred to Ben that given the true motive for this trip, his choice of lodging might well have been influenced by a subconscious urge to associate himself with two such epic lotharios.

He had time to kill and nearly called to see if Eve

could meet earlier but then decided it would look too eager. The flight from Kansas had gotten in early and despite the snow and the airport crowds of early holidaymakers and skiers, he had driven up from Albuquerque in little more than an hour. The interstate was clear, and the only hazard was that his eyes kept straying west across the ghost-white landscape to a mountain sunset of purple and vermilion.

The snow had given him the pretext to rent an SUV, a metallic red Ford Explorer, which made him feel rugged and Western, as did the red-and-black plaid woolen jacket and hiking boots and black Polartec beanie, all of which he had bought in Missoula last month when they had taken Abbie to check out the University of Montana. Ben had almost packed his Stetson but figured he wouldn't have the guts to wear it. The beanie, he believed, made him look hip and streetwise, though Abbie said it merely gave him the air of a geriatric mugger.

Whatever, he was glad he had come properly equipped. It was starting to snow again and when he climbed back into the truck it informed him that the temperature was eleven degrees below freezing. Without checking the map he nosed his way out through the evening traffic on to Paseo de Peralta.

It was nearly twelve years since he had been in Santa Fe but even in the dark with everywhere decorated for the holidays he found he could still remember the basic layout of the place and soon he saw the sign he was looking for. He turned off and drove slowly up the hill, then found a place to park and went on foot. The snowflakes were feathery and their fall through the windless air seemed hesitant, as if both time and gravity had somehow been suspended. The snow squashed pleasingly under his boots. It seemed to make his mission all the more intrepid.

Canyon Road was a Christmas movie set. There were lights in the trees and along the adobe façades of the stores and galleries. The windows bristled with greenery and tinsel and everywhere you looked there were strings of illuminated red peppers and little candles in paper bags weighted with sand. On one street corner there was even a huddle of people singing obscure carols around a little bonfire. Ben expected any moment to hear someone shout *Cut*.

He remembered the art galleries but they seemed to have spawned many more and most were still open, Aladdin's caves of warmth and color, their windows spilling quadrangles of yellow light on the snow of the sidewalk. The last time, the only other time, he had been here, Ben had vowed that if he was ever to take up painting for a living, this was where he would live. Some of the pictures on show were good, but many more weren't. And yet tourists flocked from all over the world and paid premium prices. As long as it was big and bright and lavishly framed, it seemed you could sell just about anything.

He still couldn't fully believe he was here. It was like watching some other man's boots walking him up the winding hill, some bolder or more reckless double. The same one who had made the phone calls, found the appropriately casual tone of voice, told her he was coming to Kansas anyway to visit his mother, who had been unwell, and that it was only a small plane hop farther. And, if she was interested, it might be an opportunity for them to talk about her doing some murals for the lobby of the exciting new project he and Martin had going in Cold Spring Harbor. Perhaps she could FedEx some photographs of her recent work? He had shocked himself. Who was this man? And did he truly know what he wanted?

It wasn't, of course, his first foray into infidelity. And he could remember the rejuvenating shiver of anticipation, that initial aliveness that nullified all prospect of guilt. For what, as yet, was there to feel guilty about? Twice, only twice, in all the years of their marriage had he cheated on Sarah, and he had managed to rationalize this fact to the point where the rarity of his transgression had become evidence of an almost virtuous restraint.

He knew many men, Martin for one, who were serial cheats, who never turned down any opportunity, who actively sought them out. Ben had witnessed him at work when they were away together at conferences, seen him target some likely young woman at a party or in a hotel bar. Martin claimed he could spot them from a hundred yards. Ben had watched him move in. Watched, not in awe but certainly impressed, how he introduced himself, how straightaway he made them laugh, how he listened, confided, and focused, creating an intimacy like a gardener tending a much-loved flower. And nine out of ten times—well, maybe not nine, maybe six, maybe four—he would succeed.

"The trick is not caring if you get turned down," Martin once told him. "Even the ones who say no are usually flattered to be asked."

Ben envied the ease of it, the absence of worry and commitment. To Martin it was just sex. He and Beth, who either deserved an Oscar or was genuinely the only person in Nassau County who didn't know about her husband's transgressions, would probably be married forever. But on the two occasions on which Ben had strayed—once with a young lawyer from Queens who at the time was doing some conveyancing work for him, the other with an older, married woman he had met at the tennis club—he had ended up falling in love. And mainly because he had no intention of leaving Sarah (and, more to the point, of leaving the kids, who were then still very young), neither affair had lasted long and both had ended in acrimony. It was a miracle nobody ever found out. The only person Ben had ever talked to about it was Martin.

"You know what my problem is?" he confided in a moment of rash self-pity after his tennis affair had come unstrung. "I don't seem to be able to separate love and sex."

Martin laughed.

"My problem is I've never been able to connect them."

So here he was again. In his heart, at least, a reborn adulterer. Not yet completely sure he was in love, but well on the way. And it was ridiculous, on several levels. He hardly knew the woman. And although he could tell, even at The Divide, and certainly that evening in New York, that she liked him and that there was even a little frisson of something more between them, it didn't mean a thing. Maybe he should just forget it. Be nice but businesslike. Have a drink, talk about the murals. Fly home.

But he knew, as soon as he saw her, that wasn't how it was going to be. Tired and almost color-blind from his tour of the galleries, he was sitting over a straight-up margarita in the rear corner of the bar where they had arranged to meet. It was one long room, dark and narrow, with polished wood floors and paintings on every inch of wall (there was no escape in Santa Fe, it seemed). He saw the door open and a sudden flurry of snowflakes and when they had gone, there she was. She was wearing a battered and stained old cowboy hat and a big and belted blanket of a coat in deep red and green. She took off the hat and shook her hair and knocked the snow from the brim and one of the men sitting at the bar, someone she clearly knew, said something Ben couldn't hear and she laughed and went over to the guy who put an arm around her and kissed her and she propped her arm on his shoulder and stood for a few moments talking and laughing with them all.

Then one of them swiveled on his stool and pointed

at Ben, and she looked his way and smiled and headed toward him. And he watched her walk the length of the room, the lamplight glinting in her eyes that stayed on him all the way, the smile shifting a little, fading as if some qualifying thought or warning had crossed her mind, then reasserting itself, still warm, just more composed.

He stood and said hi and she didn't reply, just leaned across the table and put her hand on his arm and pressed her cold, cold cheek to his and the smell of her almost made him moan. Lori's gallery, she said, was directly opposite and about to close. So he left his margarita, grabbed his coat, and followed her out and across the street. Lori was away but had left a message for Ben saying all fellow dudes from The Divide qualified for a ten percent discount.

Eve's paintings, two enormous triptychs in oil, hung eerily lit in a long stone-walled room at the back of the gallery. They were much more powerful than they had looked in the photographs she had sent. The larger of the two was called *The Visitation*. It looked almost biblical, its colors rich and dark, purple and indigo and deep carmine. In the outer two pictures, animals of many kinds, in paler shades of bone and stone, writhed and tangled among roots, as if swirled in a great wind. In the center panel, in a pool of light, reared a huge winged figure, part horse, part human, part reptile, almighty yet benign. Ben was shocked and moved but didn't know quite what to say except that it was wonderful, extraordinary, that it had astonishing power. He thought, but thought it better not to say, that the atrium of a Long Island insurance company office perhaps needed something a little tamer.

They went back to the bar and settled at the same table. He ordered her a glass of red wine and another margarita for himself and they talked for an hour without a pause. About the weather, about Pablo, about what they had done at Thanksgiving. About his trip to Missoula last month with Abbie to check out the university and how she was planning to spend the coming summer working for Greenpeace. And, of course, about business, those spurious murals, the pretext for his presence here this snowy and unreal night in Santa Fe. It was all so effortless. They seemed to understand each other, laughed at the same things, remembered little details about each other's lives. She even teased him, asking him where he had parked and how well he had done it.

He asked if she had eaten and she said she hadn't and that she was famished, so they took a table by an open fire in the labyrinth of a restaurant that adjoined the bar and ate shrimp and spicy grilled chicken and beans and kept on talking. She was wearing old blue jeans and a gray-green cashmere cardigan which after a while in the heat of the fire she took off. Underneath she had on a matching sleeveless top, which showed the shape of her breasts. Bare-shouldered in the candlelight, she was so disconcertingly beautiful that Ben found it hard not to gape.

Had she not felt the same, felt as comfortable and open as he did, perhaps she wouldn't have said it. It was the kind of comment that stopped men in their tracks. And, looking back on it later, Ben thought it a miracle that such a useless seducer as himself hadn't curled up in a ball and hidden under the table. But when they were through eating and, for the first time all evening, silence had fallen between them and they were just sitting there looking at each other in a way that said in neon letters a foot high *what next?* she took a drink, put down the wineglass, and said:

"So, Ben. Tell me why you're *really* here."

She said it gently and with a smile that was neither mocking nor reproachful. And instead of clenching with fear or embarrassment, with only a short pause and no waver of his eyes, he told her, simply, that he had fallen in love with her. He said that ever since the night of his birthday party at The Divide, he hadn't been able to stop thinking about her. That he had never felt so powerfully about any woman before.

This astonishing declaration (he astonished even himself) wasn't something Ben had rehearsed or intended. It wasn't his clubfooted version of the master Martin's seduction technique. And as he heard himself spilling his true feelings as if in some parody of a confessional, he was of course aware of what a foolish risk he was taking, how nothing was more likely to scare her off. But he didn't stop.

Instead, in a quiet, measured voice he went on to say that since their evening together in New York, he had been driving himself crazy, wondering what to do and how to get to see her again, that he had several times tried to write her a letter but hadn't been able to find the right words.

He was now talking mostly to his hands clasped on the table before him. Every so often he lifted his eyes to assess what effect his words might be having but all he could detect was a sort of suspended surprise. Then, just as he was finishing, she glanced at his hands and he realized that all this time he had been fiddling with his wedding ring.

He smiled and shrugged.

"Well, there you go," he said.

There was a long silence. She sat back and stared at him.

"Well," she said at last. "I don't know what to say."

"I'm sorry. You don't have to say anything."

"Oh, okay."

"No, I mean. You asked me why I was here, so you obviously knew it wasn't just about the pictures. And I thought, hell, why pretend? Just tell her."

She picked up her wineglass and drank, watching him all the time.

"So it wasn't my work you were interested in after all."

"Your paintings are wonderful."

"So do I get the job?"

"If you want it."

"Phew! Well, that's all that matters."

They sat awhile, smiling sadly at each other.

"Aren't you supposed to say Sarah doesn't understand you?"

"I think she does, as a matter of fact. Too well, probably. We're just not the same people anymore. I'd really appreciate it if you'd cover up those shoulders."

She slowly pulled on her cardigan.

"Or maybe don't," he said.

"Tell me, do you do this a lot?"

"No."

"I didn't think so."

"Thanks."

The waitress arrived and asked if they were finished and she looked a little puzzled when they laughed. Ben asked for the check. When the woman had gone, Eve reached across the table and held his hand.

"Ben, I like you very much. But I've never been involved with a married man and I'm not going to start now. If you were free, it might be different."

They kissed good-bye in the street like friends and she walked away up the hill without looking back. The snow had stopped but he had to clear a good six inches of it off the truck's windshield. He drove to his hotel in a state of boyish elation. And the next morning, as his plane banked north and east against the cloudless cobalt, he looked down on the mountains puckered like scars across the white of the desert and felt a kind of soaring clarity.

He was going home. But it was a word whose meaning had changed, a place that in his heart, he had already left. Even though she hadn't actually said it, what he had heard was that she would have him if he made himself free. And with the reckless bliss of the ignorant, he had already begun the process.

TWELVE

I t was hard to get lost in Missoula even if you wanted to. Wherever you were, all you had to do to get your bearings was look around and find the big letter M, embossed in white halfway up the steep shoulder of grass that reared on the south bank of the Clark Fork River. Though only a hill, it was called Mount Sentinel and if you had the legs and lungs and inclination to hike the trail that zigzagged up it, you could stand by the M and gaze out across the town at a travel-brochure shot of forest and mountain dusted from early fall with snow. Assuming you could take your eyes off it, if you looked down, just above the toes of your boots, laid out at the foot of the hill was the campus of the University of Montana.

It was a tranquil, pleasant place, though its older buildings, crafted in red brick a century ago, seemed to be striving for a grandeur eschewed by the more modern ones. The hub of the campus was a broad expanse of grass known as The Oval where in the summer students liked to lounge in the sun and play Frisbee. Quartered by paths of gray stone and red cobbles salvaged from the streets of downtown Missoula, it had once been graced with stately American elms that one by one had fallen to disease. Apart from a few brave ponderosas, their successors—maple, red oak, and honey locust—still looked young and vulnerable. To protect them, stationed on a plinth of gray cement at The Oval's western entrance, stood a massive grizzly bear.

He was on his hind legs, glowering into the distance, jaws parted in a silent snarl of bronze, as if sensing some imminent attack. And to those who knew their recent history, the posture was not inappropriate. For in the thirty-odd years he had stood there, the college had been under regular and rigorous assault. Conservative Montana—and that meant most of it—viewed the place as a cauldron seething with liberal poison, the most potent of which was brewed in the building just behind the bear's shoulder.

Rankin Hall stood on a base of rough-hewn rock up which twelve stout steps led to an arched double door flanked by classical pillars. In the hallway, among the posters and cartoons and notices of upcoming concerts and exhibitions, hung a framed sepia photograph of the woman for whom the building was named. In her feathered hat, high-collared shirt, and somber suit, Jeannette Rankin, suffragist, pacifist, and the first woman ever elected to the nation's House of Representatives, looked far too demure a figure to be presiding over such a hotbed of controversy. But that was exactly what she was doing, for Rankin Hall was the home of the university's notorious environmental studies program.

Born in the protest years of the Vietnam War, it took a self-effacing pride in grooming activists, who—or so its critics claimed—had gone on to wreck the state's economy by robbing it of thousands of jobs in mining and logging, with the alleged result that Montanans now had the forty-sixth lowest per capita income in the union. That the truth was, of course, more complex hadn't dampened conservative efforts to shut the program down. There were constant attempts to rein it in and slash its funding. Professors were accused of giving credits to students who demonstrated or spiked trees or locked themselves to logging trucks. And once, on the touching assumption that a wall map of Montana forests, dotted with colored pins, was in fact an official tree-spiking master plan, federal agents brandishing guns had stormed the place and later slunk out with large streaks of egg on their faces.

None of this notoriety was known to Abbie Cooper when she set her heart on coming here to college. And if it had been, she wouldn't have breathed a word to anyone, especially not her grandfather, who considered her choice not simply an aberration but almost a personal slight. Perhaps a little reluctantly, her mom had sided with him, echoing his view that it was a sin for someone of Abbie's talents not, at the very least, to check Harvard out first. Abbie's dad, predictably, was already on her side. But as a concession to her mom and grandpa she agreed to take the tour and, in a conspiring gray drizzle, trudged with a lengthening face around Cambridge and later *(Honey, come on, please, it's only down the road)* around Wellesley.

That evening, to nobody's surprise, she had

announced, with more than a touch of melodrama, that she would rather stack shelves in Wal-Mart than go to either one of them. And that was when her mom gave up and the deal was done. She would go to UM where she was duly promised a place for the following fall. She would major, naturally, in environmental studies.

The summer after her high-school graduation was the best of her life. She spent two weeks in Wyoming with Ty, working on the ranch. She had been planning to stay longer, but he was getting a little too keen and though she liked him a lot, Abbie wasn't ready for the kind of commitment he seemed to want. Two weeks earlier than scheduled, she flew to Vancouver and signed on with Greenpeace.

The work was neither taxing nor truly exciting but the people she met more than compensated and she forged many new friendships. The high points were the trips they made by sea kayak, exploring the wild inlets farther up the coast. They watched bears scoop salmon from the shallows and paddled among pods of orcas, so close you could have reached out and touched them. At night they camped at the water's edge, listening to the blow of whales in the bay and the distant howl of wolves in the forest above.

The only shadows on these long idyllic days were the seabirds they found, dead and dying in the rock pools, their feathers clogged with oil sludge. They saved those they could but most were too far gone. The sight of their suffering seemed to light a wick of anger in Abbie's heart.

She flew home in August, with just a week to get ready for UM. Her mom was edgy and fragile and there was a sadness about her that Abbie hadn't seen before. Her dad too seemed somehow different, quieter, a little preoccupied. When asked, her mom made light of it, saying they had both been working too hard and hadn't been able to take a vacation. Josh had just come home from a month with the Bradstocks on Lake Michigan and spent most of the week on the phone with Katie or moping in his room. Abbie found it all a little depressing.

The night before she was due to fly out to Missoula, her mom came into her room while Abbie was packing the last of her things. The image seemed suddenly too much for her and she broke down and cried. Abbie put her arms around her.

"I'm sorry, I didn't mean to do this," she sniffed, trying to sound cheery. "I'm just being silly. I think moms are allowed a few tears when their little girls leave home."

"Oh, Mom. I'll be back."

"I know."

"Is that all it is? Really?"

"Why? Isn't it enough? Listen, you're going to have such a fabulous time. I'm just jealous, that's all."

Abbie's room at UM was in Knowles Hall, a neat but unprepossessing four floors of brick and cement whose only flourish was a white-scalloped porch stacked with bicycles. It stood just off The Oval

207

in a walkway lined with sugar maples which now, after the first harsh frost of fall, were turning from fiery orange to red. The room itself, midway along one of six identical corridors, was furnished with beds, desks, chairs, and bookcases in plain pine, two of each, which Abbie and her roommate had arranged to give each other at least an illusion of privacy. Luckily and perhaps a little surprisingly, the two of them got along just fine.

Melanie Larsen came from a little town outside of Appleton, Wisconsin. She was a farmer's daughter and looked it. Blonde, ruddy-faced, and with thighs and shoulders that suggested she could single-handedly haul a John Deere from a bog, she too was majoring in environmental studies. Whereas the walls in Abbie's corner of the room were decorated with posters of mountains and wild animals and heroes like John Lennon and Che Guevara, Mel's had just three prettily framed photographs of her mom and dad, her four brothers, and of herself hugging a Hereford heifer who had scooped all the prizes at the local 4-H contest.

Mel was so boisterous and gregarious that in just a couple of months, their room had become a sort of social epicenter. The door was rarely closed. Today, however, it was. And the pad that was fixed to it, a pencil dangling on a string, was by now a mosaic of messages.

Hey, guys, where are you? Chuck/Rooster.

Mel, Yey! Got concert tickets! Call me. Jazza.
Abigail, yu sexee beech, wos happenin tonite? B XXX.

And so on. It was lunchtime, when normally friends dropped by with coffee and sandwiches they had just bought at La Peak, the little café across the walkway in the Lommasson Center. In ones and twos, every few minutes, friends would come drifting down the corridor and see the closed door. They would frown, maybe knock and listen for a moment, and when they heard nothing, they would shrug, scribble a message, then shamble back along the corridor to the stairwell. Abbie and Mel weren't home and nobody knew why.

Abbie was beginning to wish she was. The pain was getting so intense, she was afraid she wasn't going to last out. It came in nauseous spasms that left her close to tears. But she was damned if she was going to let them see her cry. There wasn't a part of her that didn't hurt. She hurt in places she never knew she had.

For the last five hours she had been sitting locked by her neck to a metal gate. It felt like five days. The lock was the kind they used for bicycles, U-shaped and made of toughened steel, and the crossbar to which it was fixed was so high that her spine felt as if it had stretched several inches already. Whenever she tried to relax, the lock tried to garrote her. The bruises on her neck must have swollen because the lock seemed to be getting tighter and tighter. She had to keep telling herself not to panic.

The morning had been sunny and, for late October,

unusually mild. But then the wind had shifted north and the clouds rolled in and the temperature started to plummet. The damp cold of the red-dirt road had at last found its way through the tarp they had given her to sit on and through all her layers of Gore-Tex and thermal underwear and was now rising like an icy fog into every bone of her body. All she could hope was that soon she would go numb.

"How are you doing, sister?" Hacker called.

Abbie forced a grin. Even that hurt.

"Great," she said.

"Getting cold?"

"No, I'm fine."

By now it was quite a party. Including Abbie and her ten fellow protesters, there were probably forty or fifty people and a whole fleet of vehicles parked down the hill, another one just pulling up as she looked. There were Forest Service agents, the county sheriff and a whole posse of deputies, people from the logging company, newspaper reporters and photographers, all standing around watching and chatting and waiting for something to happen. Even the perky little guy from the Forest Service who all morning had been videoing everything seemed to have run out of ideas and was now leaning on the hood of his truck looking as bored as the rest of them. The freezing air was filled with the crackle and blurt of a dozen shortwave radios and the constant underlying throb of the helicopter that all morning had been hoisting felled lodgepole out of the valley below. The truck that had just arrived belonged to a local TV station. The reporter and her cameraman were ambling up the hill toward them. Hacker started up the chant again.

Hey-hey! Ho-ho! Lawless logging has got to go!
Hey-hey! Ho-ho! Lawless logging has got to go!

"Come on, guys, let's keep the show going here!"

In its own insidious way the chant was by now almost as painful as the lock around her neck, but Abbie forced herself to join in. Using as few muscles as possible, she cranked her eyes sideways to see Scott and Mel, who were similarly secured farther along the gate. God, they looked so strong and comfortable, happy even, giving the chant all they had. It made Abbie feel like a total wimp.

Hey-hey! Ho-ho! The Forest Service has got to go!
Hey-hey! Ho-ho! The Forest Service has got to go!

At the edge of her vision, on the uphill side of the gate, she could see Todd and P.J. had again climbed into their giant papier-mâché trout costumes and were waltzing ludicrously around for the TV camera. They looked like a couple of drunken kayaks with legs. Twenty feet above them, still suspended in his harness next to the banner they had strung from trees across the road, Eric started playing his accordion again. His repertoire of four songs was beginning to wear a little thin. The banner said *Stop Killing Montana Forests.*

Hey-hey! Ho-ho! Corporate greed has got to go!
Hey-hey! Ho-ho! Corporate greed has got to go!

The TV reporter stopped fifty yards down the road to talk with the sheriff and the Forest Service people while the cameraman came up to the gate and took pictures of the dancing trout and Abbie and Mel and Scott. Abbie did her best to look tough and defiant and was vain enough to hope she might be interviewed and get her fifteen seconds of stardom. But when the reporter came up the hill, it was only Hacker she wanted to talk with.

She and the cameraman lined him up in front of the gate so the dancing trout and the banner could be seen behind him. In his confident drawl he explained that they were blocking the road to stop an illegal timber sale and that, while pretending to be clearing out fire-hazardous dead trees, the logging company was in fact, with the Forest Service's quiet connivance, clearcutting green trees.

You could tell from the accomplished way he laid down the sound bites that he had done this sort of thing before. Joel "Hacker" Hackman, veteran of a hundred lockdowns and almost as many arrests, was one of Missoula's many minor eco-legends. Balding, bearded, and built like a bear with a beer gut, he was a good fifteen to twenty years older than the rest of them. He was a UM forestry graduate of the early eighties and had never gone home to Omaha, Nebraska (*Why would anyone?* he liked to joke, before anyone else said it).

Instead he had built himself a cabin in the Bitterroots and founded a small organization called Forest Action, whose primary, if not sole, purpose was to make life as hard as possible for the Forest Service and logging companies. Abbie and Mel had met him nearly two months ago during their first week at UM when they were checking out the local environmental groups. Charmed and inspired, they had done volunteer work for him ever since, which until today had mostly meant stuffing envelopes.

Hacker had once been married and had a fourteen-year-old son he doted on but didn't see so much of nowadays since the boy had moved with his mother to Santa Barbara. Whether the woman had gotten more tired of having to bail Hacker out of jail every few months or of his legendary womanizing nobody knew for sure. He had hit on Abbie a couple of times already and the second time, late one night at a party after a little too much to drink, she had very nearly succumbed. She certainly found him more attractive than the boys she had so far met at UM, guys like Scott and Eric, who were fun to hang out with but just a little immature. In the knowing looks Hacker had ever since been giving her, Abbie could tell he considered her unfinished business.

If she was honest with herself, the prospect didn't displease her and perhaps the only thing that had held her back was a confused and faintly guilt-ridden sense of loyalty to Ty. During the two months she had been in Missoula, they had seen each other only once, when he drove all the way from Wyoming to spend a weekend with her. And though it was good to see him, he had seemed, with his hat and boots and his gentle, old-fashioned manners, a little awkward and out of place among her hipper new crowd of college friends.

The TV reporter now interviewing Hacker was a pinch-faced woman of about thirty. She was wearing a voluminous black parka with a fur hood that made her look as if she was being swallowed by a bear. She was listening to Hacker's monologue with a half-smile that somehow succeeded in being both patronizing and disapproving. But maybe she was just bored and cold, like Abbie.

"And what's with the dancing fish?"

"This creek is one of the last good spawning grounds for bull trout," Hacker said. "Clearcutting these slopes, like they're doing down there right now with that helicopter, means all the water runs off into the creek, carrying the mineral earth with it. The sediment builds up, the fish don't spawn anymore. Kills the forest, kills the fish. The kind of reckless corporate greed Montana's seen too much of."

Just as the interview was winding up, there was the sound of a vehicle coming down the hill behind the gate, then a long blast of horns. Hacker turned to look and, for the first time, the reporter seemed interested. She whispered to the cameraman to keep shooting. The sheriff and his deputies and the Forest Service people were all hurrying up the hill toward them. Abbie braced herself for the pain and managed to swivel around just in time to see the dancing trout leap out of the path of a mud-spattered red pickup. It scrunched to a halt just a few feet from the gate.

"What's going on?"

"Logging crew," Hacker said quietly.

The truck doors opened and four men got out to have a better look at what was going on. They wore feed caps and expressions of amused distaste. All but one, who from his swagger seemed to be the one in charge, looked about the same age as the protesters. But that was the only thing they had in common. Alongside them, even Hacker looked boyish. He stepped forward with a comradely smile.

"Hi, fellas. Sorry about the inconvenience. We're just peacefully protesting the illegal clearcutting that's going on here."

The foreman, if that was what he was, didn't answer, just gave him a look and walked past and came around the far end of the gate. He had a ponytail and an earring and a black circle of beard and mustache around a tight little mouth. With his thumbs tucked into the belt loops of his blue jeans, he sauntered past Mel and Scott, looking down on them as if at some lower form of life. He stopped in front of Abbie and stood there, chewing on something and staring down at her with an odd half-smile.

"Must be nice having nothing to do all day 'cept sit around on your ass," he said.

"Sure beats brainlessly butchering green trees," Abbie said.

She saw Hacker scowl and wondered why. The foreman's eyes narrowed. He sucked in his cheeks, rotated his chin a fraction, then sent a glob of black tobacco juice splatting onto the road a few inches from her right boot. Abbie had a sudden urge to kick him in the balls but decided it might not be too smart a move.

"Who are you calling brainless, you little tree-hugger bitch?"

Hacker stepped forward. The TV camera was still rolling. You could see the reporter almost wetting herself with excitement.

"Hey, guys, easy now," Hacker said.

Abbie's heart was racing. She hoped she didn't look half as scared as she felt. Thank God, just at that moment, two of the deputies and Iverson, the senior Forest Service agent, arrived. He was tall, with a gingery blond mustache and gold-rimmed glasses, and in his Stetson seemed a much more commanding figure than the tubby little sheriff still panting up the hill behind him. He had handled the protest all day with a firm but courteous good humor.

"Okay, everybody. Let's keep things nice and calm here."

"We've got no grouse with you fellas," Hacker said to the foreman. "You're just doing your job, we know that. It's your employers who need to know better."

The guy turned to face him.

"Now you're saying it too. We're just ignorant sonsofbitches."

"No, sir. I don't mean that at all. We appreciate you have to earn a living—"

"We've been working our butts off up here since five this morning and now we want to go home, okay?"

"We're sorry about that, but—"

"Just open the goddamn gate."

"Okay, gentlemen, that's enough," Iverson said, stepping between them with his palms raised, facing the logger now. "Sir, if you and your colleagues wouldn't mind going back over there to your vehicle, we'll see if we can sort something out here."

After twenty minutes of negotiation, the moment Abbie had been longing for arrived. Hacker was persuaded that the protest had made its point. Someone produced the keys to the bicycle locks and one by one Hacker freed them, Mel and Scott first, then Abbie. As he knelt down beside her, she smiled and thought he might say well done or ask how she felt, but he didn't say a word nor even look her in the eye.

When she stood up her joints seemed to have frozen and she almost fell over. But it sure felt good to be free. They all stood aside and as the loggers' pickup drove past, she saw the foreman staring at her through the glass. The look in his eyes made her hope they would never meet again.

It was a three-hour trip back to Missoula and they pulled into the first eating place they found and refueled on pizza and fries and chocolate fudge pie, all washed down with a gallon of hot coffee. Spirits were running high and they laughed and joked as they rowdily relived the day's events. Todd and P.J. kept teasing Abbie about what she had said to the logger, mimicking what she had only lately been made aware was her slightly haughty-sounding East Coast accent.

"Be off with you, you brainless tree butcher person!" Todd hooted.

It was all well intended and Abbie gave as good as she got. Eric said he was going to write a new song called "Butchers & Huggers," and she retorted that if anyone needed a new song, he did. Then they got to talking about going up to Seattle the following month, after Thanksgiving, to protest the World Trade Organization meeting. Todd, who was already making banners, said it was going to be a blast and that the whole world was going to be there. Sitting snug among these new friends, bonded by youth and adventure and giddy idealism, the chill in her bones melting in a warm, replenishing glow, Abbie felt joyful and proud and absurdly heroic.

It was dark when they came out. Weaving a route among the red-neon puddles of the parking lot to their cars, she found herself alone for a few moments alongside Hacker.

"You did good today," he said.

"Thanks."

"Has your butt thawed out yet?"

"Almost."

"But, you know, saying what you did to that guy was a mistake. You turned him into your enemy."

"He didn't exactly look like he wanted to be friends."

"Maybe not. But it's better to make him smile than spit. The rule is: Defuse, don't escalate. One snide remark and the whole atmosphere flipped."

"All I said was—"

"We all heard what you said. Thing is, you made him look like a fool and that made him mad. It's people like him we need to win over."

"I'm sorry."

"It's okay. I'm only telling you so next time you'll know."

It was Abbie's turn to feel foolish. Packed with half a dozen others in the back of Hacker's old VW camper van, she brooded awhile. Always the proud perfectionist, she never found criticism easy to take, however well meant. But she wasn't going to let it spoil her day or let Hacker know he'd gotten to her and by the time they reached Missoula she was again laughing with the others.

The plan was for everyone to go back to Todd and Eric's place, a ramshackle house on 4th Street that backed onto the river. But when they stopped at the liquor store to pick up a keg, Abbie said she needed to do some work and was going to head back to the dorm. Hacker offered to drop her off but she said she wanted to walk.

"No hard feelings," he said quietly.

"Of course not."

She said goodnight to everyone and thanked Hacker politely for the ride and for letting her come along. But she was damned if she was ever going to stuff another envelope for him. And as for going to bed with him, well. Maybe when hell froze over.

THIRTEEN

Sarah had never much cared for Thanksgiving. There was too much work and too much tension, both of which seemed to double when, every alternate year, it was their turn to have Benjamin's mother to stay. In the days when his father had been alive, her parents-in-law had always stayed home and—again, every second year—Sarah and Benjamin had been expected to fly to Kansas, where tensions of a different order applied (most of them between Benjamin and his father) and Sarah had felt more like a spectator than a participant and been able to relax a little. Had she been told that one day she would feel nostalgia for those Abilene Thanksgivings she would never have believed it.

The turkey had gone into the oven at eight-thirty and as it cooked, so had Sarah's temper. Every twenty minutes or so, Margaret came wandering into the kitchen to ask again if there was anything she could do and no matter how often Sarah said thanks, but no, really, everything was under control and going just fine, she would hover, making little comments about how the meal was being prepared. How *interesting* it was that Sarah basted the turkey so rarely or how *unusual* it was not to flour the roasted potatoes.

More to get rid of her than anything else, Sarah had

allowed her to help set the dining-room table, but even then Margaret had to go fetch the iron to get rid of the creases in the white linen tablecloth. The crowning insult was her readjustment of the center decoration of mahonia and lilies that had taken Sarah an hour to make the previous night. The poor woman was probably unaware that any of her actions could be construed as criticism, but just when Sarah was telling herself not to be so paranoid, that her mother-in-law meant well, she would catch her running a covert finger along a shelf to check for dust.

Then there were the stories, endlessly repetitive, about friends or neighbors back in Abilene, almost invariably people Sarah had never met or about something that had happened on a daytime TV show she had never seen or about some heroic or amusing escapade from Benjamin's boyhood that everyone had heard twenty times before.

Margaret Cooper was a small, rounded woman, with a tight gray perm and a constant, utterly unconvincing smile in which her mouth did all the work while her eyes remained steely. In her late seventies, she was still physically robust and meticulous in her appearance. But in the twelve months since Sarah had last seen her, the repetition had become almost ruthless. Even if you gently let her know that she had already told you something, she would insist on telling you again.

Benjamin, meanwhile, as he so often did when his mother came to stay, had disappeared. Most of the morning he had been stuck in his studio talking on the phone, probably to Martin or to Eve Kinsella in Santa Fe about those dreadful paintings she was doing for their new office block. And when he came in he went straight to the living room and slouched on the couch next to Abbie, listening to tales of derring-do in the forests of Montana. Sarah would have liked to hear them too if she had had only a moment to sit down. Abbie, bless her heart, had offered to help but Sarah had told her the most useful thing she could possibly do was entertain her grandmother and keep her out of the kitchen.

What had gotten into Benjamin lately, Sarah couldn't figure out. He used to help out but these days barely lifted a finger. Except, of course, at the gym, which had become his new obsession. Since this time last year, he must have lost about ten or twelve pounds and he claimed it made him feel a lot better, though it certainly didn't seem to have made him any happier. His face seemed to grow a little longer every day. Perhaps it was being stretched by all those newly toned muscles.

She knew how much he missed Abbie. They all did. But his way of coping with it seemed to be to retreat into himself. She hardly saw him. He got up at six every morning to go to the gym and drove from there to work. And when he came home, more often than not, he said he had work to do and carried his supper out to the studio.

And Josh was always either out with friends or up in his room talking to Katie Bradstock or playing that awful, thumping music and pretending to work. How he could even hear himself think was a mystery. So mostly Sarah ate alone now, maybe watched a little TV, and then, at about nine-thirty, went to bed and read. By the time Benjamin came to bed, she was usually asleep. They hadn't made love in nearly two months. He just didn't seem bothered anymore. On the couple of occasions that she had tried to initiate it, he said he felt too tired.

Sarah had done her best to turn things around. Books on the subject all said that combating empty-nest syndrome—or, in their case, half-empty-nest—required effort. So last weekend, when Josh was sleeping over at a friend's place, as a surprise, she had booked a table at a new seafood restaurant that had opened in Oyster Bay.

The place was crowded, the atmosphere lively, and the food terrific and Sarah tried, God how she tried, to get some kind of conversation going. But Benjamin just didn't seem to want to know. He answered her questions, sure. But he didn't ask any of his own and after about half an hour there they were, sitting in silence, looking around at the other people who were, of course, all talking and having fun. Sarah remembered how they used to joke about married couples in restaurants who sat there looking sad and bored, and how Benjamin would invent a fantasy dialogue of what might be running through their heads. And now they were that couple. It almost broke her heart.

To see him now so lively and regenerated by Abbie's presence, bantering with her as they all sat around the creaseless table, somehow only made it worse. But Sarah was trying not to think about it. She kept telling herself to smile and laugh along with the others, to be positive. It was the day when every family had an over-riding duty to be happy and not to brood on the cracks that might be running up the walls. The turkey, however inadequately basted, had been adjudged by all a tri-umph. And though Margaret had taken just one small mouthful of her pumpkin pie before gently shunting her plate away, everyone else seemed to be enjoying it. Benjamin was asking Abbie about going to the WTO meeting in Seattle the following week and what kind of protest she and her friends were planning.

"What does WTO stand for?" Margaret asked.

"It's the Whatever happened to Ty Organization," Josh chipped in.

Abbie had earlier made the mistake of telling Sarah in his presence that she had seen Ty only once since the summer and that she felt a little guilty about it. She groaned and gave him a quick, withering look.

"Josh, grow up. It's the World Trade Organization, Grandma. A club of wealthy countries that do their best to cheat the developing world and keep it poor."

"That reminds me," Margaret began. You could hear the collective sound of hearts sinking. "Benjamin, do you remember when you went on that Vietnam protest rally in Lawrence when you were at college . . . ?"

Oh God, Sarah said to herself, here it comes. The Long Hair story. Abbie and Josh exchanged a knowing smirk. Benjamin smiled wearily.

". . . and Harry Baxter saw you on the local TV news with your long hair and came into the store and told your father you looked like a girl?"

"Yes, Mom, I do."

"You know, Abbie, your father had hair right down to his shoulders."

"I know, Grandma. I've seen the photos."

"They were always protesting something or other. The war or Negro rights or whatever was in fashion at the time."

"It was called *civil* rights, Mom. And I don't think it went out of fashion."

"Whatever. Anyway, I thought he looked handsome and not a bit like a girl. But you know, Abbie, after that, he grew a beard."

"I know, Grandma. You told us."

"Did I? Oh, I'm sorry."

But she went on anyway. Telling them how, one vacation a few months later, Harry Baxter saw Benjamin with his new beard and declared that he now looked like a bearded lady in a circus.

"Next time he came in the store, I told him he could go elsewhere."

"How is Harry Baxter?" Sarah asked, pretending to be interested.

"Oh, heavens, Sarah, the old fool died years ago. Though Molly's still around. Drives around terrifying us all in one of those little electric carts they give to crippled people."

"Disabled, Mom," Benjamin said quietly.

"Crippled, disabled, it's the same thing. I can't be doing with all this finicky political correctness, not calling a spade a spade."

Sarah could see that Josh was about to make some mischievous retort and she glared at him just in time.

How they got through the rest of the day and the next day without murder or at least serious injury, Sarah had no idea. On Saturday morning, when Benjamin finally put his mother in the car and headed away down the driveway to take her to the airport and Sarah stood with Abbie and Josh in the cold sunshine, waving a cheery good-bye, it was like a ten-ton weight being lifted off their lives.

"That's absolutely the last time," Josh said, stomping away up the stairs to his room. "If she comes again for Thanksgiving, I'm out of here."

Sarah didn't bother to disagree. She put an arm around Abbie's shoulders.

"Come on," she said. "Let's make some fresh coffee. I feel I haven't had a proper talk with you since you came home."

They made the coffee and took it up the open wood staircase to the little mezzanine that overlooked the garden and the deck where they barbecued in the summer. The fall had been mild and there were still leaves on the silver birches that Sarah had planted all those years ago. They shone a bright and dappled yellow in the sunlight.

There were two cream-colored couches facing each other across a low mahogany table, and they settled on one of them with the sunshine streaming in on them. Abbie made Sarah slip off her shoes and took her feet in her lap and massaged them and told her all about college, things she had no doubt told Benjamin already but which, of course, he hadn't bothered to pass on. And though Sarah listened to every word, there was a part of her that could do no more than gaze in wonder and pride at this golden child, so beautiful and brimming with life. The massage was exquisite.

"Where did you learn to do this?"

"Do you like it?"

"It's amazing."

"Good. I figured you deserve it. Mel, my roommate, taught me. Was Grandma always like that?"

"No. It's worse, for sure."

"She doesn't listen. It's like she's just waiting to tell another of those stories about Dad we've all heard a million times."

"Perhaps that's nature's way. Making people you once loved less lovable, so it won't be so hard when they go."

"Do you think?"

"I think it's possible."

They both stared out of the window for a while. Two blue jays were playing a frantic chasing game in the birches.

"What's the matter with Dad?"

"What do you mean?"

"I don't know. Maybe it's just having Grandma around. But he seems all stressed out. Kind of detached, you know? Like he isn't really here."

"Well, things haven't been going too well at work. He and Martin have lost a couple of big projects. They're having to let a few people go. That's probably what's worrying him."

Sarah almost managed to convince herself.

"Oh. And what about you?"

"Me?" Sarah laughed. "Oh, you know. Same old same old."

"Mom, I'm a grown-up now."

"I know you are, sweetie. But honestly, I'm fine."

"You're such a bad liar."

"I'm not lying. He hasn't been that easy to live with lately, with all that's happening. And we miss you, for heaven's sake. We both do."

"Oh, Mom."

"Hey, listen. It's nothing. We'll get over it. Hell, I mean, in most ways it's absolutely terrific. Less cooking, less laundry. In fact, having you come home again is a real drag."

Abbie gave a skeptical grin.

"Let me have your other foot."

"Yes, ma'am."

That evening, after supper, Abbie asked if they minded her going out for a few hours to meet up with some old friends from high school. Sarah tried not to show her disappointment and said of course they didn't mind. Go have fun, she told her. Josh took this as a cue to inform them that there was a "kind of party" at his best friend Freddie's place and since Abbie was going out, couldn't he too? Benjamin took him aside for yet another quiet fatherly word about alcohol and pot. Twice in the last month, the boy had come home obviously stoned. He had flatly denied it but they were worried about him. Abbie said she would drop him off and pick him up later. They would be back before midnight, she promised.

Thus the scene was set for what Sarah later realized Benjamin must have been planning all the holiday and probably much longer. Maybe for weeks or even months. Within an hour both children had gone and a waiting silence fell upon the house. Benjamin would no doubt soon mumble something about needing to do some work and head out to his studio. But the minutes passed and he stayed. From the kitchen she could see him rather aimlessly tidying the mess the children had made in the living room. She called brightly to him, asking if he would like some cold turkey with some coleslaw and tomato salad.

"Sure."

Maybe he could open a bottle of wine?

"Sure."

He came through into the kitchen and pulled a bottle from the rack and stood uncorking it on the other side of the divider where she was preparing the meal. It was a long and narrow counter of polished gray granite, the sort of place every kitchen had, where things that had no other home got dumped, old magazines and stacks of letters and unpaid bills, a wide wooden bowl where they kept coins and car keys. The only sound was the saw and clack of her knife as she carved the turkey. His silence filled the room like an invisible cloud. Perhaps she should put some music on. He took two glasses from the cupboard and put them down, clink, clink, on the divider beside the opened bottle.

"Abbie seems in pretty good shape," she said cheerily.

"Yeah."

"Boy, what I'd give to be that age again."

She became aware that he was shifting nervously from one foot to the other. She stopped carving and looked at him. He was very pale.

"Are you okay?"

"Not really."

"What's the matter? Are you feeling sick?"

He swallowed. There was a long space of total silence. And then she knew. Knew exactly what he was about to tell her.

"Sarah, I—"

She slammed the knife down with a loud crack on the granite.

"Don't," she said.

"Sarah, sweetheart, I can't—"

"Don't say it! Don't you dare say it!"

"I have to go. I just can't live like this—"

"Shut up! Just shut up! What the hell are you talking about?"

He seemed for a moment to have lost his voice. There was a terrible imploring in his eyes. She was staring at him, waiting for an answer, but he couldn't hold her gaze. He looked down and just stood there, shaking his head.

"Are you having an affair?"

She heard herself. How she snarled, almost spat the word, as if she were trying to rid her mouth of a foul taste. He shook his head, still not looking at her. Like some sniveling coward. The sight made something inside her explode. She ran around the end of the counter to get at him.

"You are! You bastard! You are!"

She tore into him like a rabid animal, lashing at his head and shoulders and chest. He shielded his face but didn't step away, just let her thrash and slap and punch him. And this only fueled her fury further, that he should stand there, so wretched and demeaned, like some flaccid martyr of a fanciful God.

Then suddenly she broke away and stood there with her eyes clamped shut, clasping her head in both hands, blocking her ears too late to what she now knew, her mouth contorted in a soundless cry.

"Sarah—"

He tried to put a hand on her but as soon as he touched her, she lashed out and screamed.

"No-o!"

And then she looked at him and saw the tears rolling down his face, saw him standing there, so broken and hopeless, and she sobbed and her shoulders sagged and she reached out and drew him slowly toward her, both of them crying now. Her voice frail as a frightened child's.

"No, Benjamin, no. Please. Please, don't say it."

He put his arms around her and she pressed her head against his chest, tried to burrow into him, to find some place in him where still he might love her and want her. Begging him softly, *Please, please.* She felt his body shake in counterpoint to her own. This wasn't happening, he didn't mean it, he couldn't mean it.

"Sarah, sweetheart. I just—"

She put a hand across his mouth.

"Sshh. I don't want to hear this. Please."

And then the thought of somebody else in these arms, some other woman breathing this warm familiar smell that had always been hers and hers alone, reared and stabbed her in the chest and she clenched herself and shoved him away.

"It's Eve, isn't it?"

He hesitated then shook his head and started to say something, but she knew she was right.

"Have you slept with her?"

Her voice was like someone else's. Low and quivering, like a sheet of ice about to break.

"It's not like that, it's—"

"Have you slept with her!"

"No!"

"You liar."

"I swear to you—"

"You liar! You filthy, goddamn liar!"

He shook his head and turned and began to walk away. And the sight was so momentous that she couldn't bear it and she ran and grabbed him and turned him around and tried to get him to hold her again. Only now something had changed and even though he dutifully put his arms around her again, they were limp, uncommitted, as if some final switch inside him had been thrown.

How many hours it was, he couldn't tell. Time seemed suspended, its passing marked only in the fluctuation of their separate sorrows. She drifted around the house like a bereft ghost and he would follow her and find her, sitting hunched on a staircase or crumpled in the corner of a room they never used, sobbing or staring like a catatonic at her hands. Sometimes she would fly at him with her fists and scream at him and abuse him and the next moment she would grab him and drag him into her arms and plead with him, asking why, why, and telling him they could make it work, surely, after all these years. *She* could make it work, she could be better. If he would only give her a chance. For the children, for themselves. Please, Benjamin, *please.* Just one last chance.

Out on the deck, clinging to each other in the chill night air while the wind whisked the leaves of the floodlit birches, her sobbing subsided and a dazed and mournful calm fell at last upon them. They came in from the cold and he poured the wine that he had opened in what now seemed another lifetime and they took their glasses to the living room and sat together on the couch and talked.

She sat tense and straight-backed and in a small voice

that sometimes cracked, she asked him about Eve and he answered with care and as honestly as he could, telling her that, believe it or not, it was true that they hadn't slept together. In a phrase he had rehearsed—and which now, as he mouthed it, sounded so—he said Eve wasn't the cause of his leaving but the catalyst. He expected Sarah to erupt at any moment, or at least interrupt, but she didn't. She simply sat there, sipping her wine and watching him. And he could see something forming inside her as she heard him out, some new opinion of him, some new lens or prism through which henceforth she would see him, harder, clearer, more sharply focused.

Her silent stare was beginning to unnerve him but he tried to keep his voice calm and measured. He told her that for a long time he had been unhappy and that if Sarah was to be honest, she would have to agree that things hadn't been good between them for years. He was no longer the person she married. And anyway, for God's sake, they'd married so damned early, hadn't they? It was then that he noticed she was shaking her head. She didn't take her eyes off him, just gave this little, almost indiscernible shake of her head as if she couldn't quite believe what she had heard.

"What?" he said.

"So, that's it, is it?"

"What do you mean?"

"You share your life with someone for nearly a quarter of a century, have children, then decide you got married too young, you're not happy, and leave."

He had to lean forward to hear this, for it was uttered in a kind of breathy, shuddering whisper. But there was a new tone now that unsettled him, a gathering anger that was colder, more steely and controlled. And it frightened him. And maybe that was why he felt impelled to defend or justify himself and spoke the words he would later regret.

"I've never felt wanted by you. Never. And I look at you, at us, at the way we are. And I think, that's how it's going to be for the rest of our lives . . ." He stopped and swallowed. "And, Sarah, I can't. I just can't do it. There has to be more."

She stared at him for a long time, her chin tilted upward. It was a look of almost detached assessment, icy and regal. Then she swallowed and slowly nodded and at last looked away.

"So. When are you going to tell the children?"

"Tonight. Or tomorrow morning. Whatever you think best."

She laughed.

"Oh, please. It's your party."

"Then I'll tell them tonight."

"Fine. Oh boy, Benjamin, you sure do time things well. Happy holiday."

She raised her glass and drank the last of her wine. Then she stood up and walked to the doorway where she stopped and, after a moment, slowly turned to face him again.

"When you say I've never wanted you, you're wrong. You have always been wrong about that. What you are actually saying is I haven't loved you in the way you wanted me to love you. You are such a goddamn control freak that you even want to control the way other people love you. And I've lived with that for all these years. Trying to be what you want me to be. But nobody can ever measure up to what you want them to be, Benjamin. Nobody."

She stood there awhile, looking at him, her face quivering but defiant as she tried to hold back her tears. And then she gave a little decisive nod and turned and went.

He sat there for a moment then followed her through to the kitchen. She was scooping the uneaten turkey and salad off their two plates into the garbage. He walked over and came up behind her and tried to put his hands on her shoulders but she violently shrugged him away.

"Don't touch me."

He tried to help her clean up but she told him not to. She could do it, she said. So he went back to the living room and sat down on the couch. A few minutes later he heard her footsteps and turned to see her standing again in the doorway, looking at him. She had something in her right hand but her arms were folded and he couldn't see what it was.

"This is your home, Benjamin. I'm your wife. These are your children."

She unfolded her arms and spun what she was holding across the room so that it landed on the couch beside him. It was a framed picture of Abbie and Josh, one they'd taken on a skiing vacation in Canada two years ago. Sarah turned and disappeared and he heard the familiar clack of her shoes on the wooden stairs. He wondered if he should follow her but decided not to. In the vain hope of finding something to distract him and to shift the leaden weight in his chest, he switched on the TV and settled back to wait for the children.

Martin had already told him he must be mad. He was the only person who knew what Ben had been planning. One evening last week, he had invited Martin for a drink after work. It was something they rarely did and Ben could tell that his old friend was curious, even a little wary.

They were in a bar just off Jackson Avenue, one of those trendy new places that were all style and no soul. They were the oldest people there by a good twenty years and the music was so loud that they had to shout. They spent about five minutes making small talk about their kids and plans for Thanksgiving and then Martin cut to the chase and asked what was up.

"I'm leaving Sarah."

"You're *what?*"

Ben told him about Eve and Martin said he had half-guessed. Why else would he have been pushing those god-awful paintings, he said. He couldn't believe the two of them hadn't yet been to bed.

"So why the hell don't you just fuck her and get it over with?"

"I don't know."

"You don't know? Ben, hello? Are you out of your

mind? You want to throw everything away and you don't even know what for? Jesus."

Ben didn't really know what to say, except that things hadn't been good between him and Sarah for a long time and he felt he needed to, well, get out. Breathe. Feel alive again.

"How often have you seen her?"

"Eve? I don't know. Four or five times, maybe. We talk a lot on the phone."

"Jesus."

"She makes me feel—"

"Alive."

"Yes. As a matter of fact."

Martin shook his head and stared into his vodka martini. Then he downed it in one gulp and ordered another. Ben hadn't exactly been expecting sympathy. For many months the two of them hadn't been getting along that well. Although Martin hadn't spelled it out, Ben knew he blamed him for not bringing in more business and, in particular, for losing a project that they had spent almost two years developing. Just like the McMansion job, Ben had lost his temper with the clients and the whole deal had come unstitched. The difference was that this time it hadn't even been over a matter of principle. He just couldn't stand the people.

"So where are you going to live?"

"To begin with, I'll go to my mother's."

"In Abilene? Terrific."

"Then, if things work out with Eve, I'll get a place in Santa Fe."

"And what about us? What about work? You gonna commute every day from Abilene?"

"That's really what I wanted to talk with you about."

"You want out?"

"If that's what you want. Or maybe I just take a sabbatical—"

"A *sabbatical?* Jesus, Ben. You are one fucked-up guy."

That was the extent of the help and understanding his best friend had to offer. The next day when he came into the office he told Ben it would be better if they made a clean break of things. He coolly asked him to think about a reasonable buyout, bearing in mind the downturn in business and all the money they owed. Maybe he should get himself a lawyer, Martin added. Ben felt the first cool breeze of his new independent life, as if it had already begun.

When the kids came home, he was slumped asleep in front of *Casablanca.* The movie was ending, the plane gone. Bogart and Claude Rains were strolling off into the fog.

Sarah had heard the car and come downstairs. Ben walked out to the hallway. Josh's eyes were like an albino rabbit's and he was smiling, probably at something he and Abbie had been talking about as they came in. Abbie's smile vanished in a flash. She looked at Sarah, standing at the foot of the stairs, her face as white as her bathrobe, and then at Ben, still disoriented by sleep and trying to order his thoughts. He could see the fear creep into her eyes.

"Mom? What is it?"

"Your father's got something to tell you."

"Abbie," he began. "Josh . . ."

He stalled. His heart was beating so hard he could hardly hear himself think. All he had thought of saying seemed to have erased itself.

"For godsake, Dad, what is it?"

"Your mother and I are going to separate—"

"No," Sarah cut in. "Tell the truth. Your father is leaving us."

Abbie's face started to crumple.

"What?" she said. "You're *leaving?*"

"Sweetheart—"

"What are you *talking* about?"

She looked desperately at Sarah, a pitiful, incredulous little smile flicking on and off her lips. As if this might turn out to be some terrible, elaborate joke.

"Mom?"

Sarah shrugged and nodded.

"It's true."

Josh was peering at him, his eyes puckered in a frown as he tried to make sense of what was happening.

"Are you guys, like, serious?"

"Yes, Josh."

"Just like that?" Abbie said.

Her shoulders were shaking and she was gnawing at her fist now. God almighty, Ben thought, what am I doing? Martin's right, I must have gone mad. He reached out to her but she backed away from him, her face distorting with shock and disgust.

"Dad," Josh said. "You can't do this. I mean . . ."

He ran out of words and just stood there frowning, his mouth hanging open.

"It'll all be okay, Joshie. Honestly—"

"No! It won't be okay!" Abbie screamed. "You idiot! You're ruining our lives!"

He tried to reach her again, but this time she lashed out at his hand and turned and ran sobbing toward the stairs. Sarah didn't try to stop her, just stood aside to let her pass. The three of them stood there in silence as she ran up the stairs. The slam of her bedroom door made the whole house shake. Sarah shook her head and gave him a wry smile.

"Nice work, Benjamin."

And she turned and followed Abbie up the stairs.

FOURTEEN

Dressing up as genetically engineered fruit was Mel's idea and had once seemed a pretty funny one. They had spent every evening of the week before Thanksgiving making their costumes out of painted papier-mâché and Mel's, a scarlet strawberry with the head of a bemused-looking fish sticking out the front, was by a long way the best. Everyone who saw it just cracked up.

Mel had driven all the way up from Missoula on Sunday with the others in Hacker's camper van, the fruit suits roped precariously to the roof. It was a miracle they had arrived in one piece, which was more than could be said for Abbie's right now. Hers was supposed to be a cross between a tomato and a sheep but no longer looked like either. In the unremitting drizzle, it was fast reverting to pulp. Both its front legs had fallen off as well as its tail and the red paint had run all down the front of her sodden parka and pants. Eric and Scott, marching to her left, had already ditched their costumes and it wouldn't be long before Abbie did so too. To her left, Mel's still looked perfect. She'd probably given it a sneaky final coat of waterproof paint. And beyond Mel was Hacker, who hadn't made a costume at all, no doubt considering himself above anything so childish.

It was early morning and downtown Seattle was a vibrant sea of humanity. Thousands of demonstrators, tens of thousands, were crammed shoulder to shoulder in every street, all marching toward the convention center. And, despite the cold and the rain, everyone seemed to be having a ball, waving and shouting, laughing and chanting.

There ain't no power like the power of the people
And the power of the people won't stop!

There were people dressed as trees and elephants, turtles and whales—who all seemed a lot more waterproof than Abbie's sheep-tomato—and above them fluttered a gaudy canopy of banners denouncing the evils of the World Trade Organization. The guy in front had one with a huge picture of Dracula sinking his bloody fangs into the planet. The woman next to him was waving one that said *WTO. Fix it or Nix it.* Those who weren't chanting were blowing whistles or honking horns or ringing bells or banging drums to a dozen different rhythms.

And it wasn't just students and hippies. There were people of all ages, colors, creeds, and nationalities, taxi drivers and construction workers, cleaners and clerks. What was more, it actually seemed to be having an impact. Word was going around that they had already succeeded in stopping the opening ceremony and that all the fat-cat politicians were either cowering in their hotel suites or besieged in their limos. In fact, the whole city was under siege and the police were just standing around unable to do a thing.

It was totally awesome, like some epic carnival, the most fantastic display of solidarity Abbie had ever seen. History was being made. It was one of those world-changing events, like Woodstock or the Berlin Wall coming down or Martin Luther King, Jr., telling the world about his dream. And Abbie was actually taking part and bearing witness. In years to come she would be able to tell her children and grandchildren about it. She only wished she could feel more a part of it, more wholly involved. For, however hard she tried to block them, the images of what had happened at the weekend came flashing into her head and spoiling things.

She nearly hadn't come here at all. The previous morning, her mom had virtually had to frog-march her into the airport. Abbie had said no way, she wasn't going. They should all be together. She would stay home for the week; in fact she wouldn't go back to college at all. But her mom would have none of it.

The woman had been incredible. On Sunday morning, while the bastard went around the house quietly gathering his things and packing his bags, she held her head up and didn't shed a single tear. She was even *nice* to him, for heavensakes, helping him look for his goddamn glasses. It was obviously all a big front that sooner or later had to crack. But it hadn't. All through the day, even after he went, she had looked after Abbie and Josh, kept on hugging and consoling them, as if the hurt belonged entirely to them.

Poor Joshie. He didn't seem to know what to do. After their dad had broken the news and Abbie had fled screaming to her room, Josh had eventually followed his mom upstairs and found the two of them wailing and sobbing and clinging to each other. And he just sat himself down on the end of the bed and gazed forlornly at the wall. He was still stoned, of course, and trying to get his head around what had happened. But even the next day, even after that horrible, icy good-bye when they'd stood at the door with their mom's arms around their shoulders and watched their dad go off down the driveway, his things all stacked into the back of the station wagon, the poor kid didn't seem to know whether he was allowed to cry or had to be the big, brave man of the house.

"Abbie, listen to me," her mom had said that night, when all three of them were sitting there at the kitchen table over a supper none of them wanted and Abbie had just announced she wasn't going to fly to Seattle the next morning. "Listen to me. We are not going to let this destroy us. Life has to go on. Maybe your father'll come back, maybe he won't. My guess is that he will. But these things happen, and there's nothing any of us can do about it. He'll either come to his senses or not. Meanwhile, we get on with our lives, okay? You'll darn well *go* to Seattle, young lady, and give these—TWO creeps—"

"WTO."

"Whatever. You go there and give 'em hell. From me too. I don't know who they are or what they've done, but I already don't like them."

They laughed. A little hysterically, but they actually laughed.

Then George and Ella arrived and there was more crying, but not by her mom. Grandma was intending to stay for a few days and even she told Abbie to stick to her plans and catch her flight, though Grandpa said the whole idea of the protest was woefully misguided and clearly inspired by anarchists and communists and that the WTO was, as a matter of fact, one of the few true forces for good left in the world. Abbie was too tired and too emotionally drained to fight.

So here she was, soaked to the skin and trying to enjoy being dressed as sheep-tomato, which had now gotten so soft and gooey that the time had come to ditch it. Without breaking step, she managed to lower it to the ground and stepped almost gracefully out of it. Mel gave her a grin. She was the only person Abbie had told about her dad leaving and was under strict orders not to let the others know. The last thing Abbie wanted was for them all to start feeling sorry for her, treating her like she was some kind of invalid.

Hey-hey! Ho-ho! WTO has got to go!
Hey-hey! Ho-ho! WTO has got to go!

The rain seemed to be stopping now and as they marched forward the sky began to clear. Between the buildings she could see the ocean and port, two massive container ships anchored offshore. She had never been to this city before. Stacked steeply at the water's edge, it was even more stunning than she had heard.

Up ahead there was a billowing black pillar of smoke and as the march surged on she saw a dumpster had been set on fire and fueled with car tires. The crowd divided to pass it. Now, below the hubbub, she heard glass being smashed but she couldn't see where or what it was. To her right now, a chanting throng of demonstrators was laying siege to a McDonald's. They had a banner saying *Resist McDomination* and some were hammering on the windows and the doors. On the walls, in black paint, they had scrawled *McShit* and *McMeat Is Murder.*

The police they had so far seen had been laid-back and friendly. A couple of them, riding along with the march on mountain bikes, had even smiled and joked with them. But the ones they were now beginning to see looked altogether different. They seemed to be some kind of special riot police. They were all in black, wearing helmets with visors and gasmasks, long capes and leather leggings and jackboots. They stood still as statues, blocking off the side streets, nightsticks at the ready.

"Wow," Mel said. "Who are *those* guys?"

"It's the Darth Vader look-alike convention," Eric said. As ever, he had his accordion with him and immediately started playing the theme to *Star Wars*. Everybody around them started singing along and yelling *May the Force be with you!* If any of the cops were amused, it was impossible to tell. Their visors and gasmasks completely obscured their faces.

A helicopter suddenly thundered over their heads and they all ducked as the air vibrated to the thud of its blades. Gradually, the march slowed and then stopped and for a long time they all stood there, chanting and singing, canyoned around by the stores and office blocks, herded ever more closely by the cordons of cops and the pressure of more marchers arriving behind.

Quite how or why it all began to go wrong, Abbie never really knew. Some later blamed it on a few nervous or trigger-happy cops. Another dumpster had been set on fire and the black and acrid smoke kept drifting across the crowd so that sometimes it was impossible to see what was happening. Through the crowds Abbie could see a lockdown going on, a circle of chanting protesters, their linked arms encased in metal pipes.

Listen to the voices of the people in the street!
We don't have a vote, we don't have a seat!

And beneath this now, another voice, that with every repetition became steadily more stern and ominous. Somebody with a megaphone was telling everyone to leave the area, that they were in violation of state and city law and that all who refused to disperse would be arrested for unruly behavior.

To begin with, Abbie didn't know what the smell was. She thought it must be something burning in the dumpster. Then her eyes started to sting and in the next moment the crowd in front of her scattered and she saw a canister rolling across the ground, spewing smoke. Somebody yelled that it was tear gas. A young guy who had brought his own gasmask rushed forward and grabbed the canister and hurled it back behind the lines of police who were now starting to move down the street toward them. The cops had plastic shields and nightsticks at the ready and all but a few defiant or foolhardy protesters began to retreat nervously before them.

In just a few minutes, the whole atmosphere had changed. For the moment, the breeze was blowing the tear gas away from them, but there was the start of panic now and it rapidly began to spread.

Through a gap in the crowd, Abbie saw one of the protesters who had stood his ground being beaten to his knees by the cops with their nightsticks and the limp body of another being dragged away. Some who saw it started jeering and yelling and one or two started hurling anything they could find at the cops. But the cordon steadily advanced. Then a girl standing just a few yards ahead of Abbie jerked violently and fell and started screaming and rolling on the ground, clasping her leg.

"Holy shit!" Eric yelled. "They're shooting at us!"

Even as he said it, there was a sudden salvo of sharp pops and two more protesters cried out and fell. One was clutching his face. Abbie saw blood streaming through his fingers.

"They're firing plastic," Hacker said. He probably meant to reassure them but it didn't do the trick for Abbie. She had never felt more scared in her life. Hacker and Scott were helping Mel scramble out of her strawberry-fish, whose expression suddenly seemed a lot less amusing.

"Come on," Hacker said. "Let's get out of here."

But it was easier said than done. Except for the few who were standing up to the police, everybody was trying to leave. There were too many people and too much panic and nobody seemed to know the best way to go. With the flow of the crowd, they were being swept toward a side street but then those in front started ducking and diving. Water was gushing all over them and for a moment Abbie couldn't figure out where it was coming from. Then she saw the police truck with its water cannon and in the next moment the jet caught Mel full in the chest and sent her cartwheeling back-ward.

Abbie rushed to her and knelt beside her and asked

if she was okay, and Mel nodded but seemed too shocked to know. There was a trickle of blood coming from her nose. Hacker and Scott took hold of her, one on each side, and hoisted her to her feet. As they hauled her off, Hacker yelled to Abbie over his shoulder to stay close.

Once they had gotten clear of the water cannon, Abbie stopped and looked back for Eric. There was no sign of him. Then she spotted his accordion lying smashed on the ground. She hollered to Hacker and the others to stop but they couldn't have heard her. They were somewhere near the burning dumpster and the air was suddenly swirling again with black smoke and when it cleared and she looked in the direction she had last seen them, they had vanished.

She started to run but must have lost her bearings, because there weren't so many people now and she realized she must be heading back toward the advancing police line. Another helicopter roared over and as she looked up at it she collided with a man who was running the other way. The impact shocked her and knocked the wind from her and she gave a little whimper and just stood there, fighting for breath and trying to figure out where to run, but her head was paralyzed with panic.

That was when the tear-gas canister came skidding across the debris and knocked her clean off her feet. The back of her skull hit the ground when she fell and she saw a flash of white light. For how long she was knocked out, she had no idea, maybe only a few seconds, but when she opened her eyes again she was staring at the sky and wondering what that strange black blur was and why the air was throbbing so. Then as the world reconfigured she realized there was a helicopter directly above her and she had a sudden fearful certainty that it was going to land right on top of her. She scrambled to her knees and then to her feet and tried to run but found she couldn't because of the pain in her shin where the gas canister had struck her. The air all around her was filling fast with the tear gas and her eyes and lungs were on fire and she hadn't the slightest idea which way to run. Alone in the chaos, Abbie stood there and clamped her hands to her eyes and started to scream.

The next thing she knew, someone had grabbed hold of her arm and was hauling her away. Her first thought was that it was a cop and she yelled and lashed out at him.

"For Christsake, I'm trying to help you!"

Through her streaming, smarting eyes all she could see was the black snout of a gasmask, which made her think, despite what he'd said, that he had to be a cop. Then the snout lifted and she saw a thin, stubbled face and a pair of intense blue eyes and long black hair tucked pirate-fashion under a red bandana. He was dressed all in black but he sure didn't look like a cop.

"Here, put this on," he said.

There was a trace of an accent, German or Scandinavian maybe. Before she had a chance to argue he had taken off the gasmask and was putting it on her, pulling the goggles and snouted air filter down over her face. Almost at once the air became breathable. Through the goggles she watched him take off his bandana and soak it with water from a bottle he pulled from the pocket of his parka. He tied it like a bandit over his nose and mouth.

"Come on, let's go."

He put an arm around her and began to steer her off through the crowd. Her leg hurt but soon she forgot about it and surrendered, without a thought for the others or even for herself or where this stranger might be taking her.

Maybe it was simply that she was dazed from the knock to her head when she fell. Cocooned behind the mask, the clamor of helicopters and screams and sirens now muted, she felt strangely detached, as if the world had suddenly gone into slow motion and she was in a dream or watching it all on the TV news. All she would later remember were random images framed in the little round lenses of the goggles: a woman lying bleeding on a bed of broken glass, a Buddhist monk in a crimson robe, hunched on his knees in prayer, his shaved head pressed to the sidewalk, discarded banners torn and trampled everywhere, and an African drum with a torn skin, rolling slowly away down an empty street to the ocean.

A re you okay?"
She opened her eyes and blinked and, seeing nothing, had a rush of panic that the gas had blinded

her. She sat up and rubbed them. They felt as if someone had stripped a layer of skin from them. She looked up to where the voice seemed to have come from and saw a shadowy figure towering above her.

"Yeah, I think so," she said. "God, my eyes."

"Here, bathe them."

He knelt down and placed a bowl of water on the floor beside the bare mattress she had been lying on. While she bathed her eyes, he struck a match and lit a candle and when she looked again she saw the narrow face, those pale blue eyes. He didn't smile, just handed her a towel to dry herself. It smelled of gasoline.

"Thank you."

"Let me look at where you hit your head."

She turned so he could inspect the wound. She was wearing a big brown sweater that wasn't hers. It was rough and oily and smelled like a wet sheep. He had probably put it on her because her clothes had gotten soaked and though she didn't much like the fact that she had no recollection of him doing it, she was glad he had because the room was freezing. At least she still had her pants on.

"It's quite a bump. There's a small cut but it doesn't need stitches. Keep still while I clean it up."

He wet the towel in the bowl and gently dabbed the back of her head. The room was small and smelled of damp and the walls were cracked and peeling. The floor was of bare wooden planks, some of which were missing, and there was no furniture, just heaps of clothes and junk and old newspapers and magazines.

There was another mattress below a single window that had been blacked out with an old blanket. Abbie could hear people talking in the next room and through the half-open door she saw shadows moving on a wall.

"There. You'll live. You were concussed and passed out. You've slept for four hours. I was getting worried." He held up a hand. "How many fingers?"

"Eighteen?"

He almost smiled. He handed her a mug.

"It's tea. There's water here too. You must drink. Your leg is bruised but it's okay."

She could feel her shin throbbing.

"Thank you. Where are we?"

He shrugged. "A house. It's just a squat."

"And who are you?"

"Just a squatter."

She gave him a baleful look over the rim of the mug and this time he did smile. It was hard to guess how old he might be. Late twenties, thirty maybe. Despite the stubble, there was something fine, almost feminine, about him. He was beautiful and seemed to see her think it.

"My name is Rolf. And you are Abigail Cooper from the University of Montana."

"Been through my wallet, huh."

"Spent all the money, used the credit cards. Had a good time."

"Be my guest. It's Abbie, by the way."

He gave a formal little nod. He got to his feet and headed for the door, telling her over his shoulder that there was food in the next room when she felt like it.

"Thanks."

"You're welcome."

"And thanks also for, you know, getting me out of there today."

He turned and looked at her, gave another nod, then went out. Abbie sat awhile, cradling the mug and sipping the tea. It was too sweet but at least it was warm and comforting. She wondered what had happened to the others, whether Eric and Mel were okay. It shouldn't be too hard to find them. They had all made a note of Hacker's cell phone number in case they got separated.

When she felt strong enough, she got up and wandered through to the next room. Rolf, two other guys, and two women were sitting crosslegged on the floor around a big bowl of brown rice and vegetables, eating with their fingers. A third woman was sitting in the corner, working on a laptop. They all looked up as Abbie came in, smiling and saying hi. A couple of them replied and the others just nodded.

"Here," Rolf said, moving to make space beside him. "Help yourself."

She sat down and took a handful of rice, realizing how hungry she was. The room was bigger but almost as bare as the other, with three mattresses and more heaps of junk. It was lit with candles in jars and a flickering butane gas lamp with a cracked shade. One wall was covered with newspaper clippings and photographs and scrawled graffiti.

"Do you happen to have a phone here?" she asked.

For some reason, they all seemed to find this incredibly amusing, though quite why, Abbie didn't know. After all, the woman on the laptop seemed to be wired up to some kind of socket. Maybe it was the way Abbie had said it? She felt her cheeks coloring and hoped it didn't show.

"There's a phone booth down the street," Rolf said. "Until today we did have a cell phone but Mr. Helpful here managed to lose it." He clipped the guy next to him on the head.

"It wasn't my fault, that fuckhead cop took it."

"So, you were the guys dressed up as fruit, right?" one of the women said.

"Uh-huh."

"Why?"

"It was supposed to be genetically engineered fruit."

"Oh, right."

"Is that the kind of cool stuff they teach you about at the University of Montana?" the guy sitting next to her said. He had a tangle of dreadlocks and a silver ring through one eyebrow. Abbie wanted to punch him on the nose but decided to ignore the sarcasm and said yes, actually there were classes about the use of gene technology in agriculture, though she hadn't taken them herself.

"Fascinating."

"Yes, it is, as a matter of fact."

"And are you guys, like, big environmental activists down there?"

The question came from Rolf and because it sounded genuine and friendly and she felt he might be trying to make up for the rudeness of the others, she gave a fuller and more enthusiastic reply than perhaps she should have. She spoke directly to Rolf, telling him about Hacker, whom she figured he might have heard of (he hadn't), and about Forest Action and about the timber-sale lockdown the previous month. And though she didn't quite know why she should want to show off to him, she didn't exactly lie, but did find herself embroidering things a little, making her encounter with the loggers sound more dangerous than it was.

If not obviously impressed, Rolf seemed at least interested. And perhaps it was because she was a little in awe of him or mesmerized by those beautiful eyes that she didn't notice that the guy with the dreadlocks was grinning and shaking his head and that the two women either side of him were smiling too. By the time Abbie registered this she had already gotten a little carried away and was telling Rolf about the student "weed buster" trips when they all went up into the hills to pull up noxious weeds.

"You mean, like, to smoke?" Dreadlocks said.

Abbie stopped for a beat and narrowed her eyes at the little creep. He looked as if he had probably been smoking himself. She turned back to Rolf without bothering to answer and went on.

"It's amazing what you find up there. Three kinds of knapweed, leafy spurge, hound's tongue—"

"That leafy spurge, man, that can lift your fucking head off."

"Cut it out, man," Rolf said.

Abbie had taken enough. She turned to face the guy.

"Okay, what is it you people do that's so much more important?"

Dreadlocks just shook his head and laughed to himself.

"No, seriously," Abbie said, her anger rolling now. "Tell me, I'm interested. What do *you* do? Huh?"

"Little rich college girls, picking weeds, oh my, lah-di-dah."

"Screw you!"

"Ooh, please . . ."

Rolf told him again to cut it out then leaned forward and put a hand on Abbie's shoulder, trying to calm her. She shrugged it off.

"Abbie, it's not that we think these things you do have no value. It's just that to us, they seem a little, what shall I say? Irrelevant, marginal perhaps. Like rearranging the furniture on the *Titanic*."

"Oh, okay. Fine, thanks."

"No, seriously. I'm not being rude. Just realistic. Everything has gone too far. The big corporations are destroying the planet, and nobody's going to listen to protests or whatever. Look at what happened today. Look at what they did to you."

He reached out to touch her, but she moved and wouldn't let him.

"The governments of the industrialized world are

now run entirely by the transnational corporations. Politicians are merely their puppets. Democracy is just a sideshow. So, to have any kind of impact, to make the people who really run things stop and listen and think about what they are doing, you have to hurt them. Personally. Really hurt them."

"And that was what you guys think you were doing today?" she said sourly.

Rolf laughed. "Oh, no. Today was just fun."

The woman who all this time had been working on her laptop now came to sit down on Rolf's other side and took a handful of rice. She looked pleased with herself. From their body language, Abbie got the impression that this was his girlfriend.

"Is it all arranged?" he asked her quietly.

"Uh-huh."

"Good. Well done."

Abbie stood up. She felt a little sick and wanted to leave, get some air in her lungs. Get away from these freaks, find Mel and Hacker and the others.

"You're going?" Rolf said.

"Yes."

"Can I have my sweater?" Dreadlocks said, smirking.

Disgusted to be wearing something that was his, she quickly pulled it off and threw it on the floor. Rolf found her parka and helped her into it. It was still wet. He followed her to the door.

"Go easy on that leafy spurge!" Dreadlocks called.

She was in the doorway and turned to look at him.

"Before the revolution, asshole, learn some fucking manners."

She walked out but heard the roar of laughter. Rolf followed her down the stairs and out to the street then walked her down the hill to the phone booth. Hacker sounded relieved to hear her voice. He said they would come at once to collect her. Rolf explained how to find the place.

While they waited, they sat side by side on the steps of a derelict house. The whole area was being cleared for demolition, he said. They were going to build offices instead. He rolled a cigarette and offered it to Abbie but she declined. A mottled half-moon was hoisting itself over the rooftops and they sat for a long while without talking, just watching it move slowly into the sky.

"I'm sorry about what happened up there," he said. "The guy's an idiot."

Abbie didn't reply. She was feeling little and lonely and, for the first time in many hours, had been thinking about her mom and dad and what had happened at home and how sad and screwed up her whole world suddenly seemed. She felt tears welling but managed to hold them back and he either didn't notice or pretended not to. He asked her where she came from and it was a few moments before she trusted her voice enough to tell him.

"And you?"

"Originally from Berlin. I've lived here for twelve years."

"In Seattle."

"No. Here and there. I get bored if I stay in one place."

He took a pen from his pocket and wrote a number on the flap of his cigarette papers then tore it off and handed it to her, saying someone there would always know how to reach him. He asked for her number and perhaps because she was still slightly concussed she couldn't remember the one at the dorm, so she gave him her home number instead. Then Hacker's camper van came down the street. Scott was with him and they both made a big fuss of her. Mel was fine, they said. Eric was in the hospital where he would have to stay for at least two weeks. He had a broken pelvis, which didn't bother him half as much as the loss of his accordion. Abbie introduced them to Rolf and the three men shook hands. Then she thanked him again for helping and looking after her and climbed into the back of the van.

As they pulled away, she gave him a little wave through the window and he looked her directly in the eyes and smiled back. And she knew in that moment that one day she would see him again. She carefully folded the scrap of paper he had given her and stowed it in her wallet.

FIFTEEN

I t was the dawn of the new millennium and the whole world was brimming with hopes of happiness and peace and goodwill to all mankind. And all that bullshit. The century was a week old and already Sarah didn't like it. She was sitting at her desk in the little back office of the bookstore, trying to keep her mind on what she was reading on the computer screen, which was almost as depressing as everything else in her life at the moment. Including the weather, which was cold and damp and gray and foggy, the kind Jeffrey called slit-your-wrists weather, though he hadn't called it that today, probably because he feared she might actually do it.

The sales figures for the holiday season were even more dismal than she had feared, thanks to the chain stores and a certain online bookseller, whose name, like *Macbeth* in any theater, was not to be mentioned within these walls, thank you very much. Their prices were so ridiculous, they might as well give the damn books away. Through the open door she could hear Jeffrey patiently trying to charm a customer, the only one they'd had in the past hour and a half, a woman who was after a book but didn't seem to be able to remember the title or the author or even what it was about.

"Any idea of the publisher?" Jeffrey asked helpfully.
"The what?"
"God help us all," Sarah muttered.

Jeffrey had been fabulous. He had run the place virtually single-handed during the run-up to Christmas. Sarah had come in most days, because she couldn't stand being home alone, but she knew she had often been more of a hindrance than a help. During that first unreal week after Benjamin left and the kids had gone back to school, Jeffrey had called her two or three times every day and had always stopped by on his way home, with food or flowers or a bottle of wine. It had turned into a kind of rolling house-party or wake. As soon as her mother went home, Iris came to stay and friends kept dropping in to cheer her up, with the result that on some evenings there were half a dozen or more people in the kitchen, cooking and talking and eating and drinking and crying and laughing, none of them letting Sarah lift a finger, not even to stack the dishwasher. She talked and cried and laughed so much that in the end she was so exhausted she had to call a halt and come back to work for a rest.

"So it's a novel, but nonfiction," Jeffrey was saying. "A nonfiction novel. Hmm. Oh, you mean, something like Truman Capote's *In Cold Blood*?"

"Like *what?*"

Sarah and the kids had dreaded the thought of staying home for Christmas and the New Year, especially with all that dawn-of-a-new-age nonsense going on. Then, out of the blue, Karen Bradstock called and invited them to the Caribbean. Karen knew about Benjamin, it emerged, because Josh had e-mailed Katie. Some fabulously rich tax-dodger client of Tom's had a house on the island of Mustique, she said, and had offered it to them—for *free*—for two whole weeks. Some other friends would be there, but the place had a zillion rooms, so why didn't they come too? Sarah jumped at it.

The island was beautiful if strangely antiseptic, having nothing even vaguely resembling a local culture. According to Karen, it had years ago been bought by an eccentric aristocrat who preferred the place empty so that he could throw long and lavish parties for bored members of the British royal family. Nowadays, it was owned by a company and rigorously run as a refuge for the extremely rich.

The Bradstocks had invited two other couples from Chicago, neither of whom Sarah much took to. One of the women treated her like an invalid and kept offering to do things for her and asking with an infuriatingly caring look in her eyes how she was *feeling*. It made Sarah want to scream. It was funny how some people just didn't seem to get it. Being treated normally was best, kindness was fine, but unctuous sympathy made her feel almost homicidal.

Fortunately, Karen got it exactly right. The two of them had a lot to catch up on and, despite the other guests, found time for some good private chats. Nor was the subject inevitably Benjamin. In fact some days, even when she was walking on her own along the beach or sitting by the pool reading, Sarah often managed to go a full half-hour without thinking about him.

Young Will, who had grown about two feet taller

since she had last seen him, was now obsessed with sports and most days disappeared with his dad to play tennis or golf. Josh didn't mind. He was too infatuated with Katie and it seemed mutual. The only one who palpably didn't enjoy herself was Abbie.

She announced after just one day that she detested the place. She said it was full of fascist bankers and their bulimic, Botoxed wives and that if she saw another C-list wannabe or wrinkled has-been rock star she would throw up. It would have been more embarrassing had Karen not said she absolutely agreed and spiritedly taken her side in the debates that raged across the dinner table, with Tom and Will inevitably cast as "neo-imperialists" or "crypto-colonial dinosaurs," whatever that meant. Tom handled these skirmishes brilliantly, giving as good as he got, but always with humor. But Abbie sometimes went too far.

"God, she's so angry," Sarah said quietly to Karen after one particularly ferocious bout.

"Of course she is. Hell hath no fury. You're not the only woman scorned. However much you and Ben tell her that it's not about her and that it's just about what went wrong between you and him, she probably can't see it that way. You should have her go talk to some-body."

"A shrink?"

"Why not? Aren't you seeing someone?"

"I'm not the type."

"What's the type? You get sick, you see a doctor, right?"

"Oh, I don't know. Perhaps. Sometime."

"Whatever. It's none of my business. But maybe you should think about it for Abbie."

Sarah already had, but didn't feel like discussing it, partly out of loyalty to Abbie and partly because she felt she had bungled the whole thing. She had mentioned Abbie's anger to their doctor only the previous week when she went to see him for some more sleeping pills. He said therapy would be a good idea and that he'd be happy to put them in touch with someone. Abbie should drop by and see him, he said. But when Sarah told Abbie, she almost got her head bitten off.

"What, you mean, you think I'm crazy."

"No, sweetheart, of course not. It's just—"

"If that's what you think, just get me committed."

"Abbie, come on—"

"Mom! Okay, so I'm mad at him. But isn't it about time somebody got mad around here? I mean, it's allowed, isn't it? You're so goddamn controlled, anyone would think you didn't care."

"That's not fair."

"I'll handle it how I want. Just leave me alone."

They celebrated the new millennium at a beach bar and restaurant that protruded on wooden stilts over the water and was run by a soulful West Indian called Basil, whom Abbie had adjudged the only real human being on the entire island. Sarah had promised herself that she wasn't going to get emotional but when midnight struck and the fireworks went up and everybody was hugging and kissing and wishing each other happy new year and

266

Abbie and Josh came to find her and the three of them stood there, clinging on to one another like three lost souls, she just couldn't help herself. They all cried, even Josh, bless him. But that was the only time Sarah allowed it to happen.

Back at the house, on the answering machine, Benjamin, calling from his mother's in Abilene (or so he claimed), had left a nervous message for them, sending his love and wishing them all a happy new year. Yeah, right, Sarah thought.

He had phoned her a lot at first, and almost every time, despite herself, she had ended up crying and screaming at him. And sometimes he cried too and called her sweetheart and told her he loved her, which made her so mad she wanted to smash the phone. Because if he loved her, if he really damn well loved her, why the hell had he left? In the end, she told him not to keep saying this and asked him not to call for a while.

Then Beth Ingram dropped her little bombshell. Whether it was on purpose or not, Sarah couldn't be sure. Probably. But one day they were talking and Beth was being really sweet and consoling and then, quite casually, said something about how Sarah must have felt that other time. Sarah said sorry, hang on a minute, what did she mean *other* time? And Beth ummed and ahhed and blushed a little and then reluctantly told her she had been talking with the wife of an ICA associate at a party a while back and this woman had let slip that Benjamin had been having an affair with a young real-estate lawyer who occasionally did their conveyancing. Apparently, at work, absolutely everybody knew. Beth said she had just assumed Sarah did too.

Sarah hit the stratosphere and that very night, after too many glasses of wine, she called him at his mother's and the bastard wasn't there. Margaret said she didn't know where he was, that he was away on business somewhere. Oh, sure. In Santa Fe, no doubt, fucking that little painter whore. Fucking The Catalyst. Sarah called his cell phone and left a blistering, drunken, accusatory howl of a message, which she regretted almost as soon as she hung up and even more so in the sober light of the next morning.

The nights were the worst. When the pills didn't work and she lay alone in that vast bed with a leaden writhing in her gut, waiting for the dawn. Sometimes she would stretch a leg across and feel the creaseless cold space that howled of her husband's absence. After the first few weeks, to assert herself, she tried moving into the middle. But it felt wrong, somehow too final, as if by doing so she was admitting that he would never come back. Because he would come back, she knew he would. He couldn't just have left her like that, left his home and his children, could he? Could he?

He flew up from Kansas the week before Christmas to see the kids and bring their presents. He bought each of them a cell phone, so they could always call him, he said, which prompted a scornful laugh from Abbie. Like hell, she said. As if.

He stayed with a friend in the city and took the kids

out for dinner. He wanted Sarah to come too but she wouldn't and it was all she could do to persuade Abbie to go. The poor kid came home afterward in a flood of tears and ran straight to her room. Joshie sat wearily at the kitchen table and told Sarah that Abbie hadn't spoken a civil word the whole evening, just sat there spitting venom at her father across the table and making sarcastic remarks.

Out in the store now, she could hear Jeffrey saying good-bye to his customer and a few moments later he appeared in the office doorway, holding his hands to his head in disbelief.

"Did you hear that?"

"You were wonderful."

"I think we should give this up and open a record store."

"Oh yeah?"

"Then at least when people came in who didn't know the title or the artist or publisher, they could at least try *humming* the damn thing."

Sarah laughed. He nodded at the computer screen.

"How's it looking, boss?"

"Dismal. Let's sell records instead."

"That's not the right answer. You're supposed to say, 'Well, Jeffrey, in the circumstances, bearing in mind the state of the industry, the intensive competition, the proliferation of alternative media and other leisure entertainment opportunities or, in plainer English, the fact that nobody under thirty gives a damn about books anymore or wants to do anything that might require more than the attention span of your average hyperactive gnat, bearing all that in mind, we've done pretty goddamn well, thank you, Jeffrey.'"

"Bravo."

He bent toward her and gave her a kiss on the forehead.

"Let's close and go have a nice lunch someplace," he said.

"Good idea. And I'll have one of your cigarettes."

The theme of the day was "Express Your Humanness." At least, that's what Ben thought the woman in the leotard and red sarong had said, right at the beginning, when they were standing in that big circle, all barefooted and holding hands. He hadn't been able to hear too well because he was standing in front of a big electric fan that was blowing his hair all over the place. It might have been "Express Your Humorousness." But that wasn't, as far as he was aware, a proper word, so he was settling for "Humanness." Not that what some of those around him were doing wasn't humorous. Particularly the old guy with the gray beard, who was dressed up in purple robes and a turban, like some spaced-out elder of the Taliban, spinning all over the room with his eyes closed and pressing a bell pepper to his chest. Maybe he hadn't heard the woman's instruction, either, and was hedging his bets.

It was called "Body Choir." And Eve and Lori came here every Sunday afternoon, along with fifty or sixty like-minded souls, to express in dance and movement whatever was on the menu. The venue was a big hall with a high ceiling and a sprung wooden floor. It was right beside the railroad, so close that even when the music was playing loudly, the whole place shuddered when the trains went by.

The music was strictly new age, a lot of breaking waves and whale calls. Ben had always wondered why whale talk was always assumed to be soothing and blissful when nobody knew what the hell the creatures were saying to one another. Surely whales had fights like everybody else? Maybe they were actually yelling at each other. *You miserable humpback bastard, that's the last plankton you're ever gonna get from me. Oh, get a life, go blow some air.*

At this moment, Lori was over on the other side of the room, expressing her humanness, and perhaps a little more, with an irritatingly good-looking young guy with a ponytail. He had taken his top off, which men apparently were allowed to do but women weren't, at least, not for several weeks now, since a voluptuous Swede called Ulrika displayed her assets and a poor guy who'd had a triple bypass collapsed and had to be carried outside. Even in Santa Fe, self-expression apparently had its limits.

Another rule was that the dancing was supposed to be noncontact. But some seemed either not to know this or not to care. Several couples were writhing on the floor, so intricately entwined that it was hard to figure out which limbs belonged to whom. Ben feared for their disentanglement. They were going to end up like a knot nobody could untie. Someone would have to call the fire department.

Most people, however, like Ben, were dancing on their own. Now and then someone would sidle up and smile and dance with him for a while and then sidle off somewhere else. Eve was about ten yards away at this moment, dancing sinuously with her eyes closed and a little half-smile on her face. She was wearing a cropped white linen top and some tight red breeches that showed her hips and tummy and she looked so damn sexy, Ben's humanness was longing to express itself in a way that would have to wait.

She had been worried about bringing him along here today, saying she didn't know if it was really his kind of scene. Maybe she thought he might mock it or would be too uptight and self-conscious to take part. She kidded him that he would have to wear a leotard or at least some spandex shorts. As it turned out, he wasn't, by a long way, the oldest or straightest-looking person there and, in his gray T-shirt and faded blue jeans, he didn't feel too out of place.

For the first ten or fifteen minutes, after they all started dancing, Eve had stayed close and kept glancing at him to gauge his reaction. He wasn't the world's greatest dancer and the whole thing was, he had to admit, pretty hilarious. But he was trying to enter into the spirit of it and was almost enjoying himself. He just wished he could relax more, go with the flow, clear his head a little.

This was his third visit to Santa Fe since leaving

272

Sarah and the longest so far. Outside, the snow had gone. There was almost a hint of spring. He had been here two whole weeks now and, though he didn't quite know why—for it would be so easy to stay—he felt it was time to be going back to Kansas. They were lovers now, and at last it was okay between them. More than okay. They were in that heady, breathless state when they couldn't keep their hands off each other. He had never dared dream it might happen so quickly.

Two months ago, back in December, he had called her from his mother's in Abilene and told her in a shaky voice that he had done it, he'd left. And there was this long pause, several momentous seconds, and then she said, quietly, "Come."

And he drove down that very night, five hundred miles, through the fog and the snow, across the plains and icy slivers of Oklahoma and western Texas, and arrived just after dawn and found her house and tapped on the door. She was wearing a black woolen wrap over a white nightdress and her face was all worried and pale as the dawn. But she took him inside and stood there and held him. And he didn't want to, he'd promised himself not to—because how could she, how could any woman, want a man so raw and weak and wretched— but he couldn't help himself and began to weep. And she held him. For a long time, just stood and held him.

Then she sat him down at the kitchen table and made coffee and some poached eggs and wheat toast and sat watching him eat with her elbows on the table and her chin cupped in her hands, staring at him and gently smiling. It was as though neither of them could quite believe he was there. Then little Pablo, three and a half years old, whom Ben had never yet met, emerged from his room in his pajamas and sat at the table too and started talking to him as if it were the most natural thing in the world to find him there.

But then, when big things happened, people rarely behaved the way you'd expected. Ben's mother and sister to name but two. Right or—more probably—wrong, he had felt he couldn't tell either of them over the phone that he had left Sarah. He had to tell them in person. He called his mother from New York to say he was coming to stay and, of course, she was thrilled. The night he arrived she cooked his favorite pot roast dinner, just for the two of them.

Naturally, Ben knew she would be upset at what he had to tell her. Any mother would be. But she had always so adored him and believed in him, affirming his every action and decision, even those he knew himself to be wrong, that her reaction that night, when finally after supper he broke the news, took him completely by surprise. She was distraught, furious, coruscating. She even struck him on the arm. How could he leave his wife and children? How *could* he?

"You made a promise!" she wailed through her tears, which seemed shed as much in anger as in grief. "A promise! You go back, Benjamin. Do you hear me? You go back! You made a promise!"

Eventually she calmed down and wept as he tried gently to explain why he had left. Not that it was possible, without telling her things he had no wish to hear himself say or, for that matter, share with anyone, least of all his mother. He spoke instead in coded clichés, saying that *for many years now,* although they had put a *brave face* on it, he and Sarah had not been *happy together,* that things hadn't been *good between them,* that they had both *changed* and *grown apart.* And at last these homilies seemed, if not to convince her, at least to soften her to a kind of sad acceptance that the deed was done and that no amount of chiding would undo it. All she wanted, she said through her tears, all she had ever wanted, was for him to be happy.

If his mother's reaction surprised him, his sister's nearly blew him off his feet. He drove to Topeka to have lunch with her the following day. Sally was five years his senior, enough to ensure that as children they had never really gotten to know each other. Aware he was the object of his mother's blatant favoritism, he had always treated his sister a little delicately, as if she might, justifiably, resent him. He was relieved, on those rare occasions when he saw her, that she didn't seem to. Not yet, anyhow.

Sally was what used to be called a handsome, rather than a pretty or beautiful, woman. She had their father's intense brown eyes and heavy brows. She was taller than she seemed to want to be and stooped a little, as if she were carrying some invisible load on her shoulders. She had married an accountant named Steven, a man so momentously boring that Abbie had even christened a verb for him. To be *Stevened* by someone or something or to feel *Steved out* or *totally Steved* had long been absorbed into their lexicon of family slang. Sally and Steve had two children who sadly seemed to have scooped most of their genes from their father's end of the pool. Both had become accountants.

Ben had expected to take her out to a restaurant but instead Sally had prepared lunch for them in her trim kitchen, with its lace curtains and collection of ceramic frogs on the windowsill. Steve was at work, so it was just them and the frogs. Again, Benjamin waited until the meal—grilled pork chops followed by lemon meringue pie—was over before telling her his news. He knew as he spoke, from the way her eyes were narrowing, that he wasn't going to get away lightly. When he finished, there was an ominous, quivering silence.

"What gives *you* the right?" she hissed.

"How do you mean?"

"What gives you the right! To leave."

"Well—"

"I mean, we're *all* unhappy! Every couple I know. I don't know of a single goddamned marriage that I could put my hand on my heart and say was happy."

Ben shrugged and shifted a little on his chair.

"Do *you* know of any?"

"Well—"

"Do you? I mean, really happy? I don't. It's part of the package, Benjamin, you idiot! Get real! Do you think Mom and Dad were *happy?* Do you?"

"Well—"

"Of course they weren't! Nobody is. But that doesn't

276

mean you just up and leave. Oh my, I'm *so* unhappy, boo-hoo, so hey, I'll just walk out on my wife and my kids. For Christsake, Ben, get real!"

Ben felt paralyzed with shock. But she hadn't finished. In fact, she'd barely started. She went on to give him a scorching lecture about how he was a victim of this ridiculous, upside-down consumer culture in which everyone was constantly being bombarded with the pernicious promise of happiness and, even worse, being told at every turn that they had the goddamn *right* to be happy. And if they weren't, they could be, if they just got themselves a new car or a new dishwasher or a new outfit or a new lover. The messages were everywhere, Sally said, in every magazine you picked up, on every dumb TV show, fueling greed and envy, making people dissatisfied with what they had, persuading them they could change it and be *happy* and successful and beautiful, if only they had some gorgeous new *thing* or a new girlfriend or a new face or a new pair of silicone tits . . .

If he hadn't been so amazed or so starkly implicated in the diatribe, Ben might have given her a standing ovation. As it was, he lowered his eyes and nodded and tried to look suitably admonished. And half an hour later, having twice denied that there was somebody else, somebody *new,* for by now he was too scared to admit it, he kissed her good-bye and walked to the front gate with a stoop in his shoulders that almost matched hers. Not *Steved* but thoroughly and ignominiously *Sallied.*

The dancing was over now and the Body Choristers were all in a circle again, only this time they were sitting on the floor with their eyes closed, silently holding hands. Ben was holding hands with the whirling Taliban who seemed to have taken something of a shine to him. He was wondering where the guy had put his pepper.

After another twenty minutes or so, during which anybody who wanted to could share thoughts about how it had been for him or for her, the session broke up. Everybody put their shoes back on and Lori came over and gave Ben a hug and then Eve arrived and they both gave her a hug.

"Was that good?" she asked him nervously.

"Terrific."

She gave him a skeptical look.

"No, honestly. I really enjoyed myself."

He put an arm around her shoulders and she put hers around his waist. She smelled all warm and sweaty and delicious. Lori was standing there, assessing them, beaming at them.

"You know something?" she said. "You guys look so great together. You even look like each other."

"Is that a compliment?" Ben and Eve said at the same time.

"Yes."

Pablo had gone to stay with his father for the weekend, so they had the house to themselves. Ben lit a fire in the arched stone fireplace in the bedroom while Eve made them some green tea whose taste he was at last beginning to like. The late winter sun was angling onto the white quilt of the bed through the window and filling the room with a soft amber glow. They slowly undressed each other, nuzzling each other's necks like cats as they did so, then lowered themselves onto the wedge of light that lay athwart the bed. Her skin tasted of salt and he kissed her shoulders and her breasts and beneath her arms and traveled the long hollowed curve of her belly with his hand and found her warm and open.

The fear that had blighted their first couplings was banished now, confined to a shadowed recess of his mind. There were times, still, when it would try to summon him, with whispers of inadequacy and plangent taunts of guilt and betrayal. But whereas once he would have paid heed and answered and wiltingly gone, now he could usually block the sound from his ears. Had Eve not been so patient with him, so forgiving and apparently unfazed by his early failures as a lover, he would long ago have crawled away in shame. But she seemed to understand and hushed the faltering self-pity of his efforts to explain.

Inside her now, a stranger still to her shape and feel, he watched the pale tilt of her chin, her parted lips, the shuttered lashes of her eyes beyond, her hair thrown like a spill of ink across the pillow and the shadow of their conjoined selves moving slowly, slowly, on the roseate rough plaster of the wall. He was here now, with her. He was here.

SIXTEEN

I t was less than a year since she had last been here. But like so much else in Abbie's life, during those months the place had been utterly transformed. She and Ty were standing their horses on the crest of the same bluff where they had ridden with his father two summers before and watched the golden eagle soaring above the river. They had ridden here by the same route, loping through the sage on the same two horses. But that was where any similarity ended. The landscape over which they now looked out belonged to a bleaker planet.

"My God," she murmured.

"I said you wouldn't know the place."

Even the mountains, on this close, gray May morning seemed altered, darker, more broodingly distant. The river was low and ashen and its banks looked as if they had been sluiced with whitewash. Downstream, where the breaks had once babbled and sparkled among the willow scrub, there was now a desert of shingle and baked mud, all patched with white where the salt water had dried. The water that had killed the Hawkins' colts and the cattle.

"See the cottonwoods down along there? By now they should all be in leaf. They're dead. Every last one of them. We figured they might make it, but they haven't. And down there? Where Dad took you to see those colts? This time of year those meadows would be so thick with flowers you couldn't walk through without getting your clothes all yellow. Look at it now."

It was arid and brown and crusted with salt, a few sorry tufts of bleached grass trying to cling on.

"Nothing'll grow down along there now. The hay fields up along have gone too. The river's poisoned and now the land is too. The water that's released from the drilling kills everything."

Abbie just sat there in the saddle, shaking her head.

"I can't believe it."

Ty laughed.

"Boy, you haven't seen the half of it. Come on, I'll show you."

He reined his horse around and urged it forward and they loped back the way they had come, past the gash of red rock and down through the sage. Instead of turning left to the ranch, they bore right and headed toward the mountains, up a winding valley, dotted on either side with boulders and gnarled limber pine, some of which, Ty's father had told her, were more than a thousand years old.

As they rode up the valley she could hear a rumbling sound that got louder and louder until they came around a bend and Ty eased his horse to a standstill and she rode slowly up alongside and stopped too.

"Well, there you go," he said. "Used to be good pasture. Now the topsoil's gone, nothing's going to grow here, even when they're gone."

Up ahead of them, a wide dirt road had been gouged across the entire width of the valley and the far side of it was a sea of dried-out mud, churned and rutted with tire tracks. There were power lines and pipes and a cluster of white-topped cement plinths that Ty said were the wellheads.

The rumbling noise was coming from some low white-walled buildings with generators and drilling rigs and some strange-looking trucks parked beside them, all surrounded by a chain-link fence, posted with signs saying *Danger* and *Keep Out.* Ty said this was a compressor station and that there were others, farther on, and tanks too where the water released by the drilling was supposed to be contained. Which was a joke, he said, because they were always leaking and overflowing. And they were poorly fenced too, so that keeping horses and livestock away was a nightmare. Just one of many, he added wryly.

It was the weekend, so there was nobody about. But any other day, he said, they would be dodging trucks every few minutes and wouldn't be able to see the place for dust.

"This is where Daddy used to hold his horse clinics. He always said, with the mountains up yonder and the forest and all, it was the prettiest place on the ranch and if ever anyone started moaning about how much he was charging, as soon as they got up here, they'd stop. One woman once said she'd pay that much for the view alone."

He looked away and went quiet for a while. Abbie could guess what he was thinking about.

She had been able to tell from his tone of voice on the

phone two days ago that something was wrong. At first she assumed he was just acting all hurt because it had been so long since she had last called him. The truth was that the only person she ever called these days was her mom. Since going back to school after that god-awful trip to Mustique, she had become something of a hermit. She never went out and her friends, all except Mel, had by now virtually given up on her. She had buried herself in her studies, holed up day after day in her room or in the college library, reading about how the world was being ruined. Getting angry seemed to help her feel less sorry for herself. But hearing what Ty had been through made her feel selfish and guilty. On the phone, when she'd asked him what was wrong, there was a long pause and then he told her quietly that his father had suffered a stroke.

Abbie had bought a used car with the money her grandpa had given her for that very purpose for Christmas, a little dark blue Toyota, and she drove it to Sheridan the very next day to see him. She knew she wouldn't remember the way on the gravel roads out to the ranch so they arranged to meet at the Best Western. He looked pale and drawn and hugged her so hard and for such a long time that she knew he was at the very edge of himself.

He said he ought to tell her what had happened before they went out to the ranch, because he didn't want his mom to have to hear it, so they walked along Main Street and found a little plaza and sat together on a bench. There was a bronze statue of a cowboy there, with long hair and chaps and a rifle resting across his shoulder, as if he might at any moment have cause to use it, and Ty stared at him while he told her what had happened.

It was in February, he said. Just a couple of weeks after the bulldozers moved in and started cutting the road. His mom and dad had refused to sign the surface-damage agreement that McGuigan Gas & Oil had sent them. Instead they had hired an attorney and were asking for further assurances about putting the land back the way it was.

Then one morning, unannounced, two guys drove up to the ranch house and said the diggers would be arriving the following day and that within the week they'd be drilling. The attorney did what he could but it was hopeless, Ty said. Like talking to the deaf. The gas company just didn't want to know. Next day, as promised, in came the bulldozers and soon the whole place was a quagmire.

"They had these guys working up there, ten or twelve of them, some crew they'd brought up from Mexico, all of them illegal. And McGuigan didn't bring in any kind of backup, not even portable toilets, so these guys were up there, just doing their business out in the meadow. Dirty toilet paper blowing all over the place, even down at the house. It was just plain revolting.

"Dad and I would go up and try and reason with them but most of them didn't even speak English and even the ones that did said it had nothing to do with them and we should call the office, but nobody there wanted to

284

talk to us either. And all the while Mom's just, you know, crying her eyes out, breaking her heart . . .

"Anyhow. Eventually, Dad managed to get hold of J. T. McGuigan himself on the phone, the CEO or president or whatever the hell he calls himself. Down in Denver. And this guy starts yelling and saying Dad only has himself to blame, that he should have signed the goddamn surface-damage agreement.

"He flew up two days later and there was this meeting at the attorney's office and McGuigan, who turns out to be this big bull of a fella, ex-Marine or some such, starts hollering and poking his finger at Mom and Dad . . . Hell, Abbie, I should have been there, but I had to be in Bozeman that week.

"So, Mom's real upset and Dad's trying to calm her down and all. And she keeps saying to McGuigan, *You can't do this, you can't do this to us.* And it all goes quiet and he walks right up to her and points his finger in her face and says, *Listen lady, let me try and explain. It's like you and I are married. I can do whatever the hell I like to you, whenever or wherever I choose, and you just have to go along with it.*

"And that same night, Dad had his stroke."

As they walked back to their vehicles Ty told her that his father had come home from the hospital about a month ago but that he had lost the power of speech and was pretty well paralyzed.

"Just sits there all day in front of the TV. He never used to watch it but it's hard to know what else to do with him. We talk to him, read him things. We reckon he knows what we're saying and that he's still in there somewhere, locked up inside himself, though sometimes . . ." Ty stopped for a moment and swallowed. "Sometimes, I kind of hope he isn't."

"How's your mom?" Abbie asked softly, realizing as she said it what a dumb question it was.

"Kind of how you'd expect."

Just as Ty had said, when they got up to the ranch house, his father was slumped in his chair, staring at the TV. Abbie said hello but his eyes didn't even flicker. It was a wildlife documentary film. A pack of hyenas was trying to snatch a little warthog from its mother. Martha gave Abbie a big hug and welled up but managed not to cry. Over supper they kept up a brave and brittle cheeriness, Martha asking Abbie all kinds of questions about college and telling her how bad she felt that Ty had given up his studies at Montana State. Maybe Abbie could persuade him to go back, she said.

"Oh, Mom," Ty said wearily. On the TV, the hyenas were having their supper too now.

"The thing is, Abbie, he thinks he's indispensable and that his poor old mother can't run this place without him."

"I do not."

They changed the subject. Then Martha delicately asked after Abbie's mom. Ty had obviously kept her up to speed.

"She's okay, thanks. Doing a little better. She's started smoking, which is kind of strange. Hasn't done it for more than twenty years."

"Don't give her too much of a hard time."

"I'm not. It's her life."

"And your dad. How's he doing?"

"Okay, I guess. I don't really know."

Abbie nearly added that she didn't care either, but didn't.

He e-mailed her the whole time and though to begin with she had sent him short, mostly vitriolic replies, she now didn't bother. Three or four times a week he would call her cell phone but she usually just let it ring and then listened to his message, which was always the same bullshit. How much he loved her and missed her and wanted to talk with her and could he fly up and see her, maybe next weekend or the weekend after or any time that suited? And sometimes, just to get him off her back, she would take the call and say coldly that she was really busy and no, sorry, but it wasn't convenient for him to come, not that weekend nor any other foreseeable. She didn't know how long it would be before she would stop wanting to punish him. Maybe when the sound of his voice no longer made her seethe with a resentful anger. The fact that she missed him terribly only stoked it further. He had always been there for her, ever her staunchest supporter and mentor. And she loathed how weak and rudderless she felt without him.

Ty came to her room that night and though their lovemaking was laced with a mutual sorrow, it brought at least an obliterating comfort. Yet afterward she found she couldn't sleep and lay with her head on his chest listening to his soft snoring and, somewhere off in the darkness, the distant yipping of a coyote.

One of the ranch dogs had had a litter of puppies. Ty had found homes for all but three who were now some twelve weeks old. One of them, a scraggy little mutt with three white paws and a kink in his tail, took a shine to Abbie, just trailed around after her and wouldn't leave her alone. None had names, so Abbie called him Sox. Ty said she should take him back to Missoula with her but though she was tempted, she said no, she couldn't possibly.

She stayed for two days and on the second, when the gas men were back at work, she witnessed for herself the constant passage of trucks up the valley and the clouds of dust they churned. Ty said they were going to try to file suit against the company even though their attorney said they didn't stand a chance and might as well instead just sit there setting fire to hundred-dollar bills for the next two years.

The morning she left, Abbie said good-bye to Ray and kissed him on the forehead and he made a little noise as she did so, but she figured he was probably just trying to clear his throat. Martha made her promise to come back soon. Ty led the way in his old pickup back down into Sheridan and they parked up just short of the interstate to say good-bye.

From the passenger-side footwell of his truck he gently lifted out a cardboard box containing the puppy and a blanket and he put them on the backseat of the Toyota. Abbie tried to protest but he knew her too well and wouldn't take no for an answer. If it didn't work out, he said, all she had to do was bring the little critter back. He asked about her plans for the summer and Abbie said she hadn't really made any. She was probably going to hang around for a while in Missoula, find a job of some kind. Maybe go back home for a week or two to spend some time with her mom. Except, with Sox now, how exactly that was going to work out, she had no idea.

"Our kennel rates are pretty reasonable," Ty said.

He put his arms around her and held her awhile, neither of them speaking, just the roar of the trucks going by.

"I love you, Abbie."

It was the first time he'd said it to her, the first time anyone, except her mom and dad, had ever said it. And she nearly burst into tears but didn't, just hugged him and gave him a kiss. She felt bad for not saying she loved him too, but it wasn't true and she didn't want to lie. As she drove away, she saw him in the mirror, standing sadly by his truck, watching her leave. The puppy was already asleep.

The UM campus had that lazy, school's out and summer is a-coming feel about it. Even though the semester was officially over, nobody seemed to be in too much of a hurry to leave. The cottonwoods along the Clark Fork were in their best vibrant green, the weather clear and balmy, the very air abrim with promise. Students pedaled the dappled shade on bicycles or strolled the few blocks to Rockin' Rudy's to browse the records or to Bernice's Bakery or Break Espresso for iced mochas and bagels or simply sprawled in the sun on the lush spring grass of The Oval, chilling out and making plans.

Mel and Abbie had cleared all their stuff from their room in Knowles Hall and dumped most of it at Todd and Eric's house on 4th Street, where Abbie was staying until she figured out what she was going to do for the summer. Everybody else had made their plans weeks, even months, ago.

Mel and Scott had already left for Peru. They'd tried to persuade Abbie to join them but she wasn't going anywhere without Sox. Eric and Todd would any day now be heading down to Idaho where they had fixed themselves jobs as white-water raft guides on the Salmon River. After six weeks in plaster, Eric's hip had mended well and though he limped a little, he figured he would still be able to handle a raft with half a dozen people on it. Hell, he said, if Meryl Streep could do it, so could he. To torture the guests around the campfire, he was taking his new accordion.

Thus, by the beginning of June, Abbie and Sox had the house to themselves. The place clearly hadn't been cleaned in years, the windows so filthy you could barely see out. There wasn't even a vacuum cleaner, so Abbie borrowed one and spent the next three days cleaning and scrubbing. It made her feel like her mother but at least it kept her mind off things. On the third morning, just after Sox had discovered an entire fossilized pizza under the living-room couch, her phone rang. The caller's number was local, but one she didn't recognize.

"Housewives Anonymous?"

"Abbie?"

She almost hung up.

"Dad. Where are you?"

"I'm at the Holiday Inn."

"What, in Missoula? What are you doing here?"

"Abbie, you know why. I've come to see you."

"But why didn't you let me know? It's just that, you know, at the moment, I'm kind of—"

"Abbie, sweetheart. Please."

He asked her where she was and could he come see her. For reasons she didn't herself fully understand, she didn't want him to. Probably it was just to hurt him, to deny him knowledge to which he might think a father had some right. She said she would meet him in the hotel lobby in an hour and hung up.

At once she regretted it and nearly called him back to say she wasn't coming. But she hadn't seen him in five whole months, not since that appalling dinner before Christmas. And she didn't want to make him think it was any big deal. No, she would go. Show him how little he figured in her life now.

It was at most a ten-minute walk across the bridge and she spent the other fifty in an accelerating spin, her heart racing, worrying about what she was going to say to him and how mean she should be. She took a shower and washed her hair and then spent at least twenty minutes trying to decide what to wear, all the while cursing herself for being so stupid because who cared? Really. What the hell did it matter? She put on a dress, then changed it for another, then settled for blue jeans and a white long-sleeved T-shirt.

Sox was getting pretty good at going for walks now. He didn't even really need a leash, just tucked in behind her. But the traffic on the bridge could be scary, so she put him on the leash to be safe.

She saw her dad before he saw her. In fact, once he looked straight at her but didn't recognize her, presumably because he didn't know about Sox or because she was wearing sunglasses and had cut her hair. He was standing outside under the big cement portico and a busload of guests had just arrived, so it was busy. He was thinner and his hair was longer. He kept nervously checking his watch. Then he saw her.

"Hey!"

He walked over to her and put his arms around her and kissed her and it took every atom of willpower she possessed not to succumb, not to dissolve and cling to him. But somehow she managed. All she gave him in return was a token hug. She wasn't going to give him more. No kiss, no tears. Nothing. He held her by the elbows to inspect her. Abbie could see that he was trying hard not to cry.

"How are you doing, baby?"

"Fine. How are you?"

"I'm good. All the better for seeing you. Hey! And who's this? Is he yours?"

"Uh-huh. He's called Sox."

He squatted to ruffle the dog's ears and Sox squirmed and jumped and kept trying to lick her dad's face.

"Hey, little fella, I already washed."

He suggested that maybe they could go have lunch somewhere but Abbie said that with the puppy that wasn't possible. Instead they walked up to North Higgins to buy sandwiches and juice, then came back down to Caras Park and sat on the grass looking over the river and had a picnic. There was a sculpture of some huge trout which for some reason seemed to spook Sox. He stood barking at them then saw a squirrel and chased it up a tree, below which he sat for the next half-hour, staring up at it with his head on one side and giving an occasional whimper.

Her dad asked her lots of questions about college and what she had been up to and she gave him flat, factual answers, not overtly rude, just cool. Informative enough, but utterly unembellished with anything that might be construed as enthusiasm or emotion. And she kept her sunglasses on so he couldn't see her eyes. She could tell that it was gradually getting to him, because after a while he seemed to run out of questions and the life to drain from his face and in the end he just stared out across the river, silently chewing his sandwich.

"So how's *your* new life?" she asked sourly.

He turned and looked at her for a few moments before he spoke.

"Abbie, I'm so sorry."

She gave a little laugh and looked away.

"I know how much I've hurt you. All of you."

"Oh, really?"

"Of course, I do."

"You know what? I don't think you've got the first fucking clue!"

"Abbie, come on—"

"No, *you* come on! You've destroyed us. Everything we had. And you think you can breeze up here and say a few nice little things and make it all better again. Well, you can't, okay? You fucking well can't."

She had never in her whole life sworn at him and the violence of the word shocked her as much as they clearly shocked him. Not to mention those around them. People were staring at them now and she was grimly gratified to see how that bothered him. Let them stare, let them hear, let the bastard squirm. She was close to tears now and abruptly stood up and strutted across the grass to gather Sox from his squirrel vigil beneath the tree. When she came back her dad was on his feet too.

"Sweetheart, please . . ."

"What?"

"We're not the first family this has ever happened to."

"Oh? And is that supposed to make us all feel better?"

"No, of course not. All I mean is that—"

"Dad, listen. You didn't tell me you were coming—"

"You'd have told me not to."

"Well, anyway, I've got to be somewhere."

"Really?"

"Yes. What, are you saying I'm lying or—"

"Then can we meet later, have dinner maybe?"

"Sorry, I can't."

He looked so crushed and wretched, she almost gave in. Almost.

"Abbie—"

"Dad, I've got to go, okay?"

With Sox cradled in her arms, she stepped toward him and gave him a peck on the cheek. He tried to hold her but she wouldn't let him and pulled away.

"Bye."

"Abbie . . ."

She turned and walked briskly toward the bridge and then up the steps to the street, without once looking back. She wondered if he might follow her and when she was halfway across the bridge she looked back and down toward where they had been. But he was walking slowly away across the park, his head bowed, going back to the hotel.

Later, when she had stopped crying, she called her mother and told her what had happened. She said how upsetting it had been and how unbelievable and selfish of him it was, just showing up like that, out of the blue. As if, after what he'd done, he could just snap his fingers and everyone had to come running. Her mom listened and made all the right noises, but Abbie had the impression that she wasn't being heard with quite the sympathy she deserved.

"I mean," she said, "don't you think it's amazing?"

"Honey, he's your dad."

"What?"

"He loves you very much. Maybe you should give him a break."

"Oh, like, you mean, *I'm* the one who's being unreasonable?"

Her mother sighed and in a weary voice said no. She tried to explain what she meant but Abbie didn't really want to listen. Jesus. For a woman to be making excuses for the guy who just walked out on her was surreal. What was she, some kind of doormat? Her mom changed the subject and asked if she was coming home soon. Abbie said she hadn't yet decided but would probably stay in Missoula and find a job.

"How about Josh and me coming out there to see you? We could go someplace nice together."

"Sure."

"Okay, well, let's both think about that. Oh, and I nearly forgot, some guy called for you, said you'd met in Seattle. Ralph, I think he said."

"Rolf."

"Rolf, that's it. He's calling back. Is it okay to give him your cell number?"

Abbie thought for a moment. He hadn't crossed her mind in months.

"Sure," she said. "I don't mind."

SEVENTEEN

E verybody was crowded against the rail on the right-hand side of the boat—the port side. Or was it starboard? Josh could never remember if it depended on which way you were facing. A lot of people had brought binoculars and just about all of them had cameras. His dad had forgotten to bring either, which, as far as Josh was concerned, was cool. Some idiots were even taking photos right now, of absolutely nothing, just a wide expanse of ocean on which the only signs of life were three other stationary boats crammed with similar idiots. You could see the pathetic little flashes of their cameras. As if that would be enough to light the tail of a whale half a mile away. In the unlikely event of one ever deciding to surface. Josh imagined these people back home showing friends their vacation pictures. *And here's one of the ocean with nothing in it. And here's another . . . and another.* The whole thing was probably just one big scam anyhow. They'd been out here for two hours already and seen nothing but a few bored seagulls. There probably hadn't been a single whale sighted off Cape Cod for a hundred years.

"Over here! Look!"

Somebody behind them on the other side of the boat—there was always some smartass—was yelling and pointing and everyone turned and then started to run toward him. Josh had even considered playing the trick himself, waiting until everybody's back was turned and then yelling *Thar she blows!* And they'd turn and he'd say *Suckers!* or *Aw shucks, you just missed it.* He looked at his dad and the two of them exchanged an amused grimace.

"Sorry," his dad said. "Not exactly heart-stopping is it?"

"It's cool."

They strolled after the others.

It had been a strange few days. Just the two of them spending all this time together. It wasn't something they had ever done before. Vacations had always been the four of them, like at The Divide, and at first it had felt odd not to have Abbie or his mom around. His dad at first had seemed stiff and awkward, as if he didn't really know what they should do or even talk about.

The original idea had been for Josh to fly to Kansas and see his grandma, then go on to Santa Fe and spend some time with his dad and Eve. Even though it might have been a little strange seeing the two of them together, Josh would have felt okay about it. In fact, he was quite interested. But his mom had totally freaked at the idea, so his dad had changed plans and instead rented a ramshackle house on Cape Cod, just on the edge of Provincetown. It was big enough to sleep about eight or ten people. Maybe it was the only place he could get or maybe he had been hoping Abbie and her new boyfriend might at the last minute change their minds and come.

They had never been to the Cape before and Josh

didn't think he'd be hurrying back. Provincetown turned out to be a big vacation place for gays—which was absolutely fine by him—but in the evenings, when he and his dad went out for dinner and walked down the street together, Josh kept imagining people were staring at them. Especially when his dad, as he sometimes liked to, draped an arm over his shoulders. Josh felt like carrying a placard saying *Listen, it's my dad, okay?*

Even driving up here they seemed soon to run out of things to talk about, at least those trivial or neutral things that had nothing to do with the separation or—as apparently it was soon to be, once the papers or whatever had gone through—divorce. It was kind of dumb, like an elephant was sitting in the room and everybody was too scared to mention it. They talked about school, about friends, about Josh's college plans for next year (he didn't much want to go anywhere, as a matter of fact, but at gunpoint he would probably try for NYU). He knew his dad would much rather be talking about what had happened to them all, but for at least the first couple of days, he didn't seem to know how to raise the subject. Josh nearly said, "Dad, it's cool, go for it, let's talk, I don't mind." But he didn't, just watched the poor guy fidget and twist himself up into ever tighter knots until the only topics of conversation they had left were the weather and a whole list of boring things he had picked up from his Cape Cod travel guide.

"Apparently Norman Mailer has a house here," his dad said one morning while they were having breakfast in the squalid little kitchen. The place smelled like something furry had died under the floorboards.

"Who's Norman Mailer?"

"Josh, you really don't know? Your mother would be appalled."

Josh shrugged.

"Is he, like, some famous gardener or something?"

"He's one of America's greatest writers."

"What did he write?"

There was a long pause, then his dad gave a slow, sheepish smile.

"You know, son, I can't remember a single book he wrote."

"Did you read them?"

"Never. Not one. Don't you dare tell your mother."

Finally, last night, they'd gotten around to mentioning the elephant. And it was good. The only thing was, his dad kept asking him how he *felt* and didn't seem to believe it when Josh said he was fine, really he was. It was as if what his dad wanted to hear was that he felt totally screwed up and needed therapy. That he was putting on some big front, just to be cool or brave, and that underneath he was tearing himself apart with hurt and anger.

But it wasn't like that. Of course, seeing his mom so upset all the time was tough and sometimes really pretty heavy, like that night a couple of weeks ago in Montana, when she broke down with Abbie and Josh had to sit there on the bed and hold them both while they wailed and sobbed their eyes out.

But the truth was, he wasn't angry with his dad. He just felt sorry for him. The poor guy had left because apparently he wasn't happy, but leaving didn't seem to have made him any happier. Sometimes, when Josh glanced at him and caught him in an unguarded moment, his face was as long as a shovel. Of course, Josh felt sad about what had happened, but it didn't make him angry or even resentful. In fact, he worried that this meant there must be something wrong with him, that he was somehow emotionally deficient. Perhaps he should be feeling what Abbie was feeling. Perhaps he should be spending this week screaming abuse at the guy, telling him what a disgrace he was, what a terrible father and husband and example he was.

But Josh didn't feel that way. It was all so goddamn confusing, he couldn't figure out what he *did* feel. Except a little ashamed and guilty sometimes. Because, if he was absolutely honest, he didn't really mind too much that his dad had left. Wasn't that a shocking thing to admit? But it was true. Apart from the fact that it had made everybody else so unhappy, Josh didn't actually *care*.

In a way, if anything, it had made his life better. He wasn't in his dad's shadow anymore. The guy wasn't there, on his case the whole time, telling him to go easy on the weed and not to drink or stay out too late. Or giving him a hard time over some paper he hadn't handed in on time. Suddenly, from troublesome teenager, he had been transformed into man of the house. He was the pillar now, the rock, the one who fixed the fuses and chopped the wood and shoveled the snow off the porch.

Of course, Josh didn't so much as hint at any of this when they talked last night in the little restaurant where they had ended up going almost every night because everywhere else was too noisy and crowded. On the one hand his dad might have been happy to hear it, of course. On the other, it might have upset him to discover he wasn't too badly missed or, in truth, missed at all. So Josh sat there and listened while his dad kept apologizing and then did his best to answer all those questions about his mom and Abbie and how they were doing, trying to give it as positive a gloss as possible so the poor guy wouldn't beat himself up even more. Because what was the point in telling him how broken and wretched the two of them really were? And how weird was that? There was Josh, still a year to go in high school, playing the rock, the man of the family, even with his dad, for heavensakes.

The week he and his mom had spent with Abbie had been about as much fun as one of those asthma attacks he used to get when he was little. Josh hadn't seen his sister since the beginning of the year, when they came back from Mustique (which would forever be engraved on his heart as the place he had at long last lost his virginity under the palm trees to the luscious Katie Bradstock). The change was pretty staggering. Abbie had cut her hair all short and dyed it black and was dressed like something that had crept out of a crypt. His mom was brilliant. She hardly batted an eye, even told her how nice she looked. Abbie was clearly a little disappointed.

But it wasn't just her appearance. It was how she now talked and what she talked about. Her every sentence was peppered with swear words. The whole week she never stopped going on and on about how the world and everything in it was fucked and beyond hope. How the big corporations were fucking everything up, the rivers, the forests, the entire fucking planet. And we were all going along with it and happily letting them.

It started the moment they flew into Missoula when she gave their mom a hard time for renting an SUV. It was something they had always done in Montana and never before had Abbie questioned it. As their dad used to say, in the West, unless you drove a truck, you weren't getting your money's worth.

"Do you have any idea how much fucking gas these things burn?" she said.

"No, honey," their mom said calmly. "How much fucking gas do they burn?"

"You get, like what, twelve miles to the gallon? And do you know how much carbon dioxide and other shit they pump into the atmosphere?"

"I imagine it must be quite a lot or you wouldn't be so upset."

Josh suggested Abbie should chill out a little, which was a big mistake and had precisely the opposite effect. She flew into such a rage that their mom went quietly back to the Hertz desk and rented a Subaru instead.

There was no way they could go stay at The Divide. There were too many bad memories for their mom, though Abbie said later that they ought to have gone just to exorcise the ghosts and give the finger to their dad. Instead they had booked into a god-awful dude ranch called the Lazy Spur, an hour out of Missoula. The food was grim, the people grimmer, and the horses were about a hundred years old and kept trying to bite everyone. Abbie had brought Sox along and paid no attention to the rule that dogs weren't allowed in the rooms or anywhere else on the ranch. She and the owner got into a big fight about it and probably would have come to blows if their mom hadn't stepped in to negotiate a compromise.

Their mom figured some of Abbie's anger and much of her new dark view of the world must have something to do with her new boyfriend, the German guy she had met in Seattle. Josh thought he sounded pretty cool and was sad they didn't get to see him. Rolf traveled a lot, Abbie said, and that week was up in Eugene, Oregon, visiting with friends. She later let it slip that actually he had come back to Missoula two days before Josh and his mom were due to fly home.

"Can't we at least meet him?" his mom asked. "Just to say hello?"

"He doesn't do that kind of thing," Abbie said.

"He doesn't say hello?"

"He doesn't do, you know, the meet-the-parents thing. All that bourgeois shit."

"Ah. Well, you do it for us, okay? Say hi from the bourgeois shits."

"Yeah, right."

After the Lazy Spur and a week of Abbie's anger, Cape Cod with his dad had turned out to be almost fun. Whale-watching was hard to avoid if you were staying in Provincetown because there wasn't much else to do, especially when the weather was so miserable and the house had no TV and there wasn't a single movie on anywhere that you hadn't already seen. Come to think of it, maybe that was why there weren't any whales around, not even gay ones. They'd all gotten too bored and gone off someplace else.

Just as the thought slid by, somebody at the rail hollered and everybody started babbling and craning their necks and looking through their binoculars.

"There, look!" the woman yelled. "At ten o'clock!"

For a second Josh didn't know what she meant and had a sudden fear that they might all have to stay out here another five hours but then he realized she was giving the direction. And now he could see it. It was three or four hundred yards away and about the size of an ant, a black lump slowly rising from the water.

"Look! Look at him spouting!"

Then the captain, or chief whale-watcher or whoever he was, woke up and started telling everybody over the loudspeaker what they'd already seen for themselves. It was a right whale, he said, which was the name the whalers had given it on account of its blubber being so rich in oil. In other words, it was the right one, the best one to kill, a name the poor old whale must have been pretty proud of, Josh imagined, until he figured out the implications.

He felt his dad's hand on his back now.

"Well, there you go, Joshie. Worth the wait, huh?"

For a moment Josh thought he was being serious, then saw the grin.

"Absolutely."

"What do we think about the whales, save them or not?"

"I think . . . save them."

The creature was diving now, its great tail hanging there in the air for a moment, then slowly sinking in a surge of foam. And that was the last they saw of it. The darned thing never came up again. But it had made scores of people's day and they all sailed home with smiles on their faces, their lives just a fraction enhanced.

They drove back home the next day, chatting and listening to music and occasionally stopping, with appropriately affectionate jokes at Abbie's expense, for both Starbucks and McDonald's. Their talk about the elephant two nights ago seemed to have loosened things up between them and Josh felt, for the first time in as long as he could remember, totally relaxed in his father's company.

"I know it'll be awhile," his dad said as they stood by the car, waiting for the ferry to take them over to Long Island. "But sometime I'd really love you to come down to Santa Fe and, you know, meet Eve properly."

"I'd like that."

Neither of them said anything for a few moments, just stood there watching the boats out on the Sound, the seabirds whirling, the ferry coming in.

"Are you guys going to get married?"

His dad laughed. Josh didn't know why. Just nervous maybe.

"It's too early, Joshie. Your mom and I aren't even divorced yet."

"I know, but you and Eve are, kind of, living together, aren't you?"

"I'm staying with her now, while I look for a place of my own."

"Are you going to work down there?"

"I hope so, Josh. I'm talking to some people, got one little job going. I want to get back to designing houses. It's what I always enjoyed doing, but for some reason I stopped. Got a little lost, I guess."

He seemed to drift off into his thoughts. Down by the water a Stars and Stripes was billowing in the breeze, the hoist wire clinking against the pole.

"Maybe I should think about becoming an architect," Josh said. He didn't really mean it. He just wanted to please his dad and it was the first thing that popped into his head.

"Really?"

"Yeah."

"That's great, Joshie. I had no idea. You used to draw well. And what was that game you were always playing on your computer?"

"SimCity."

"That's it. Boy, you were so good at that."

"I still play it sometimes."

"You do?"

He put a hand on Josh's shoulder.

"I think you'd make a fine architect."

As they drove closer to Syosset, their conversation faded. Even in the late-afternoon sunshine, the shadow of their fractured home seemed to reach out and silence them. Josh led the way into the house and his mom made a big fuss of him without once looking at his dad, who had slunk in behind and was standing there, timidly waiting. At last, after she had asked Josh a hundred questions about the trip and told him that his hair needed a wash, she turned and looked toward his dad and gave him this funny, formal little smile.

"Hi," she said.

"Hi, sweetheart."

They touched cheeks. Like a pair of glancing icebergs.

"We saw a whale," Josh said. It was the sort of thing a four-year-old might say.

"You did?"

"Yeah. It was a right whale."

"Well, hey, I'm sure glad it wasn't a wrong one."

Josh picked up his bag and at the foot of the stairs turned and looked back. His dad smiled and gave him a peace sign.

"Almost peace, man."

And with his one and a half fingers, Josh replied.

He took his bag up to his room and left his parents standing like strangers in the hallway. He heard his mom say something in a hushed and angry voice and then his dad wearily replying. It was about some letter she had received from his lawyers. Josh didn't want to know. He put on some music and called Freddie on his cell phone to ask him what everyone was doing that night and did he have something good to smoke.

EIGHTEEN

T he sad thing about it was that you never really got to see the full glory of your labors. You had to sneak in, set things up, and then get the hell out as fast as you could without being seen. The whole idea was that by the time the place went up in flames you were out of town and miles away. Of course, you got to see the pictures of the charred remains in the newspapers the next day, but it wasn't the same as seeing the whole thing go boom.

The part Abbie liked best was spraying slogans on the walls and across those big showroom windows. This was basically her job, while Rolf set the fire. It was one long rush of adrenaline, knowing that at any moment some security guard could come strolling around the corner. She had gotten quite inventive with what she wrote. Her best efforts to date were *Fat Lazy Polluters* and *SUVs = U.S. GREED*, which had a kind of rhyming thing going. Rolf said she shouldn't get too clever in case people missed the message. For example, *Despoilers* and *American Avarice* were too obscure, he said. He also made her vary what she wrote and the style she wrote it in, so the cops would think there were a whole lot more cells operating than there really were. The only thing it was important to keep repeating was *ELF.* Or better still, if time and space allowed, spell it out in full: *Earth Liberation Front.*

The one thing he was really strict about was not spending too long at the location. Hanging around was how you got yourself caught, he said, so Abbie didn't argue. He was probably the first person in her whole life whose instructions she felt happy to follow and whose every opinion she respected, usually without question. He knew so much, it was almost scary, like he had this amazing computer in his head. You could ask him absolutely anything—about politics or the environment or international affairs or the human rights record of the most obscure country you could think of—and he inevitably knew the answer. She loved to sit or lie beside him and just listen to him talk.

Abbie knew her awe and compliance had something to do with his being ten years older than she was. And it obviously also had something to do with what was going on between them sexually. From the very first time, he had completely blown her away. His body was so lithe and beautiful. She let him do things to her that she could never have imagined she might like. Things that, had anyone told her about them before, would have shocked, even disgusted, her. It was as though he had unlocked in her some secret room to which she now went willingly and unbidden.

Of course, she wasn't dumb. She knew he'd found her at a time when she was vulnerable and almost driving herself crazy with rage and grief. But in a few short months he had given her this incredible new sense of purpose, made her feel that she had some value again, convinced her that she, that they together, could have a real impact on the way the world was. And for all these things, whatever happened, she would always feel indebted.

They had spent the summer, except for the week her mom and Josh came out, either on the road or living at the house on 4th Street, which they'd had entirely to themselves. During that time they had hit two SUV dealerships—one in Sacramento and the other in Portland—burning a total of eighteen vehicles. Portland had been amazing. Apparently people could see the flames more than a mile away. It was on the front page of all the newspapers and even made the lead for a few hours on CNN. They watched it in a motel room just outside of Seattle where they holed up for two days, laughing and eating takeout and fucking until Abbie hurt so much she just couldn't go on and they curled up like wounded animals and slept.

Their most recent outing, two weeks ago, hadn't been such a success. They had driven down to Reno to burn some condos being built on land that was supposed to be protected. But something had gone wrong and the fire just fizzled out. Two of Abbie's best pieces of graffiti still made the local news, however. She had sprayed *Stop Raping Nature* and *You Build It, We Burn It*, which would have been a little more impressive if they actually had. Rolf had gotten really mad about the fire failing and had ever since been trying to figure out what went wrong. He normally used cotton rags soaked in diesel oil and a delayed ignition which was basically a cocktail of hair gel and granulated chlorine, the kind people used for cleaning swimming pools. He said he was going to find something better for next time.

Now it was late August and people were starting to drift back to Missoula. First Eric and Todd had showed up, then Mel and Scott, all bubbling with stories about their summer adventures and consoling Abbie because she'd been stuck in Missoula and must have had such a boring time. It was good to see them again and amusing to have such a secret. Everyone was nice to Rolf. But Rolf wasn't interested and as the house filled up, he just quietly removed himself. He said he had to go away for a few days. He never told her where he was going and she never asked, though this time she had a pretty good idea. While he was gone, he said, maybe she should try to find someplace else for them to live, just the two of them.

With the autumn semester about to start, it was late to be looking. Anywhere at all decent was already taken. After three days, Abbie found them a room in a run-down sprawl of a house on a corner of Helen Street. The building was clad in mildewed clapboard and the room itself was dark and smelled of damp. It was on the first floor but had its own entrance at the top of a rotting wooden fire escape which poor Sox at first had trouble negotiating. There was a bathroom the size of a closet and a kitchen area whose every surface was layered with grease. Mel helped her move her things in and then the two of them gave the place a thorough clean and a coat of white emulsion and for five dollars got some red-velvet drapes from the Salvation Army store on West Broadway. By the start of the following week, when Rolf called to say he was coming home, it almost felt like it.

He never said what time he would show up and, again, Abbie had learned not to ask. Sometimes he would arrive at five in the morning and just slip into bed beside her and make love to her. Today was the second day of classes and Abbie was supposed to have a two-hour biology lab which she decided to cut. With Sox in the wire basket behind her, she cycled over to the Good Food Store to buy something special for supper.

Rolf was a strict vegetarian and so now Abbie was too, though all her lofty principles could still be jeopardized by a waft of broiled chicken or bacon frying in a pan. She decided to make parmigiana, one of his favorite dishes. She bought tomatoes and basil and eggplant and buffalo mozzarella and Parmesan, all of it organic (which he wasn't quite so adamant about, but almost).

Hacker was giving a party that night and Mel called and tried to persuade her to come. She said the whole gang was going. Why not bring Rolf along? If he hadn't turned up by then, she could leave a message telling him to come.

"Oh, you know, I think I'll stay here," Abbie said. "I've got a paper to write and . . ."

"Abbie, come on, it'll be a blast."

"I know, I just don't feel like it."

"You two are like an old married couple."

"I know, soon I'll be knitting him a sweater."

Everybody was curious about Rolf. All anyone knew was that they had met in Seattle, that he was the guy who had "saved her" when things turned nasty. Mel said how romantic it was and had already nicknamed him The Knight, as in shining armor. They were all curious to know what he did and where he came from, so Abbie told them what Rolf had told her to say: that he was doing a Ph.D. at Washington State on International Social and Environmental Change but was taking rather a long time about it. It even took a long time to say, she would joke then quickly steer the conversation to something else. Even if she had wanted to tell them the truth, Abbie wouldn't have been able to come up with much more.

She laid the little table with candles and a bottle of wine and cooked the parmigiana and made a salad and had it all ready to serve at eight o'clock. And when, two hours later, after she'd taken Sox for another walk down to the park and up along the river and gotten home and Rolf still hadn't come and hadn't called her on the cell phone, she took the meal out of the oven, because it was getting too dried up, and sat at the table and ate alone, reading her book. It was a biography of Fidel Castro that Rolf had said she should read. Though she would never have dared tell him, she was finding it more than a little heavy going.

He turned up at eight-thirty the next morning, just as she and Sox were coming out the door and about to head over to the campus where she had a couple of errands to run before class. As usual, he had a different vehicle. They were nearly always vans, unmarked and nondescript. This time it was an old gray Nissan. She never asked how or where he got them.

Abbie waited on the little deck at the top of the fire escape and watched him walk up the steps toward her, Sox beside her, squirming and wagging his tail, not yet confident enough to go down to greet him. Rolf didn't smile or say anything, just kept his eyes on her until he reached her. And when he did, he walked straight past her and she followed him back inside and closed the door and he turned and still without a word slipped his hands inside her jacket and held her by the hips and kissed her, then led her by her wrist to the bed and fucked her.

They were sitting crosslegged on the floor, the street map spread before them along with all the photographs Rolf had taken. He had numbered each picture and written neat notes on the back, detailing what it showed. The video footage they were now peering at on the little folding screen of his camera was a lot less clear because he'd had to shoot from inside the back of the van. He talked her through it, explaining what they were looking at.

The street was lined with trees, cars parked along either side. The neighborhood was smart but not as upscale as Abbie had expected, just like any average white-collar suburb. The houses weren't huge, but they were well spaced, set back a little from the road. There were landscaped lawns, smart cars parked in the drive-ways. But there weren't fences or gates or any of those "armed response" security signs. The camera was zooming in now.

"Is that the house?" Abbie said.

"Uh-huh."

Rolf froze the frame.

"The street is quiet," he said. "At night there's hardly a car. After midnight only two or three every hour."

"Is that his car in the driveway?"

"They leave it there to make people think there's somebody at home. There are lights inside on time switches to give the same impression. They go on and off at precisely the same times every night."

"It's not exactly a palace. I thought it'd be a lot more fancy."

"Don't feel too sorry for him. They have a palace in Aspen and another in Miami where his wife spends most of her time. This place he uses only when he is in Denver and, even then, most nights he's across town fucking his mistress."

"How come you know all this?"

He gave her a baleful look and didn't reply. It was the kind of question she wasn't supposed to ask. There was obviously some sort of information network to which he had access, but all he'd ever told her was that he *knew a few people* who could find things out for him.

She had once asked him if the woman at the squat that night in Seattle, the one in the corner working on the laptop, was one of them. But Rolf said these were things they shouldn't discuss, that it was safer for her not to know. Abbie tried not to let his secretiveness bother or hurt her, but it did. It made her feel patronized and that he didn't fully trust her.

"Okay," she said. "But how can we be sure that whatever night we do this, nobody will be there? I mean, they've got kids, right?"

"Two boys. Both away at college. Anyhow, I have the house phone number. There's a pay phone just three blocks away. All we have to do is call. If someone answers, we leave."

He unfroze the picture. They were looking at a different place now, a narrow lane overhung with trees, like a tunnel. A concrete wall running along one side, with gates and dumpsters.

"The front of the house is too exposed and there are movement-activated security lights. This is the alley at the rear. There may be lights on the back of the house too, but if they come on, nobody will see. The whole yard is surrounded with trees."

The picture was shaky and dim but as the camera was lifted to peep over the top of the wall, Abbie got a vague impression of the rear of the house. A swimming pool with a little whitewashed summerhouse, a sloping lawn with flower beds, some glass doors.

"There must be some kind of alarm."

"In the house? Of course."

"So how do we set the fire? If you break a window, the alarm will go off."

He smiled.

"They have a cat. Don't worry, the woman takes it with her wherever she goes. Right now it's probably sunbathing in Florida. But in the kitchen door there is a little flap. We strap a can of gasoline to Sox's back and send him in."

"We *what?*"

He grinned. Rolf didn't often make jokes and when he did they weren't ever that funny but she still felt dumb for not getting this one. Sox was on the couch, with his head on his front paws, watching them. Rolf ruffled the dog's ears.

"The mutt has to start earning his keep sometime, right?"

"Oh, baby, who's Poppa calling a mutt?"

She gathered Sox up and cradled him. He wriggled and tried to scramble up to lick her face.

"I'll have to work something out when I see it," he went on. "I've got some better ignition sorted out but maybe this time I'll have to use gasoline. Cut a hole and feed in a pipe. Anyhow, that's my problem."

Abbie's heart was already galloping. This was a bigger deal than anything they had done so far. And while SUV dealerships and empty condos were somehow anonymous, this was personal. They were looking at the home of J. T. McGuigan of McGuigan Gas & Oil, the man responsible for trashing Ty's ranch and ruining his parents' lives and livelihood. And now the bastard was going to pay for it. They would burn his house to the ground. Abbie only wished—well, almost wished—that McGuigan could burn with it.

But the ELF was strict about the use of violence. She knew the guidelines by heart. It was legitimate to inflict *economic damage* on those who profited from destroying the environment. But you had to take *all necessary precautions against harming any animal, human or nonhuman,* a definition that sadly seemed to cover even criminal pigs like J. T. McGuigan.

Until June, when Rolf had first disclosed to her his secret life—or, at least, a little of it—Abbie had never even heard of the ELF. What he told her made her suspect he was just doing his usual evasive man of mystery thing. But she gradually came to conclude that there probably wasn't a lot more to tell. The group was modeled, so Rolf told her, on the Animal Liberation Front, which targeted fur farms and vivisection labs. ELF members were people who believed, as he did, that the environmental movement had lost its way, had been emasculated and taken over by lawyers and organizations that had become almost as big and bad and bureaucratic as the very corporations and government departments that they were supposed to be fighting.

The ELF had no centralized structure, Rolf said, no leadership or hierarchy. It was just people following their own consciences, acting individually or in cells, as the two of them were doing. And as long as they kept within the guidelines, they could strike wherever and whenever they chose.

Torching McGuigan's house had been Abbie's idea and she was pleased and proud that Rolf had so readily embraced it. She was doing it for Ty and his parents, taking revenge on their behalf, sending a signal to McGuigan and all the other greedy, bullying, destructive bastards that what they were doing was not acceptable and would not be tolerated. There was, of course, another motive which Abbie would never dream of mentioning to anyone and only barely acknowledged to herself. It was that, by doing this for Ty, she might in time feel a little less guilty about rejecting him.

When she had gotten back from seeing him in May, he had called her almost every day, asking her to come again or saying he could come to Missoula. But she kept making excuses and now he hardly ever called. She hadn't told him about Rolf or even hinted that there was somebody else in her life now. Maybe it would have been kinder if she had. But she didn't want to hurt him and was too much of a coward. In any case, she had the impression that he had guessed. But, really, what the hell did it matter? That was then. He belonged to her old life. He was a sweet guy but she couldn't be doing all that *I love you* shit.

Rolf switched off the camera and clicked the screen shut.

"So," Abbie said. "When do we do it?"

NINETEEN

I t was just how he had said it would be. They had driven by three times now in Abbie's Toyota and seen the lights come on and go off at exactly the times he said they would. The car was parked in the driveway just as it had been in the video. Around midnight they drove back out along the highway a couple of miles to a gas station and bought some sandwiches and fruit and a bottle of water, then found a little park and took Sox for a walk and let him do his business.

Rolf always moaned about her bringing the dog along but Abbie refused to go without him. He was their lucky mascot, she said. And good cover too, because he made them look kind of homey, like a little family. And so far, on all three of their outings, the little guy had been good as gold, just curled up in the car and waited. The only concession Abbie made was to remove the collar tag with her phone number on it in case he got lost.

The weather all week had been sunny and warm but it was late September and the nights were getting crisp. The forecast had predicted clouds rolling in from the west and now they were, slowly blotting out the stars. They had left the van on a quiet street near some derelict land close to the freeway and at a quarter before two they went to collect it and parked the Toyota there instead. They put on their dark-colored jackets and checked that they had all they would need, then drove back and made a final pass of the house in time to see the upstairs lights go off at precisely nine minutes past the hour, just as Rolf had said they would. They parked near the phone booth three blocks away and Abbie waited in the van, humming a random little tune to calm herself while she watched him dial the number. He stood there, listening for a while, then hung up and walked casually back and got into the car again.

"Just an answering machine," he said.

"Hope you left a message."

She was trying to pretend she wasn't nervous. He didn't answer, just gave her one of his looks and started the engine. It occurred to her that some people left their answering machines on the whole time, even when they were at home. But she didn't say anything. He'd already told her she was too neurotic about it and that he knew for sure that nobody was there. He'd checked. The wife and kids were away and McGuigan had flown down to Houston for some gas industry conference.

They took a different route back, through streets that looked much the same and when they reached McGuigan's street they drove on past and turned instead into the alley behind. Rolf shut off the head-lights and they cruised slowly down the tunnel of over-hanging trees, peering into the backyards of the houses and seeing not a single sign of life.

They stopped short of McGuigan's back gate and turned off the engine and sat in the darkness and low-ered the windows and listened. Somewhere, back along the alley in one of the houses they had passed, a dog was barking. But soon it seemed to grow bored and stopped and all Abbie could hear was the urgent pulsing of her own blood. Sox was curled up watching them with wide eyes from his little bed in the back, wedged in beside the plastic containers of diesel and gasoline and the black backpack with all Rolf's tools and ignition stuff in it.

They put on their gloves and their black beanies and Abbie checked her pockets again for the two aerosol cans of black paint. She had already figured out what she was going to spray on the walls of the summerhouse, to which, Rolf assured her, the fire wouldn't spread.

"Ready?" he said.

She nodded.

"Cell phone off?"

"Uh-huh."

"Okay, let's go."

The back gate was locked but the wall wasn't hard to climb. Rolf jumped up and swung himself over and she handed him his bag and the fuel containers. Then he hoisted himself again and helped her up and over the wall and down into the yard. They crouched there for a few moments while their eyes got used to the darkness, their breath misting in the cool air. Abbie looked up. The clouds were thickening, a few stars glinting in the gaps. Rolf put the backpack on and picked up the two fuel containers.

"Keep close," he whispered.

He moved quickly away to his right, keeping low,

with his knees bent and his head and shoulders hunched forward. There was a path that led directly to the pool and the lawn but he led her instead over to the side of the yard and they headed up toward the house under the cover of the trees that grew along the fence, weaving among the bushes and the flower beds.

If there were any security lights they hadn't yet come on. And soon Rolf was leading her past the pool and the summerhouse and over a low concrete wall and then along the edge of the lawn until finally they reached a paved terrace and the house itself and still no lights came on. Rolf put down the containers and swung the pack off and lowered it gently between his feet. They stood awhile, panting now, their backs flattened to the cold brick wall, listening. There was a distant drone of traffic but nothing more.

The door with the little flap in it was just four or five yards from where they now stood. Beyond it, jutting from the rear of the house, was some sort of sunroom or conservatory, with half-closed blinds and glass double doors. Rolf was about to move forward when, peering through the darkness, Abbie saw something. Inside the sunroom. In the shadows. The head and shoulders of someone standing there, looking out. She put a hand on Rolf's shoulder.

"There's somebody in there."

He turned to look at her and she motioned with her eyes and he followed her gaze and for a long moment they both froze.

"It's a just a plant, for Christsake," he whispered.

He was right. She could see it now. It was just a rubber plant or some sort of palm. The room was full of them. She felt foolish.

"How many times do I have to tell you?" he said. "They're away. Come on now, you bring the cans."

He picked up the backpack and moved toward the door and squatted down beside it. Abbie followed with the fuel containers. She stood watching over his shoulder while he gently put a finger on the flap. It moved. Rolf looked up at her and grinned.

"See? He wanted to make things easy for us. Go, quick, do your stuff, this won't take long. Stay down there, I'll come find you."

He began to unfasten the backpack. Abbie turned and headed back the way they had come, toward the summerhouse, still feeling like a complete idiot and so busy chastising herself that she forgot about the little concrete wall and tripped and fell headlong into a bush. One of the branches poked her in the face, narrowly missing her left eye, and she nearly cried out but somehow managed not to. She scrambled to her feet and made her way, more carefully now, to the summerhouse.

One of the walls was covered with ivy but there was another, facing the back of the house, that was perfect. It even looked as if someone had cleared and whitewashed it specially for the occasion. She pulled the black aerosol can from her jacket pocket and got to work.

Rolf had warned her not to write anything that might

connect them in any way with Ty's parents' ranch or even with the area, so she sprayed two large black *ELF*s, one in each top corner, and along the bottom wrote *Nature Destroyer* and *Oil Greed, No Need*. Then, right across the middle of the wall she started to write *Gas Gluttons Shall Be Punished* but when she got to *Be* the paint ran out. As she was fishing the other can out of her pocket, she heard a rustle and a click behind her.

"What the hell do you think you're doing?"

She almost lifted off the ground in fright. A flashlight was shining straight into her eyes and for a moment she couldn't see a thing. Then she saw the muzzle of the shotgun. He had it pointed right at her chest.

"Don't move. Don't you fucking move! Okay? Just stay right where you are. I already called nine-one-one, okay? The cops are on their way, but if you move I'll blow your fucking head off."

Dazzled in the glare she could only get a dim impression of his face. But he was young, in his early twenties, maybe. She noticed he wasn't wearing any shoes.

"Jesus, are you a girl?"

She nodded. And in that same moment she caught a glimpse of something moving behind him. If there was anybody with him, he surely would have called out. Maybe it was Rolf. It had to be. She tried not to let her eyes so much as flicker.

"What's this?"

He was trying to read the wall behind her.

"ELF? Who the hell are you?"

And then she saw for sure that it was Rolf. He was

326

creeping up behind the guy, getting close now. Just the slightest sound, the snap of a twig, and the guy would swivel and shoot. Maybe she should say something, try to distract him, make sure he didn't hear.

"Listen," she said. "I'm sorry . . ."

"You're sorry? Hey, that's good."

"Would you mind not shining that in my face?"

"Don't fucking move, I said!"

"I'll pay."

"What?"

"I'll pay. For the damage. Really. It's just a joke, you know . . ."

Rolf was right behind him now. He had something in his hand, a club of some kind, a piece of wood or a wrench maybe. But as he lifted it, there was a flash and a great thud up at the house and the guy turned to look and saw Rolf standing there about to hit him. He ducked to one side so that the blow missed his head and hit him instead on the shoulder. Rolf lunged for the shotgun and grabbed hold of the barrel. The guy dropped the flashlight and Abbie leapt forward and jumped onto his back and tried to get her hands around his neck.

The back of the house was all lit up now, flames leaping and darting from the kitchen door and the window beside it and then there was a second, much bigger, explosion and the sunroom windows blew out and now the fire was raging there too. Rolf and the guy were struggling for the gun, grunting and yelling and cussing, and Abbie was still on the guy's back, yanking his head with all her might and pulling his hair. He hollered and screamed and tried to throw her off but still didn't loosen his grip on the shotgun.

Then the gun went off. Abbie felt as if she had been kicked in the chest by a horse. The blast seemed to shred her eardrums. For a moment everything went still. Wide-eyed, she watched Rolf stumble backward, the house blazing behind him, and she was sure it was he who had been hit. Her arms were still locked around the guy's neck but he wasn't struggling anymore and so she slowly loosened her grip and through her ringing ears heard him groan and felt him start to crumple beneath her. He sank to his knees and she stepped back and by the light of the fallen flashlight saw the dark stain spreading on the back of his sweatshirt.

Then he began to make this terrible gurgling noise and she walked fearfully around him to stand with Rolf and saw the blood come rushing from the singed and smoking hole in the young man's chest.

"Oh God," she said. "Oh my God."

He was staring down at himself in disbelief and then he slowly lifted his eyes and stared at Abbie and opened his mouth as if he wanted to tell her something.

Rolf grabbed her arm and began pulling her away.

"Come on."

"We can't just—"

"There's no time!"

He dragged her after him, down the path, toward the gate. Abbie tried to run but kept looking back at the man and at the flaming house beyond and twice she stumbled and Rolf had to stop and haul her from her knees. They reached the gate and it wasn't locked, just bolted, and he slid the bolts and swung it open and then they were out in the alley and running toward the van. They hadn't locked it for this very reason, so they might make a quicker escape. He opened the passenger door and pushed her inside and slammed it shut again then ran around to the driver's side and got in and dug for the keys in his pocket.

"Shit," he said. "Shit! Shit! Shit!"

He couldn't find them. There was a yell outside, someone shouting "Hey! Hey!" and they both looked back and through the rear window of the van saw a man running up the alley toward them. Rolf had found the keys now and was putting them into the ignition. The engine started first time but whoever was chasing them had reached them now and as the van started to pull away he wrenched open the back doors.

"Stop! Stop, you motherfuckers!"

He was no youngster, in his forties maybe, but big and athletic-looking. He was trying to climb into the back of the van which by now was moving away fast. Sox, about whom until that moment Abbie had completely forgotten, was standing in his bed barking. She reached out for him but he was too far away and too terrified to come. The guy had a knee on the sill of the van now and was trying to get the other one in. But they were at the end of the alley and Rolf yanked the wheel hard to the right and as they swerved out into the street, the van skidding and squealing and tilting on two wheels, the guy lost his grip and went tumbling like a rag doll away across the street. And with him went everything else in the back of the van, including Sox.

"Stop!" Abbie screamed. "We lost Sox!"

"Are you crazy?"

"Sox has gone! He fell out!"

"No way."

"Rolf, you've got to stop!"

She tried to grab the hand brake but he lashed out and shoved her away and she banged the back of her head against the window.

"You bastard!"

"Shut up! Just shut the fuck up!"

She looked back but the dog was nowhere to be seen. Abbie looked down at her hands and saw that there was blood on them. She started to wail.

In just a few quick seconds everything had turned upside down and gone spiraling out of control. She couldn't believe it was happening. Her head was a slide-show carousel: the blazing house, the guy kneeling there, staring at the smoking hole in his chest, that look in his eyes when he stared up at her.

Through the streaming blur of her tears she looked across at Rolf. He was breathing hard, his face warped with concentration as he drove them in a manic rush through the maze of streets. Houses, storefronts, the glare of headlights strobing by, an ambulance now, its sirens blaring and lights all flashing.

"We've got to go back."

"Just shut up."

"It was an accident. We can tell them. We have to go back and tell them."

"Abbie, shut up."

"Rolf, if the guy dies! They'll think we killed him."

"He's already dead, you idiot!"

They were out on the highway now and he slowed a little, his eyes darting between the road ahead and the rearview mirror. There were more sirens now, then flashing lights ahead, two police cars coming fast toward them. But they whipped past without slowing.

"For fuck's sake, stop crying," he said.

There were signs to the freeway now. Another police car came by and then the road was clear. Rolf slowed and checked the mirror then quickly turned left into a side street and took two more turns and soon they were driving down alongside some derelict land and parking up behind the Toyota.

"Come on," he said. "Abbie, come on! Move!"

But she couldn't. All the power had drained from her limbs. She couldn't stop staring at her hands. She had tried to wipe the blood off on her pants but there was still some under her nails and in the creases of her knuckles.

Rolf quickly got out and unlocked the Toyota then ran back and dragged her from the van and down the side-walk to the car, all the while looking around to see if anyone was coming or watching. He dumped her in the front passenger seat and shut the door. She heard him open the trunk and take something out and there were a few moments of silence until the trunk slammed shut and he was climbing into the driver's seat beside her and starting the engine. He did a quick U-turn and braked alongside the van and lowered his window. The van's window was open too and he struck a match and tossed it through and at the same time stamped on the gas pedal. Abbie looked back and a second later felt the air compress and saw the van explode into flames behind them.

And soon they were out on the freeway, arcs of orange lights flashing overhead like the gates of hell as they headed out of town and into the waiting darkness. And so filled was her head with the image of her alien bloodied hands, that to where and to what if any kind of life, she neither knew nor cared.

TWENTY

I f there was one thing Eve had always hated more than being photographed, it was being asked questions about her work. So being interviewed for some local cable station was a double whammy. The reporter looked about fourteen years old and had already confessed that he usually covered basketball stories and didn't know the first thing about art. And he wasn't being falsely modest. He really didn't.

She was pinned against one of her new paintings, not one she would have chosen to talk about; in fact she didn't really like it and wouldn't have included it in the show if Lori hadn't forced her to. But the camerawoman liked the color and said that if Eve stood in front of it, the background was better and they could get some guests into the shot as well as that nice potted plant over by the window.

"So," the fourteen-year-old was asking. "Do you do it in, like, little bits, you know, like, work on a little section of it first and then do another little section and so on? Or do you, like, do the whole thing in one big go and then, kind of, fill it in?"

Eve could see Ben leaning against the wall, with his glass of red wine. He was talking with Lori but she knew from the way they were smiling that they were eavesdropping on the interview. The bastards.

"Well, I guess it varies from picture to picture," Eve replied. "With this one, I had a very strong idea of the shapes I wanted and the way they were going to relate with each other. And you just, kind of, go with the flow. And inevitably something will happen that changes what you intended, you know, an accident of some kind."

The boy looked mystified.

"You mean, like, a car accident?"

"No, I mean, something that happens on the canvas. You make a mistake and suddenly, if you stand back and look, it's better than what you planned."

She could tell he hadn't the faintest idea what she was talking about. Maybe she should start talking about basketball.

The gallery was cooler and quieter now that people had begun drifting out into Canyon Road. It had been a great party, though Eve had hardly known a soul. She knew that Lori had been working hard on her list, trying to drum up new clients, so it hadn't just been the usual crowd of friends and hangers-on who came only for the pinot noir and canapés. To deter freeloaders, a lot of the galleries served nothing more potent than punch at show openings but Lori had managed both to keep the wine flowing and to sell a lot of pictures. All evening Eve had seen her scurrying around sticking little dots onto the paintings. Quite a lot of them were red too, which meant money had changed hands and the deal was as good as done. The green ones, of which there were more, meant the picture was reserved for a week with no deposit, so they weren't worth getting too excited about. It usually meant someone had drunk too many glasses of wine and tomorrow would forget all about it.

The fourteen-year-old, thank heaven, seemed to have run out of questions now. Eve had long ago run out of answers.

"Thank you very much," he said.

"You're welcome. Thank you so much for coming."

The boy wandered off with his camerawoman to take some more pictures of the paintings and Eve walked over to Lori and Ben, pulling a face as she came up to them. He handed her his glass of wine and she took it and drank.

"That was so impressive," he said.

"Bullshit. With you two standing here smirking, I couldn't string two thoughts together."

"Neither could he, so you were perfectly matched."

He put his arm around her and kissed her on the cheek. Lori leaned toward her.

"We have sold a truckload of paintings," she said in a conspiring whisper. "Have you seen? Twenty-three, maybe twenty-four. Fantastic."

"And Lori says she'll only be taking five percent this time," Ben said.

"In your dreams, pal."

They laughed. Then Lori said she had to go and help Barbara, her assistant, who was over at the desk in the front room taking deposits and doing the paperwork. Eve looked up at Ben. He looked so handsome in his black linen shirt and white chinos. He still had his arm around her and now gave her a little squeeze.

"I'm so proud of you," he said.

"Oh, go on."

"You should have heard some of the things people were saying. They were just knocked out."

"They were?"

"Yeah, they said it was the best pinot noir they'd ever had at an opening."

She pinched his arm.

"No, honestly. Everybody was just in awe. You could have sold those two wolf angels twenty times over. That woman from LA in the red dress and the earrings? She just stood there staring at them for about ten minutes. She was nearly in tears."

"That might not be good."

"It was. She loved it. She was having a cathartic moment."

Eve smiled and reached up and kissed him.

"I love you," she said quietly.

They had dinner at El Farol with Lori and her latest boyfriend, Robert, who worked at some hi-tech military installation in San Diego and often had to come to Los Alamos for meetings that were so top-secret he was hardly even allowed to tell himself about them. He was a thin little guy with gold-rimmed glasses and a pointy face and a habit of bombarding you with facts that were interesting enough but didn't lead to any kind of real conversation. Ben could do a great impression of him.

"Do you know how many humans there are in the world?" Robert asked between spoonfuls of crème brûlée.

Everybody had forgotten.

"Six billion."

He paused a moment, for appreciation.

"Do you know how many birds there are?"

Nobody did.

"A hundred billion."

He repeated it, in case somebody had missed it.

"Do you know how much of the earth is land and how much ocean?"

"No," Ben said. "But I've a feeling we soon will."

Robert chose to ignore that. Eve caught Ben's eye and tried not to laugh.

"One third land, two thirds ocean. That means one hundred and ninety-one square miles of land. Which means . . ."

He paused for effect. Ben, dead serious, leaning for-

336

ward as if riveted, was pressing his knee against hers, trying to make her laugh.

". . . two-point-five birds per acre."

They all did their various best to look amazed and edified.

"Where does Lori find them?" Ben asked afterward, as they walked up the hill to the car. "I mean, what does she see in the guy?"

"She says he's incredible in bed."

"Really? Jesus. Does he whisper sweet facts and figures in her ear?"

"Uh-huh. Apparently it's an amazing turn-on."

"Oh really?"

"Absolutely."

He thought for a moment, then put his lips close to her ear.

"Did you know that Polynesian is almost an anagram of oily spanner?"

She gave a little moan.

"All it needs is another R."

"Stop, stop."

They walked on awhile, the strike of their footsteps echoing off the adobe walls, his arm cozily around her. The night was clear and close to freezing, the fall shading to winter. God, Eve thought, they had been together nearly a year. And it was two years, almost to the day, since that night in New York when they saw *Kiss Me, Kate* and had dinner. At times it seemed like the blink of an eye and at others like a lifetime.

She had never expected it to be easy. She had known

from the outset, even when they first met, that he had an aptitude for sadness. And she sometimes wondered if it was this very trait that had attracted her. For though she had never knowingly done it before, she was aware that it was possible for a woman to confuse love with pity and to take a man on in the hope of saving him. Or to see him as a sort of challenge, persuading herself that she and she alone could rescue him and mother him and make him happy. She didn't think she was that kind of woman, in fact she hoped to God she wasn't. But how could one ever be sure?

In fairness, Ben wasn't that kind of man either. And Eve preferred to think that what she had fallen in love with was the man she had glimpsed behind the sadness. The man who, day by day, Ben seemed more able now to be. Like he was tonight, so easy and light and funny. When he was like that there wasn't anyone in the world she would rather have been with.

But there had been occasions when she had wondered if they would make it. She had never met a man so susceptible to guilt. He was a double-major at it, a professor of guilt. And during those first few months after he had left Sarah and was living in Kansas and coming to Santa Fe for a week or two at a time, he was giving himself such a hard time that she'd almost had to ask him to stop visiting, at least until he sorted himself out. He seemed to have this bottomless pit into which he poured everything he could conceivably blame himself for and then every day would climb down into it and wallow around.

It wasn't just about Sarah and his kids. A lot of the time it was about his mother. Living with her was driving him to distraction. He would get angry with her for going on about him and telling the same stories again and again of some wonderful thing he'd done when he was younger and he would end up saying something hurtful and then spend the next week feeling guilty about it. It even irritated him that in no time at all she seemed to have forgotten her first reaction to his leaving Sarah and had set to work rewriting history. He'd once heard her on the phone telling a friend that he'd never been happy with Sarah and that, actually, he was a saint for staying so long.

The prime source of his guilt was, of course, Abbie. Eve could remember trying to comfort him, back at the beginning of the year, telling him that it was only a matter of time, that in a few months Abbie would start feeling better and understand his side of things a little more. But that hadn't happened. If anything the girl's hostility had entrenched and solidified. He'd come back from Missoula almost broken. Eve felt like phoning the girl to tell her to grow up and stop being so damn selfish, but of course she didn't.

Since then, Ben had been trying to learn to live with the fact that his daughter, for the foreseeable future at least, was lost to him. He had at last listened to Eve's advice and found himself a therapist. The only other time he'd done it was after his father died and then it was only two or three visits. She'd heard him speak dismissively of what he called the whole *shrink culture.*

On the whole, he said, people just ought to *get on with it*. But he'd obviously come to the conclusion that he couldn't and had gone out and found a guy he liked and now dutifully visited twice a week.

He didn't tell Eve too much about their sessions but apparently they talked a lot about how, in almost every area of life, the things you did soon became the only things you could do. Grief and guilt could easily become habits as much as picking your nose in the car. Guilt, the therapist said, was nature's way of getting you to reconsider or rescind something you had done. But if you were sure, really sure, that you didn't want to rescind, then it was just like some playground bully that had no other purpose than to make you feel bad. When Ben felt lured to his pit of guilt, the therapist suggested, maybe he should just pause on the brink, have a look down and decide if, today, he really wanted to get wet.

He still took a good wallow now and then, but it wasn't daily anymore. And as the summer passed, Eve had watched him grow looser and brighter. Pablo adored him and it seemed mutual. He had a natural way with kids and Eve loved hearing the two of them talk and laugh and enjoyed watching them do all the *boy stuff,* throwing a football around or playing softball or pretending they were sumo wrestlers.

When he'd first moved down here, Ben had been adamant about finding a place of his own and kept going to see houses and apartments that were never quite right. To begin with she didn't discourage him.

Until then, the longest they had lived together was a couple of weeks and although it had worked fine, it somehow seemed too early, too significant, to have him move in permanently. But he was easy to live with, presumably because he'd had so many years of practice. And soon, with barely a word being said about it, they both came to accept that he was there to stay. He had, however, rented a room down the street which he now used as an office.

Eve had to work on him a little, to stop him from being so fussy and fastidious. He liked everything in its proper place, while she was more relaxed and left things lying around. Well, okay, she was untidy. Sometimes she would catch him clearing up after her or checking that she had locked the car door (she never bothered) and she would stand there and give him a look and he'd put his hands up and apologize.

"Why do you have to lock the door?"

"People steal things."

"I haven't locked a door in ten years and nobody ever stole a thing."

"Then you're very lucky."

She tried to get him to acknowledge that what he saw as sensible precaution could also be construed as expecting the worst to happen. And if you expected the worst, it had a funny habit of not wanting to disappoint you.

"So give me an example," he said.

"God, there are so many."

"Just one."

"Okay. Making Pablo wear a helmet when he rides his bicycle."

"But he could fall off, for heavensake."

"See what I mean?"

"You're really telling me that putting a helmet on him makes it more likely he'll fall?"

"Uh-huh. Probably."

"Eve, you know that's baloney."

"Maybe, maybe not. But kids have got to learn. You can't protect them from everything. Like the other day when he was climbing that tree and you got all uptight about him falling."

"He could have broken his neck."

"He didn't."

Ben shook his head. She went and gave him a hug.

"Listen, honey," she said. "All I'm saying is this: If you have negative thoughts, you invite negativity. Positive thoughts have power."

He didn't quite concede, but at least it seemed to make him think. A few days later he mentioned that Sarah had once accused him of being a control freak. He asked Eve if she agreed and got depressed for two whole days when she said, in the nicest possible way, that she did. But he was getting better, he was trying, he really was.

He missed his friends, she knew, and felt hurt and rejected by the many who, in his view, had blindly allied themselves with Sarah, leaping to judgment without even attempting to hear his side of the story. The one he had been most hurt by was his old partner and best buddy Martin. After taking Josh to Cape Cod, Ben had gone to collect Eve's paintings that had been commissioned for the Cold Spring Harbor office block. Martin had refused to hang them and they had stood gathering dust in the ICA garage. He had kept Ben waiting in reception for twenty minutes and then had been cold and brusque and treated him almost like a stranger.

But whereas, before, something like that would have set Ben back a week, he rarely now allotted it more than a day. For a man who all his life had cared so inordinately about what others thought of him, Eve had an idea of the effort this required. Even when he e-mailed Abbie, as he did almost every day, or called her and left a voicemail without ever once getting a reply, he refused to let it drag him to the pit anymore.

They were home now. They parked the car and walked through the little arched adobe gateway with its creaking bleached-pine door into the garden. There was not a breath of wind and the chimes on the cherry tree hung silent. There were still yellow roses along the rails of the deck outside the kitchen door and Eve picked one as she passed and put it to her nose. The petals were brittle with frost but still there was a trace of scent. She handed it to Ben.

Maria, the babysitter, was asleep on the couch in front of the TV and Eve had to lay her hand on the girl's shoulder to wake her. Ben had forgotten to take his cell phone and had left it in the bedroom and Maria said it had rung several times but that she hadn't felt she should answer it. They paid her and the girl went home and while Eve went to check on Pablo, Ben walked through to the bedroom to listen to his voicemail.

There were three messages, of increasing urgency, and all from Sarah. Would he call her? It was important. Where the hell was he?

Sarah had thought it was somebody playing a trick on her. Jeffrey was always calling and putting on some funny voice, pretending to be the fire department or some famous irascible author or the Nassau County gigolo service, offering her a weekend special. So when the phone rang and the man introduced himself as Special Agent Frank Lieberg of the FBI, without missing a beat she said, "Yeah, sure, and I'm J. Edgar Hoover and you're fired, buddy." There was a pause and then he asked, more diffidently this time, if he was indeed talking to Mrs. Sarah Cooper and that was when she figured it had to be for real.

"I'm sorry," she said. "Yes, I am—I mean, yes, you are."

"Mrs. Cooper, are you the mother of Abigail Cooper, a sophomore student at the University of Montana?"

It was like the toll of a bell. She felt as if every ounce of breath had suddenly been squeezed from her lungs. In a quiet voice, she managed to say yes, she was.

Agent Lieberg asked her if she knew where Abbie happened to be and Sarah said, well, at school of course, and would he mind telling her what this was all about? She was standing in the kitchen and had been making herself some supper. Her knees had gone all shaky so that she had to prop herself up on the counter. On the TV across the room, Al Gore was kissing his wife and waving to a cheering crowd somewhere in Florida.

She hadn't spoken with Abbie or had an e-mail from her in more than a week, but that was how it mostly was nowadays. Sarah had, in fact, tried phoning her that very morning. As usual, the call went straight to voice-mail and she left another message, cheerful and chatty, asking her to call but trying not to lay on a guilt trip.

"Mrs. Cooper, I'm calling you from our Denver office. This is something that would be best handled face-to-face and I would like to arrange for some colleagues of mine in New York to come see you. Would that be convenient?"

"I guess. But what's this all about? Has something happened to Abbie?"

"Mrs. Cooper—"

"Listen, for heaven's sake, you can't just call up out of the blue and then not tell me—"

"My colleagues will tell you all they can. At the moment all I can say is that we urgently need to talk with Abigail—"

"Abbie."

"To ask her some questions relating to an incident that took place last weekend in Denver."

"In Denver? What kind of incident? Is she okay?"

"As of now, we have no reason to believe she isn't. We are having difficulty contacting her. Mrs. Cooper, is

Abbie's father with you at the moment?"

"He doesn't live here anymore. What kind of incident?"

He wouldn't tell her any more. His colleagues would be there within the hour, he said. He wanted to know if there would be anybody else with her and she told them that by then her son would be home.

Sarah at once called Josh on his cell phone and asked him to come home quickly, then put in her first call to Benjamin but only got his goddamn voicemail. She tried Abbie again with the same result. She went online and did a search for incidents that had happened the previous weekend in Denver. But she didn't have enough information to narrow it down and found nothing that rang any kind of bell.

The two FBI agents showed up just before eight. Except that they had no hats, they could have come from central casting. Dark suits, neckties, snappy haircuts. They didn't want anything to drink and it was even a job to get them to sit down at the kitchen table. Josh and Sarah sat opposite them and listened. And as she heard what they had to say, it was as if her heart was pumping all the blood from her veins and filling them instead with liquid dread. Her hands were clasped tightly on the table, the knuckles white. Josh gently put his hand on her forearm and kept it there.

A young man had been murdered, shot in the chest, his father's house burned to the ground. Two people had been seen fleeing in a gray van that had later been found, burnt out. Another man who had tried to stop them was in a coma with severe head injuries. A dog had been seen falling from the van and was so badly hurt that it had later been put down. There was a veterinarian microchip implanted in the back of its neck. On the chip were the name, address, and phone number of its owner, one Abigail Cooper of Missoula, Montana. Abbie hadn't been in class or at her apartment or been seen anywhere on campus or in town for ten days.

They asked some questions about Abbie's political views and whether, to Sarah's knowledge, she was a member of any radical environmental groups. All Sarah could come up with was Greenpeace which for some reason made them smile. They said they were talking about more extreme groups such as the Earth Liberation Front, which Sarah had never heard of.

The truth was that whereas a year ago Abbie had talked constantly about all her environmental work, the meetings she went to, and the campaigns she was involved in, lately she hadn't. In fact, in the summer, she had given the impression that she now considered it a waste of time. *Like rearranging the furniture on the* Titanic, Sarah remembered her saying. Some strange maternal instinct told her it might be wiser not to mention this.

The two agents asked if they could see Abbie's room. And so dazed was she by all she had heard, Sarah led them without question up the stairs. She stood in the doorway watching while they looked around. With its posters and photos and bric-a-brac, its trophies and staring echelons of stuffed toys, the place already seemed like a shrine. They asked if she would mind if they took some strands of hair from Abbie's hairbrush on the dressing table. It might help them eliminate her daughter from their inquiries, they said gently. They wanted some recent photos too. Sarah saw no reason to refuse.

By the time Benjamin called, she was in bed. She had taken a pill but it hadn't worked, even on top of the bourbon she'd had before coming upstairs, so she had switched the light back on and was trying to read. But her head wouldn't stop fizzing. She'd read the same paragraph five times already. Apart from Benjamin, the only person she had called was Iris. She didn't want anyone else to know. Iris had said all the right things, that it was probably all some terrible mix-up or misunderstanding. She offered to fly up in the morning but Sarah said no. She promised to call again the moment there was news. When she heard Benjamin's voice, something inside her snapped.

"Where the hell have you been?" she yelled. "I've been trying to reach you all night."

"I'm sorry, I—"

"Christ, I've been driving myself crazy here."

"What's the matter?"

She felt bad for giving him such a hard time, because, really, how was he to know? But she couldn't help it. It was weeks since they had last spoken and even then it was about the divorce, some sneaky new thing he and his lawyers were trying to pull. Of course, whenever she tried to confront him, it was always the lawyers' fault, never his. She told him about the FBI agents and everything they had said. He listened in grave silence, occasionally asking her to clarify something he hadn't understood.

"I'll fly up there first thing," he said when she had finished.

"Where? To Denver?"

"To Missoula. We've got to find her. Somebody there must know where she is. Are you okay?"

She swallowed, her eyes filling with tears.

"Sarah?"

"What the hell do you think?"

"Why don't you fly out there too? We can meet in Missoula."

"What about Josh? I can't just leave him here."

"Okay, maybe I'll come to New York first."

"Benjamin, don't be so ridiculous! What on earth would be the point of that?"

"No. Okay."

He went all hangdog on her. She could imagine him standing there, looking all forlorn. Then the thought knifed into her head and she couldn't stop herself from blurting it out.

"Is she listening to all this?"

For a moment, there was silence. He didn't seem to understand who she meant or else was pretending not to. The two of them were probably in bed together.

"Well, is she?"

"No, Sarah," he said wearily. "She isn't."

TWENTY-ONE

The young cop unhitched the plastic *Do not cross* tape that was rigged up across the foot of the wooden staircase then stood aside for them to pass. Agent Jack Andrews nodded and thanked him and led Ben up the steps past the layers of moldy clapboard to the little landing outside the apartment door. There was a panel of cracked glass in the door with a dirty net curtain draped inside across it. Agent Andrews unlocked the door and led the way inside.

The place was cold and cramped and smelled of damp. The only concession to luxury was some over-long red velvet drapes. There was a dog's bowl on the floor with some food in it.

"Student life, huh?" Andrews said.

Ben shrugged and nodded, tried to smile.

"You haven't been here before, then?"

"No. She was living in a house on Fourth Street last time I was here. That was back in the spring."

"We've been there. You didn't see her too often then."

"Since her mother and I split up, she hasn't really . . . No, not too often. Is this how it was when you first came here?"

"Some things have been taken away for analysis. A computer, some papers, photographs, a few other bits and pieces. Everything else is pretty much as it was."

"Are you allowed to do that? I mean . . ."

"Yes, sir. We are."

Earlier, in his office, back across the river in the Federal Building, he had already told Ben about the other incidents. The arson attacks where similar graffiti had been sprayed on the walls. They had taken place in three different states, which was one of the reasons the FBI was involved. The other reason was that these were clearly acts of ecoterrorism.

Ben had just laughed. Terrorism? Sacramento, Reno, Portland? The idea of Abbie whizzing all over the West, setting fire to things, was too absurd for words. And as for this Denver deal, Jesus. Andrews had smiled sympathetically and looked down at his notes. Then he asked about her boyfriend, the one who called himself Rolf. He wanted to know if Ben had ever met him or spoken with him and Ben said that neither he nor Sarah had.

They had gotten all Abbie's cell phone records and were painstakingly going through every call she had received or made since she got it. There were some calls from a number in Sheridan, Wyoming, Andrews said, from the home of a Mr. Ray Hawkins. Did the name mean anything to Ben?

"That would be Ty. If I remember rightly, his dad is called Ray. Ty and Abbie were close for a while. Though, lately, I don't know. My wife would know more about that."

Ben walked around the little apartment, without knowing what he was looking for or why indeed he had asked to see the place at all. But, God knew, he had to do something. Andrews's cell phone rang and he pulled it out and went out the door to answer it. All Ben could hear were many repetitions of *yes* and *okay* and *right* and then he was back in the room again, putting the phone back in his pocket.

"Mr. Cooper, I have to tell you that our Denver office have this morning released your daughter's name and photograph to the media. I didn't know it was going to happen that soon."

"Jesus Christ."

At that moment the cop appeared in the doorway.

"Sir?"

Andrews walked over to him and the cop quietly told him something.

"Okay, thanks."

The cop went back down the staircase. Andrews turned to Ben.

"We better get going. There's a TV crew on its way."

"What? Jesus."

"We need to go."

But they were too late. As they came down the staircase, a truck and a van with some kind of satellite thing on the top were pulling up in the street, the doors opening and people piling out with cameras and microphones. The cop put out his arms to try to hold them back but it was too much of a job for one man.

"Mr. Cooper? Mr. Cooper? Could we have a word, please? Mr. Cooper?"

Andrews tried to shield him as they walked to the car.

"Please, ladies and gentlemen," he said. "If you could just let us through? Thank you, thank you very much."

But it was no good.

"Have you heard from Abbie, Mr. Cooper?"

"Gentlemen," Andrews said. "Mr. Cooper will no doubt be issuing a statement later. He's not in a position . . ."

"Do you have any idea where Abbie is, Mr. Cooper?"

They were at the car now. Andrews was opening the passenger-side door for him but everyone was crowding in and jostling him. Ben managed to lower himself into the seat but didn't duck low enough and bumped his head. Andrews was trying to shut the door but the reporter had the microphone stuck in under Ben's nose.

"Mr. Cooper, did Abbie do it?"

"What the hell do you think?" Ben shouted. "Of course she didn't do it!"

The door slammed and he hit the lock and tried not to look at the camera and the faces still calling their muted questions through the glass. He felt like a criminal. Andrews was in the driver's seat now and starting up the engine.

"I'm so sorry."

Ben was too shaken to speak. He just shook his head in disbelief.

The thing is, Mr. Cooper, we haven't seen that much of her lately," Mel said. "Since she and Rolf started seeing each other, they just, kind of, hang out together, just the two of them."

They were sitting in a corner of a rowdy restaurant

called The Depot, up near the railroad. The walls were hung with paintings of the Wild West, though done with irony in bright neon colors, pinks and purples and lime greens. The music was loud but at least it meant they could talk without being overheard. Mel was facing him across the table with her boyfriend, Scott, while Ben was sitting next to the older guy with the beard who they'd introduced as Hacker, though apparently it wasn't his real name. They'd all ordered steaks, the biggest Ben had ever seen, to which the three of them had by now done justice. Ben had barely touched his. He just wasn't hungry.

It was Mel he had wanted to talk with and when he'd arrived here—late, after another long and devastating phone conversation with Sarah—he had been surprised to find the others waiting with her. Mel had sounded wary when he'd called her that afternoon, after the media nightmare had at last subsided. Perhaps Abbie had told her bad things about him. Or perhaps she was just shocked, like everybody, by what was going on. At first she was reluctant to meet, but she eventually agreed. Scott and Hacker had no doubt been enlisted as moral support. By now, though, everybody was feeling a little more relaxed.

"So can you tell me about Rolf?" Ben asked. "All we really know is that she met him in Seattle."

"You know, Mr. Cooper," Mel said. "We hardly ever got to meet him. Said hi a couple of times. That's really all."

"Is he a student here or what?"

Mel glanced a little nervously at Scott and then they both looked at Hacker, as if he should be the one to answer. Hacker cleared his throat.

"No. He put it around that he was doing a Ph.D. at Washington State. But it's not true. I know a lot of people there and nobody's ever heard of him. In Seattle he was living for a while in a squat with a few others. That's where we picked Abbie up after she got hurt in the demo. I got a friend of mine to check the place out. There's nobody there anymore."

He took a drink of his beer and went on.

"Tell you the truth, I don't think his real name is Rolf at all."

"Why's that?"

"Mr. Cooper, I've been involved in active environmental stuff for quite a few years now. Been known to do a little monkey-wrenching myself, now and then."

"Monkey-wrenching?"

The three of them shared a smile.

"You never read *The Monkey Wrench Gang*? Edward Abbey?"

"Oh. No, actually, I haven't. But I know what you mean. Spiking trees, that sort of thing."

Hacker pretended to look shocked.

"Perish the thought. Yeah, that sort of thing. Anyhow, you get to know people. There's like a kind of network. And once in a while some character drifts in who clearly has his own agenda, if you know what I mean. Word kind of gets around."

Ben didn't know what Hacker was talking about and

his face must have shown it. It was as if the guy was trying to tell him something without having to spell it out. Hacker looked at Scott and Mel. Scott nodded and Hacker leaned closer to Ben and went on.

"A few years ago there was some pretty heavy stuff going down. Some in Oregon, mostly northern California. Letter bombs in the mail, pipe bombs, that kind of deal. Most of the targets were federal agencies, the BLM, the Forest Service, logging and mining companies. Nobody got killed but quite a few were injured. Some senior executive of a lumber business got his arm blown off. Thing is, there was a guy around at that time who a lot of folks figured was involved. Slight European accent, German, Swiss maybe. Rangy, kind of good-looking. Called himself Michael Kruger or Kramer, some name like that. Eventually three or four people got arrested, went to jail for a long time. He just vanished."

"You think that's who Rolf is?"

Hacker held up his palms.

"I don't know. Maybe. Maybe not."

"Have you told anybody about this?"

Hacker laughed.

"The cops, you mean? No, sir."

"Well, is it okay if I do?"

Hacker sat back and picked up his beer and gave a wry smile.

"Man, I figure they know all about it already."

Ben asked him what he meant, but Hacker wouldn't elaborate. He just asked Ben if the FBI was intending to issue Rolf's photograph and details as they had Abbie's. Ben could only repeat what Andrews had told him: They hadn't yet gotten any ID on the other person involved that was strong enough to go on. Hacker gave a skeptical laugh.

"Yeah, right," he said. And finished his beer.

As they said good-bye in the street outside the restaurant, Mel shook his hand and said she was sure Abbie wouldn't have done anything stupid and that everything would be all right. Ben smiled and said he knew it would. She kissed him on the cheek and turned briskly and walked off with the others. Which was just as well because for some reason this small gesture of affection made the tears come rushing to his eyes and he cried all the way back to the hotel.

Sarah had told him to call her after meeting them, no matter how late it was. So back in his room, lit only by the bedside lamp and the flickering blue of the muted TV, he dialed the number that had once been his. But all he got was the answering machine. The voice was still Abbie's, recorded at least two years ago.

Hi, you've reached the Cooper residence. We're all far too busy and important to talk with you right now, but please leave a message and if it's really witty and cool, we'll get back to you. Bye!

"Sarah?"

He thought she might pick up but she didn't. He left a brief message then decided to try her cell.

"Benjamin?"

"Hi. I tried the house number."

"We're at Martin and Beth's."

"Joshie too?"

"Yes. We had to get out. It was like a siege. News-paper reporters, TV crews. We had to sneak out the back. It's a total nightmare."

She sounded numbed, fragile, right on the edge.

"They said on the news she's wanted for murder." And now her voice cracked. "Oh, Benjamin . . ."

"Sweetheart."

She was sobbing. He could hardly bear to hear it.

"Oh, sweetheart."

"Please come. Please."

It was one of those perfect fall evenings, clear and warm and still, everything saturated in a golden light. The maples in the Ingrams' backyard were a blaze of amber and red, their shadows leaning long across the lawn. Sarah had been staring at them for a full five minutes. She was out on the deck, leaning against the wall by the open doors to the kitchen, smoking another cigarette. It was getting out of hand. She had smoked half a pack today already. She was going to stop. Tomorrow.

"Sarah?"

Beth was standing at the door. She had taken the day off work to stay with her.

"He's here."

Sarah followed her inside and through the kitchen to the hallway then across the polished woodblock floor and the elongated triangle of sunlight that fell on it through the window halfway up the staircase. Beth opened the front door and walked out into the glow, the cab pulling away down the driveway, Benjamin standing there in his long stone-colored raincoat, putting down his bag so Beth could give him a hug. Sarah stood in the doorway, shielding her eyes against the sun and watched him walk toward her. He looked tired and strained around the eyes and he was giving her this beautiful, brave, sad smile. Oh God, she thought. At such a time, their world so suddenly askew, how could he not be hers?

He opened his arms and she clung to him as if to life itself, her shoulders, her whole body shaking as she wept. He held the back of her head against his chest and stroked her hair as he always used to. And when at last she could look up at him, he kissed her on the forehead and gently wiped her tears with his fingers and neither had yet spoken a word.

Beth was watching them, mopping tears too. They followed her into the house with their arms still around each other and in the hallway stood again and hugged.

"You smell of airplanes," she said.

"It's my new cologne, kerosene for men."

"Oh, Benjamin. Tell me this isn't happening."

"Is Joshie here?"

"He wanted to go to school."

"Are the reporters still camped out at the house?"

"I drove by around two this afternoon," Beth said. "There were still one or two. Alan says once you've made the statement, they'll probably leave you alone."

Beth had put them in touch with a lawyer friend of

hers named Alan Hersh who specialized in high-profile cases where there was a lot of media interest. He had been liaising on their behalf with the police. The plan was to hold a press conference the following morning at which Benjamin and Sarah would appear and read an agreed statement. Hersh even wanted Josh to be there too. Sarah was dreading it.

They went into the kitchen and Beth made them sit down and poured them each a glass of wine and though it wasn't even yet six o'clock they put up only token resistance. Benjamin asked after the Ingram boys who were both away at college. Beth said they were doing just great. They soon ran out of small talk.

"Did you hear they arrested Ty today?" Sarah said.

"They *what?*"

"I had a call from his mother. She was in a terrible state. The father of the boy who got shot in Denver owns the company that's been drilling gas on their ranch. They've had a lot of trouble with him. Apparently he's ruined the whole place. The police know about Ty and Abbie and all the calls he made to her cell phone. They seem to think he must be involved in some way, maybe even that he was the other one in the van with Abbie."

"Ty?" Benjamin said. "No way."

"That's what I said. But they say he has a motive."

Sarah also relayed what Hersh had told her that afternoon about taking care what they said in their phone conversations and e-mails, that there was a "strong possibility" that they were being monitored to see if Abbie might try to contact them. Her bank account and credit cards would already have been closed, he said. And Benjamin's and Sarah's accounts would no doubt be under scrutiny too in case they attempted to forward money to her.

"They can't do that, surely?" Benjamin said.

"He said it was safe to assume we would be under surveillance."

"What, everyplace we go? All the time, somebody's going to be tailing us? Joshie too? At school?"

Sarah shrugged. Benjamin shook his head.

"I don't believe that. Beth, do you?"

"Maybe I've seen too many movies."

Josh arrived back from school and Benjamin got up and gave him a long hug. Then Martin came home and the five of them had supper and tried to talk about other things but it all seemed a little phony. Martin and Benjamin hadn't spoken in a long while and though they both made an effort there was clearly a mutual residue of hurt.

And the phone never stopped ringing. The FBI and Alan Hersh wanted to finalize the details for the press conference and e-mailed them a draft of the statement. Sarah and Benjamin and Beth all went into the den and stood around Martin at his computer, reworking it then e-mailing it back. All it basically said was what a wonderful girl Abbie was, how proud of her they were, and how they were convinced of her innocence. It ended with a direct appeal to her to come forward and help clear things up. *We love you, honey,* it concluded. *Please come home.*

"You realize it has to be you who reads it out," Benjamin said.

"I can't."

"Sweetheart, I'll be there beside you. Joshie too. You know I'd do it, but with the way things have been between Abbie and me, she needs to hear it from you."

Sarah argued for a while but she knew he was right. Somehow she would have to find the strength.

The Ingrams' house had a guest annex that jutted in a typically Martinesque flourish into the back garden. It had its own deck and three double rooms, each with its own bathroom. The arrangement neatly got Beth off the hook about who was going to sleep where. Sarah and Josh had the previous night each taken a room and Ben had already put his bag in the third. After the late TV news—on which, thank heaven, there was no mention of Abbie or the murder—the Ingrams said goodnight and retired and the Coopers made their way upstairs to the annex.

They sat, all three of them, for a while on Sarah's bed and talked. Josh told them about the video he and Freddie and some of the other senior-year kids were making at school. Then he got up and said goodnight and went to his room. Benjamin seemed to take this as his cue to leave too. Now that it was just the two of them, he suddenly looked awkward and he stood up and stretched. Tomorrow was going to be a long and heavy day, he said. And he bent and kissed her on the cheek and walked toward the door.

"Don't go," Sarah said quietly.

He turned and looked at her.

"Sleep here. Please. I need you with me. Just tonight."

He shut the door and came back to the bed and sat beside her and put his arms around her and held her.

They undressed discreetly, like strangers. It felt odd to see his wash-bag beside hers in the bathroom and all the things she recognized but were no longer in her life. His razor, the little red leather manicure set she had once bought him, the deodorant he always used. When she came out of the bathroom he had already turned off the bedroom lights and she slid into bed beside him and for a long time the two of them lay there, separately staring at the ceiling and the slowly configuring shapes and shadows of the room.

"I miss you, Benjamin. So much."

"Oh, sweetheart."

"I get by without you. From day to day. But it's as if . . ."

She had to swallow hard. Don't cry, she told herself, don't cry.

". . . as if there's only half of me now. The other half has gone."

He rolled toward her and put his arm around her. And at his touch, of course, she couldn't help but cry.

"I love you, Benjamin."

He would probably think, later, that she must have planned it. But it wasn't so. There was no plan. Just the slow, inexorable conjunction of two wounded souls.

She turned toward him and put her arm around his waist and felt the warmth of his body, the familiar shape and angles of him, the press of his chest against her breasts. Her cheek against the roughness of his jaw, her lips in the softer hollow of his neck. She breathed the ever-remembered smell of him.

"Sarah, listen, we—"

"Ssh. Please."

She had already felt him stir against her thigh and now she pressed her pelvis into him and felt him swell and harden. She reached down and lifted her nightgown and reached for him inside his shorts and held him and felt him quiver. And now he'd found her mouth and was kissing her and raising himself across her and upon her, tugging down his shorts and lowering himself between her opened thighs and sliding up and into her.

And he was hers again. If only for this sorrowful and stolen night. He was hers.

TWENTY-TWO

Abbie had been to San Francisco only once before. It was on a family vacation when she was about twelve years old and they had stayed in a hotel that turned out to be a place where people came to recover from cosmetic surgery. Everybody had been wearing bandages, some with their heads and faces completely wrapped, trying to eat their breakfast through the slits that had been left for their mouths. Her dad said it was like an audition call for *The Invisible Man.* It was high summer but they never once saw the sun because the city was shrouded in a damp fog. Even so, they'd had fun, done all the tourist things, the streetcars, the cable car, browsed the stalls on Fisherman's Wharf, bought the T-shirts.

This time it was a little different.

She was standing in the dirty little corridor outside the manager's office, just along from the restrooms, waiting for her money. There was a single bare light-bulb and the walls were gloss red with lots of little white patches where notices had been ripped off and the paint had come away with the tape. The only one left said *Private, Keep Out* on which some great wit had inserted the word *Parts* after *Private* and, for those who didn't get it, scrawled an obscene illustration beneath.

At the other end of the corridor, she could see the smoky red glow of the bar where the jukebox, as usual, had been commandeered by the heavy-metal freaks. They always played it so loud she'd had to learn how to lip-read to take people's orders. When her shift ended, it was normally at least an hour before her ears stopped ringing.

It was after midnight and she had already been waiting five minutes. Behind the locked door, Jerry the manager, all two hundred and fifty disgusting pounds of him, was counting out the tips while at the same time talking on the phone to one of his crass friends. Which was presumably why it was taking so long. Multitasking was not among his gifts.

"Far out," he was saying. "Okay, you got it, big man. I gotta go. Yeah. Later."

The door was being unlocked now and as it swung open she saw Jerry, propelling himself on the castors of his chair back to the desk where the money stood divided into five little stacks among a decaying clutter of old burgers and pizza and coffee cups and God only knew what lived among them. The office, like everything else at Billy Z's, including the kitchens, was a health hazard. Who Billy Z was or might have been Abbie had no idea. Maybe he ate something off the menu and died. Or survived, which was why he was famous.

"Hey, Becky, sorry about that."

Abbie just nodded. He picked up one of the stacks of bills and handed it to her. Abbie counted it.

"There's only eighteen dollars here."

He took a bite of the burger and shrugged.

"It's been quiet."

She wasn't going to argue. She stuffed the money into her coat pocket and turned to go.

"You okay?"

"What?"

"You don't say a whole lot."

"So? I don't get paid to."

"Hey, chill, babe. Whatever."

She wanted to throw something at him but instead just gave him a look and turned and walked out.

"Love you too!" he called after her.

The fat jerk had kept her waiting so long that she

missed her bus back to Oakland. She ran down the hill but it was already pulling away up onto the freeway, so she sat on the wall and lit a cigarette and waited for the next. Apart from the traffic up on the freeway, the only sign of life was a black cat, sitting on the sidewalk across the road, outside the salvage yard with its stacked towers of flattened cars. He was grooming himself at the edge of a pool of cold light cast by a solitary street lamp. Every so often he would freeze and fix his yellow eyes on Abbie for a few moments, then nonchalantly go back to licking his paws.

"Hey, boy," she called softly. "Come on now, come over here."

But, of course, he didn't.

It was nearly April but the night was cold and damp and still felt like winter. Maybe it was the weather that was making her feel so down. When it was clear and sunny she found life a lot easier to handle but when it was like this her spirits seemed to plummet. And when that happened all she could think about was calling her mom.

The last time she had heard her voice was on the TV, begging Abbie to give herself up. It was pretty heavy watching it though Abbie couldn't remember all that much about it because she was a little out of her head with the pills Rolf had given her. It was just after they'd gotten to LA and were holed up with some people he knew there. One day had blurred into another, weeks into months. Just lying there on the bed with the drapes closed and the TV always on, Rolf bringing her food or something to smoke or making love to her. She couldn't even remember Thanksgiving or Christmas. But she could still conjure the image of her mom and dad and poor Josh standing there, so pale and nervous and brave in front of all those reporters, cameras flashing and microphones bristling, her mom saying how they knew she was innocent and how much they loved her.

Maybe, if her head had been clearer, she might have called them right then and there or even walked into a police station and announced who she was. Not that Rolf would have let her out of his sight long enough to do either. She knew he'd been worried that she might do something stupid like that. He'd kept telling her that they had to give things time to blow over, let all the media madness die down. And, of course, as always, he was right.

The house where they had first laid up was in Whittier, out in the endless sprawl of eastern LA. It was a run-down but not overly rough neighborhood, the kind of place where people minded their own business and the cops kept away unless someone got murdered. There were two guys and a woman living in the house and Abbie was never quite sure what they did. Two went out every morning, as if to work, but one always stayed home. From the regular flow of visitors, she figured they were most likely dealing drugs. She knew one of the guys had a gun and she figured there were probably others. But they were all kind to her, much kinder than those creeps she had met at Rolf's squat in Seattle. They treated her with sympathy, even with respect.

Then again, she was no longer just a rich little college kid on leafy-spurge patrol.

Little by little, the horror of that night in Denver began, if not to fade, at least to settle into what Rolf called its *context*. What had happened was an accident, he kept telling her, and she mustn't buy into the way the media distorted these things. He said—and Abbie believed him—that he felt bad about McGuigan's son dying. Knowing his parents were away, the boy had apparently brought his girlfriend home. He must have looked out, seen Abbie, and come out with the shotgun, walking straight past Rolf. Luckily, when the house went up, the girlfriend had gotten out. The boy getting killed was a sad and serious fuckup, Rolf said, but on the front line these things sometimes happened. And it was important to remember what his father had done to Ty's parents, how he'd ruined their lives and the lives of countless others. It was J. T. McGuigan, more than anyone, who bore the responsibility for his son's death, not they.

Rolf said all this before they had seen the news about the cops arresting Ty. That was the moment when Abbie had cracked and almost turned herself in. She had even put on her coat and was about to head off down the street to find a phone, but Rolf had stopped her and held on to her while she hollered and screamed and tried to hit him. How could those idiot cops think Ty had any-thing to do with it? Rolf said it was probably just a trick by the feds to get her to come forward. And it turned out he was right because a few days later Ty was released.

Luckily, he had several witnesses to prove he'd been in Sheridan on the night the McGuigan boy died. Though, according to the newspapers, the bastard feds still hadn't ruled out some kind of conspiracy charge.

She begged and begged to be allowed to call her mom, but Rolf wouldn't let her. Soon, he said, but not yet. It wasn't safe. He did, however, allow her to write a letter, which he carefully vetted in case she gave something away. All she really said in it was that she was okay, that what had happened was an accident, and that she was sorry for all she was putting them through. Rolf said they couldn't mail it from LA. He sent it to someone he knew in Miami who in turn was supposed to mail it on to New York. Whether it ever got there, Abbie didn't know.

The cat across the street was still cleaning himself. What little interest he had shown in Abbie's coaxing had vanished. The bus was coming now. She stood up as it slowed and when it stopped beside her and the doors hissed open, she climbed aboard. There were maybe half a dozen other passengers. It was only as she was walking toward the back that she noticed that two of them were cops.

One was a man, the other a woman, and they were sitting side by side chatting. By the look of it, both were off duty and on their way home. The man was watching Abbie's approach with what was probably only the most casual kind of interest but it was enough to make her heart start thumping. Rolf had told her the worst thing you could do was to appear nervous or furtive.

She looked the guy straight in the eye and smiled and he smiled back then looked away.

Abbie settled two rows from the rear and sat watching the backs of their heads. They were still talking, though about what she couldn't hear. Then the guy laughed and Abbie figured she was in the clear.

She looked out the window through her own reflection which, even after all these months, could still startle her. The dark brown hair cut short and stiffened with gel, the eyebrows dyed to match, the little rectangular black-rimmed spectacles with their plain glass lenses, the silver stud on the side of her left nostril. She didn't know why the sight of a cop still sent her into such a panic, for she could hardly recognize herself. You wouldn't guess she was even a distant cousin of the happy, blonde princess whose high-school graduation picture had been plastered all over the newspapers and shown night after night on the TV before they'd gotten tired of the story and, thank God, moved on.

All Rolf had done was grow a beard and trim his hair. And he hadn't really even needed to do that. Once the idiots had figured out that *Abbie Cooper's ecoterrorist accomplice* wasn't Ty after all, they had issued an artist's impression of Rolf so wildly inaccurate, it was a joke. The only thing that vexed him was their estimate of his age, which was "mid- to late thirties."

Within a week of reaching LA, he had fixed up new identities for them. He was now Peter Bauer and Abbie was Rebecca Jane Anderson. She had the driver's license, Social Security number, and credit cards to prove it. Though soon she was going to have to start over and learn to be somebody else because Rolf wasn't happy with the quality of the forgery of their licenses and was working on getting some better, more expensive ones. They were going to cost a thousand dollars each, which was why Abbie was having to wait tables at Billy Z's.

Rolf was still cagey about telling her too much about how he came by such documents. It was always "a friend" somewhere. But in the three months they had spent in LA and the two and a half here, listening and watching and eventually being given things to do on her own, she had learned a lot.

She knew, for example, that the best way to get a new identity was to check out newspaper obituary columns. She had seen this in a movie once and thought they must have made it up, but it was true. All you had to do was find someone of a similar age then apply by mail for an officially certified copy of his or her birth certificate. It was amazing, but when people died, it could take the authorities months, years even, to find out.

And getting a credit card was child's play. People were always receiving mailings asking them if they wanted a new card and nine times out of ten they just threw them in the garbage. All you had to do was rummage around in dumpsters to find one, fill in the form, notify a change of address, and bingo, they sent you the card. Of course, you didn't want to hold on to it for too long, in case you got busted, so you had to spend hard and fast then ditch it and get yourself another. Rolf said using them to get cash from ATMs was risky because the machines were all fitted with cameras. So instead they just bought stuff and sold it. It didn't even matter what you bought because Rolf always knew how to shift it, but they stuck mostly to electronic stuff, computers and cameras and phones, nothing too big or bulky.

It surprised her, when she thought about it, even shocked her a little, that she had taken so readily to what Rolf called living *on the outside*. If she was honest with herself, it excited her. Sometimes, in moments of fanciful exhilaration, she liked to think of them as a kind of eco-warrior version of Bonnie and Clyde— though she knew better than to share such romantic nonsense with Rolf.

And it wasn't as if anybody really got hurt—at least, with the credit-card scam. Rolf said people's liability for fraudulent use of their card was limited to fifty dollars. So it was the credit companies, the fat-cat corporations, who took the hit, not their customers. And, as he said, since the greedy bastards were themselves ripping everybody off the whole time anyway, why should anyone feel sorry for them?

They had moved to San Francisco in January and after living for a while in a horrible squat in Mission, had now at last moved to Oakland and had a place of their own. It wasn't much, just a one-bedroom apartment in a godforsaken neighborhood, but Abbie had cleaned it and painted it and made it livable, just like she had in Missoula. Rolf laughed at her, saying he despaired of her bourgeois values. But she told him she didn't care what he thought (which wasn't true) and anyhow why was it bourgeois not to want to live in squalor with fleas and lice crawling all over you? With a little more money, she could have made the place look great.

They were happier now. Now that the trauma had subsided and it was just the two of them again. She loved taking care of him and cooking for him and finding him little gifts. Every Friday, without fail, she would buy fresh flowers and put them in a jug on the kitchen table. And though he told her it was a waste of money and pretended he didn't care about such trivial things, she knew he secretly did. The times she liked best were the weekends when they would drive out of the city and hike for miles in the hills or the forest or along the coast. They would talk and laugh and make love. She had told him many times that she loved him, though he hadn't yet said it to her. It simply wasn't in his nature to say such things. But she was sure he did. On a cold and windswept beach, two weeks ago, he had drawn the outline of a heart in the sand and written within it their linked initials.

To help pay for their new documentation, Rolf too had now gotten himself a job. He was working in a bar down on Fisherman's Wharf and though the pay wasn't any better than Abbie's, he was actually earning fifty times that amount. She hadn't known anything about it until the other morning when she found this funny little device lying on the bedroom floor. It was black and looked like a pager or some fancy little cell phone. When she asked him what it was, he just smiled and for a long time wouldn't tell her. She wouldn't let him have it and he chased her all around the apartment until she threatened to flush it down the toilet unless he told her.

"Okay," he said. "It's a skimmer. Now give it to me."

He came toward her but she held up a hand and with the other lowered the thing toward the water until he stopped.

"And what's a skimmer?"

He sighed and pointed out the little slit in the side. If you swiped a credit card through it, he said, it downloaded all the information on the card's magnetic strip. If you knew where to go, you could sell the information for fifty dollars per card. Rolf, needless to say, knew where to go. He said he could get one for her to use at Billy Z's, but Abbie said she wouldn't do it. It was too brutal and brazen, too personal, she said. To rip people off like that, when you'd just been serving them and smiling and trying to earn a decent tip, seemed wrong. Rolf shook his head and laughed.

The bus had reached Oakland now and Abbie's neighborhood was the next stop. Everybody except the cops had gotten off. And, for the first time, the woman turned and looked back at her and Abbie had a stab of paranoia. Maybe they knew about her. Even if they didn't, she shouldn't let them know where she lived. Maybe she should stay on the bus until they got off then catch another one back. But, shit, it was late and she was so tired. She told herself not to be so stupid.

As the bus began to slow, she got up and walked to the front. But in her nervousness she forgot about the traffic lights at the foot of the hill. They were on red and the bus stopped and she reached the doors much too early so she had to stand there, right in front of the cops. They were staring at her and she was trying to look as if she either didn't know or didn't care. She turned up the collar of her coat.

Then one of the cops spoke and although she didn't hear what he said, she knew he had to be talking to her. She looked at him.

"I'm sorry?"

"I said, don't worry, spring'll soon be here."

"Oh. Yeah. Hope so."

The bus was moving again now. Abbie smiled and looked away, hoping that was the end of the conversation.

"Working late?"

She nodded, trying to look tired, just cheerfully resigned.

"Yeah. That's right. You too, huh?"

"Yeah. But not tomorrow. Tomorrow I get to patrol the golf course."

"Great."

The bus was stopping now, though it seemed to take an eternity for the doors to open. But at last, with a loud hiss, they did.

"Goodnight," she said as she stepped off.

"Goodnight."

The living-room lights were off when she got home,

just the shimmer of the TV coming from the doorway to the bedroom. She called his name as she double-locked the door but there was no answer. She walked through to the bedroom and saw him lying on the mattress they'd salvaged from a dumpster. He was working on his new laptop but shut the lid as soon as she came in.

"Hi," she said.

"How many times do I have to tell you not to call me Rolf?"

"Sorry. You still call me Abbie."

"I know that when it matters I won't get it wrong."

She took off her coat and knelt beside him on the bed.

"What makes you think I will?"

"You're new to all this. You have to practice these things."

"Yes, sir."

She kissed him on the forehead and then more fully on the lips, but there wasn't a flicker of response.

"Somebody's gotten into bed the wrong way," she said. "What have I done?"

For a moment, he didn't reply, just stared at the TV that stood on a crate behind the door. The sound had been turned off. President Bush was strolling on a ranch somewhere, dressed like a cowboy, an absurdly small black dog trotting along beside him.

"We've got to get out of here," he said.

"Why? I mean, what's wrong with this place?"

"I mean the city, for godsake."

"Leave San Francisco?"

"Have you been drinking? Why are you so goddamn slow?"

"Jesus. What's the matter with you?"

He turned away and got off the bed and went into the bathroom.

"Rolf—I mean . . . Please, tell me what's happened."

"Somebody's been talking. I don't know who. Maybe you."

"What?"

"I don't know. I heard today. The feds here have been asking questions. Anyway, whatever, we have to leave. Tomorrow."

"And go where?"

"I don't know. Chicago. Maybe Miami."

"Did the new IDs come through?"

"That fucked up too. And we have no money. You're going to have to get some from those rich parents of yours."

TWENTY-THREE

Josh had more or less gotten used to the idea that it was all over between him and Katie Bradstock. He'd seen her only once since she went off to Ann Arbor. They still sent each other e-mails but his were always a lot steamier than hers. Maybe that was the problem. Some of the sexy stuff he wrote, about intimate things they had done with each other or might yet do, which Josh thought might really turn her on (it sure turned him on writing it), she didn't even bother to acknowledge. He was, like, *I remember the shadows of your nipples in the moonlight.* And she would reply, *On Monday we played basketball and then all went to Wendy's.* She probably had a new boyfriend at college. That had to be it.

Then he figured that, since Abbie went on the run, maybe Katie was embarrassed, thinking everything they said was being monitored by some pervy little FBI creep. And maybe it was. Come to think of it, hell, he was embarrassed too. Anyhow, Katie Bradstock and her moonlit nipples were five hundred miles away in Ann Arbor and he was in Syosset and he had to face it: It wasn't going to work. As Freddie had been telling him for months now, long-distance relationships sucked.

Which was why it came as such a surprise when he got her letter saying she had to meet him. It was obviously something important and secret too because she sent it to him at school and said not to tell his mom and dad anything about it. Getting a letter at school was kind of embarrassing because nobody got letters at school and everyone was like, *Hey, Josh, so who's the love letter from?* The only person he told was Freddie, who stroked his chin and asked how long ago it was since he and Katie had seen each other.

"I don't know, like a couple of months or something. Why?"

"Like, eight or nine weeks, that kind of deal?"

"Yeah, I guess. Why?"

"And you had sex?"

"Yeah, of course." He tried to sound nonchalant and

manly. In fact, it had been fairly disastrous. "Why?"

"She's pregnant."

Jesus Christ! Josh spent the next three days in an agonized haze. That had to be it. Why else would she be so secretive? He would have called her on her cell phone straightaway but she had expressly forbidden it. Instead she gave him a number he didn't recognize and told him to call it at one o'clock precisely that coming Thursday. He should do this from a pay phone, she instructed, and make sure nobody was watching or listening. Jesus Christ!

When Thursday came and he called the number from one of the booths outside the school cafeteria, she picked up immediately. There was a roar of traffic, so he figured she was probably at a pay phone too.

"What's going on?" he said.

"I've got to see you. I can get a ride to New York this weekend. Saturday afternoon. Bloomingdale's. Can you make it?"

"Yeah, I guess. Katie, what the hell's all this about?"

"I can't tell you now. The cosmetics floor, okay? I'll be by the Clarins counter. Two o'clock. Have you got that?"

"The what counter?"

She impatiently spelled it out. He swallowed.

"Katie?"

"What?"

"Are you, like, pregnant?"

"*What?* No, for godsake. Of course not. Listen, I've got to go. I'll see you on Saturday. And Josh?"

"Yeah?"

"Make sure nobody's following you, okay?"

Only then did it occur to him what it might be about. Man, he was so dumb.

"Is this about Abb—"

"For godsake, Josh, shut up. I've got to go."

And she did. And now here he was, lurking in Bloomingdale's. He'd gotten here an hour early and had already walked every corner of the store, glancing over his shoulder, looking in mirrors, going up and down the elevators and escalators, scanning the faces for anyone who might be looking at him or studiously ignoring him. It was a miracle the store detectives hadn't grabbed him.

Until now, he hadn't taken all this surveillance stuff too seriously. He could just about believe they read e-mails and that the phones at home were bugged, maybe even his cell phone too. And for a few weeks after Abbie went missing, on the way to and from school, he'd kept an eye out for anyone watching from a parked car or a van with darkened windows, like it always was in the movies. But he soon concluded that if they were spying on him, they must be pretty damn good at it, because he never saw a thing. And they must be pretty damn bored too. Jesus, even *he* found his life boring. How much worse must it be for the poor suckers who had to watch him live it?

Freddie, who was a major computer freak and into all kinds of geeky techno stuff, said it was all done electronically nowadays anyhow. Cameras on satellites, so powerful they could zoom in on a zit. Well, if that was true, there wasn't a whole lot Josh could do about it now. On the train in from Long Island he had kept an eye out for anyone suspicious and even did a couple of laps of Penn Station before getting a cab over to 55th and Park Avenue. Then he'd woven a convoluted route to 59th and Lexington, with darted looks over his shoulder, even double-darted looks, before plunging into the store.

And now, at last it was two o'clock and there was the Clarins counter and there was Katie Bradstock, blonde and gorgeous and looking oh-so-worried in her tight little brown jacket and fur collar and black combat pants and silver trainers. The sight of her made Josh's heart lurch. She saw him and smiled, but her eyes were immediately scanning for who might be behind him. He put his arms around her and kissed her and she made a brave little attempt to respond but he could feel how taut and frightened she was.

She told him to follow her and walked away so fast he almost had to run to keep up. And soon they were out into the April sunshine and walking at top speed along the sidewalk. There was a Starbucks that she had clearly scouted out before, because she just went straight inside. While they waited for their coffees to be made, he tried to make small talk, told her about his getting accepted at NYU and how he was actually starting to look forward to it. But she didn't seem inter-ested. In fact, she barely seemed to register what he said. And it wasn't until they were settled in the back corner and out of earshot that finally she spoke.

"I saw Abbie."

"You *saw* her?"

"She came to Ann Arbor. Last week. She came to the house on McKinley—"

"What, she just, like, knocked on the door?"

"Josh, you're going to have to keep quiet and let me talk, okay?"

"Sorry. Okay."

"She had been watching the place and followed me. I had a class that morning. And when I came out of the hall, she followed me again and when I was on my own, she came up behind me and quietly said, *Katie?*"

"Jesus Christ."

"I didn't know who it was. I swear to God. She looked so different. Her hair, everything. Like ten years older. She was wearing glasses and this old black coat. I said, *I'm sorry, do I know you?* And she gave this funny little smile and said, *Katie, it's me, Abbie.*"

She was leaning close to him now, talking in a low voice that wasn't quite a whisper but almost and all the time looking over his shoulder and around him in case someone was watching.

"What did you do?" Josh said.

"We went for a walk and found somewhere to sit and talk."

"Did she tell you what happened?"

"Not really. She said it was all a terrible accident. They thought there was nobody in the house. They were just going to burn it down—"

"*Just* burn it down. Oh, that's okay then."

"Listen, you asked me, okay? I'm telling you. She said it was to show the guy's father, the one who owns the gas company, that he couldn't treat people the way he'd treated Ty's parents. Nobody was supposed to get killed."

"Why doesn't she give herself up then?"

"She said maybe she should have, but now it's too late, nobody would believe them."

"So she's still with Rolf?"

"Yes. She says she loves him and he's all she has left in her life."

"Oh, man."

"Josh, she needs money."

"How the hell's that going to work? My mom says the FBI watch every cent we spend."

"Abbie said your grandfather would know how to come up with a few thousand dollars in cash they wouldn't be able to trace."

"A few thousand dollars!"

Josh shook his head and looked away. Outside the clear spring sunshine made this all seem so surreal. He looked back at Katie and saw that she was crying. He took her hand in both of his.

"Do you have any idea how much this scares me?" she said.

He put his arms around her and held her. Her hair smelled fresh and wonderful. God, how he wished . . . She sat up and found a tissue in her pocket and dabbed her tears and the run mascara, composing herself. Then she reached for her purse and pulled out a sealed brown envelope.

"She said to give you this. I don't know what it says and I don't want to. I'm having nothing more to do with this, okay? I don't want my life ruined too. Or my mom and dad's. I love Abbie, or the person she was, but I told her not to contact me again. And Josh . . ."

She swallowed and seemed for a moment unable to go on. She wiped her eyes one final time and closed her purse.

"I don't want you to contact me again either."

"Katie—"

"I mean it. Don't e-mail me, don't call me. Ever. Okay?"

She stood up and kissed him on the forehead then walked briskly to the door and out into the sunlit street and disappeared.

Josh sat there for a long time, staring at the envelope in his hands, his head whirling with so many different thoughts and emotions it was hard to focus on any of them or on anything else. Man, what a total fucking mess it all was. He sighed and opened the envelope. There was a single sheet of yellow paper in it, torn from a legal pad and tightly folded. It wasn't much of a letter. In Abbie's elegant handwriting, all it said was:

Josh. Be at the corner of 58th and Madison at 3 p.m. Be SURE you are not followed. Destroy this now. A.

He threw it in the trash but then had second thoughts

and fished it out and took it instead to the restroom and flushed it. He looked at his watch. He had nearly twenty minutes to get there but he still ran the first two blocks until he nearly got knocked down disobeying a *Don't Walk* sign. The blast of angry horns brought him to his senses and he walked the rest of the way, taking deep breaths to calm himself but without much success.

He got there with five minutes to spare. But by three-twenty, nothing had happened. And by now every passerby, every passenger in every passing car, had become an FBI agent, even the huddle of tourists across the street who had been there for the last five minutes, pretending to be looking at a street map. Shit, one of them was even taking a picture of him! The cloudless sky was full of satellites, zooming in on his zits.

Just as he was reaching the conclusion that nothing except his own paranoid delusion was going to happen, a cab pulled up beside him and the door opened and a woman in dark glasses beckoned him to get in. Fraught with fear and fantasy, his first instinct was *no way*. But as he backed away, she took off her shades and he realized he was looking at his sister.

"Hey, how *are* you!" she said, making space for him to get in beside her. "Come on."

But the happy tone, the kind you might use with a friend you hadn't seen for some time, had thrown him and he stood for a moment gaping like a moron until she smacked the seat sharply with her hand and slipping out of character for a moment, mouthed for him to hurry the fuck up and get in.

He obeyed and shut the door and as the cab pulled out into the traffic, he sat staring at her, his mind groping for something to hook on to behind this stranger's mask. He began to speak her name but she interrupted him.

"Hey, it's so great to see you!"

And at last he realized that she wanted him to act too.

"Yeah, great. How've you been?"

She leaned forward and casually told the cab driver to head into the park then settled back into the seat and looked at him and smiled.

"Oh, fine," she said. "You?"

"Terrific."

He said it flatly, barely bothering to veil the sarcasm. The shock of seeing her was giving way to anger now. How dare she think she could pull his strings like this. Who the hell did she think she was?

"Well, that's great," she said brightly.

She glanced at the driver, met his eyes in the mirror, and he looked away. Then she swiveled to take a quick look out of the rear window, checking—Josh, of course, knew the routine now—if they were being followed.

"It's okay," he said.

She smiled at him, more nervously now. Josh shook his head and looked away out of the window.

Halfway across the park she asked the driver to stop and let them out and from the way she sat there Josh realized she expected him to pay. She must have been in the cab for some time because it cost thirty-five dollars, forty with the tip. It almost cleaned him out. It made him madder still and she noticed.

"I'll pay you back," she said quietly.

"Yeah, right."

They walked up the hill into the park, neither of them saying anything. Everybody was out enjoying the spring sunshine; joggers, rollerbladers, tourists taking those dumb horse-and-buggy rides. Some of the trees were in blossom, the leaves of others a luminous, unreal green. Josh was still seething. She slid an arm inside his and he nearly elbowed her away but didn't.

"How's Mom?"

"Oh, she's just . . . on top of the world. Never been better."

"Josh—"

"Christ, Abbie!" And now he did shrug her arm away, more violently than he meant to. "What the hell are you *doing?*"

A guy coasting by on a skateboard turned to look at them.

"Josh, please—"

"I don't care. Whatever stupid fucking game you think you're playing, we don't have to play it too. Do you understand? Do you?"

She looked away and nodded. She was wearing her shades and the black coat. She was so pale, her neck all bony and thin. Somehow the black hair made her look like a refugee, some starved survivor of a nameless war.

"Do you have any idea what you've put Mom through? And Dad? And me and Katie and everyone? Do you know how many people's lives you've wrecked?"

"I can imagine."

"Oh, really? And now you get in touch just because you need money. Jesus, Abbie. You're unbelievable."

"I wrote a letter."

"When? We didn't get any letter."

"I wrote Mom a letter, months ago."

"Well, it didn't arrive."

They strolled on in silence for a long time. A guy was playing soccer on the grass with two little girls, a pregnant woman lying in the shade of a tree, cheering them on. Josh glanced at Abbie. She was looking the other way but he could see the glint of tears on her cheeks below the sunglasses.

"Oh shit, Abbie."

He put his arms around her and held her and she buried her face in his chest and wept. Her quaking body felt frail as a bird's, as if he could snap her bones were he to squeeze too hard. And her smell was strange and musty, like clothes stored too long in the attic.

"I'm sorry," she murmured. "I didn't want to do this."

"It's okay."

He was close to crying too. Damn it, he hadn't cried since junior high and he wasn't going to do it now.

"We just miss you, for Christsake. It's like you've left this great big hole in all our lives. Mom's been so brave but underneath she's kind of broken and terrified something else will happen and . . . Oh, shit, Abbie, I don't know. Everything's just so totally weird and messed up. Things aren't supposed to be like this."

"I know."

"Why don't you just give yourself up? Whatever happens, it can't be worse than it is now."

"Oh, yes it can."

"Listen, everyone knows it must have been Rolf who—"

She pulled away from him, took off her glasses, and with a fist violently rubbed away her tears.

"You don't know anything about him. You never even met him."

"I know, but—"

"So don't go saying things! You don't know what happened. Nobody does. It was an accident. Everyone thinks he must be this bad guy and led me astray and all that bullshit but it's not true. He cares more about what goes on in the world than anyone I ever met."

She was angrily wiping the lenses of her sunglasses, but with her fingers and thumb, smudging them, like a madwoman. He gently took them from her and cleaned them properly with the tail of his T-shirt, then handed them back. She wouldn't look him in the eyes until she put them on again.

"Listen, I don't have long. We need to talk about the money."

"Abbie, you need help."

"What I fucking well need is money!"

Josh sighed. She looked nervously around her then started walking again and he followed and fell into step beside her.

"Do I ask Mom? Do I tell her I saw you?"

"I don't know. You tell me."

"I don't know. Anyway, they've got tabs on all our accounts."

"Then sell something."

"*Sell* something?"

"Or talk to Grandpa. He knows about money. Probably launders it for his fat-cat clients all the time."

He asked her how much she needed and nearly choked when she said twenty thousand dollars. She wouldn't tell him what it was for and got angry again and strode off ahead when he tried to press her.

By now they had reached Central Park West and she led him across and into the streets beyond. Josh realized they were on some sort of mission and asked her where they were headed and she told him they were going to RadioShack, where he would buy himself a prepaid cell phone so that she could contact him. She wasn't going to come into the store, she said, so he would have to make sure he got the right kind, one that could be activated without having to give any kind of ID or address. It would cost around a hundred dollars, she said, and he should pay cash, so there would be no record.

When Josh complained that after their taxi ride he didn't have that kind of money on him, she told him—sarcastically, as if he was an idiot—that this was why they were going first to an ATM, where, while he was at it, he could get out some extra cash for her. Josh had a lifetime of practice being bossed around by his big sister, but there was something about this fractious, half-crazed stranger with her calculated list of instructions that made him want to grab hold of her and shake her to her senses. But he didn't.

Abbie probably wouldn't have paid any attention anyway. All the earlier emotional rawness seemed to have vanished. This was clearly the business she had come to do and she seemed to have it all figured out. The prepaid phone was to be used only for her to leave messages, she went on. No one but the two of them must know the number or even that he had the phone at all, not even their mom. Once it was activated, he should keep it switched off, except once each morning and evening to check his voicemail. However, he must never, *never,* do this at home where calls of every kind were obviously being scanned.

They found an ATM on Broadway and he took out two hundred and forty dollars and gave her a hundred. Then they walked a few blocks to RadioShack and while she waited in a coffee shop Josh went in and bought a prepaid phone for a hundred and twenty dollars with thirty minutes of talk included, no questions asked.

When he went to find Abbie in the coffee shop she was getting edgy and said she had better be going. She made a note of his new phone number then handed him a sheet of yellow paper on which she had written two columns of letters and figures. In a voice so quiet he had to lean in close, she told him this was the code she would use. It shouldn't be disclosed to anyone. Every number from zero to nine was randomly allocated a letter of the alphabet. When she needed to speak to

Josh, she would call his new cell phone and leave a message of two words; the first would be a coded phone number and the second would give him the date and time he should call it. If it didn't work out, he should try again an hour later, then an hour later and so on. He should never, she said, use anything but a pay phone and always be totally sure he wasn't being watched. Josh's head by now was whizzing with too much information. But he still couldn't resist asking if all this James Bond stuff came from Rolf. In response he got only an irritated sigh.

The coming Wednesday she would leave him a message with a number he should call at one o'clock the following afternoon. This should give their mom enough time to sort out the money.

"She'll want to talk with you herself," Josh said.

Abbie looked away and thought about this for a moment.

"Please," he said. "Just let her hear your voice."

She nodded.

"Okay. Let her make the call. But only from a pay phone at the time I tell you. And somewhere safe where she's certain she's not being watched. Make sure she understands how careful she's got to be. And tell her if she starts giving me a hard time, I'll hang up, okay?"

Jesus, Josh thought. Give *her* a hard time? And all this *be careful* shit. Didn't she think by now he might have gotten the message? But he said nothing, just nodded.

Now she was on her feet and walking out and for a moment he thought she was going to leave him just like that without even saying good-bye. But she turned and waited for him and, as he came up to her, gave him a sad little smile in which he thought he glimpsed the sister he once knew.

"Thanks, Joshie."

"It's okay. I just wish . . ."

"I know."

She kissed him on the cheek and turned and quickly walked away. There was a subway station at the end of the block and he stood watching while she wove her way through the crowd like a frail black ghost toward it. He thought she might look back but she never did. The sidewalk was sunlit but the entrance to the subway lay in the sharply angled shadow of a tall building. And he watched her cross the threshold of the shadow and start to go down the steps until at last the darkness devoured her.

TWENTY-FOUR

Her father had been on the goddamn running machine for about ten minutes now and however he might be feeling, Sarah didn't think she could take much more. His eyes were fixed on the mirrored image of himself on the wall in front of him, though why, she had no idea, for it wasn't anyone's idea of a pretty sight. The sweat was streaming off him, his breasts under the sodden T-shirt wobbling with every stride, while his cheeks puffed in and out like a cantankerous blowfish.

It was her own fault for coming down here. His morning workout was sacrosanct. And this, the Sunday-morning version, doubly so. He had said no twice already, last night when she arrived and again this morning. But before driving home, she had to give it one more go.

"Dad, couldn't you just—"

"Sarah, I've told you. It's out of the question."

"Please, just listen to me for a minute."

"I've listened. I've heard. And the answer's still no."

"Stop!"

If she had thought about it, she wouldn't have dared do it. But in the same moment that she hollered, she whacked the off button of the running machine and her father lurched forward and had to grab the rails to stop himself from falling.

"What the hell's the matter with you?"

"Goddamn it, Dad! I need your attention here."

She didn't speak to her father like that and she almost apologized. But it seemed, for a moment at least, to have done the trick.

"Sarah, we've already gone through it ten times over."

"This is your granddaughter, for heaven's sake!"

He stepped off the machine and snatched up a towel from the chair.

"It's not just Abbie," he said, patting himself dry. "You've *all* gone crazy. How many times do I have to say it? What you're asking is illegal, Sarah. Illegal."

"So when has that bothered you before?"

"I beg your pardon?"

"Oh, come on, Dad. Don't give me that. Don't tell me you've always played it by the book. What about all those shady bond deals, all that offshore stuff, those trips to the Cayman Islands. I'm not a complete idiot."

"How dare you."

He picked up his robe and headed for the stairs up to the kitchen. She was more shocked by what she'd just said than he was. It was as if some protective, mother-animal override had clicked in. But seeing as it had, she wasn't about to stop. She was following him up the stairs now and into the kitchen. Her mother was sitting at the breakfast counter, pretending to read the news-paper. From the arched eyebrow and the delicate tilting of the glass as she sipped her orange juice, Sarah knew she must have heard what had been said down in the gym. This was new territory and her mother was inter-ested. Her father was at the refrigerator, pouring him-self a glass of water.

"Dad, talk to me."

"I've said all I have to say. And you've said more than enough."

"Listen, I could have told you it was for me."

"Well, maybe you should have. What's she going to use it for? Making bombs? Killing more people or what?"

"You know Abbie wouldn't do that. What happened was an accident."

"Then she should give herself up and tell the truth."

"Well, maybe she will. If we can just establish some kind of contact."

He drank his water and poured some more. He wouldn't look at her.

"Dad?"

"What?"

"If it was me out there, scared to death and starving . . ." She bit the inside of her lip. Damn it, she wasn't going to cry. "Would you do it for me?"

Her mother, still pretending to read her newspaper, muttered something. Sarah's father turned and glared.

"What was that?"

"I said, of course, you would."

He drained a second glass and put it down on the counter with a clunk, then mopped his face and neck again with the towel.

"I'll give you ten thousand."

"Fifteen."

"All right, fifteen. But that's it. I don't want to hear anything more about it. It's for you and what you do with it is entirely up to you."

Sarah walked over to him and put her arms around him.

"Daddy, thank you."

"I must be out of my mind."

Sarah had imagined it might take him a day or two to sort things out, but after he'd showered and dressed he went quietly to his safe in the den and within the hour she was driving home with the money bundled up in a yellow plastic bag in the trunk.

By now she had gotten used to keeping a constant eye on the rearview mirror to see if she was being tailed and not once had she seen anything even vaguely suspicious. Today, however, everyone was suspect. And it wasn't just cops she was worried about, it was robbers too. Every pedestrian waiting at the lights was suddenly a potential mugger or carjacker. It was just how Josh said it had been for him on his way to meet Abbie.

Sarah knew something serious had happened the moment the boy walked through the door yesterday evening, after his mysterious—and utterly implausible—"shopping trip" into the city. He had taken her outside onto the deck and told her quietly what had happened. And as soon as Sarah felt she had gotten as much out of him as she was going to get (for he was such a poor liar and she was sure there was more he hadn't told her), she had packed an overnight bag, gotten into the car, and driven directly to Bedford. She'd wanted Josh to come too, thinking his eyewitness account of meeting Abbie might sway things with her father, but Josh made some lame excuse about having promised to see Freddie. The poor kid was clearly still fazed by seeing his sister, so Sarah hadn't pressed him. Though now, on her way home, besieged by phantom cops and carjackers, she wished she had.

Only then did it occur to her that they ought to tell Benjamin about Josh seeing Abbie. He had a right to know, though she didn't much relish the prospect of calling him. The last time they had talked it had been little short of catastrophic. After that night before the press conference when they had made love, she had stupidly managed to persuade herself that things would somehow change. That the shock of what had happened with Abbie would chase away his madness and bring him back. He loved her, she knew he loved her. The way it had been that night, it was obvious. Men couldn't fake those things.

But after a few days, off he'd gone. Back to Santa Fe. And, as the weeks and then the months went by, she knew she had deluded herself. Nothing had changed. Except that the loneliness and sorrow seemed somehow immeasurably deeper. And she felt so stupid, so goddamn stupid, for letting it happen that night. And how could he make love to her like that, so tenderly, so penitently, when he didn't mean it, when he clearly didn't have the slightest intention of coming home, how *could* he?

But if she felt foolish then, it was nothing compared to how she made herself feel last month when she came home to an empty house after a week in Pittsburgh with Iris. The weather had suddenly gone wintry again and the furnace had given up the ghost so there was neither heat nor hot water. Josh was out partying and so, it seemed, was everybody else she called—Martin and Beth, Jeffrey and his boyfriend, Brian. She put on two sweaters and a coat and lit a fire in the living room and drank a whole bottle of Chianti, then opened another and did what she had vowed never to do again: the late-night drink-and-dial thing.

Benjamin answered the phone with his mouth full, clearly having some cozy, candlelit dinner *à deux* with The Catalyst. And Sarah launched into him like a volley of tomahawks, accusing him of everything she could think of, even things she knew he hadn't done and never would do. How he had never loved her, never loved any of them, how all he'd ever cared about was his work and his goddamn ego. And how he had ruined and wasted her life, stolen all those precious years when she could have been doing so many better, more worthwhile things, had a proper, fulfilling career, instead making all those sacrifices only to get it all thrown back in her face.

She could tell from the background sound that he must have walked off to another room, somewhere more private, to spare The Catalyst's blushes. After a while his attempts to get a word in edgewise grew more assertive.

"Sarah, listen. Listen a moment. Please. I'm going to hang up now."

"Yeah, why don't you? Go and fuck the bitch, like you did me that night. And fuck yourself too while you're at it."

It must have been quite a shock for all those FBI phone-tappers, playing their endless late-night game of poker or whatever it was they did to while away the hours.

She hoped the memory of what she'd said might haze with the hangover but it hadn't. And though she had tried ever since to pluck up the courage to call him and apologize, she hadn't been able to. But now that they had heard from Abbie, now that Josh had actually seen her, there was no excuse. Somehow, without alerting suspicion, Benjamin had to be told.

That afternoon, the money stashed in the washing machine (it seemed appropriate and, for want of a safe, as good a place as any), she gave Josh a wink and asked him to come out into the garden to help her do some planting. She had no idea if the FBI had bugged the house as well as the phones. They'd certainly had ample opportunity. There had been so many agents in the place these past months, going through Abbie's things and asking a million questions about her so they could "profile" her, chances were they'd planted something. Until now there hadn't been anything worth eavesdropping on, but now that there was, Sarah wasn't taking any risks.

Josh didn't know about her abusive call, so while sparing him the lurid details, she told him. It was amazing how much he had grown up since his father left. Abbie had always been the one with whom Sarah had discussed important emotional matters. But Josh had revealed himself to be every bit as good a listener and wiser, if more sparing, in his counsel. Before Sarah even thought to suggest it, Josh said that he would be the one to call Benjamin.

He had it already figured out. So as not to alert any eavesdroppers, he would tell his father that there was a lot to sort out about his going to NYU—forms to fill out and so on. By the by, he would mention that Sarah was embarrassed about their last phone call and suggest that while he was in New York maybe the three of them could have lunch or dinner. It seemed to Sarah a fine plan.

They went inside and Josh ran up the stairs to his room to make the call while Sarah tried to focus on preparing supper. Within five minutes he was down again. It was all fixed, he said. Benjamin would fly in on Friday. They would have dinner. He sent her his love.

J osh wouldn't say how he knew which number to call. He said he had promised Abbie that he wouldn't tell anyone and that it was safer that way. When he arrived home from school the previous evening he'd handed Sarah a piece of paper with the number on it. It was a New Jersey area code and probably, he said, a pay phone. Somewhere like a mall or a gas station.

All week Sarah had been racking her brains to think of the best place to call from and had finally opted for Roberto's, a restaurant she and Benjamin often used to go to. There were two cowled phone booths at the back, beyond the restrooms, and always enough bustle and noise from the kitchen to mask any conversation. It was also only a few blocks from the bookstore. So on Thursday morning at twelve-fifteen, as if on a whim, she announced to Jeffrey that she was going to buy him lunch.

The place wasn't crowded but as one o'clock drew nearer it began to get busier. They ate their Caesar salads and chatted about business then Jeffrey started telling her about a new French movie he and Brian had been to see at the Angelika Film Center. Sarah did her best to look interested, although every time anyone went toward the restroom all she could think about was what would happen if, at one o'clock when she went back there, both phones were being used. She looked at her watch. Four minutes to go.

"Are you okay?"

"Sorry?"

Jeffrey was frowning at her.

"You seem a little distracted."

"No, I'm fine. Jeffrey, I'm so sorry. I just remembered. I was supposed to call Alan Hersh this morning. It's apparently something important and I completely forgot. Will you excuse me a moment?"

"Sure."

She picked up her purse and got up and walked back across the restaurant, weaving her way among the tables where suddenly every face seemed to be staring at her. She felt like Al Pacino in *The Godfather*, on his way to get the gun. Both phone booths were free. She chose the one farther from the restrooms. It was two minutes before one o'clock. She put her purse down on the little stainless-steel shelf and took out a sandwich bag of quarters and Josh's piece of paper. And as the second hand of her watch ticked toward the hour, her breathing fast now and shallow and her hands trembling so badly she almost spilled the coins, she picked up the receiver, inserted the money and dialed.

"Hello?"

Sarah gasped and swallowed and for a moment couldn't speak. To hear the voice, after all these long months, overwhelmed her.

"Mom?"

"Hello, my love."

"Oh, Mom."

From the small, faltering way she said it, Sarah knew she wasn't the only one fighting tears. Suddenly, stupidly, she didn't know what to say. There was both too much and nothing.

"Baby, how are you?"

"I'm okay. How are you?"

"I'm okay too."

There was a long moment of silence. Sarah could hear music playing in the background, then the blare of a horn. She longed to ask where Abbie was, but knew she shouldn't.

"Mom, I'm so sorry."

"Oh, baby."

"Listen, we only have a short time—"

"My love, come home, please—"

"Mom—"

"Everyone will understand, if you just tell them what happened—"

"Don't! I told Josh you mustn't do this!"

"I'm sorry, I'm sorry."

There was another long pause.

"Did you get the money?"

"Abbie, honey—"

"Did you?"

"Yes."

"Good. Now listen very carefully. I'm going to tell you what to do. It's very important you do everything exactly as I tell you. Do you have a pen?"

There was a man coming down the corridor now. Sarah turned her back and wiped her tears and reached for her purse. She assumed he must be on his way to the restroom. But he wasn't. He was going to use the other phone.

"Mom?"

"Yes. Hold on a moment."

She found a pen but her hands were shaking so much that she knocked her purse off the shelf and its contents spilled across the floor.

"Damn!"

The man, a nice-looking young guy in a brown sports coat, squatted beside her and helped her scoop everything up. He looked her directly in the eye, maybe a little too directly, and smiled. Could he be . . . ? She thanked him and stood and picked up the phone again.

"Sorry," she said, striving for a jauntiness that even to her own ears sounded half-demented. "I just dropped my purse."

"Are you ready?" Abbie said.

There was a tap on Sarah's shoulder and it startled her so badly she almost cried out. The guy was holding her lipstick. She smiled and took it and thanked him.

"Is there somebody there?" Abbie asked anxiously.

"It's okay."

"Who is it?"

"Don't worry, everything's under control."

She knew she had to sound light and breezy now. Just in case. The man probably wasn't an agent. They wouldn't do it like that, so unsubtly. Would they? She could tell Abbie was on the verge of hanging up. But she didn't. She asked if Sarah was ready then started dictating her instructions.

When Sarah got back to the table, Jeffrey said he'd been about to call search and rescue. He had already almost finished his pasta and had asked for hers to be taken away and kept warm. The waiter had seen her return and at once brought it back. She had never in her whole life felt less like eating. Jeffrey asked if everything was okay and she said yes, thanks. Everything was fine.

TWENTY-FIVE

Ben reached the mall a little after seven-thirty, a good hour earlier than he was supposed to be there. He was worried about the traffic and worried too that in the dark, if it was one of those massive places with twenty acres of parking, he might get lost and blow the whole thing. In fact it turned out to be even bigger than he expected, but more by luck than brilliance he found the right spot without any trouble at all.

Zone M, row 18, at the far corner of the lot, across

from Petland and Old Navy. He could even see the black trash can, the third from the left, in which he was supposed to dump the bag. There didn't seem to be any security cameras, which was probably why Abbie had chosen the place. It occurred to him that she might already be here, watching him from somewhere even now. If she was, it was probably best not to peer or snoop around too much in case it scared her away.

He drove around the lot, slowing here and there for shoppers pushing their loaded carts out to their cars and then he pulled out onto the highway again and drove west for half a mile until he saw the red flashing neon arrow and a sign that said *Bar Rodeo*. He pulled in and parked then went inside and sat at the bar and ordered himself a beer.

He was pretty certain he hadn't been followed. He'd slipped out of a side door at The Waldorf, where he was staying, then crisscrossed Manhattan in three different cabs, walked through Macy's and out the other side, then taken a fourth cab to the car-rental place. Any agent who'd managed to keep up with all that, then trail him through the traffic all the way out here to Newark, deserved immediate promotion.

Bar Rodeo was pretending, none too convincingly, that it was somewhere out west. There were a few cowboy pictures on the walls and a rather forlorn-looking fake buffalo head that seemed to be watching the ballgame on the TV above the bar. The barman was wearing a red satin waistcoat and one of those little black Maverick neckties and greeted every customer with a no doubt obligatory if slightly halfhearted *howdy.*

Ben still hadn't quite recovered from the shock of it all. He'd flown to New York expecting to talk about college with Josh and make peace with Sarah. And here he was, furtively preparing to dump fifteen thousand bucks in a New Jersey trash can for his terrorist daughter.

At the noisy restaurant last night in Oyster Bay, just as he'd started to think the peacemaking with Sarah was going rather better than he'd dared hope, she and Josh had looked at each other, nodded, then leaned forward over their steaks and broken the news.

By then, of course, they were both many fathoms deeper into the conspiracy than he was. Josh kept saying things like *blowing her cover* and *making the drop,* as if he were already a paid-up member of the Mob. Ben just sat there with his eyes growing ever wider. While Josh was more into the mechanics of it all, Sarah was into the psychology. She couldn't stop going on about Rolf.

"She's obviously completely in thrall to the guy," she said. "Joshie said she was like this totally different person. And I could hear it in her voice. All hard-edged, kind of manic. She needs help, Benjamin. We've got to get her away from the guy."

Ben didn't need convincing. Only two weeks ago he'd had a visit from a new FBI agent from Denver who had apparently taken over the case from Frank Lieberg. The guy's name was Kendrick and he seemed a much more sympathetic character than any of the other agents they had so far had dealings with. At one point he had even gotten out his wallet to show Ben some pictures of his own daughter and said he just couldn't begin to imagine how he'd cope if something similar happened to her.

What had happened to Abbie, he told Ben, was a classic case of infatuation, what had come to be known as Patty Hearst or Stockholm Syndrome: a young woman from a loving, well-off family who at a vulnerable moment becomes besotted with a charismatic man, inevitably older and more experienced. The man convinces her that the values she has grown up with are wrong-headed and morally corrupt, and leads her into a way of life in which criminality becomes a romantic, even a thrilling, moral alternative. There was usually an element of wanting to shock or outrage or even to punish parents. And often, Kendrick added, a little uncomfortably, a strong sexual element, which blurred reality and tied the woman ever more closely to her new mentor.

Ben had gone on to cross-examine him about Rolf and was depressed to learn how little they still seemed to know. It was more than six months since he'd passed on what Hacker had told him that evening in Missoula, about Rolf possibly being the Michael Kruger or Kramer who had been involved in those bombings some years ago. Kendrick said they had checked out every possible connection but found nothing that cast new light on the guy's true identity.

Partly because of their last incendiary phone call and partly because he didn't want to upset her with things she must have already more or less figured out for herself, Ben hadn't told Sarah any of this. And last night, at dinner, it hadn't seemed appropriate, particularly in front of Josh. But there they were, talking about *making the drop,* concocting a plot in which Ben somehow seemed to have emerged as the lead player and which (though he didn't know chapter and verse) could no doubt get him sent to jail if he got caught. God help us, he'd thought, our golden child has made criminals of us all.

Sipping his beer and distractedly watching the ballgame above the young barman's head, Ben kept thinking Sarah might after all have been right. She should probably be doing this, not him. Even before she went on the run, Abbie had made it clear that she didn't want to see him. In her new volatile state of mind, the sight of him tonight was likely to send her into a rage. Seeing her mother, on the other hand, might just conceivably soften and touch her. Abbie, of course, was expecting Josh to deliver the money and the sweet kid would have willingly done so. But there was no way Ben and Sarah were going to let that happen. After talking it over last night, examining the idea from every possible angle, they had all agreed it should be Ben. Physically, he was the strongest. And, if it came to it, he might be able to grab hold of her, overpower her, maybe get her into the car and make her see the sense of turning herself in. Maybe.

He thought of Eve and had a sudden urge to call her, then remembered that on Abbie's instructions he had left his cell phone at the hotel in case the cops used its signal to track him. Anyway, he had spoken to her only a couple of hours ago, without giving any indication of what he was about to do. She had told him something that had unsettled him a little.

Yesterday evening she had found Pablo in front of the TV, watching a videotape that he said he'd found in the bedroom closet. It seemed to be a transfer of a home movie. Eve was mystified. Two young kids she didn't recognize, a boy and a girl, were splashing around in the shallows on a beach somewhere. Then the camera panned around and there was Sarah in a swimsuit holding up her hands and trying to get out of shot, Ben's voice chiding her and laughing from behind the camera, telling her she looked great and should stand still.

It was one of the tapes he had secretly packed when he left. He'd tried watching it once when Eve was out but found he got too choked up and stopped. Pablo, of course, knew Ben had two grown-up kids but insisted these young ones were different and wanted to know when he was going to get to meet and play with them.

It was a quarter past eight now. Ben finished his beer and paid and the barman said *Y'all hurry back soon, y'hear?* Ben said he definitely would.

Outside, it was almost dark. The air was cool and clear and the neon signs along the sides of the highway shone sharp in many vibrant shades. Ben drove slowly out of the lot and headed back toward the entrance to the mall and did another circuit of the stores. They were all still open, though the cars were fewer than before. In zone M there were probably thirty or forty vehicles but they all seemed to be empty. Maybe she would come on foot.

On his second circuit, the clock on the dash turned to 20.28 and this time when he reached Petland, he turned into zone M and cruised slowly toward the corner and row 18. There were only two cars within twenty yards of the third trash can and nobody visible in either. He would be able to park right next to it. A little farther away, across the dividing strip of concrete, in zone L, an old couple were trying to lift something heavy from a cart and into the back of an old station wagon. But they were the only people anywhere near.

He stopped by the space and reversed so that the rear of his car was within three or four yards of the trash can. As the clock flicked to 20.30, with the engine still running, he got out of the car and walked around and stood by the trunk, taking one last quick look around him. The old couple in zone L were arguing but neither of them gave him so much as a glance. Ben quickly opened the trunk, took out the yellow plastic bag, and in one quick move, dumped it in the trash can. Then he shut the trunk and, exactly as Abbie had instructed, got back into the car and drove away.

As he crossed the lot, back toward the road that passed in front of the stores, he kept looking in his mirror and all around him for any sign of her. But he saw none. In front of Old Navy, he stopped to give way to a passing car and then pulled out behind it and followed it slowly around the corner. And as the parking lot behind him slid out of his mirror, he took a last glance over his shoulder. But nothing had changed. No new car by the trash can. No new people.

She had to be somewhere watching. There was no car following him but he wanted to give the unseen eyes the impression that he was still obeying orders and so he followed the white exit signs painted on the road as if he was going for good.

But he wasn't. He'd already figured it out. There was a slight rise about three hundred yards along the highway and after it some lights. By the time he got there he would be out of sight and far enough away and she would assume he had gone. But at the lights he would take a right turn and then another right which would bring him into the far end of the mall again where he could pick up the internal road and make his way back to the parking lot.

In no more than about three minutes he was coming past JCPenney and Bed Bath & Beyond and up ahead now, across a little link road, he could see Petland. He had to wait for three cars to go by and he peered through the darkness at the people inside but none of them was Abbie. And now he was across the link road and drawing closer to Petland and looking to his right he could see a white car, a little Ford, crossing the lot to the far corner of zone M, much farther away from the stores than you would need to go if all you wanted to do was park. It had to be her. He knew it was. But he was still too far away to get anything more than a vague impression of the driver.

In zone L, which was closer to where he now was, he could see the old couple still trying to maneuver whatever it was into the back of the station wagon. On impulse, instead of driving on to zone M, he turned sharply into the entrance to L and made his way toward them. The white car was almost at the trash can and Ben had a sudden stab of panic that if she saw him she might just turn around and go. It was dark enough by now and she wouldn't, of course, recognize his car. But he wasn't going to risk being seen too soon and he quickly turned the wheel and parked in a slot between two tall SUVs. He got out and started to run.

The white car was pulling up beside the trash can. There seemed to be only one person in it. Ben ran as fast and as low as he could, trying to keep the old couple's station wagon between him and the white car. But he could see the driver's door opening now and someone getting out. It was a man. Abbie had told Sarah she would be picking the money up herself. But this had to be Rolf. How stupid they were not to have thought of it. He wouldn't trust her to do this on her own. He'd want to do it himself. And how could they be sure he was going to give it to Abbie? The bastard was probably going to steal it. Ben felt a sudden, uncontrollable surge of fury.

The guy was walking to the trash can, taking a quick look around him as he did so, trying to look casual. Ben was about twenty yards away, bounding low and fast like an ape, trying to keep the station wagon between himself and the trash can. But the old woman had spotted him now and was tapping her husband on the shoulder, clearly terrified that they were about to get mugged. Ben put up his hands, trying to tell them it was okay, not to worry, and luckily neither of them said a word. He was past them now and closing quickly on Rolf who had hoisted the bag of money out of the trash and was heading back to the car. Ben was only ten, eight, five yards away now.

"Look out!" someone called. It was a woman's voice and it came from the white car. Ben looked and saw a face at the back window and in a moment realized it was Abbie. She must have been lying out of sight on the backseat. But her call had alerted Rolf and he turned and saw Ben closing on him, almost within reach. He began to run toward the driver's door.

"Stop!" Ben yelled. "You lousy little sonofabitch!"

Rolf was clambering into the car but Ben managed to reach him before he could shut the door. He grabbed at the guy's leather jacket and got a twisted grip on the lapel and tried to haul him out. Abbie was screaming from the backseat.

"Go! Go! Just go!"

Rolf was thrashing at him, trying to punch and elbow him away.

"Give me back my daughter, you bastard!"

The car was moving away but Ben lunged forward and grabbed the guy's leg and wrenched it so that his foot came off the gas pedal. He lunged for the keys but missed.

"Dad, don't! Don't do this!"

"Abbie, please!" Ben shouted. "All I want is to talk! Please!"

"Let go!"

"Please, Abbie! I just want to talk! Tell him—"

That was when the guy's fist hit him full in the face, right between the eyes. Ben saw a sudden flash of light and then he was falling back, crumpling, the back of his head cracking against the ground, the door swinging and slamming shut above him and the car moving away in a shuddering blur of white.

And through the warped and thickening haze of his concussion, the last thing he saw was the face pressed against the rear window, looking back and down at him, the strange black hair, the shocked and wide and fearful eyes of his daughter.

TWENTY-SIX

Of all the images of that September morning—the planes slicing in, the flames against the lucent sky, the crumbling towers—the one that etched itself most deeply in Eve's mind was the billowing cloud of dust that chased and engulfed the fleeing crowds. For it seemed to roll ever on and out to engulf the watching world beyond and when eventually it cleared, every life was somehow reconfigured.

Eve hated the clarion invasion of news or what generally passed for it. And in summer and early fall when Pablo came in to wake her, she would put on some music and open the doors to the deck and let the sound stream out and the sun stream in. Her taste in music was capricious though mostly determined by what she was currently painting. That morning, she might have chosen Mozart or Tom Waits, Beth Nielsen Chaplin or the chanting of Tibetan monks. But she opted instead for Bach, the Goldberg Variations.

Pablo had dragged a chair under the cherry tree and was standing on it to refill the feeder jars for the hummingbirds. Eve was lying on her back on the deck in her nightgown doing her morning stretch routine. Through the music she dimly heard Ben's cell phone ring but thought no more of it until he appeared in the doorway. She could see from his face that something had happened and her first thought was of Abbie. The call was from Sarah, he said. Something terrible was happening in New York. The NYU dorm on Water Street, just three or four blocks from the World Trade Center, had been evacuated. Josh was missing and wasn't answering his phone. Sarah was almost hysterical.

For what seemed like an eternity, as the horror unfolded on TV, they called everyone they could think of in Manhattan in the hope that Josh might have contacted them. Nobody had heard a word. Cell phones didn't seem to be working anymore. Maybe one in twenty calls was getting through. At last, almost half an hour after the second tower collapsed, Sarah called again. He was alive. The windows of the dorm had blown in and everyone had grabbed what they could and gotten out. Josh had gone to see if there was anything he could do to help and had then made his way uptown to Penn Station where at last he had managed to call her. The boy was only half-dressed and coughing and shocked and covered in dust, Sarah said. But, thank God, he was okay. He was on the train and coming home.

It was many weeks before the Coopers came to grasp that although the day had spared them the loss of a second child, it had almost certainly cemented the loss of their first. The fragment of hope they had clung to, that Abbie might wake from her madness and give herself up, now all but dissolved. With luck, sound lawyerly advice, and a lenient judge, she might once have been able to elicit understanding, even some modest sympathy. But as the world hardened and retrenched and prepared itself for war, all delicate distinction that might once have been made now vanished. There were no longer any shades of gray, only the glaring divide of good and evil. And Abbie was irredeemably consigned to the black beyond.

Ben's first inkling of this came in a phone call one evening from Dean Kendrick. It left him reeling. After the usual pleasantries, Kendrick had asked a whole string of what he called *routine* questions, about any possible connections Abbie might ever have had with Arab or Moslem countries. Had she ever traveled in the Middle East? Did she, to Ben's knowledge, have any friends or acquaintances of those particular ethnic or religious backgrounds at high school or college?

"Give me a break, Dean," Ben said.

"I know, Ben, I'm sorry. But unfortunately it's a fact that there are often links between these various terrorist groupings—"

"Terrorist groupings!"

"Ben, I know how hard it is for you to think of Abbie in that way, but she is a terrorist. She wrote the initials of a terrorist group on walls. It's a fact. We have to check every angle."

Since that dreadful night in Newark, there had been no word from Abbie. Ben had a hunch she wasn't even in the country anymore, that she and Rolf must have slipped into Canada or Mexico or gone even farther afield and were using the money to start a new life. Ben had come back to Santa Fe looking like a prizefighter, with two black eyes and a broken nose. Eve worried more, of course, about the deeper wounds the night had inflicted.

But curiously, as the months went by and the reality of Abbie's new status beyond the pale began to sink in, something seemed to shift in him. He didn't talk with Eve about it much, though she knew he talked of little else with his therapist. But from what he said, she got the impression that the events of that night had helped him draw some sort of line. He told her once that the face he had seen in the car window belonged to someone else, a stranger he no longer recognized as his daughter. Only by seeing her had he truly been able to know this. And since there was nothing he could do about it, the choice was clear: He could surrender himself to grief and go on blaming himself and make his life and the lives of those who loved him unbearable, or he could surrender to life itself and embrace all, both the new and the old, that was good and unsullied.

What seemed to help most in this process was his work. From a slow start—many phone calls and unproductive meetings and unpaid spec work that came to nothing—he now had some good contacts and a couple of projects that excited him. A young Hollywood film producer had asked him to design a house on twenty acres of rolling pine scrub desert beyond Tesuque, with views all around of the mountains. Ben by now had read every book ever written about Southwestern architecture and adobe and many more besides, about "building green" and all the many things that could now be done to make a house more environmentally friendly. He never said, but Eve knew that he wanted to build the kind of house for which his daughter might have felt proud of him. When he handed in his drawings the young producer was ecstatic. They began to build the following spring. Eve had never seen Ben so galvanized.

That July, for the first time, Josh came to stay. Naturally, Eve was nervous. But she knew enough wicked stepmother stories to realize that the worst thing she could do (though it wasn't in her nature anyway) was to try too hard to be liked. She needn't have worried. Although he only came for a long weekend, Josh was easy and open from the outset and this touched her and made Ben so happy that he couldn't stop talking about it for days. It was the first time she had seen Josh since that fateful week at The Divide and she barely recognized him. He was taller but no longer awkward, as if he had at last grown into what he was meant to be. And apart from the new haircut that looked as if it had been done in the dark by a vengeful Marine, he was a lot better-looking than she remembered.

Pablo wouldn't leave him alone. He woke the poor guy up every morning at seven o'clock and was forever dragging him out to play soccer or softball or Frisbee or to hunt for bugs and lizards down in the jungle by Eve's studio. After Saturday breakfast at the Tesuque Village Market, Ben drove them all out to see the house, which in less than three months was already starting to look spectacular. Josh seemed genuinely impressed. He kept saying how *amazing* it was and though Ben tried to sound suitably modest, you could see him grow an inch taller every time.

On Josh's last night they had a barbecue and sat out late on the deck under a marbled gray moon, two days short of full. Pablo had long ago crashed out and Ben, no doubt deliberately to leave Eve and Josh alone together, had disappeared inside with the dishes. They stared for a while at the glowing embers of the brazier, the cooling air of the garden shrill with the rhythmic clamor of insects.

"Pablo's a cool kid."

"He is. He thinks you're pretty cool too."

They smiled at each other then looked again at the fire. She could tell he wanted to say something else but maybe didn't know how to.

"And you guys, you and Dad, you seem . . . good. Happy, I mean."

"We are."

"I'm glad."

"Thank you, Josh. That means a lot."

"You know how everybody talks about feeling happy or unhappy as if it's something that just, kind of, happens?"

"Uh-huh."

"Well, sometimes I think it isn't like that and that maybe we can all decide, you know, choose which we want to be. Either happy or not. Do you know what I mean?"

"I absolutely do."

I ris had been watching the boy mowing Sarah's lawns for at least five minutes. She was looking out the open doorway to the deck but standing back a little in the shadows, presumably because she didn't want the object of her lustful gaze to notice.

"Jeez, look at the muscles in those arms," she said.

"Iris, you're technically almost old enough to be his grandmother, do you realize that?"

"Don't be ridiculous."

"He's seventeen, for heaven's sake."

"Really? You're kidding me."

"I'm not."

"God, what's happening to the human race? Boys look like men at seventeen."

The mower was a little sit-on John Deere and Jason, tanned and blond and ripplingly stripped to the waist, was expertly swinging it around the silver birches, leaving little islands of longer grass, just as Sarah had asked.

"Want some more iced tea?" Sarah asked.

Iris didn't seem to hear.

"Hey, Mrs. Robinson. Do you want some more tea?"

"Oh, yeah, okay."

She walked back to the table and Sarah filled her glass. They had just finished lunch. It was too hot to eat out on the deck. Iris had come to keep her company while Josh went to Santa Fe to meet The Catalyst. Which was okay. It was going to happen sometime and Sarah didn't feel as bad about it as she had expected. And having Iris here for the weekend had been great. It felt like old times. Just the two of them, no kids, no husbands. They had eaten out three times, slept in the same bed, cried through a whole tub of chocolate-chip ice cream while watching *The English Patient* and talked until their jaws ached. Mostly about marriage and men and how touchingly unevolved they were as a species. But also about Sarah's future, for she had at last decided to sell the bookstore. Well, *sell* wasn't quite the right word.

Last month, Jeffrey had delivered one of his periodic "time I quit" speeches. These moments usually passed, eased with praise and a raise or a few more shares. Only this time he sounded as if he almost meant it. Brian had apparently been going on again about moving to California, which Jeffrey said should be taken about as seriously as a character in a Chekhov play saying she wanted to go to Moscow. With all of a second's reflection, Sarah had said: "You know what, Jeffrey? You stay and I'll quit instead."

It took him a while to realize that she wasn't kidding. She said that since he had anyway more or less been running the show for the past few years and already owned forty-nine percent of the business, he might as well have the rest of it. That was, if he wanted it. Poor Jeffrey didn't know what to say. More for his pride than her profit, they figured out a deal whereby he paid a few thousand dollars up front for Sarah's fifty-one percent and then something extra down the line, for what he insisted on calling her *consultancy arrangement*, which seemed to involve little more than reading advance book proofs, organizing a few author events, and having lots of lunches. Iris thought she was nuts but Sarah didn't care. It was time to move on.

"But what are you going to *do?*" Iris asked again now, over her iced tea. It was about the eighteenth time. Sarah lit another cigarette.

"I don't know. Travel a lot. With you, if you'll come."

"You betcha. Let's go to Venice."

"It's a deal. And I'll read. Maybe even try writing something. Get fit. Stop smoking—"

"Have an affair with Jason the Mowerman."

"Uh-huh. Or his kid brother."

"Seriously, how long is it since you had sex?"

"Last night, with you. Didn't you notice?"

"Sarah, I'm serious."

"Apart from that night with Benjamin?"

"Less said about that the better."

"I don't know, nearly three years, I guess."

"God."

"It's the companionship I miss, not so much the sex."

"I know, but wow. Three years. I'd go bananas. Why don't you try speed-dating?"

"Iris, give me a break."

"I guess, you just kind of shut yourself down."

"That's exactly right. Listen, if the right person shows up, fine. I could do that now. I'd like it. But I'm not going out there looking for it."

"Not even out to the garden?"

"You're a bad person."

Iris went home to Pittsburgh that same afternoon. And a few hours later Josh arrived and neatly deflected every question she threw at him about The Catalyst and what her house was like and what her little boy was like and so on. His discretion was frustrating but she respected it, though whether it stemmed from protectiveness toward her or loyalty to his father, she wasn't sure.

She and Benjamin had seen each other only twice in the fifteen months since the night of the money drop, though they had talked a few times on the phone. She would never forget the sight of him standing there on the doorstep, his shirt torn and covered with blood, his eyes mere slits in a swollen Neanderthal face. And then sitting in the kitchen, while she bathed his wounds, saying again and again how stupid he was, how he'd blown it, how if he'd only gotten hold of the keys or had some kind of weapon or slashed the tires . . .

When he came to Josh's high-school graduation the following month, the swelling had subsided but his face around his bloodshot eyes was still a palette of blue and purple and yellow and the boxer's bump on his nose would probably be there forever. He was brave to have come because he knew Sarah's parents would be there. They barely acknowledged his presence and left straight after the ceremony. In the evening Josh went off to a party and the two of them had dinner and of course spent most of it talking about Abbie. But in a way that was different. It was as if something had been clarified or crystallized by what had happened that night at the mall. Although it remained unspoken, there seemed to be a mutual acceptance that the girl was beyond reach and redemption, a conclusion duly stamped and sealed a few months later by the fallout of Nine-Eleven.

Sarah knew it was insane to see it in such terms, but what happened on that morning, those terrible hours when Josh was missing, seemed now like a perverse kind of trade: Her son had been spared and her daughter was gone, probably forever.

I t was funny the way people protected themselves, Josh thought. Like, if you didn't talk about something, it didn't exist or would go away. They were both like that now, both his mom and his dad. Not once during the four days he was in Santa Fe had anyone mentioned Abbie's name. And he couldn't even remember the last time his mom had talked about her. He couldn't believe they didn't still think about her the whole time. He was sure they did. Maybe they just didn't want to talk about her in front of him, in case he got upset. Hell, who knew, maybe they were right. No amount of talk ever changed a thing.

Going to Santa Fe had been nowhere near as bad as he'd feared. In fact he'd enjoyed it, especially fooling around with Pablo. Though it was pretty weird seeing his dad with this new family, putting his arm around Eve just like he used to put his arm around Josh's mom and doing things with Pablo as if he was the kid's real dad. It was funny though how quickly you got used to it. And Eve was nice, really nice. He hadn't known quite what to expect, whether she'd be wary and cold and treat him like an enemy or be all gushy and overdo things trying to be his new best friend. But she hadn't done either. She'd just been easy and friendly and hadn't pushed things at all. And he actually liked her. Of course, she was kind of gorgeous too and he could understand—well, almost—why his dad had done what he had.

The only time he felt he might have blown it a little was when he asked if he could see what she was working on at the moment and she took him down to the studio and showed him these huge paintings of naked men and women. She said they were inspired by erotic statues from temples in India and Josh didn't know what to say, just stood there like a moron, trying not to look too embarrassed.

He felt bad about not telling his mom more but it didn't seem right and he knew that whatever he said it would only make her unhappy. Like, if he said Eve was lovely and she and Dad seemed really happy, how was that going to go down? And if he lied and said Eve was a bitch and they both seemed miserable as sin, would that be any better? Then she would just think what a double fuckup the whole thing was or, even worse, start building up her hopes that his dad might come back. No. Best not to say too much.

The two of them had supper and then Freddie called and asked if Josh was coming over and just as Josh was saying no, he'd been away and was going to stay home to keep his mom company, she hollered from the kitchen and said for heaven's sake, Josh, go. So he showered and put on a clean shirt and drove across town to Freddie's.

Freddie Meacher's parents were seriously rich. He didn't have just a room, he had a whole apartment over the garage where his dad kept all these amazing cars, including two Porsches and an Aston Martin. Freddie had always been allowed to do pretty much what he liked. His parents clearly knew he did drugs but never gave him too hard a time about it, just let him get on with his life. Josh hadn't seen so much of him since they'd both gone to college. Freddie was at the University of Colorado in Boulder which he said was the coolest town on the planet with the best-looking chicks he'd ever laid eyes on. And judging by the two who'd come to stay for a few days, he wasn't kidding. One of them, Summer, was his girlfriend. She had long, golden legs and a knowing smile.

Josh was jealous as a jilted skunk. Katie was still the only girl he'd ever slept with and by now that was such ancient history that it almost didn't count. There were plenty of girls he liked at NYU and some of them even liked him, but not, sadly, in the way he wanted them to. He was trying not to feel too sorry for himself, but he couldn't help thinking it was a sad state of affairs that sex for a guy his age, not too bad-looking nor entirely socially dysfunctional, should still consist of furtive trips to sketchy websites or hunching over a crinkled copy of *Hustler* magazine.

Summer's friend Nikki (Josh was prepared to bet she signed it with a little heart or flower or smiley instead of a dot over that last letter) was pretty hot too, though with a quieter kind of vibe. And after a few joints, the four of them sprawling on the couch in front of Freddie's mile-wide flatscreen TV, watching some newly issued DVD of *Apocalypse Now*—the director's wife's hairdresser's cut or some such—Josh, for a few thrilling moments, when her head nestled on his shoulder, thought he might have a chance. But she had just fallen asleep.

Later they went out to the pool for a swim and Summer and Freddie swam naked and Josh pretended he had a cold and didn't want to go in, just in case his unruly dick again made a fool of him. Instead, he sat on the terrace playing with Freddie's GameBoy and Nikki (thank God, wearing a bikini) sweetly came and sat beside him, toweling her hair, and started asking him a whole lot of questions about Abbie. He'd gotten used to it by now, playing the brother of the famous Abbie. It wasn't a whole lot different from how it had been all his life, except now the golden princess had become the big bad wolf. And the quality of the answers he gave depended entirely on who happened to be asking. With Nikki he was prepared to be as generous as possible. Though not, of course, as truthful.

"Has she ever been in touch?"

"Nope."

"What, like, she's never written your mom and dad or called?"

"No. Never."

"My God, that must be so terrible for them."

"Yeah. It's been tough."

"And for you, my God."

Josh set his jaw manfully and nodded, ignoring the little voice at the back of his head that was saying, *You scumbag, using this as a way to try to get yourself laid, how low can you sink?*

Nikki was originally from Boston, but her parents had moved to Colorado when she was still in junior high. She said she loved it there, the mountains, the hiking, the snowboarding. Josh ought to come out some time, she said, with Freddie. Not wanting to sound insular or ignorant or overly urban, Josh told her about their vacations in Montana and said he'd always wanted to go snowboarding in Colorado. Vail or someplace cool like that. The truth was, he'd never been on a snowboard in his life. Sometimes, especially when he was trying so hard not to stare at a girl's breasts, these things just popped out of his mouth.

But what did one more lie matter? They were all liars now. Abbie had seen to that. And the biggest lie of all was the one he played out every single day with his mom and dad. Because holding something back, keeping such a powerful secret from them, was every bit as bad, if not worse, than actually telling them something untrue. Abbie *had* been in touch again. He had spoken with her twice. And hadn't told a soul.

He still had the prepaid phone she'd made him buy and he checked it every morning, just as she'd told him. The very next day after his dad came home looking like he'd fallen foul of Mike Tyson, there was a message, two words which when decoded gave him a number to call. And he'd gone to a pay phone and called it, at precisely the right time, and listened for ten minutes while Abbie cursed and ranted and called their dad every obscene word Josh had ever heard. She'd gone on and on about there being only fifteen thousand dollars in the bag, *only fifteen fucking thousand, the cheap fucks!* He nearly hung up but didn't, just stood there with his head bowed, listening and taking it, until eventually she seemed to run out of steam and said, *Okay, well that's it. Tell them from me they won't get a second fucking chance, okay?* And he nearly replied, *What, you mean, not until you want some more money?* But, again, he didn't.

And he kept on, every day, religiously checking his secret phone—the one which still, amazingly, nobody except Abbie knew he had—and for eight months there was nothing. Until last Christmas Day at his grandparents when he dutifully snuck down to the tennis court to check his voicemail and heard her voice, not angry this time, just frail, giving the coded two-word message. He called the next day and, again, listened for ten minutes. Only this time she didn't curse or call anybody names. She just cried. Sobbed for ten long minutes, saying how lonely and sad she was and how she wanted to kill herself. And Josh did his best to comfort her, but what could he say? Except a lot of *Oh, Abbie* and *Don't, please don't, it'll be okay, it's just because it's Christmas . . .* What a dumb thing to say, really.

He didn't even tell her to come home or suggest that she should turn herself in, because he didn't want her to yell at him. At least this time she sounded human. But he did ask her where she was and she told him not to be stupid. This time the number wasn't a pay phone but a 704-area-code cell phone. It meant nothing. She could have been calling from anywhere. And when he later tried the number again, bracing himself each time in case she answered and bawled him out, all he ever got was an unavailable tone.

It was after three in the morning when Josh drove carefully home from Freddie's. Nikki had given him her number but he figured that was about all he was ever going to get. Maybe he'd call her sometime. Or not. He'd already done the long-distance heartbreak thing and didn't feel inclined to try it again.

His mom's light was still on and as he tiptoed up the stairs and past her door she called his name and told him to come in. She was propped up in bed, reading, a half-empty glass of milk beside her on the night table. As he came in she smiled and took off her glasses and patted the bed for him to sit and he did so, trying not to look her too directly in the eye. He didn't feel that stoned, but he probably looked it.

"Good party?"

"Yeah. Wasn't really a party. We just hung out, you know."

"How's Freddie?"

"Good."

"How's he getting on at college?"

"Fine."

"Well, that's great. Are you okay?"

"Sure. Just tired, you know."

"Give me a hug."

He leaned forward and put his arms around her and they held on to each other for a long time. She felt bony and fragile. He was always telling her she needed to eat more, but it never made any difference. She didn't seem to want to let go of him. And when she did, he saw there were tears in her eyes.

"I love you, Joshie."

"I love you too."

TWENTY-SEVEN

Abbie leaned her aching back against the white-washed wall of the weigh station and stared out through narrowed eyes over the vast flat fields where a hundred hunched figures were still picking the rows, their shadows long and black in the mellowing sunlight. A truck was heading in from the highway, trailing a cloud of luminous gold behind it. Abbie looked at her watch and saw it was coming up to six o'clock. She was going to be late.

There were still about a dozen pickers ahead of her in the line waiting to have their last trays weighed and get their money. Her tray was at her feet and as the line moved forward she shunted it with her boot across the baked earth and one of the supervisors yelled at her and told her to pick it up and she cursed him under her breath but did so. No matter how tired you were or that it was twelve long, hot, backbreaking hours since you'd started work, you weren't supposed to put your tray down in case the strawberries got dirty. As if they weren't contaminated enough by all the toxic chemicals they sprayed them with. She would never eat another strawberry in her life.

It was early September and three whole weeks since she had seen Rolf. But she was going to see him tonight and her heart beat faster at the thought of it and at what she had to tell him. She hadn't taken a test, but she didn't need to. She was already sure. She was two

434

weeks late and she was normally never late. And this morning, for the first time, she had gotten sick. How he was going to take it, she didn't know. She was hoping it might make things better between them. Of one thing she was sure, however. Come what may, whatever he said, whatever pressure he put on her, she was determined to have the child.

She would have to find the right moment to tell him, of course. Maybe they could go down the coast, to Big Sur or somewhere, and find some nice place to stay, spend a little of the money they'd earned.

It had been Rolf's idea that they should spend some time apart. He said he needed space and when she asked him what he meant, he'd just gotten mad at her. He was working on a construction site in Fresno, earning two or three times as much as she was for many fewer hours. At least, that's what he'd told her he was doing the last time they saw each other. Nowadays she never really knew. She no longer had a cell phone and on the three occasions she'd been able to call his he hadn't answered. Abbie only hoped he was going to be in a better mood this time, that he would be nicer to her, not fly into a rage with her so easily.

She'd had time to reflect on why things weren't so good between them anymore. It was more her fault than his, she knew. She was too possessive, too needy and jealous. After that first time she'd found he was cheating on her, when they were living in Chicago, she'd tried so hard to change, not to see it as such a big deal. It wasn't important for him, so why should it be for her? But in Miami, when she'd actually caught him at it, walked in on him and found him in bed with that little Cuban bitch, all her noble reasoning had collapsed.

If she was honest with herself, she'd known all along that there were other women. Rolf said she should grow up, that she was the victim of her own pathetic bourgeois background. They didn't own each other, he said, and if she wanted to have other lovers herself it was absolutely fine by him. That hurt her too, though she didn't really know why. She didn't want anyone else. Especially not now. Well, tonight and tomorrow and all weekend she would make a special effort and they would find each other again and things would again be good. And when he knew about the baby it would all be different.

"Next!"

In front of her now, her new friend Inez was swinging her tray onto the scales and the sour-faced bastard on the other side was checking its contents and throwing out any berries that in his indisputable opinion had been damaged. Inez challenged him on a couple that looked perfect but he just gave her a blank look and didn't even bother to justify himself, just yelled out the weight to the guys sitting beyond him at the trestle table, one with the clipboard and the other with the money, then swung the tray off the scales and stacked it.

"Next!"

Abbie always got a little anxious at the weigh station, just as she still did at post offices and banks or anyplace where she felt her identity was being scrutinized. Apart from a handful of students (which was what, if anyone ever asked, she pretended to be), she was the only non-Hispanic and the men at the pay table always seemed to look at her more closely than they did at the other women. Sometimes they tried to flirt with her but she just kept her eyes down and never engaged. She knew she didn't really need to worry too much. Every single picker here was working illegally. Nobody was going to ask any awkward questions. In any case, today the guy seemed interested only in her strawberries.

"These are all dusty."

"The hell they are."

"What did you say?"

"I said they're not. And if they are it's because of that truck that went by just now. You ought to tell them to slow down."

The guy threw most of the top layer of berries out, ignoring her complaints, then gave her a baleful look and yelled out the weight.

"Next!"

The man with the clipboard asked for her name.

"Shepherd."

He logged the last tray and hit a few buttons on his calculator and the man beside him then counted out her day's pay: forty-eight dollars and twenty cents. He pushed it across the table and Ann-Marie Shepherd of Fort Myers, Florida, gathered it up and stuffed it into the pocket of her skirt and followed Inez into the shower block.

Inez's English was only a little less primitive than Abbie's Spanish but the two of them had become close. They had met on Abbie's first day of picking when she still hadn't found anywhere to stay. In the evening Inez had hauled her into the back of a crowded truck that drove them up into the hills above the Salinas Valley. Abbie could hardly believe her eyes when they got there. She knew this was Steinbeck country but not that so little had changed.

There was a whole camp of Mexican fruit pickers, all illegals, living in the woods. The lucky ones had found caves for shelter but most just slept out in the open, with plastic garbage sacks over them to keep off the dew. She couldn't get over how kind and generous they were. They found her a blanket and a mat to lie on and a plastic sack and gave her food and water. It was strange how those who had the least always seemed to give the most. She spent the night listening to the yip of coyotes and it made her think about Ty.

After a few days, Inez managed to find them somewhere nearer to the fields, a garage with its own sink and toilet, which they shared with ten others, each paying four dollars a night for the privilege. Inez was only a year older than Abbie but already had two kids who lived with her mother back home in Santa Ana. She missed them badly. Their father had run off when she was eight months pregnant with the second but she didn't seem to hold it against him.

"Men," she said one night when they were sitting outside under the stars, sharing a cigarette. "They cannot help themselves. They don't know who they are or why God made them. You cannot hate them for what they don't know, only pity them."

Abbie hadn't told her she was pregnant, though the morning sickness was going to make the secret a tricky one to keep.

Because it was Friday night and everyone felt flush, there was a truck going into Salinas and when the two of them had showered and dressed they climbed up into the back and sat squeezed among a dozen others, all but a few of them men. Abbie wanted to look her best for Rolf and was wearing the pretty black-and-red cotton print dress she'd bought in a street market in Miami. She rarely looked in a mirror nowadays but this evening Inez had forced her to and Abbie was pleasantly surprised. It was like looking at someone she hadn't seen for years. She didn't dye her hair anymore and it was longer and going blond from all the sun she'd been getting. She'd never had such a tan in all her life. The only thing that dented the image was the state of her hands. They were calloused and ingrained with dirt, the fingernails bitten short.

Inez was all dressed up too and so were the three young men sitting opposite. They were flirting with her. Abbie couldn't understand what they said but she got the drift. One of them seemed more interested in her than in Inez and kept staring. He said something to the others who looked at her with a sort of shy assessment then nodded.

"What did he say?" she whispered to Inez.

"He said you look like a movie star."

She was supposed to be meeting Rolf at seven-thirty at a bar in the Oldtown district, near the Fox movie theater, but it was half an hour's walk from where the truck dropped her and by the time she got there it was after eight and he wasn't there. She found a table near the window so she could see out into the street and ordered a soda and took her book from the old duffel bag that held all her few worldly possessions. But an hour passed and darkness fell and still there was no sign of him. By then the glances of the men in the bar were making her uneasy so she got up and went for a walk, telling the woman behind the bar that if anyone came looking for her she would be back.

Just before ten, when she was half-sick with worry and wondering where she was going to sleep, she saw his car pull up across the street, the little Ford they had bought in Florida with the last of her grandpa's money. As he sauntered across the street, talking on a cell phone, he saw her in the window and gave a little nod but not a smile. Abbie got up and went out to meet him but had to stand there, stupidly on the sidewalk beside him, waiting while he ignored her and finished his call.

"Yeah. Okay. You too. Bye."

He snapped the phone shut and slipped it into his jacket pocket and she put her arms around his neck and kissed him on the lips.

"I thought you were never coming."

"I had some things to see to."

He didn't say how pretty she looked, in fact he barely

gave her a glance, just walked past her into the bar and said the place looked like shit and they should go someplace else.

They found a restaurant farther along the street, a darker place with wooden booths and little red candle jars on the tables. They sat in a corner and ordered two beers and he drank his in two long drafts and ordered another. The food was poor but Abbie wasn't going to let it spoil things and she told him all about the fruit picking and the good people she had met and the harsh conditions they lived in. Rolf nodded as if he knew all of this already. He hardly said a word and sometimes didn't even seem to be listening.

"Are you okay?" she said at last.

"Sure. Why?"

"I don't know. You're just kind of quiet."

"I'm tired, that's all."

"Did you miss me?"

Even as the words came out of her mouth, she knew it was the wrong thing to say. He sighed and cast his eyes upward in contempt.

"Yes, daaarling, I missed you terribly."

He said it with such a sneer that she had to bite her lip and look down at her plate, but she said nothing. Tears for Rolf were simply a sign of weakness and she knew better than to cry. But he must have seen how hurt she was for he reached out a guilty hand and took hold of hers.

"I'm sorry. But you know how I feel about all that bourgeois shit."

"Like missing someone you care for."

He moved closer and put an arm around her and kissed her temple.

"I'm sorry. I missed you. Okay?"

She nodded and swallowed bravely and smiled.

"Can we go somewhere? Just for the weekend?"

"Where?"

"I don't know, someplace by the ocean. I want to walk beside the ocean."

"I have to be in Seattle on Sunday."

"Can I come?"

"No."

He had never told her much but these days told her nothing. But Abbie knew from the newspapers some of the things that had been going on and that he was probably involved. From the Canadian border to northern California there had been a string of arson attacks, mostly on logging and biotech companies, the damage running into many millions of dollars. He said it was too risky for her to be involved anymore but Abbie suspected the real reason was that in Denver she had failed him, shown herself too weak and fearful.

There was a time when the harshness of this verdict had hurt her. But no longer. The truth was, she didn't want to be involved. She still admired his passion and resolve. But these actions that she had once considered so heroic now seemed only futile and dangerous. And counterproductive too, because all they succeeded in doing was to generate sympathy for the greedy corporations that were the targets. Anyhow, Rolf had no doubt found some other young woman to help him. And probably to fuck as well, but Abbie tried not to think about that. She needed him now, more than ever.

"Then let's go somewhere just for tonight and tomorrow," she said. She kissed his neck and put her hand on his thigh. "Please. It's been so long."

They drove south for about an hour and just before Big Sur, meandering high around the cliffs, they found a little place that looked out over the highway to the ocean. There was a blue neon *vacancy* sign in the window and they pulled in and parked. An old woman sat asleep in front of a blurred TV behind the reception desk and they woke her and got themselves a room.

Abbie put down her bag and turned to him and as he shut the door behind him she saw in his eyes a darkening glint she didn't recognize.

"Rolf?"

He ripped the dress from her shoulders then threw her facedown on the bed and fucked her so violently and unlovingly that she screamed at him to stop but he didn't. She managed to twist around and lashed out at him and he hit her hard across the face with the palm and then the back of his hand, the first time he had ever struck her. Then he grabbed her by the throat so tightly that she thought he was going to strangle her. And she was so scared, not just for herself but for the child within her, that she stopped struggling and let him do what he wanted to her until he was spent and rolled off her and slumped beside her.

How long she lay there listening to his breathing she

couldn't tell. But when at last she was sure he was asleep and she had summoned enough courage, she edged herself, inch by inch, away from him and off the bed and silently gathered her things, freezing every now and then when he shifted. She took the car keys and a roll of dollar bills from his jacket and thought about taking his phone too but didn't. The warm, wet run of him on her thigh almost made her retch. She tiptoed naked to the door and let herself out, praying with every quivering breath that it wouldn't creak and it didn't.

The moon was angling in along the bleached wood walkway outside and she dressed hurriedly beside her shadow on the wall then walked barefoot across the cool, gray gravel to the car. It was parked on a slope under some ragged pines maybe fifty yards from the room, close enough, she figured, that he might hear the engine start and get to her in time. There was not a breath of wind and the only sound was the distant barking of a dog. She threw her bag into the back then quietly climbed in and put the shift to neutral and the car rolled slowly down toward the highway, the gravel crunching beneath the tires.

As the car nosed onto the highway she turned the key and the engine sputtered to life. Out on the ocean a trail of reflected moonlight shimmered to the horizon. She eased the car out onto the highway and gently accelerated away, heading back the way they had come. How long the journey would take she wasn't sure. But she already knew where she would go.

She drove all through the night, working her way north until she found I-80 and headed east and watched the sun lift out of the Sierras, hazy and red and implacable. Just after Reno the sickness kicked in and she found a truck stop and threw up and washed herself and sluiced from her body all trace of him. She walked back to the car and lowered the seat and slept until woken by the heat and the glare of the sun.

It took eight hours just to cross Nevada, the names on the signs whipping by, Lovelock, Battle Mountain, and Elko, the Humboldt River curving and flashing beside her. Sometimes, to get gas or something to eat or simply to break the mesmerizing miles, she would exit the interstate and pass through forlorn and desiccated towns with boarded storefronts and sprawling trailer camps and the plundered carcasses of cars. Then across into Utah, the highway straight as a spear through the flat forever of the desert that glowed pink to each horizon as another night rolled in.

She passed Salt Lake City a little after midnight and by then, even with the windows wide and the night air rushing in about her, cooler now and sweetly laced with sage, her eyelids began to droop and her chin to jolt against her chest and she knew she had to stop. She branched off the interstate and found a cheap motel and was so tired she almost gave her real name but corrected herself in time and the boy at the desk jokingly asked if she'd forgotten who she was and Abbie smiled and said it was true, she had.

She had driven most of a thousand miles and, looking at the map the next morning, figured she had half as many more yet to go. She had considered calling ahead but decided not to. Maybe their phones were still being tapped. And anyhow, maybe he wouldn't be there and his mother would answer instead and Abbie wouldn't know what to say. Not that she yet knew what to say to Ty after three long years and all the heartache and trouble she had brought into his life.

She crossed the Continental Divide in the early afternoon and at Rawlins forked north to Casper. And as the sun was starting to slide into the Bighorn Mountains, at last, she turned off the interstate and drove into Sheridan. She cruised along Main Street, past the little plaza where she and Ty had sat that day and talked, the bronze cowboy still standing sentinel with his rifle resting on his shoulder. She found a place to park and on the paper she had picked up at the motel wrote the note that she planned to leave in the mailbox at the end of the driveway. She scrapped her first two attempts. The apologies sounded too futile and self-pitying. At the third attempt she wrote two simple lines.

Ty, I'll be by the bronze cowboy Monday noon.
If you don't show up, I'll understand. Love, A.

After such an absence she worried that she might not remember the way out to the ranch and lose herself in the labyrinth of gravel roads but even in the fading light it all came back to her. She passed a truck coming the other way with McGuigan Gas & Oil written on its side and the name clicked the well-worn connection in her head to the image of the man's son dying on his knees with the blazing house behind him. And as she drove on through the clarifying cloud of dust the truck had stirred, she wondered how she could ever have come to such a sorry state of mind and damaged so many lives.

When she stopped at the end of the Hawkins' driveway, a flash of white caught her eye and peering up to her left through the twilight she saw a small herd of deer, mothers and fawns, below a stand of aspen, watching her. She thought they would run into the trees but they didn't, just stared as she walked to the mailbox. She stopped there and stood awhile, tapping the sealed envelope with her fingers and staring back at the deer. And whether it was something in their gaze that dared her or merely the encroachment of another lonely night, she didn't know, but instead of leaving the note she took it back to the car and steered around and headed up toward the house.

As she knew they would, the dogs came running and hollering. And even before she had parked, there was a face at the kitchen window and the outside light went on. When she opened the car door the dogs at once seemed to remember her and stopped their barking and started to bounce at her and she got out and squatted and stroked them and let them squirm and lick her face. There were footsteps on the porch now and she looked up to see Ty heading out toward her across the gravel.

"Hi there, can I help you?"

Abbie stood up before him and saw the shock on his face as he recognized her. He stopped in his tracks.

"My God," he said quietly.

"I'm sorry. If you want me to, I'll go."

"I can't believe it."

"I didn't know where else . . . Listen, I'll go."

But he was walking toward her now and she just stood there unable to move and watched him. Without a word he put his arms around her and she started to quake and would probably have fallen had he not been there to hold her. He stroked her hair and let her cry and all she could say was his name and that she was sorry, so sorry, again and again, until he gently hushed her and walked her slowly toward the house. His mother was waiting on the porch but Abbie's eyes were too blurred and the light too dim for her to know if she was welcome here or reviled. Then Martha stepped forward and took her from Ty and embraced her as if Abbie were her own, patting and soothing her.

"You poor child," she murmured. "You poor, poor child."

It was almost more than Abbie could take. To have her first hot tub in years, the feel of fresh towels, the smells and sounds of supper cooking, all these mundane things, familiar yet forgotten, opened the cell in which she had locked all memory of home and family. Martha found her fresh clothes and piled on her plate more food than Abbie was used to seeing in a week. And only when she could eat no more and the table was cleared and the three of them sat staring at each other with a fond yet wary disbelief did they begin to speak of what had happened and what might happen now.

Abbie had already noticed Ray's empty chair in front of the TV and Ty now told her that it was almost two years since his father had died and that his passing was a mercy for them all. After the stroke he had never uttered another word. Abbie said how sorry she was and that she wished she had known him better. Then she took a deep breath and began to tell them about that night three years ago in Denver. And she tried to tell it plainly, without self-pity or the embellishment of any justifying motive, told them simply what had been intended and how events had gone so tragically awry.

And Ty and his mother listened to her with just an occasional question and listened too to the censored account of her subsequent life that Abbie said seemed like a fog in a valley from which she had only now managed to climb. And though she spared them the worst of the darkness and spoke of Rolf as if he were but a phantom of that fog, she said she had come to understand what madness was and could live with it no more.

Then Martha got up from the table and went to the sideboard and came back with what looked like some sort of scrapbook.

"Mom," Ty said. "Please, not now."

"I think Abbie needs to see this."

She placed it on the table in front of her and Abbie opened it and saw at once what it was. Page after page of pasted clippings from newspapers and magazines, telling of Ty's arrest and imprisonment, police pictures of him looking pale and haunted, name and number hung around his neck. And Abbie's ubiquitous graduation face beaming alongside. The headlines screamed his guilt: *Denver terror murder arrest, Sheridan man is terror girl Abbie's lover, Terrorist Tyler held for murder.* There were pictures too of Ray and Martha, smeared by association. Even the later stories about Ty's release—much smaller and tucked away inside, for naturally the news was less exciting—somehow still managed to point a lingering finger of guilt.

Abbie closed the book and looked up. They were both staring at her. She couldn't find her voice.

"I needed you to see what you did to us," Martha said.

Abbie nodded.

"I don't know what to say."

Martha nodded and gave her a sad smile and reached across the table and took her hand. Ty was biting his lip. He reached out and took Abbie's other hand and for a while the three of them sat conjoined in separate reflection while the old wall clock ticked away the sorrowful silence.

"I feel so ashamed," Abbie said at last.

"I know you do, child. Ty must speak for himself, but I forgive you. All that matters now is what you're going to do about it."

"Did Ray ever know about all this?"

She meant, of course, Ty's arrest and whether it had contributed to his father's death, but she couldn't bring herself to spell it out.

"I don't think so," Ty said quietly.

Martha stood and gathered up the scrapbook.

"I'll be going to my bed now. You two will no doubt want to be doing some talking."

She kissed her on the forehead and left them.

Abbie needed air. The two of them walked out across the yard and past the stables and along the dirt road that ran above the meadows. The sky had clouded and a breeze was funneling up the valley. It felt cool against her face and carried the first faint scent of the coming fall. Every now and then, far away above the mountains, the clouds flickered blue with muted lightning. Ty put his arm around her shoulders and for a long while they simply walked and neither of them spoke. They stopped by a gate and leaned side by side on the rail, staring down the slope where the shapes of horses stood dark and still against the sun-bleached grass of the meadow.

In a low voice and not trusting herself to look at him, Abbie said she wished she could undo all the harm she had brought him and that there was some way she might make amends. She said she knew his mother wanted her to turn herself in and that she wanted to and would, but that right now she felt like a child high on a rock above the ocean, wanting with all her heart to jump but too afraid.

"You know, it's probably still not safe for you to be here," Ty said, still staring out into the darkness. "How much they bother with us these days, I don't know, but I doubt they'll have forgotten. I think they still listen to our phones."

"I'll go in the morning."

"No."

"Ty, there's something else I have to tell you."

He looked at her.

"I'm pregnant."

He looked at her for a long time and she saw the pain in his eyes and some new emotion forming that she couldn't yet decipher. He stepped closer and held her by the shoulders.

"There hasn't been a day in three years that I haven't thought about you. Even through all that happened I never once stopped loving you. And whatever happens, I'll always be there for you. It's right that you give yourself up. And for the child's sake you have to. But give me a few days first. Please, Abbie."

"Oh Ty, how can we—"

"Just a few, just the two of us. We can figure out what you're going to do, then do it the right way. I know somewhere we can go."

TWENTY-EIGHT

Boulder was every bit as cool as Freddie had said it was. In fact, for Josh's taste, it was way too cool. Everybody was so damn beautiful, he felt like the ugly duckling. All the guys were tall and blond and pumped and tanned and the girls all had perfect smiles and diamonds in their navels and looked like they'd just stepped off the catwalk. It was like a starter colony for some alien super-race. Or maybe it was just

Freddie's crowd. What the hell, Josh thought. He was here and the weather was beautiful and Nikki—God alone knew why—still seemed to be interested, so he was just going to go with the flow and enjoy himself.

Flying all the way to Colorado for Freddie's twenty-first hadn't been that easy a deal to swing. He'd had a major dustup with his mom about it. On reflection, he hadn't been too smart. He should have asked her rather than just announced that he was going out for the whole week. It wasn't worth going all that way for anything less, he told her, and he could easily borrow notes on all the classes he was going to miss. He regularly missed most of them anyway, but felt it better not to mention that. Anyhow, she went ballistic and for the last week of the summer vacation they hardly spoke. Eventually they reached a compromise. Josh would fly out on the Thursday and be back at NYU the following Tuesday.

Freddie shared a house just off Spruce Street with three other guys, all of them as chilled and rich and good-looking as he was. The place had become famous and was known as the Temple of Doom because of all the incense they burned to camouflage the smell of grass and the Oriental drapes and statues and the fact that there didn't seem to be a single chair in the whole house, just cushions and mattresses around the walls.

It was Saturday night, the night of the party, though in fact the party had already been going on ever since Freddie and Summer and Nikki picked him up at Denver airport two days ago. The house was packed. For reasons best known to himself Freddie had hired some Japanese caterers and waitresses dressed as geishas were walking around bowing to everyone and handing out sushi and little tots of warm sake, of which Josh had already drunk too many. The effect wasn't unpleasant, though, on top of the beer and the joints that kept coming around, it had the potential to go that way. It seemed not so much alcoholic as paralytic. He couldn't feel certain parts of his body anymore and when he turned his head, his face seemed to stay where it was for a moment then swing into place. He was lying on a heap of cushions with Nikki and a few others who were all talking and laughing and clearly having a great time. But the music seemed to be turning a little sour and he was breaking out in a cold sweat.

"Are you okay?"

Nikki was frowning at him.

"Kind of."

"You're white as a sheet. Come on, let's get you some air."

She helped him to his feet and led him by the hand through the crowd and out into the hallway which was just as crowded but not so hot.

"Listen, I don't want to be a pain," he said. "I'll just go outside for a while."

"I'll come with you."

"No, really. Thanks. I'll be okay. I'll just walk around the block."

"Are you sure?"

"Yeah. I'll come back and find you."

He found his jacket where he had left it with his bag,

stuffed under the bed in Freddie's room, then made his way to the front door and down the steps to the street. The mountain air felt cool and good and he filled and refilled his lungs with it half a dozen times as he walked along the sidewalk, trying to negotiate as straight a line as he could. By the time he reached the mall on Pearl Street he was starting to feel better and he walked the whole length of it, looking at the store windows already full of colorful winter clothes and snowboarding stuff, then walked back along the other side doing the same.

His head was clearer now and his hands felt cold and as he stuffed them deeper into his jacket pockets he felt the old prepaid cell phone that, loyally or stupidly, he still carried wherever he went. He hadn't checked it since leaving New York and didn't really know why he bothered with it at all anymore. Abbie hadn't been in touch since that Christmas two years ago when she'd cried and said she wanted to kill herself. For all he knew, she might have done so but that was something he tried not to think about. He took the phone out of his pocket and switched it on and a few seconds later, to his great surprise, there was a beep and up came the little sign that showed he had voicemail.

But it was so long since he'd had to use it that he'd forgotten the damn code. And the piece of paper that spelled it all out was back in New York, slipped between the pages of an old dictionary. As Abbie spelled out the two words a second time, he started to panic. The first word told him the number and the second when to call it. But, goddamn it, that was all he could remember. He kept pressing repeat and listening to it over and over again but it didn't help at all. Then he heard a prompt saying that there was a second message. It was Abbie again. She said she had been waiting for him to call but maybe he didn't check this phone anymore or maybe he'd forgotten the code. She gave him a number and asked him to call it at six on Sunday evening. Her voice sounded little and hesitant. But somehow more normal. Not strident or bossy or hysterical like before.

"I hope you get this," she said. "If I don't hear from you I guess I'll have to find another way of reaching you. Please try to call. It's kind of important. Don't tell Mom and Dad yet. I love you, Joshie."

On his way back to the house he listened to it four more times until he knew the whole message by heart. What could be so important? She probably just wanted more money. Well, at least she was alive. The thing that puzzled him most was the *I love you* at the end. He couldn't remember her ever saying that to him, at least, not since he was a little kid. Back at the house the party was chilling out a little. The geishas had gone. He looked around and found Nikki. She seemed to be with some other guy, one of the blond gods. She asked Josh how he was feeling and he told her he was fine. Someone handed him a joint and he passed it on without taking a puff. And for the rest of the night, so his head would be clear tomorrow for the call, all he drank was water.

Each morning when she opened the cabin door and walked along the creek and beyond the trees to where the land fell sharply away and you could look east down the valley and west to mountains, she always expected something to have changed. But the signs that marked the passage of these precious days were all but imperceptible. The yellow shimmer of the aspens perhaps a shade more vibrant, their white stems starker in the mellowing sun, more snow on the mountains, the sky a deeper blue. Each day the world a fraction more exquisite.

The last few hundred yards of the trail that zigzagged up to the cabin were too steep and rocky to drive, so they parked Ty's truck in among the trees below. The cabin was one room, twelve feet square, with a potbellied stove and two small windows. It was basic but cozy, just a bed, a small table, and two chairs. There was no power and they got their water from the creek. Outside, along one of the side walls, was an open lean-to where they chopped and stacked the firewood and hung the saddles and bridles. And behind, beyond the outhouse, was a small corral where they kept the horses.

They rode mostly in the early morning and again in the late afternoon when the sun flooded the land with an amber glow. Sometimes they took a tent and food and rode the whole day, high into the wilderness, where the canyons echoed eerily to the bugling of elk. In the chill of the evening they would light a fire and cook then sit huddled and blanketed, her head against his chest, and stare at the flames and the spiraling of sparks into the vast and sequined sky.

The rediscovery of tenderness, not just in him but in herself, sometimes almost overwhelmed her. He would hold her shoulders when she got sick in the mornings and cradle her in his arms each night when she slept. She knew that people treasured most what soon they would not have. And perhaps it was only the concrescence of another life within her that made the slow decay of these stolen golden days and the looming of winter endurable.

The cabin was on several thousand acres of land bought some years earlier by an aging TV talk-show host. He had built himself a fancy ranch house down the valley and flew in for two weeks every summer with a different wife or girlfriend. The place was locally nicknamed the Ponderosa because he'd decorated it like a set for a western and, just in case anyone thought he was a phony, decorated the land with a little herd of buffalo and a few fine horses, all of whom needed looking after. That was why he had built the cabin, tucked out of sight, up a snaking, rocky trail a mile more into the mountains, and had hired Ty's friend Jesse Wheeler to live there.

Abbie remembered him from that last summer at The Divide but only faintly. Ty said he was a quiet soul who liked the solitude up here on the Front, but not fifty weeks of it at a stretch, so he was always looking for someone to stand in for him and give him a break.

When Abbie had shown up in Sheridan and Ty had called him, Jesse couldn't believe his luck. During the summer he'd finally found himself a girlfriend. If he could spend a couple of weeks courting her, he said, he might just be able to talk her into marrying him. Ty told him to take three. Jesse left the cabin key under a designated rock and was gone before they got there.

They had driven from Sheridan separately, Ty in his truck and Abbie following in Rolf's car which now stood concealed in one of the barns down at the ranch. She felt bad about taking it and worse still when Ty, checking the trunk, found Rolf's laptop wrapped in a towel inside the spare wheel. Abbie thought they should find some way of returning it but Ty wouldn't hear of it. He said there was sure to be evidence on it that would help her defense when she turned herself in. They took it up to the cabin and switched it on but it asked for a password. Ty put it in a plastic sack and hid it in the outhouse.

In the two weeks they had now been here, Rolf had been the only source of tension between them. Ty couldn't understand how she could love a man who had treated her so cruelly. Abbie hadn't told him the half of it and sometimes had trouble understanding it herself. To Ty it was all so black and white: The guy was evil and to blame for all that had happened. It was a clarity she envied and might have gotten closer to sharing had it not been for what was happening inside her. Though barely yet formed, the baby seemed to blur her vision of both present and past, tempering even the shock and violence of the night she had fled.

Whatever Rolf had done, however heartless and harsh he had sometimes been, no other human being had ever touched or possessed her so intensely. She was aware, of course, that he had found her at her most vulnerable. But how could that possibly explain her feelings for him now, more than three years on? The fact was she still admired his resolve, envied his fearlessness and independence. And though, in her most objective moments, she had to acknowledge the darkness in him, surely the fact of her love for him suggested something matching in herself? Resilient to reason, that darker part of her still saw him as a warrior, whose seed now lodged within her. And their child would be the best of both of them.

To talk with Ty about a subject so hurtful with any sort of candor was naturally impossible. But it ran like a brooding river beneath their many long discussions about how best to organize her surrender.

More than anything, Abbie wanted to see her parents. And not through the glass of some heartless prison visiting room. She had to see them before she gave herself up, had to be able to hug them and hold them and say she was sorry. To her mother, for everything of course, but especially for being so selfish in her rage and grief and for giving so little support when her dad had walked out. But also to him. For what had happened that night at the mall and for being so cruel to him before her life unhinged.

Ty considered the issue from a more practical angle.

He believed that if she could first contact her parents, they might be able to broker some kind of deal. These things happened all the time, he said. With good attorneys, they could secure the promise of some lesser charge in exchange for Abbie giving herself up. The corollary, of course, was that, with the help of whatever might be on the laptop, most of the blame could be shifted to Rolf. But the first step, they agreed, was to call Josh.

Choteau, the nearest town, was small enough for strangers to be noticed. So they drove another forty-five minutes to Great Falls and found a pay phone and Abbie called Josh's prepaid cell and left a coded message. They came back the following evening and waited for the phone to ring but it didn't. They didn't want people to start noticing them so they found a gas station across town with an outside phone and no security cameras and this time she left Josh a fuller message without the code.

When they came back the next evening, while Ty filled up with gas, Abbie stood by the phone, with her finger discreetly on the hook, pretending she was on a call. And at six on the dot the phone rang and it was Josh. She told him she was going to turn herself in and he got all excited and said how it was *so* the right thing to do and how incredibly happy their mom and dad were going to be when they found out. Abbie said he mustn't tell them until things were a little more figured out. She told him where she was and only then did he announce that he was in Colorado. He said he would come collect her, he would borrow a car and drive straight there or he'd fly or get a bus or whatever. But he would come, he said, there was no way he wouldn't come. Abbie told him to keep the phone switched on and she would call him in a couple of hours when he had checked things out.

To pass the time they drove to a supermarket and got a few things they needed, then they walked awhile. Clouds were rolling in from the west and Ty said the air had the smell of rain. They found a place to eat and by the time they were done it was coming up to eight o'clock and Abbie went to the phone and again called Josh. He said he couldn't find a car to borrow, so he'd booked himself a flight from Denver to Great Falls the following afternoon. He gave her the flight number and the arrival time and Abbie said Ty would be there to meet him. With all the security at airports nowadays, she didn't want to risk being recognized.

"I'll see you tomorrow," she said.

"Okay. Hey, Abbie?"

"What?"

"Almost peace, man."

"Almost peace."

She hung up and was about to walk away. Across the restaurant she could see Ty talking with an old cowboy at the adjoining table. She picked up the phone again. This might be her only chance to do what she had been thinking about doing for days. She didn't know if she had the guts. But he had a right to know, both about the baby and about what she was intending to do. If he got angry or tried to bully her, she would simply hang up. But at least she would have told him. With her heart thumping, she took some more quarters from her pocket and dialed Rolf's cell number. He answered on the first ring.

"Yes?"

"It's me."

"My God. Where are you?"

"Rolf, listen—"

"I've been so worried. Are you okay?"

"Yes. Listen, there's something I—"

"I've been driving myself crazy. Baby, I'm so sorry about what happened. I don't know what it was, I was out of my head that night with all the shit that's been going on. Please, Abbie. Please, come back."

The sweet contrition in his voice almost floored her. She had been braced for him to yell at her.

"I can't," she said. "I'm going to turn myself in."

"You're *what?*"

"Rolf, I'm pregnant. And I'm going to turn myself in."

There was a long pause.

"I was going to tell you that night, but . . ."

"Oh God, Abbie. I am so sorry. Listen, I've got to see you."

She swallowed hard. Her eyes were fixed on Ty and for the first time he turned around and briefly looked at her.

"I don't think that's a good idea."

"Please, Abbie. We have to talk about this. We can

work something out. I know we can. Where are you, baby?"

"Rolf—"

"Tell me, please. I'll come straightaway."

"No. I'm going home. Josh is flying up from Denver to get me."

It was more than she'd meant to say, but he didn't pick up on it.

"You're not going home, you're going to jail. Maybe worse. You can't have our baby in jail."

"I can. They work these things out."

"Abbie, surely I have some kind of say in this?"

"If you want to make things right, do what I'm doing. Turn yourself in. Tell them what happened. It can all be okay, I know it can."

"Abbie—"

"I've got to go now."

"Baby, please—"

"I love you."

She hung up, tears flooding down her cheeks. *Our baby,* he'd said. She turned quickly and ran into the restroom and doused her face with cold water and tried to calm herself. She'd done what she had to. The rest was up to him. When she came out Ty was standing there waiting for her. He looked very worried.

"Are you all right?"

"Yeah. I just got a little tearful. Josh just said some really sweet things, that's all." She laughed, unconvincingly, wiping her eyes. "God, these hormones!"

"Is he coming?"

"Tomorrow."

When they left the restaurant the sky had clouded over and a cold wind was gusting from the north. By the time they reached Choteau it had started to rain.

TWENTY-NINE

Josh had never known such rain. It was like a monsoon. You could hardly see through it. Ty had kindly brought him a slicker to wear but it reached almost to his ankles and on the final scramble up to the cabin he caught a foot in it and almost fell. What with the rush and roar of the creek, Abbie couldn't have heard them coming, but she must have been watching for them and seen Ty's flashlight because as they walked toward the cabin the door flew open and she ran out to meet them. She wouldn't even wait for him to take off the slicker, just threw her arms around him and hugged him and held him and wouldn't let go.

She had the place all prettily lit with candles and the stove going and supper already cooked. Ty had shot a pair of grouse at the weekend and Abbie had stewed them up with vegetables and wild berries. Josh hadn't eaten all day and could have finished the whole pot by himself. They pulled the table close to the bed and Abbie perched there between them while Josh and Ty took the two chairs. There was so much to discuss that nobody seemed to know where to start, so they just ate and talked about nothing instead, about the rain and how his flight had been and about Freddie's party.

He had never seen Abbie looking more beautiful. She was totally transformed from the raven-haired witch she'd been that day in New York. She had a kind of glow to her, which Josh was somehow aware happened when you got pregnant, along with throwing up and wanting to eat lumps of coal. Ty had broken the news on the way here from the airport and thank God he had, because it had knocked Josh almost speechless for about ten minutes. He just sat there like an idiot, saying *Wow* and *Jeez* and shaking his head. Ty didn't need to say how *he* felt about it. The sadness was written all over the poor guy's face. What a goddamn tragedy the whole thing was. And yet here she was, radiant and happy in the candlelight. Pregnant and about to go to jail. Josh was having trouble getting his head around it.

The stew was good and by the time he'd downed a second plateful and chewed on the bones, they at last got around to talking about more important matters. Ty and Abbie had clearly spent a long time thinking things through so Josh just listened carefully to what they had to say. They figured the best place for Abbie to turn herself in was New York and because flying with her fake ID was too risky, she and Josh would drive there in Rolf's car. Ty had done a little work on it and was sure it was sound enough to make it. He said they were welcome to take his tent and sleeping bags if they wanted. Driving all the way across America was something Josh had always fantasized about. But never in a million years could he have guessed that this was how he'd end up doing it, with a sister at his side who was wanted for murder.

Abbie said that because the phones of family and friends were possibly still being tapped, they should wait until they got there before telling anyone. She could hole up in a motel or someplace until Josh told their mom. Their dad would fly up from Santa Fe, they would have their reunion and then get down to contacting lawyers and all the rest and take it from there. Josh asked a few questions but as far as he could see, it all made sense. All they had to do was drive carefully.

"So when do we go?" he said. "Tomorrow?"

Abbie looked at Ty and took his hand and Josh suddenly saw in the poor guy's face how hard it was going to be to lose her again.

"We figured we'd have just one more day," Ty said quietly. "It'll give you a chance to rest up some. You've got a fair few miles to go."

They had already rigged up a makeshift bed for Josh in the corner and after clearing the dishes they blew out the candles and settled down for the night. Tired as he was, Josh couldn't sleep. His head was whirring with all that was going to happen. So he lay there staring at the fading glow of the stove and listening to the rain hammering on the roof.

Once Abbie cried out *No, I won't!* in her sleep and Josh heard Ty quietly soothe her. The cry unsettled him and set him off wondering what she might have been dreaming. He conjured an image of her in handcuffs and a pale blue suit, being walked by guards down a long corridor toward a big steel door, faces watching through bars on either side. He did his best to banish it but it wouldn't go. And in a fitful half-sleep, it morphed into pictures far worse, plucked from movies and violent video games and the darker reaches of his mind. He woke in a chill sweat and forgot for a moment where he was. There was a first merciful glimmer of dawn at the window. The rain had stopped and all he could hear was the rushing of the creek.

The day was cold and blustery with sudden bursts of sun and low clouds scudding from the north, their shadows rolling like giant tumbleweeds along the valley. Ty said it felt like the first true day of winter. After breakfast he lent Josh a jacket and the two of them went outside to feed the horses and get some wood for the stove.

"Do you want to ride with us?" Ty said. "We could bring up another horse from the ranch."

"You know what? I think it would be good for the two of you to have this day to yourselves. I'll go into town, get a few things for the trip."

"You don't need to do that."

"I'd like to. I was never much of a rider anyhow. Abbie was always bigger on the outdoors than me. I'm more of a town kind of guy."

Ty smiled and put a hand on his shoulder.

"Thanks, man. I appreciate it."

"I just hope, one day, you guys'll be able to, well, you know . . ."

He didn't know how to finish but Ty seemed to understand.

"Yeah. Me, too."

They broke open a bale of hay for the horses and leaned on the rail in silence for a while, watching them feed. Then Ty took a short-handled ax from its slot in the lean-to and began expertly to split some logs while Josh stood admiringly by.

"How good are you at computers?" Ty asked.

"Okay, I guess. Why?"

"Do you know if it's possible to crack a password?"

"I think you can get around them if you know how. My friend Freddie would know for sure."

Ty swung the ax and left it embedded in the chopping block. He walked across to the outhouse and came back holding something wrapped in a black plastic sack.

"This is Rolf's laptop. There's sure to be all kinds of things on it that could help Abbie's case. She still can't see straight about him, so she's not too keen on the idea. It might be best not to mention it, but I figure we'd be crazy not to try taking a look. Maybe you could give your friend a call."

Josh borrowed the truck and drove to Great Falls. He found a mall and bought himself a warm jacket and some food and drink for the trip, then called his mom on his regular cell phone to say he was safely back in New York. He gave her a parent-friendly account of Freddie's party and even got a little cocky and—with just the right tone, sulky but virtuous—said the class he'd just been to was so boring it hadn't been worth coming back for. He was such a good liar, it was almost scary.

He'd tried three times to call Freddie and left a message each time, but it wasn't until mid-afternoon, when he was sitting in the corner of a bookstore coffee shop, with the laptop powered up in front of him, that Freddie called him back. Josh pretended the computer belonged to a dumb friend at NYU who'd forgotten his password. Freddie asked a few questions about the make and the model and how old it seemed to be, then told him to take notes in case they needed to do it again and proceeded to talk him through, step-by-step. In about five minutes up popped the Windows screen and Josh was in. Freddie got him to check if the individual files were encrypted. They weren't.

"Freddie, you're amazing."

"I know. That'll be two thousand dollars."

"You got it."

For the next two hours, with his heart racing, Josh rummaged through the files. There was a lot that meant nothing to him, but plenty more that did. File upon file of names and addresses and phone numbers; details of companies, their individual depots and warehouses, lumberyards, and laboratories; notes that seemed to be based on observation about security and phone and power lines; and, most intriguing of all, tucked away in an alphabetical contacts file under C for *cops,* a list of about two dozen names and numbers. He tried to access Rolf's e-mail filing cabinet but found himself blocked by another password.

He would have gone on, but it was coming up to six o'clock and he ought to be heading back. Abbie and Ty would be getting worried about him. The only thing he still wanted to do was make a copy of what he'd seen. In case the computer got lost or broken or stolen. Without turning it off, he hurried back to the mall and bought a flash drive no bigger than his thumb and copied as much as it would take.

It was past eight o'clock and getting dark when he drove into Choteau. The gas gauge was almost on empty, so he pulled into the station on Main Street and filled up. When he went inside to pay, his hands were so cold that he dropped a whole lot of coins on the floor and they ran everywhere. The girl behind the counter kindly came and knelt beside him and helped him gather them all up.

"Not the best night to be out," she said.

"No, unless you're a polar bear."

She laughed. As he paid, she asked him if he was just passing through and he said he was and for some ridiculous reason added that he had just driven down from Canada and was on his way to see his dad. When he came back out to the truck, the wind had dropped and it was starting to snow.

It was freezing hard too and on the road out to the mountains he skidded twice on patches of ice and was glad when the surface turned to gravel. Once, coming too fast around a corner, he almost plowed into a herd of deer and then he took a wrong turn and had to backtrack, cursing himself all the while for leaving his return so late. By now they'd be halfway up the walls with worry. As he drove past the ranch house and the barns, the land opened before him, transformed to white.

A mile farther, when he got to the place where the road came to an end, he was surprised to see a car parked under the trees where he'd been intending to park Ty's truck. Josh pulled up behind it and got out to have a look. There was nobody inside and nothing to show whose it might be. He searched for a flashlight in the truck but there didn't seem to be one. It seemed dumb to carry all the supplies he had bought up to the cabin only to have to haul them down again tomorrow, so he left it all, along with the computer, in the truck and locked the doors. It was snowing steadily now and very cold. He pulled the hood of his new jacket over his head and set off up the trail.

He looked for footprints but it was too dark to see and if there were any they were probably already covered by the snow. He kept wondering whose car it might be. It didn't look like a police car and if it was the cops, surely there'd be a whole bunch of them, wouldn't there? Maybe it was a neighbor who'd dropped by or someone who'd gotten lost. Or maybe Ty's friend Jesse had come back. That had to be it. It was only when he reached the top of the climb and the cabin came into view that Josh got the feeling something was seriously wrong. Someone was shouting. Then a figure crossed the window. And it was neither Abbie nor Ty.

He was pacing to and fro across the cabin, the flames of the candles ducking as he passed and throwing jagged shadows on the bare wood walls. The two of them sat at the table as he'd told them to, watching him warily. Ty looked calmer than she knew he must be. Abbie was still in shock.

"How dare you? How fucking *dare* you?"

"Listen," Ty said. "I've said I'm sorry. When he comes back, you can have it. Just take it and go."

"Don't you fucking tell me what to do."

Rolf looked at his watch again then peered out the window where all there was to see was the steady windless falling of the snow. The sight of him walking out of the twilight when they were leading the horses into corral had almost made her faint. How he could possibly have found them, she still didn't know and was too afraid to ask. The look in his eyes shattered at once any fond hope that the baby might have changed things. She must have been out of her mind to imagine it might make him want to give himself up.

If only Ty hadn't been so goddamn pigheaded about what was on the laptop. She could still barely believe what he'd done, sending Josh off with it like that to call Freddie, without even mentioning it to her until they were out on the ride and it was too late to stop it. He'd been trying to convince Rolf that it was all quite innocent, that the computer just happened to be in the truck and that he could have it as soon as Josh got back. But Abbie could see that Rolf wasn't buying it. The first sight of Ty had sent him into a rage and the missing laptop had given him an excuse to stoke it to a full-blown fury. He hadn't hurt anyone yet, but the promise of violence was in his every word and action.

"Where the fuck is he?"

"It'll be the snow," Ty said. "Maybe the roads are blocked."

Rolf looked out of the window again and in that same moment Ty darted another quick glance toward the foot of the bed and only now did Abbie understand why. It was where he kept the loaded shotgun. You could just see the protruding ribbed end of the butt. She glared at him. For the love of God, surely he wouldn't be so dumb?

"Okay, that's it," Rolf said. "Put your coat on."

"What?" Abbie said.

"I said put your coat on. We're getting out of here."

"No way," Ty said, standing up.

"Was I talking to you? You just stay where you are. Sit down and shut up."

He snatched Abbie's red ski jacket from the back of the door and threw it at her.

"Put it on!"

"Listen," Ty said. "Can we just be reasonable here—"

"Shut the fuck up."

"You're not taking her anywhere."

Ty took a step toward him and Rolf turned to face him.

"If you don't sit down, I'll fucking kill you."

Abbie hurriedly put on the jacket.

"It's okay, Ty. I'll go. We'll see Josh on the road and he can have his computer and go."

"There's no way I'm letting you go with him. He's done you enough harm already."

"Why don't you tell your little cowboy hero here to mind his own fucking business?"

He swung open the door and grabbed Abbie by the shoulder to steer her out. Ty made a lunge but Rolf saw it coming and hit him hard in the stomach then gave him a shove that sent him sprawling across the room, crashing into the table and knocking it over and the candle with it. Abbie screamed. Ty was badly winded but was getting to his feet again.

"For godsake!" Abbie yelled. "I'll go. Just stop!"

The door was open now, the falling snow silently framed against the black of the night. Ty was moving sideways toward the bed.

"Ty, no!"

She shouldn't have cried out because Rolf's eyes at once scanned across to the bed and he saw the butt of the shotgun. In the same instant Ty dived for it and Rolf leapt at him and grabbed him around the hips and managed to drag him away before he could reach it. Dear God, she thought, please, not again. They were both on the floor now, trying to punch and grab each other's necks and hair and Abbie just stood there by the doorway, screaming like a woman possessed for them to stop. But Rolf had tucked his knees up now and he jerked backward and kicked Ty hard in the chest then made a grab for the shotgun and got hold of it and started to pull it out from under the bed.

When the snowy figure burst past her through the doorway, it took her a moment to realize who it was. Josh flung himself on top of Rolf and got his arms around his neck and wrenched back his head.

"Abbie, go!" Ty shouted. "Just get out of here! *Go!*"

She didn't need telling again. To watch three men she loved trying to tear each other to pieces was more than she could bear. She turned and ran out into the snow and around the side of the cabin and saw the horses still tethered to the rail where they'd left them when Rolf arrived, an inch of snow on their saddles. She untied hers and swung herself up and onto him and reined him hard around and jabbed him with her heels and he launched himself like a racehorse from the starting gate, up the trail and into the trees.

She didn't know where she was going and didn't care and, even if she had, her eyes were too blurred by snow and desolation to see more than a dim impression of the trail ahead. She kept her head low, her cheek against the horse's snowy mane, and simply let him run. She knew the broad lay of the land by now but not at night nor shrouded as it was by snow. As he galloped ever on and upward, the stems of lodgepole strobing darkly past, she heard beneath the thud and scuffle of his feet a deeper, sharper sound and then a rolling echo and she knew the shotgun had been fired and she cried out and in her anguish heeled the horse yet faster.

The trail veered to the left and down and suddenly they were splashing through a stream then leaping and jerking up the bank beyond, the horse stalling and skewing and scrambling, rocks clacking and clattering loose beneath his hooves. And now they were running again, the slope steeper than before, much steeper, the horse's breath rasping and coughing like an engine choked with rust.

They were out of the trees now and high and the land was leveling out. Below her, to her right, all she could see behind the swirl of snow was a chasmic black and she realized that they must be on some kind of spine or ridge. And a second after the thought occurred they were suddenly on rock or ice or both and the horse's hooves were skidding from under him and he lurched and squealed and she felt herself being launched like a missile from the stirrups into the darkness then hitting the slope and falling, tumbling, twisting, cartwheeling down and down, the snow flying and fluffing all around her and into her mouth and eyes. There was a sudden splintering shock of pain in her leg and a crunch in her shoulder and then her head hit something hard and the world went whiter than the snow and slower and she was sliding, slipping, gliding down. And her last sensations of the night and of the world were a long and weightless drop, like the twirl of a broken feather, and the icy embrace of water bubbling and closing above her.

THREE

THIRTY

They had been hearing the elk bugling all morning but not until now had they seen them. There was a herd of about twenty females down below them along the creek in the shadow of the valley and a big old bull with a fine rack of antlers standing watch. Sheriff Charlie Riggs gently reined his horse to a standstill on the ridge and Lucy, following on her cute little paint with its fine new saddle, came alongside and did the same. Charlie pointed down the slope and handed her the binoculars.

"There you go," he said. "See 'em?"

The sun was in her eyes and he took off his hat and used it as a visor for her.

"Yeah. Wow, he's big."

"Yep, he's your main man, for sure."

"How many points on those antlers?"

"You're the one with the eyesight."

"Seven, I'd say."

They had been out for nearly three hours now and as the valley slowly filled with shadow you could feel the air growing cooler. They were making their way down to the trailhead where they'd left the trailer. Working weekends was one of the reasons things had gone wrong with Sheryl, so when he'd picked up Lucy that morning he'd thought it best not to mention that they were going to ride up around Goat Creek. Anyway, it didn't feel like work and Lucy certainly didn't see it that way. She knew, for sure, as everybody around these parts knew, about the girl's body being found back in the early spring. But that was six months ago and nobody talked about it much anymore. What his daughter didn't know—and Charlie wasn't about to tell her—was that the elk were grazing the very spot where they'd cut Abbie Cooper from the ice.

When the creek unfroze at the end of April they'd combed it for clues but found nothing. And ever since, all through the spring and summer, Charlie had come up here again and again. Sometimes he rode, either with Lucy or alone, and sometimes he just hiked around. How many hundred miles he'd covered he had no idea but he must have walked or ridden every trail there was in a twenty-mile radius as well as a lot of untrailed land besides, scanning the ground for anything that might have been left or dropped or hidden. But in all those miles and hours he hadn't found a single darned thing to cast a glimmer of light on how the poor kid might have died.

His obsession with the case had become something of a joke around the office. He could see the look on some of the deputies' faces when he asked them to follow up on some tenuous line of inquiry or hunch he might have had. Even the folks down at the Grizzly Grill, where

Charlie ate supper when he got bored of reading alone at home or had forgotten to get food in, had started teasing him about it, asking if he'd caught his killer yet. *No,* he'd say. *Not yet. But I'm on your case, buddy.* The truth was, he didn't have either the time or the resources for such a case and should probably have handed it over months ago to the state DCI guys down in Helena.

"So why does one male have all those females?" Lucy asked.

"What makes you think it's that way around? Maybe they're holding him hostage."

"Da-ad."

"Have they taught you about genes and all that stuff at school yet?"

"Of course they have."

"Okay, well. As I understand it, the male's role is to spread his genes as far and wide as possible, so the strongest one tries to stop all the other guys from getting to the females."

"That's not fair on the females. The younger bucks are a whole lot cuter than that big ugly old thing."

"Yeah, and some day one of them'll beat him up and take over."

"And the females don't get any say at all?"

"Nope."

"That's sexist."

"I guess it is. Probably makes life a whole lot easier though. Come on, I'm getting hungry."

They eased the horses forward along the ridge and wound their way slowly down into the twilight of the trees where the air was cooler and smelled of fall. It was around this time last year that they'd had the big freeze and that heavy dump of snow. And though he had nothing to prove it, Charlie figured that might well have been when Abbie got herself killed. Throughout the winter there had been a number of thaws and refreezings. But from what he could gather, from Ned and Val Drummond and a few others, hunters and rangers and folks who liked to ride their snowmobiles up here, that first heavy snowfall and the ice that came with it had never fully cleared from the creek.

And that was pretty much all he knew. For six long months of work, it wasn't exactly going to win him a Detective of the Year award. All early leads had come to nothing. With the idea fixed in his head that she might have died at the time of that first heavy snowfall at the end of September, he'd trudged around town asking if anyone had seen any strangers at that time. The only sighting that seemed remotely promising was a young guy who'd filled up at the gas station on the very night of the storm. He'd paid cash and dropped all his coins on the floor. He had apparently told the girl at the register that he'd come down from Canada to see his dad and she'd noticed that the top part of his right first finger was missing.

Charlie had gotten all excited because they had security cameras there, both inside and on the forecourt. But it turned out they only kept the pictures for a month and these had long ago been wiped. She couldn't remember what kind of vehicle he'd been driving but added helpfully that he seemed nice and not at all like a murderer.

For a while Charlie thought he was on to something with Ty Hawkins, the boy from Sheridan whom the FBI had at first mistakenly assumed to be Abbie's accomplice. Charlie discovered that Ty was a friend of Jesse Wheeler, who looked after the Ponderosa. It was at the top of the next drainage and a fair few miles north of Goat Creek, but Charlie had nevertheless gone up there to see him.

He was glad he made the effort. Jesse seemed a little wary and fidgety when Charlie talked with him. It turned out he'd met Abbie once himself, about six or seven years earlier, at some dude ranch where he used to work summers. He swore he hadn't seen her since and swore he hadn't seen Ty in a long while either and that never in the three years he'd been working there had Ty once visited with him. But Charlie wasn't completely convinced.

He drove over to Sheridan and talked with Ty himself and couldn't help but feel sorry for him. As a horseman himself, Charlie knew of Ray Hawkins and had many years ago seen him in action at one of his famous clinics. Not only had the poor kid lost a fine father, not only had their ranch been drilled and trashed for coalbed methane, not only had he been wrongly jailed for several weeks and his name blackened as a terrorist, he had, quite clearly, also just lost the love of his life.

In his eyes and in his voice when he talked about Abbie, you could see that her death had plain broken his heart. He said he hadn't seen her in years. And

Charlie believed him. All his instincts cried out that the boy could no sooner have killed her than have murdered his own mother. There wasn't a bad bone in him. Even so, Charlie had to do his job. He asked Ty if he could take a DNA sample and had it sent off to the crime lab in Missoula to be tested against the paternal DNA of Abbie's fetus. And, thank God, there was no match.

They'd reached the trailer and the truck now. And Charlie watched while Lucy expertly led her pony up the ramp and then he did the same with his own horse. As they drove back through the fading light into town, he felt the sadness fall upon him the way it always did at the end of a day with his daughter, when he had to take her home to her mother. As his grandma used to say, what a muddle life was. What a mess and a muddle.

E very few weeks, even if there wasn't anything new to tell them (and there rarely was), Charlie would call the Coopers. Just to keep in touch and let them know the case was still open and active. He had grown to like them and admired the dignified way they seemed to be handling the loss of their daughter. He once, tentatively, almost said as much to Ben and would never forget the little pause and the exact words of his reply.

"The real loss happened four years ago. At least we know now where she is."

Charlie was careful to call both of them, but Sarah was the one he especially liked to call. Though he hardly admitted it to himself, she was the reason he was reluctant to hand the case over. Though he had only met her that one time in Missoula, when she came to collect the body, the image of her had stayed in his head. He enjoyed the sound of her voice on the phone, kind of regal and creamy, a little husky, the kind of voice a man could fall in love with. Sometimes they talked for half an hour or more, much longer than he could spin out any news of the so-called investigation.

In one of their conversations, about a month ago, she had somehow discovered he was a big reader and, what was more, that they had a few favorite authors in common. He imagined her taste was probably a lot classier than his own, but when he told her he loved Elmore Leonard and Pat Conroy and Cormac McCarthy, she got excited and said *The Prince of Tides* and *All the Pretty Horses* were two of her all-time favorite books. She said it was such a pity that she had just sold the bookstore, because she could have sent him proofs and new books she had come across.

The next time they talked, the day after Charlie and Lucy had ridden up Goat Creek and seen the elk, Sarah told him she was trying to write something herself. About Abbie. And that she was planning a little research trip to Missoula. She asked him if he ever had cause to be there and he lied and said he often did. Maybe they could meet up, Sarah said. Charlie said he'd like that very much and then got worried that this didn't sound sufficiently professional so added that he hoped there might be some *developments* by then that he could tell her about.

She called a few days later to tell him the date and said she'd booked herself into the Doubletree, just across the river from the university, and would he like to have lunch or dinner on the Tuesday? He lied again and said he had a lot to do that day and couldn't make lunch but dinner would be fine. The food at the Doubletree was by all accounts terrific, he said. He spent the following ten days trying to stop thinking about it.

He got there three quarters of an hour early and strolled along the river by the cottonwoods whose leaves glowed yellow in the dusk and then over the little wooden footbridge to the campus where he stood watching some boys practicing football under the floodlights.

He'd had a haircut and put on his best jacket, the beige corduroy, with a pale blue snap-button shirt. He'd wondered awhile about coming in uniform but decided it might make him look too stiff. Instead, for a touch of businesslike authority, he took his briefcase with him into the restaurant and arrived a few minutes late, as if he might have been held up at some important meeting.

She stood up and smiled and held out her hand.

"Hello, Charlie. It's so good to see you."

Her hand felt cool. He said it was good to see her too. She was wearing black jeans and a white shirt under an open navy cardigan, a single string of pearls around her neck. She had a slight tan and had done something different to her hair, but maybe he only thought that because the last time it had been bedraggled by rain. She looked stunning. He had never dined with a woman so classy and beautiful in his entire life.

. . .

I t was so sweet how diligently he had kept in touch, Sarah thought. Maybe it was standard procedure when they were dealing with the parents of a victim as opposed to those of a criminal. By her death, Abbie had, of course, neatly switched categories.

He was telling her about the ride he'd had with his daughter a couple of weeks back, and how, looking down that slope, he had become even more convinced that Abbie must have fallen. It was obvious he hadn't anything new or important to tell her, but Sarah hadn't expected it, nor did she mind. He was such a nice guy and she was enjoying his company. It was some time since she'd had dinner on her own with a man and she could tell by the way he looked at her with those kind blue eyes that he was a little smitten.

He had asked her already how her research had been going. She had been here two days and had met up with some of Abbie's teachers and friends, all of whom had been warm and generous and helpful, especially Mel and Scott, who had stayed on at UM to do postgraduate work. The only thing that had been a little hard to take was hearing that Mel was five months pregnant. They were going to get married at Thanksgiving.

Sarah didn't tell Charlie much about what she was planning to write, partly because she was shy about it and partly because she wasn't altogether sure herself. Iris had called it an *exercise in closure* and she was probably right.

"So is Lucy your only child?"

486

"Yeah. But she's got enough spirit for twenty. Ran the household from the age of about six months. Kind of full-on, you know?"

"I do. Abbie was like that."

"I'm sorry, I—"

"Charlie, please. It's okay, really."

He looked so embarrassed that she put a hand, briefly, on his.

"Tell me more about her."

He did and with a little prompting got to talking about his marriage and how it hadn't worked out and that it was probably more his fault than Sheryl's. He said that if he had the chance over again he'd do things differently, pay more attention, be there more. Then, almost out of nowhere, he asked her how Benjamin was and she had to say she didn't really know, but that she thought he was okay.

The truth was, they had only spoken a couple of times since the funeral and on each occasion it had been oddly formal, a little stilted. Sarah had a pretty good idea why. It was what she had said to him on the plane, about Abbie's death being his fault. She couldn't believe she had said such a terrible thing. Being here again in Missoula these past couple of days and talking about Abbie with Mel and Scott and the others, she'd had time to reflect and something inside her had shifted. She had even been thinking that she should probably write to him and apologize.

"He has a new life, a whole new support system, you know?"

"I'm sorry."

"Charlie Riggs, if you don't stop apologizing, I'm going to start getting cross with you."

He smiled. She finished her wine and he poured her some more.

"We're both divorced, single adults," she went on. "We should be able to talk about these things."

"Absolutely."

"So Sheryl got married again. Why not you?"

"Well. Partly work, I guess. You know, I've got a patch of almost two and a half thousand square miles to cover. Makes you kind of tired just looking at the map. And the other thing, I guess, is that there's not too much choice. There's plenty of cattle and critters, trees, and empty space out there on the Front Range, but not a whole lot of people."

Sarah smiled and for a moment they just looked at each other.

"How about you?" he said.

She laughed.

"How old are you, Charlie?"

"I'm forty-four. No, forty-five."

"How old do you think I am?"

"I was brought up not to speculate on such matters."

"Go on, guess."

"Hell, thirty-nine maybe?"

"You're so full of . . ."

He smiled at her and took a sip of his wine.

"I'll be fifty next fall."

"I don't believe that."

"It's true. Sometimes I feel a lot, lot older. And sometimes I feel about eighteen."

"How old do you feel tonight?"

"About thirty-nine."

He laughed.

"The thing is," she went on, "available men of my age, I mean, suitable men—and believe me they're not too thick on the ground—all want to date women twenty years younger."

"Well, I'd say, if they're that dumb, they don't qualify as suitable."

She'd been wondering what she'd say if he asked her to go to bed with him. Not that he was likely to. He was too polite. Which was a pity, because the idea appealed to her strongly. If anybody was going to make the move, it would have to be her. But she'd never done such a thing in her life. And she'd probably end up regretting it anyway.

"On the other hand," he said. "To be honest, living on your own has a few things going for it. You can leave the dishes without anyone getting mad at you, slop around, you know. Read all day if you want to."

She took the cue (though she doubted it was so intended) and steered out of the danger zone by asking him what he was reading at the moment. And for the rest of the meal all they talked about was books. She promised to send him a novel that she had just read. It was by a young Mexican writer and the best book she'd read all year.

"There's something else you can do for me too," he

said, after she had let him win the fight over who should pay the check.

"And what might that be?"

"I'd like some better pictures of Abbie. You know how people can look so different sometimes? How you can show someone two pictures of the same person and they'll recognize one and not the other? Well, if I had a couple more to show around, maybe it'd help trigger folks' memories a little better."

Sarah reached to the floor for her purse.

"I've got some with me, if you like."

She took out the little plastic envelope she always carried. There were probably a dozen photos in it of Abbie and Josh. Though none of Benjamin anymore. She handed them to Charlie and he carefully went through them.

"This'd be Josh, of course."

"Uh-huh."

"What's he up to at the moment?"

"In his final year at NYU. And after that, well, we're all waiting to find out. He's had a lot to handle these last few years."

"He looks like a nice guy."

"He's more than that. He's amazing."

He turned to the next picture. It was of Abbie and Josh during that final vacation at The Divide. They were in close-up, grinning and doing their *almost peace* signs.

"Josh again, huh?"

"Yes. He lost the top of his finger in a car door when

he was little. The peace sign's a sort of family joke. Almost peace."

Charlie nodded but kept staring at the picture. Then he gave an abrupt little smile and quickly flipped through the last few pictures.

"Some of these would do just fine," he said. "Could I get copies made?"

"Of course, take them. As long as you let me have them back."

"Thanks," he said. "I'll do it tomorrow."

THIRTY-ONE

J osh had been hoping Nikki might call, so even though he was in class, where there was a strict rule that cell phones should be turned off, his was on vibrate. He was sitting at the end of the back row, near the door, so that if she called he could slip out, as if to the restroom.

The class was on something called the Age of the Enlightenment, about which Josh remained completely in the dark. The woman had been droning on for half an hour and he'd been trying to take notes which already, when he looked down at them, meant absolutely nothing to him. Things like *crumbling of feudal edifice, perfectibility and progress, humanized theological systems.* Josh had his elbows on the desk, head heavily propped on his fists in case he nodded off.

"Diderot, however, saw religious dogma as absurd and obscure," she now declared.

Absurd and obscure, he wrote. Then he felt his phone start to wobble in his pocket and he stealthily slipped it out, expecting to see Nikki's name on the screen. But it was a number he didn't recognize. He let it go to voice-mail.

Only when he was outside in the cold November sunshine, eating a turkey-salad sandwich as he walked back to the apartment, did he check the message. When he heard who it was, he almost choked.

"Hi, Josh. This is Sheriff Charlie Riggs from Choteau, Montana. I'm in New York and I'd be real grateful if you could maybe spare me half an hour of your time. There's a couple of things concerning your sister that I thought you might be able to help us with. You can call me back on this cell number. The subject's kind of sensitive, so I'd appreciate it if you didn't mention this call to your mom and dad just yet or anyone else. Look forward to hearing from you. Bye now."

Josh felt his world start to tilt. Oh man, he thought. Here we go. They've found Rolf's body.

He called the number and tried not to sound frightened, just interested and helpful. The guy seemed friendly. Best not to get too paranoid. They tried to figure out where to meet but his mind was racing too fast to think of anywhere, so the guy suggested the Brooklyn Bridge. He said he'd only once before been to New York and someone had told him the view from the bridge at sunset was spectacular. What *was* this? Josh wondered. Was the guy just here on vacation?

They arranged to meet at four o'clock at the Manhattan end of the south-side walkway.

"How will I recognize you?" Josh asked.

"I'll be the one with the star and the Stetson."

"Right."

"I'm kidding. It's okay, I know what you look like."

That got him even more paranoid. How could he know what he looked like? Four o'clock was two hours away and Josh spent them in his room at the apartment. It was in a run-down block just off East Broadway and he shared it with three guys from NYU, all of whom he liked well enough but wasn't that close to. Luckily, nobody else was home. He thought of calling Freddie but decided not to. He'd told him a little, but not the whole story, not about what really happened with Rolf. Ty must have talked. That would be it. Maybe he should call him? But then, maybe they had a wiretap on him in case he did just that. Jesus, he thought. Oh Jesus.

Quite why he did so, he wasn't sure, but at three-thirty, when he'd put on his coat and was heading for the door, he stopped and went back to his desk. He knelt down and reached underneath and felt for the little package taped behind the drawer. And he ripped it clear and put it in his pocket and set off.

Charlie was leaning on the rail, watching the sun creep down toward the skyline. The city looked amazing, the sun flashing on cliffs of glass, the lights of the skyscrapers starting to twinkle. He was trying to figure out where exactly the World Trade Center had been but he didn't know the geography well enough to place it.

He saw Josh walking toward him and even from a hundred yards in the low glare of the sun he could see how scared the poor kid looked. He was wearing a black parka and a red beanie pulled down to his eyebrows. As he came closer he caught a glimpse of Sarah in the boy's pale face. Charlie stepped toward him and held out a hand.

"Hello, Josh."

"Hi."

The boy's handshake was weak and cautious. They didn't teach kids how to shake hands anymore. Josh quickly stuck both hands back into his pockets and didn't seem to want to look him in the eyes. Charlie nodded at the view.

"Quite a sight, huh?"

"Yeah."

"I was trying to figure out where the towers were—"

"Over there." Josh pointed, without a great deal of interest.

"Shall we take a walk?"

"If you want."

They set off, strolling side by side along the boardwalk, the traffic roaring below them, taillights flickering in the cracks between the planks.

"What's all this about?"

"Well, these past few months, we've been trying to figure out what happened to Abbie. How she came to be where we found her, who she might have been with, that kind of thing. And I thought you might be able to help clear up a few things for us. Is that okay?"

"I guess."

"How well do you know Ty Hawkins?"

"Not really at all. He was a wrangler at the ranch we used to go to. He and Abbie had a thing going for a while."

"I know."

"And the cops got it wrong and thought he was involved in that thing in Denver."

"Uh-huh. When was the last time you saw Ty or spoke with him?"

Josh shrugged, keeping his eyes straight ahead.

"I don't know."

"Roughly."

"Years ago."

"Is that really true?"

"Yeah, why? Does he say something different?"

Charlie didn't answer. He was trying to give the impression that he knew a whole lot more than he did. He didn't even really know why he'd started with the question about Ty, but it seemed to have touched a nerve.

"When was the last time you saw your sister?"

He saw Josh swallow.

"Same. Years ago. Like everyone else."

"So why would you have been in Choteau at the end of September last year?"

Josh turned to look at him, frowning and shaking his head as if he didn't understand.

"What do you mean? I wasn't."

"Yes, you were."

Josh didn't say anything. A happy group of Japanese tourists were having their picture taken against the sunset. It was getting cold. Charlie and Josh negotiated a way around them and didn't speak again until they were clear.

"Josh, unless you're going to level with me, this is going to be a whole lot harder for the both of us. Now, I know you were in Choteau and I know you were in Great Falls."

Josh said nothing.

"Josh," Charlie said gently. "I've seen your cell phone records."

The boy closed his eyes for a moment, clearly cussing himself.

"And the flight records. You flew in from Denver. The cameras at the airport recorded pictures of Ty Hawkins meeting you there. You were also caught on camera in the gas station when you dropped all those coins. The gal who helped you pick them up has identified you from photographs. So let's save ourselves time and cut the bullshit, okay?"

Charlie stopped walking and Josh halted a few paces ahead but didn't turn to face him. He still had his hands thrust deep into the pockets of his parka.

"Tell me what happened, Josh."

What was the point in lying anymore? The guy seemed to know most of the story anyway. And

496

more lies would probably only make it worse. For everyone. He wasn't going to make the same mistake as Abbie. If she'd only come clean straightaway and told everyone they hadn't meant to kill the McGuigan boy, she might still be alive. He let his shoulders slump and walked to the rail and leaned there staring out at the river and the harbor. Charlie Riggs came up beside him and did the same. Josh took a deep breath and began.

"Abbie wanted to turn herself in. When she found out she was pregnant, she ran away from Rolf. She told Ty the guy had been treating her badly, hitting her and . . . I don't know. Anyhow, she went to Ty's place and the two of them holed up in a cabin somewhere out of Choteau, up in the mountains."

"Jesse Wheeler's place."

"Ty's told you all this already, I guess."

"I'd like to hear it from you. All of it. How long were they there?"

"I don't know. Two weeks maybe. They were trying to figure out the best way for Abbie to turn herself in, you know, how to give herself the best chance of not going to jail forever. I tell you, she was a totally different person from how she was the last time I . . ."

He realized he was tripping himself up on a lie he'd already told.

"The last time you saw her? And when was that?"

Josh sighed. He might as well come clean.

"The spring before Nine-Eleven. Here in New York. She wanted money. She was, like, crazy. Like somebody I didn't know. Anyhow, September last year, she called me. I was in Colorado seeing a friend of mine. So I flew up to Great Falls and . . . well, you know."

"What did they want you to do?"

"Bring her home. Back here to New York. Fix up a meeting with Mom and Dad. The idea was they'd sort out the lawyers and all that, see if they could make some kind of deal. She looked so pretty. It was Abbie again."

"How were you going to get her here?"

"Rolf's car. Her car, I guess. The one she took when she left him."

"Did you ever get to meet Rolf?"

Josh gave a little sour laugh and looked away. This was it. The point of no return. Maybe he should stop now.

"Josh?"

He turned. The sheriff was staring hard at him. He seemed like a decent guy. He probably knew every-thing.

"Yeah, I met him. The night of the snowstorm. He just showed up, out of the blue. How he found out where they were, God knows. I mean, it doesn't get much more remote than that place. Ty figured maybe Abbie must have called him or something. Or that he knew about me coming up from Denver and followed us back. I guess we'll never know."

"Go on."

"Ty found the guy's computer hidden in the back of the car and I went to Great Falls that day to see if I could get into it. Like, crack the password."

"And your friend Freddie helped you."

Josh looked at him nervously.

"Josh, I saw your phone records, okay?"

"Oh man, don't do anything to Freddie. He didn't know. Please."

"We'll come back to that. Go on."

"When I got back to the cabin and it was snowing and all, there was this car there and it was him. He was in the cabin, waiting for me to come back with the goddamn computer. Jeez, was he mad. Out of his mind. I guess it was finding Abbie with Ty and everything. And the computer. They tried to pretend it was all a mistake, that it just happened to be in the truck, but he knew something was going on. I think he knew we were going to use it against him. That guy, I tell you. He was like a maniac, ranting and raving . . .

"And then he tried to take Abbie. And that's when Ty made his move and I ran in to help him. Rolf was pulling Ty's shotgun out from under the bed and I just leapt on top of him and everything went crazy. The three of us, just wrestling and punching and fighting."

"What was Abbie doing?"

"Ty yelled at her to go, anywhere, just get away. And she ran out to the corral and took one of the horses and . . ."

He felt the tears surging in his eyes now. Shit! He didn't want to cry but he couldn't stop himself.

"It's all right, Josh. Take your time."

The sheriff put a hand on his shoulder and kept it there. Josh took a deep breath. The sun was disappearing in a final blaze of orange and red.

"Anyhow. Her going made him even madder. And, man, he was strong. I mean, Ty's a strong guy, but Rolf, hell, he was something else. He kind of dragged us all through the doorway and out into the snow and around the side of the cabin. He kept hollering Abbie's name, you could tell he wanted to go after her. I had my arms locked around his neck and he and Ty were struggling for the gun, both trying to wrench it out of each other's hands. Then Rolf kind of swung me around and sent me crashing into the rails of the corral and I broke clean through them.

"I think I must have gotten knocked out for a moment because the next thing I know is I'm lying there in the snow and the two of them are by the broken fence, still wrestling with the gun. Then Rolf kicks Ty's legs from under him and Ty loses his grip on the gun . . . oh, man."

"It's all right, son. Easy now."

"He was going to kill him, no doubt about it. Ty's on the ground in front of him and the guy just lowers the barrel, points the gun right at him and tries to pull the trigger. I swear to God. But the safety catch was on and while he tried to find it, Ty grabbed hold of his leg and I got up and charged, just hurled myself right at him. And I knocked him sideways and he kind of twisted around and fell back. And the gun went off. It was a miracle nobody got hit. But Rolf, he . . ."

Josh could see it now. And hear it too. The guy crashing back against the broken rail, the dreadful scrunch of skewering flesh, his face suddenly changing, the look of stunned horror in his eyes.

"I didn't mean for it to happen, I swear. It was just the way he fell. There was this jagged end where the rail had broken off, like a spear of splintered wood, still nailed to the post. And he landed with his back right on it and . . . For a moment we didn't know what had happened. He just went all still. And then we saw the blood and . . . the point sticking out through the front of his shirt. Oh, Jesus."

He started to sob now and it was a while before he could go on.

"We pulled him free and Ty ran and got a towel and we tried to stop the bleeding, but it was no good. All we could do was stand there and . . . watch him die."

The twitching body, the clawed hand reaching out, the unstoppable flood of blood.

The sheriff was still holding him by the shoulder, patiently waiting.

"What happened to Abbie?"

"We never knew. The horse came back without her. We rode out the rest of the night, calling and calling. But the snow was coming down so thick, you couldn't hear or see a thing. No tracks, nothing. We had no idea where she'd gone. We spent the next two days looking for her. Not a thing. Not a single thing."

"And what did you do with Rolf?"

"We . . . we wrapped him up in a plastic sheet and put him in the trunk of his car, the one they'd hidden in the barn. The blood on the snow, oh man, I tell you. We boiled water, God knows how many gallons, and tried to melt it away, then shoveled fresh snow over it and still the red came through. Ty knew this big lake or reservoir, about twenty miles south. Up in a kind of canyon. Real deep, he said it was."

"I know it."

"Anyhow, that third night, after we'd given up looking for Abbie, and we'd cleaned up the cabin and mended the rails, gotten everything back the way it was and, at last, the blood wasn't showing anymore, we drove up there. I drove Ty's truck, he drove the car with the body in the trunk. It was amazing we made it, what with all the snow. We pushed it off a cliff into the water.

"He'd rented the other car, the one he arrived in, at the airport in Great Falls. I left it there the next day and flew home. And that's it."

For a long time they both stared out and said nothing. There was a narrow band of fire across the skyline where the sun had gone down. The buildings were all alight. Below them, under the boardwalk, the flash and roar of the rush-hour traffic. Everybody going home. Josh wondered what the guy was going to say. He'd obviously have to arrest him now.

"Who knows about this, apart from you and Ty?"

"Just you."

"You haven't told anyone?"

"I'm not that dumb."

"Not even your mom and dad?"

"Are you kidding? Can you imagine what it would do

to them? Finding out that both their kids are murderers? No way."

"It doesn't sound like a murder to me, son."

"One's enough."

For a minute or more neither of them spoke.

"What happened to the computer?"

"We put it in the trunk."

Josh pulled from his pocket the little package he'd taken from beneath his desk. It was the flash drive. He handed it to the sheriff.

"That's a copy of what was on it."

Charlie lay all night in his bed in the little downtown hotel room listening to the traffic and watching the lights and shadows travel the ceiling in ever-changing patterns. He'd never found it easy to sleep in cities but tonight he had nothing to blame but his own troubled head. It felt like a casino machine on which the same thoughts reassembled in a different order every time you played and never let you win.

He knew, of course, where his duty lay. He should let events be dictated by the due process of the law. That was what it was there for and that's what he had always done. The car and the body would have to be hauled out of the lake and Josh and Ty would have to be arrested and charged with the killing. The chances were that a court would go easy on them. If Josh's account of what happened was believed, that it was self-defense, the two of them would probably walk free.

But there was never any certainty. The case would be

coast-to-coast news, just as it had been when they found Abbie's body. Some smart, ambitious prosecuting attorney might well sniff fame or political advantage in painting events quite differently. And in the current climate of fear, the brother and former lover of a notorious terrorist could easily get tarred with the same brush—as Ty had already once discovered to his cost. The poor guy was broken as it was. How could he survive another such ordeal? And what about the Coopers? What about Sarah? Hadn't they all suffered enough?

Charlie cussed himself for leaving Josh. They'd walked off the bridge and caught a cab back to the boy's apartment, agreeing to meet again in the morning. Charlie had wanted time to think things through. But time was exactly what Josh didn't need. He'd be terrified now. What if he'd run off or, God forbid, done something worse?

That was enough. He was driving himself crazy. He got up and took out his phone and started to dial Josh's number and then realized it was four in the morning and snapped it shut again. He dressed and put on his coat and went out through the drab fluorescent lobby to the street and started walking. Block after block, light after light, *Walk, Don't Walk,* the options pounding through his head with each step.

Two hours later, as the eastern sky paled behind him, he found himself by the water again, staring out across the Hudson to the spangled black bank beyond. And he knew at last what he was going to do. Absolutely nothing. He knew the place where they had pushed the car into the reservoir. The water there was green and opaque and very deep. The guy wrapped up in the trunk had gotten no more and no less than he deserved. He could stay where he was.

In his pocket Charlie had been fingering the little flash drive Josh had given him. He knew he should check what was on it. Or maybe not. He took it out and looked at it. Then, as hard and as far as he could, he threw it out across the river. And he neither saw the splash nor heard it.

THIRTY-TWO

It was Iris's idea that they should have a combined party to celebrate their fiftieth birthdays. Sarah hadn't been planning to have one at all, preferring to let the dreaded date skulk by as unacknowledged as possible. At first she brushed the proposal aside. It would involve too much work and too much stress. And it was completely impractical too, because Iris's friends were all in Pittsburgh while hers were in New York. No problem, Iris said. They would throw the party in New York. She had too many people to ask anyway and it would be a clever way to cull a few. She hounded her and bullied her and in the end, just to get some peace, Sarah reluctantly agreed.

The date was set for the Saturday after Labor Day, which fell precisely between their two birthdays. In June Iris came to stay and they scouted half of Nassau

County for a venue but couldn't find anywhere they both liked that wasn't already booked. Sarah's parents offered their house in Bedford and were a little offended when she said thanks, but no. Held there, it would feel like a twenty-first and she was a grown-up now. Just when she was starting to hope that they might be able to call the whole thing off, up stepped Martin Ingram with an offer they couldn't refuse.

He was building a restaurant, a sort of brasserie, on a fabulous site in Oyster Bay and he wasn't just the architect, he was going to have a fifty percent share of the business too. Barring disasters, to which Martin rarely fell prey, by early October it would be finished but not yet open. It had wonderful maple floors and a vast mezzanine with a wraparound window through which you could see the ocean. It would be good for business to let people see it, he said, and they could have it for free. Sarah had to concede that it was perfect.

They hired a professional party planner called Julian McFadyen who was so cute and clever that Iris almost went into a swoon every time they met to discuss things. He did everything, including sending out the invitations, and made it all seem so effortless and enjoyable that as the day drew near, Sarah found she was actually looking forward to it. There was only one issue that troubled her.

It was just after Labor Day and Iris had flown in to finalize a few things with the adorable Julian, who she still refused to accept was gay. It was early evening and they were sitting out on Sarah's deck and Julian, having raised the subject of toasts and speeches and sensing some disagreement, had tactfully withdrawn so they could discuss it.

"Why do we have to have speeches at all?" Sarah said.

"Because that's what happens. Honey, how often do you get to stand in front of a hundred people being told how fabulous you are? And if I told Leo he couldn't make a speech he'd do it anyway."

"Well that's fine. But what about me? Who's going to do mine?"

"Josh could. Martin could. Hell, *I* could."

"Oh, Iris."

"Listen, we won't make a big deal of it. I'll tell Leo short and sweet."

"When has Leo ever done short and sweet?"

"We'll put up a clock like a game show. Three minutes and bong!"

"Everyone'll just be feeling sorry for me. I can't stand all that *poor old Sarah, still on her own* stuff."

"Oh, give me a break."

Sarah stubbed out her cigarette.

"I don't want Martin talking about me."

"Then ask Josh. He's a big boy now."

"You know how shy he is."

Josh was in Santa Fe spending a few days with his father. Sarah promised to ask him when he got home.

Since he graduated that spring, Josh had astonished them all. Out of the blue he'd announced that he wanted to be a lawyer. He'd cut his hair, bought himself a suit, and all summer had been working as an intern at Alan Hersh's firm in the city. He regularly came home buzzing with news about cases and clients and esoteric points of law that Sarah had to pretend to understand. Soon they were going to start paying him to do some paralegal work. If all went well, next year he'd go to law school. Meanwhile, on the weekends, he earned a few dollars helping Jeffrey at the bookstore. To see him so involved and invigorated was as thrilling as it was surprising. Sarah sometimes wondered if she'd missed the spaceship landing on the lawn.

Benjamin said the same. Of late they had been speaking more regularly. Instead of always calling Josh's cell phone, he now often called on the house line and it was usually Sarah who answered. He seemed less wary of her now, probably because she was warmer with him. Their shared wonder and admiration at Josh's transformation had helped draw them closer.

"What did we do wrong?" he'd said the other night, when he called to check out Josh's flight times.

"How do you mean?"

"I never dreamt I'd have a lawyer for a son."

"I know. Maybe we should have been more supportive of his marijuana habit."

"I don't think he missed out too much in that department."

The more compelling reason that they were easier now with each other was Sarah's letter. At Christmas she had written to apologize for what she'd said about Benjamin being to blame for Abbie's death. They were words uttered, she said, in a moment of deranged grief and despair. He sent her back a card, a serene photograph of sky and ocean. All it said was *Thank you, with my love, always, Benjamin.*

It helped too, of course, that he now knew about Charlie Riggs. Sarah and Charlie had taken a week's vacation in June. They had driven down to Colorado and stayed in a heavenly hotel in the mountains. They had ridden together through high meadows filled with flowers and hiked a stretch of the Continental Divide trail to a spring where one stream ran east and the other west. And they had at last become lovers. Sarah liked him very much. How serious it was ever going to be, she didn't know, and neither of them was pushing it. She had asked him to come over for the party and after cross-examining her to see if she truly wanted him there, he had said he would come.

Josh, for reasons Sarah couldn't quite fathom, seemed keener than she was that it should work out, even though he'd never met the guy. Perhaps it was because it would take the pressure off him a little, having to look after his poor, lonely, old mom. She had to remind him of his sometime refrain that long-distance relationships sucked. He said she'd better move to Montana then and Sarah laughed, as if she hadn't already considered the idea.

L eo had been going on about Iris for about twenty minutes and though some of the stories were funny (especially the one about her coming to haul him off the golf course in front of all his friends), it was, as Iris liked to say, enough already. Josh could see people giving each other little glances. Still, it gave him a good excuse to be brief.

The party seemed to be going well. Freddie, who was above him, leaning on the mezzanine rail with Summer and Nikki, had already voted it the best *old folks* party he'd ever been to. The food was great, he said, and even the band wasn't bad.

As Leo embarked on his eighteenth story, Josh went through his notes once more. He thought he had it pretty well straight. It was amazing how much better his memory was since he'd stopped smoking grass. He looked around the room for his mom and saw her standing with Martin and Beth Ingram and Charlie Riggs. She was wearing a black silk dress that showed her shoulders and she looked absolutely gorgeous. She and Charlie had hardly left each other's side all evening. It was great to see her looking so happy.

When she'd introduced them, Charlie and Josh had, of course, shaken hands as if they'd never met.

"Your mom's told me a lot about you," he said.

"Likewise."

"How're you doing?"

"I'm good. Thank you."

During the ten months that had passed since their walk on the bridge, Charlie had called him maybe a dozen times to see how he was getting along. He never made a big deal of it, always had some little joke or a funny story to tell. The last time he'd called was in

June, just before his vacation with Josh's mom in Colorado. Charlie clearly had something important to ask but didn't seem quite able to spell it out. Then Josh realized he was in fact being asked for his blessing, which he duly tried to bestow.

Watching them standing there now, across the room, listening to Leo's speech, Josh thought what a fine couple they made. He hoped, with all his heart, that it was going to work out for them. His mom must have felt his gaze, because she turned and looked at him and smiled and pulled a discreet face to indicate it was time somebody banged the gong on Leo. Luckily, it wasn't needed.

"And now, ladies and gentlemen, although I could go on all night . . ." There were calls of *Please, no, spare us.* ". . . I'm going to hand over to that handsome young man over there who all of you know—and if you don't, believe me, you soon will—Mr. Joshua Cooper!"

Everybody clapped and cheered and Josh stepped forward and walked across the room. Leo handed him the microphone and Iris gave him a kiss on the cheek.

"You look fabulous," she whispered. "Go kill 'em, kid."

Then everything went quiet and Josh felt a spasm of nerves. He looked at his notes, took a deep breath, and cleared his throat. The microphone made a little squawk of feedback, then settled.

"Thanks, Leo. I don't have many jokes to tell you about Mom. Growing up with Mom was a serious business."

There was a little laugh, but not what he'd hoped for.

"I could tell you how I threw up all over her first edition of *Tender Is the Night*, but I was only two and don't really remember doing it."

Now they laughed. That was more like it.

"Or I could tell you about the day she dropped the car keys down the drain outside Kmart and the fire department had to come and drill up the road and take us all home in a fire engine."

A great laugh.

"Best day of my life, as a matter of fact."

They roared. This wasn't so tough, after all. He glanced up at the mezzanine. Nikki grinned and blew him a kiss. Josh stuffed his notes into his pocket.

"The truth is, growing up with Mom wasn't a joke, it was just plain happy. Every single day. She ran the bookstore, ran the house, helped us do our homework. To be honest, with me, it wasn't so much *helped*. She actually did it. The only A's I ever got were when Mom had done my homework. In fact, everything I don't know about literature is thanks to Mom. She always made everything seem like fun. Even when, I guess, it wasn't so much fun for her."

He paused and looked across at her. She was smiling and he could see that she was trying hard not to cry. He wondered if he ought to skip the next bit, but he went on anyway. Ghosts didn't go away however much you tried to ignore them.

"And if Abbie was here tonight, she'd say the same."

You could have cut the silence with a knife.

"She loved Mom with all her heart. Just as I do. Because our Mom has been the best any kid could ever want. She's beautiful and funny and incredibly wise and clever. And she has the biggest heart any Mom ever had. She was always there for us. Always. And she still is."

Christ, everybody was crying now. He even felt like crying himself, but that might be a bit of a bummer. He'd been intending to go on to say something about the other ghost in the room, his dad. Nothing dramatic, just a little mention, but maybe he'd better quit while he was ahead. He looked around and Julian McFadyen discreetly handed him a glass of champagne.

"So. If you've got a glass, let's all make a toast. To these two great, incredibly old, and incredibly wonderful women. Iris and Sarah."

Everybody repeated the toast then the whole room erupted in applause and suddenly Josh was being mobbed and kissed and cuddled and his back was being slapped and for the best part of five minutes, he didn't really know much more, except, finally, when the crowd parted and he saw his mom, tears streaming down her face, opening her arms to him. And he went to her and hugged her and held her for a long time.

"I love you," she whispered. "I love you so much."

Lying in his bed much later when the party was over, tired but too wired to sleep, Nikki snoring softly beside him, Josh thought what weird creatures human beings were. How they could be all these different things at the same time, feel all these conflicting emotions. Love and hate, joy and despair, courage and fear. It was like we were some great whirling disc, of every imaginable color, on which the light constantly shifted and danced. He pictured all those faces, young and old, laughing and crying at his speech. It didn't seem to matter how old you were, seventeen or seventy, the disc was always there, whirling away. Maybe all that happened was that as time went by it just got a little easier to figure out the colors and know for sure which one you were looking at and what it might mean.

He was probably only thinking this way because he wasn't taking those damn pills anymore, the ones his doctor had prescribed last year after what happened with Abbie, the ones that leveled the world into a kind of muddy sameness. Josh preferred the whirling disc any day. The only downside was that he didn't sleep so well now.

He used to think it was because he was frightened of what he might dream. When he was little he used to have a list of about ten or twelve things that he would recite to himself at bedtime—witches, werewolves, Mrs. O'Reilly (the kindergarten cleaning woman with the glass eye and whiskers), that kind of stuff. The idea was that if he thought about them, he wouldn't dream about them. And for at least six months after he came back from Montana that fall, even after Charlie Riggs had come to see him and told him he wasn't going to do anything and that he would talk with Ty and it would be their secret, Josh had every night deliberately pictured Rolf twitching and bleeding in the snow and rising slowly from the lake, his leprous face half-eaten by fish.

Perhaps because his conscious summoning of these pictures was so vivid, the dream had never come and he no longer bothered with this nightly incantation. Charlie had worried that the burden of the secret might be too great, but it didn't seem that way now. To see his parents both happy again in their divided lives was compensation enough.

He was drowsy now. He thought about waking Nikki so she could go back to the guest room. But it seemed too cruel and he liked her lying next to him and anyway his mom was cool about these things now and wouldn't be embarrassed if she found out. He closed his eyes and with the disc of life still whirling in his head, but more slowly now and fading gently into the distance, he fell at last into a dreamless sleep.

B en could have driven the route with his eyes closed. But in the six years that had passed since he lived here, there were already changes. Different stores popping up along the strip malls, a new office block by the railroad station, Bahnhof's Deli sadly closed down at last, a kids' cooking school there in its place. They had planted a row of cherry trees around the edge of the park, sturdily staked and wrapped to the knees in white plastic to protect them. Memories at every turn of the road.

And now there was the house he'd built, all those years ago, looming out of the silver birches they'd planted, the leaves already starting to turn. The Korean dogwood in the driveway looked leggy and a little tired. Maybe they should have put a magnolia there instead. It wasn't such a bad house, though he'd do it differently now. He saw Sarah at the window and by the time he had parked the little Honda he'd rented at the airport she was coming out of the front door. He got out and walked to meet her.

She looked lovely. A blue linen skirt and a cream cashmere V-necked sweater. She was carrying a bunch of white lilies. Ben had chosen the same. His were lying on the backseat.

"You look nice," he said.

"So do you."

She put her hand on his arm and kissed his cheek and he noticed she was wearing a different scent from the one he always used to buy her every Christmas.

"All set?" he said.

"Uh-huh."

He opened the passenger-side door for her but for a moment she didn't get in. She was frowning at the dog-wood.

"That damned tree," she said. "It's got to go. I was thinking I might put a magnolia in there. What do you think?"

Ben nodded thoughtfully.

"Yeah. I could see that."

"They take such a long time though. You know, to be any good."

She got in and he shut the door.

The cemetery was on the other side of town but the morning traffic wasn't too heavy and the sunlight was of the kind that could make even Syosset's meaner streets seem mellow and calm.

"I hear Josh was a knockout at the party."

"He had them eating out of his hand. I tell you, if he's that good in court, he'll be one hell of a lawyer."

It was Josh who had designated this last day of September as the date on which Abbie should be formally remembered. It was the day of the big snowfall two years earlier in Montana and it seemed to them all a more fitting anniversary than the random date of her funeral. That wretched day that all of them would rather, but would never, forget. The photographers and film crews all lined up waiting in the parking lot, jostling and yelling questions in the rain as he walked with Sarah to the waiting black sedan, her face beneath the netting, wet and whiter than their buried child.

The parking lot was all but empty now and they left the car and walked with their twin bouquets of lilies through the gates and past the uniformed attendant, who smiled and gently nodded them through. The sprinklers on the perfect green grass were whirring and flicking rainbows across the sunlight and making oval patches on the path that led up the little hill to Abbie's grave.

"How's Eve?"

Ben wondered if he'd heard correctly. It was the first time she had ever asked.

"She's fine."

"Are you two going to get married?"

"I don't know. Maybe. It's not something we talk about a lot."

"But you do talk about it?"

"Hey, what is this?"

She laughed and shrugged.

"It's okay. I wouldn't mind."

"Well, I appreciate you saying that."

"You're welcome."

They walked awhile in silence. A young gardener was clipping the roses and he smiled and said good morning as they passed.

"God, he's making a mess of that," Sarah whispered. "Why don't they teach them how to prune properly?"

Ben laughed.

"What about you and the sheriff?"

She gave him a look.

"Me and the sheriff. He's nice. It's early days."

"I'm happy for you."

She tucked her arm inside his and they didn't speak again until they reached the grave. Josh had already been here before going in to work. His pink roses were propped against the simple granite headstone. They laid the lilies side by side and stood in silence looking down at them, their arms still linked.

"Josh told you, didn't he?" she said quietly.

"About the phone call? Yes."

Two nights ago, he had called Ben in Santa Fe. He said he had something important to say that for a long time he'd kept to himself for fear of upsetting them. He had just told his mother and now wanted to tell him. It was about Abbie. Before she died, Josh said, she had phoned to say she'd run away from Rolf and was going to give herself up. She wanted to say how sorry she was to all of them for what she had done. And to Ben especially for being so cruel.

"I wonder if he just made it up to make us feel better," Sarah said.

"I don't know. I don't think so."

He put an arm around Sarah's shoulders and she put hers around his back and gave him a little hug.

"Do you see what he's written there?" she said.

Ben put on his glasses and knelt beside Josh's bunch of roses. There was a little card attached. It said simply, *Peace.*

Center Point Publishing
600 Brooks Road • PO Box 1
Thorndike ME 04986-0001 USA

(207) 568-3717

US & Canada:
1 800 929-9108